Born in 1946, **Ibrahim Abdel** [   ]
Alexandria. He has combined ([   ]
out his literary career, and is the author of numerous novels and
short-story collections. He was awarded the Naguib Mahfouz Medal
for Literature in 1996 for his novel *The Other Place*. *Clouds over Alexandria* is the final part in the author's Alexandria series, following *No
One Sleeps in Alexandria* and *Birds of Amber*.

Kay Heikkinen is a translator and academic who holds a PhD
from Harvard University and is currently Ibn Rushd Lecturer of
Arabic at the University of Chicago. Among other books, she translated Naguib Mahfouz's *In the Time of Love* and Radwa Ashour's *The
Woman from Tantoura*.

Clouds over Alexandria

Ibrahim Abdel Meguid

Translated by
Kay Heikkinen

hoopoe

AN IMPRINT OF AUC PRESS

First published in 2019 by
Hoopoe
113 Sharia Kasr el Aini, Cairo, Egypt
200 Park Ave., Suite 1700, New York, NY 10166
www.hoopoefiction.com

Hoopoe is an imprint of the American University in Cairo Press
www.aucpress.com

Dar el Kutub No. 19359/17
ISBN 978 977 416 867 3

Dar el Kutub Cataloging-in-Publication Data

Abdel Meguid, Ibrahim
        Clouds over Alexandria / Ibrahim Abdel Meguid—Cairo: The
    American University in Cairo Press, 2019.
        p. cm.
        ISBN 978 977 416 867 3
        1. Arabic fiction—Translation into English
        892.73

1 2 3 4 5   23 22 21 20 19

Designed by Adam el-Sehemy
Printed in the United States of America

When suddenly, at midnight, you hear
an invisible procession going by
with exquisite music, voices,
don't mourn your luck that's failing now,
work gone wrong, your plans
all proving deceptive—don't mourn them uselessly.
. . . . .
As one long prepared, and graced with courage,
as is right for you who proved worthy of this kind of city,
go firmly to the window
and listen with deep emotion, but not
with the whining, the pleas of a coward;
listen—your final delectation—to the voices,
to the exquisite music of that strange procession,
and say goodbye to her, to the Alexandria you are losing.

Constantine Cavafy, "The God Abandons Anthony"

1

TIME WAS FLYING IN THE second half of 1975, and news of President Sadat dominated the headlines. He traveled to France, and France announced that Mirage jets would soon circle the skies over Egypt. From there he traveled to New York, and the American president, Gerald Ford, announced that Egypt would be supplied with American weapons. President Sadat gave a speech at the United Nations, suggesting that the Palestinian Liberation Organization be included in the Geneva Conference that would be held to discuss the situation in the Middle East. Egypt and Israel were then separated in these discussions, which were to result in the second withdrawal, the evacuation of the Israeli army from southern Sinai, and the return of the oil fields. Syria, the Palestinian Liberation Organization, and the Soviet Union were all displeased with the separate discussions and with the strong rapprochement between Sadat and the West.

On his return, Sadat announced in England that the West could supply Egypt with weapons that the Soviet Union could not provide. During Sadat's visit, the world-renowned actor Omar Sharif had announced in New York that he was returning to Egypt and that he would build a resort on Alexandria's North Shore. The film *The Summons*, based on the novel by Yusuf Idris, was being shown at the Cinema Rivoli in Cairo and Cinema Radio in Alexandria, while the Cinema Royale in Alexandria was showing *One Flew over the Cuckoo's Nest*, which had been preceded by the fame of the actor Jack Nicholson, and of course of the producer, Miloš Forman. The play *The Lesson's Over, Stupid* continued its successful run in the Bab al-Luq Theater in Cairo.

It was announced that three women had been arrested, each of whom had married two men. Also winter fashions for men appeared, with big jackets boasting two large patch pockets and wide lapels. The Ministry of Supply announced that there would be no change in the price of meat, and that it would not exceed three-quarters of an Egyptian pound per kilogram, under a dollar for a pound of meat. An initial announcement was made of the creation of seven new cotton-trading companies, whose shares would be offered to the public, as a first step on the path to the new capitalist state. Additionally, it was announced that the creation of political parties had been turned down in favor of retaining the concept of platforms for various political tendencies within the Arab Socialist Union, the only national political organization since the time of Nasser. So far the number of platforms had reached forty, and it was said that they were a good beginning toward bringing people together and toward the formation of parties later on.

In broad daylight a drunk attacked some girls from the Wardian Secondary School in Alexandria as they were leaving school. At the end of September Daria Shafiq died, a woman who had been an important pioneer in movements for women and for patriotism as well. She was a daughter of the city of Tanta who had obtained her doctorate from the Sorbonne in France, who had translated the Quran into English and French, and who had published the magazine *The New Woman* during the forties. She fell from the balcony of her home in the Zamalek neighborhood of Cairo; it was rumored that she committed suicide because of the isolation in which she found herself living. Around the same time the governor of Alexandria announced the beginning of the reclamation of a large part of Lake Maryut in the area of Muharram Bey, which would be filled in with garbage from the city to create an international park.

In western Alexandria, the neighborhood of Dekhela experienced an invasion of people arriving from the Delta and from Upper Egypt. It was a neighborhood far from the city, with no high buildings but with a lovely, peaceful coast, and its women and girls were known for their fair complexion, their round faces, and their wide eyes. The new arrivals built in the southern part of the neighborhood, on low, sandy land that the people of Dekhela called 'The Mountain.' They built little houses in narrow streets, haphazardly planned, usurping the land or buying it from its Bedouin owners, who had taken possession of it ten years before but did not live there.

The Dekhela neighborhood had previously witnessed the exodus of its Greek citizens, during the sixties, as well as the departure of a number of artists, men and women, who spent the summer there. They closed their houses and went out to Agami, about the time of the foundation of the company Microsoft in the United States, and the appearance of the first personal computer ever made available on the market.

Three days earlier the sweeping miknasa storms had begun, dumping heavy rains on Alexandria. That's how it is every year during the last ten days of November: black clouds slam together and clash forcefully, and sudden bolts of lightning fill the sky over the city, followed by rolling, jarring rumbles of thunder. Who guards the city tonight but the angels on high?

The rain is ceaseless. It's illuminated by flashes of lightning high in the sky, and closer to the ground by the light of the street lamps. The noise is continuous as the rain pounds on the flat roofs of the houses or the asphalt streets, and the water pours onto the sidewalks from the gutters or from balconies, to be devoured by the drains that wait for it from year to year.

The sound of the wind, so quarrelsome moments before, dropped over the city, though it still mixed loudly with the sound of the waves along the shore of Alexandria. In the apartment of Yara's family her father and mother sat in front of the television, enjoying the warmth emanating from the air conditioner turned to the heat setting, and waiting for the film *Night Train* that would be shown soon. Her mother and father loved the dancing of Samia Gamal, "The Lady" as they called her, which was not at all vulgar, and they loved the acting of Stefan Rosty, who took evil to its extreme in this film.

Yara's brother Fuad, as usual, was away on a long voyage with the merchant ship where he served as an officer, heading for South

America. He would return months later, to begin a new voyage around the world. That's the way it was with the officers who graduated from the Merchant Marine College, which his father had chosen for him, and which he had taken to.

Yara's room had an ebony wardrobe that her father said was a work of art, and she knew that in fact it was just that. He had bought it along with a lot of other furniture for the house, from some of the Jews who left the city after the Suez War in 1956. Her father always said that he had refused to pay its owners anything less than its value at that time, which was much more than its original price. They were in a hurry, fleeing from Nasser's politics; but some of them, as her father always said, were his friends, speculating with him on the Egyptian Exchange in Manshiya. The Exchange was officially closed on Sunday and on Muslim and Christian holidays, but it closed also on Saturday and on Jewish holidays, because of the large number of Jews who worked in it. He would laugh and say shamelessly, in front of Yara and her mother, "We used to learn love, when we were boys, with the girls from the Jewish school in Shakkur Street." His mind would always wander from them then and he would speak distractedly, as if he were watching a film in the air before him. He would speak of the agents who filled the cafés in Muhammad Ali Square, specifically on the right side when you faced the Exchange, where the cafés and the wide sidewalks were also crowded with money changers as soon as the square was light, even before sunrise. Then he would close his eyes on what he saw, and fall silent.

Aside from the wardrobe there was a clothes tree in Yara's room, also of ebony; it had eight hooks, four above and four shorter ones below, and a few pieces of clothing were hanging from it. Yara was sitting now at a desk in the French style, inlaid with copper, each of its legs carved with a woman lifting a bunch of grapes to her mouth. In front of the desk were two chairs inlaid with mother of pearl, as was the chair she was sitting on. In the corner was a low, round Persian table from the fourteenth century, which her father had bought at auction in Tawfiq Street (Urabi Street after the July Revolution), where there were antique shops and the Hannaux Store, which had a cafeteria celebrated throughout Alexandria for its beauty.

On one side of the room was a copper bed with a small nightstand next to it. On the desk were books, notebooks, a holder for pens, and a small radio. She had announced more than once that she would not move the dial away from the music station, which she had not known existed until her boyfriend Nadir told her about it. "It looks as if I'm going to spend my life reading and writing and listening to the music station," he said. He told her about classical music, which he had come to love, and about the magical time with light music that began at two in the morning and went until six. It was rare that any announcer interrupted that program, and mostly it was from the sound tracks of films he had seen before. Yara did as Nadir did, and she said, going beyond his description, that the music did not glide down from heaven but rather opened the doors of heaven to her, so that she flew with it in the white clouds among the angels.

The first time they had declared their love was the previous year, when they went to the Antonius Garden. They found that the public was not allowed to walk in it. *Why?* It became a military zone after the defeat of 1967. *But we won the October War!* It's still a military center, and it's still restricted. That's what the soldier said, seeming surprised by their questions. They spent the day in the nearby zoo, just a few steps away.

The visitors were few that day and the air was springlike, with blossoms opening on their branches. The very instant that Nadir decided to gather his courage and ask for a kiss, she anticipated him and gave him a quick kiss on the lips. His eyes flew open in overwhelming pleasure, a magic he had not experienced before. This was his first kiss. The pleasure went from his lips to his whole body, and he closed his eyes in ecstasy and said "Allaah!" He found himself thinking about the lovely taste of women. Then he opened his arms again, this time shouting "Allaah, Allaah!" He spun around and nearly fell. She steadied him with her hands, laughing and saying, "There are people around us!" But she let him put his arm around her shoulders and they walked leaning on each other. Then she put her arm through his and the tender warmth of her breast traveled to his arm and then to his spirit, with a pleasure he could truthfully say he had never known before.

Now Yara smiled as she sat in her room. She was tempted to open the window to see the lightning in the sky, to see the rain rushing toward the earth. The fleeting lightning appeared behind the shutters and the glass of the high window. These were bahri buildings, facing the sea, Italian in design and overlooking the eastern port. The sound of the royal palm reached her, its fronds moving in the wind. If only for an instant she wanted to see the ships anchored far off, as they moved on the water, rising high and falling down again. She wanted to see the small feluccas closer in and how the waves pulled at them, too, even though she knew they were held in place by great heavy metal anchors, maybe by more than one for each boat. She wanted to see the Citadel of Qaytbay at a distance in the dark, and the lights of the Greek Club even though it had closed its doors, and the Yacht Club. Was there anyone in them now?

She opened the glass gently and the cold air penetrated the cracks of the wooden shutters. "Crazy," she said to herself as she shut the glass again. Once more she asked herself if she could open the shutters without her mother and father noticing. But their absorption in *Night Train* would not keep them from hearing the air entering the room.

Softly she closed the door of her room, which had been ajar; that way the sound might not reach them. She opened the glass and grasped the knob of the shutters, finding it very cold. She opened the shutters a little and a strong, cold wind rushed over her face and chest. What did Yara want tonight?

She wanted the wind to carry her, to fly with her to the sky. She was smiling in happiness. She had opened the shutters enough to see the darkness before her covering everything in the eastern port before her, and she saw the Citadel of Qaytbay, darker than its surroundings. Who would believe that in its place once stood the Lighthouse of Alexandria, four or five meters taller than the Citadel? It had been anchored there for centuries, guiding the ships, announcing that it was one of the Seven Wonders of the World! Had lovers gone to it by day as they now went to the Citadel? But the sound of the thunder was continuous, so she closed the window hurriedly, amazed at her own madness.

The music of *Boléro* filled the air in the room. She really wanted to dance. She had seen a ballet dancer once on the television program *With the Ballet*, dancing to the beautiful music of Ravel. She began to move her legs to the rhythm of the music. When would she have the freedom of a butterfly? She went with Nadir to the Nuzha Gardens to kiss him and be kissed, and to the Smouha neighborhood, where there were thickets of trees and open spaces and very few houses, which all seemed to be uninhabited. No one saw them in the great broad spaces filled with camphor and willow trees, date and banana palms, as they hugged and kissed each other. Every time Nadir's thoughts would stray, despite the delight that moved through them, and he would say, "When will we be together between four walls, without worrying that anyone will see us?" She knew he was inviting her to the apartment he lived in with his friends, their classmates in the college. She would pat his hand without answering, repressing her inner desire, a great urge to say yes. But now she laughed as she sat at her desk. She glanced at the book of modern philosophy, opened to the lesson on Nietzsche, and said, "It's a night for Superman." But before she returned to studying she heard a light tapping on her door, which then opened. It was her mother, her eyes wide in surprise and confusion.

She whispered, "Kariman!"

Yara was even more surprised. Her mother continued:

"She's standing outside. I saw her from the peephole after she rang the bell. Were you expecting her?"

Yara's surprise grew. "No. Why would she come in this weather?"

Her mother answered, "Hurry, go open the door for her."

Yara crossed the living room where her father sat, absorbed in the film, as her mother went back to sit next to him. Both of them were dressed for a winter evening at home, with a neat robe over their pajamas. In front of them was a dish of cashews, pistachios, and walnuts, all the nuts that had disappeared from Egypt

7

for so long during the time of Nasser, and that had returned now to invade the market with high prices.

It was after ten, and Nadir was still sitting in the small, dimly lit lobby. He felt as if it were an old place where no one had come before. He had been waiting for more than an hour, hearing a continuous sound of moaning that came from some unknown source. The intelligence officer who had come to his house at about five in the afternoon had given him a small paper, summoning him to appear at the State Security headquarters on Faraana Street at eight-thirty. It only took a moment at the door, when he went out to see who was knocking and came back dumbfounded. His father had just finished the evening maghrib prayer, his mother was in the kitchen preparing a platter of fish, and his little brother was also in the kitchen, hurrying the food. His father saw him frowning and asked him,

"Who was at the door?"

Nadir did not answer for a moment, looking distracted. Then he said, "No one. Someone who made a mistake with the address. He wanted our neighbors."

He fell silent and went to his room. It was a simple room with an old bed, an old desk, a metal wardrobe, also old, and wooden shelves on the wall holding a small number of books. He usually borrowed books from the college library or the municipal library. If he couldn't buy newly published books, he borrowed most of them from Amm al-Sayyid, who sold books at the Raml station. He would borrow them for a penny a book, or two pennies, or five if the book was expensive. Dostoyevsky's novels stood out amid the other books because of their large size. Really, why did he insist on buying them, when he could have borrowed them also? Why did he always read them on cold winter nights, when the sound of the rain was ceaseless, like tonight? He dreamed of a day when he would visit Russia and stay up until morning during the icy, sleepless nights.

He had just finished reading *Dr. Zhivago* today, after a week of pleasure and pain. He paused over the last poems, over everything in them. Now he recited to himself:

The darkness of the night still reigns
and the time has not yet come
for the sky to scatter its stars
that cannot be counted.

Always, when Lara was running before him in the open fields, in the
buildings besieged by ice and death, in the war and the internment
camps, the name of his beloved Yara and her face moved above the
pages of the novel, and he found himself saying "Yara, Yara." He
often read "Lara" as "Yara," and pushed away his anxiety over the
separation that afflicted Lara and Zhivago.

At that moment in his room Tchaikovsky's *Marche slave* filled the
air around him, coming from the radio. As usual he was surprised
at the announcer who called it "March of the Slaves," not realizing
that "Slav" is the name of a people and does not mean "slaves." He
remembered what Dr. Hussein Fawzi, that Egyptian Sindbad, had
said during one of the music lessons he presented every Thursday
on Channel Two on the radio, about how Tchaikovsky had written
this orchestral music when Orthodox Serbia had risen against the
Ottoman state in 1876. Orthodox Russia had stood with Serbia,
and had sent its soldiers to fight on its side, and the music was
a glorification of the Slavs against the Ottomans. But that didn't
matter now. He was confused and didn't know what would happen
tonight. The man who had brought him the summons must be
walking now in the wind and rain, or standing on the deserted
Maks beach, waiting for the bus. Was summoning him important
enough for this man to rush out so urgently in this weather? What
would happen if he didn't go?

An hour of Arabic music began with the song of Muhammad Abdel Wahhab, "The Night was Calm," composed by the
poet Ahmad Shawqi. To his great surprise, Nadir found himself
forgetting the matter of the summons, and thinking instead about
how the tune of the song was based on the same melodic interval
as the *Marche slave*. The discovery surprised him and he smiled. He
thought about how he had not realized that before, nor had any

of the music critics who were always accusing Muhammad Abdel Wahhab of stealing from Western music. But he liked the fact that Muhammad Abdel Wahhab had known the music of Tchaikovsky very early in his career.

Nadir was pleased that he could realize this, despite the anxiety that engulfed him over this sudden summons. He was capable, then, of facing the summons. But he asked himself again why he had not asked the intelligence officer the reason for the summons. The man wouldn't have answered. Nadir had taken the paper from him, frowning, as if he had been expecting it. All that he had noticed was the large palm of the man's hand, unusually large, as he handed him the paper.

Nadir noticed *Dr. Zhivago* open to the last page in front of him, and he closed it. A delicious aroma of fish came to him as his mother opened the door of the room and said, smiling,

"A platter of fish to swear by! Come and eat."

"I'm not hungry."

She was surprised. "What? Dad bought bluefish today especially for you. He bought two kilos for three Egyptian pounds, all at once!"

He did not move from his place. Looking into his eyes, she asked him, "What's wrong, Nadir? What's on your mind?"

"I have an important errand. One of my friends is sick and I have to visit him."

"In this weather?"

"Forgive me, Mama. Anyway you know I like rain."

She didn't look convinced. He saw that on her face, and said, "Fine. Bring the food to me here."

He thought that would solve the problem of eating among them when he was preoccupied. She returned quickly with a tray bearing a big plate holding two large bluefish, grilled, and another plate with red rice. The two bluefish were surrounded by slices of tomato and onion and pepper and a few slices of potato. Did he really not have any appetite for this meal he loved?

He began to eat slowly, then he could not resist. He must show his mother the pleasure she was used to from him when she cooked fish. He would never leave her worried, thinking about what was keeping him from eating her food that he loved.

He finished and dressed quickly—pants, a shirt and over it a pullover, and a chamois leather jacket. He left the house after telling his parents that he would spend the night with his friends, after he visited the one who was sick. They knew that he spent most nights during the school year with his friends from outside Alexandria, in the apartment they rented close to the college. In the beginning his father wasn't happy with that, but he saw that he spent all his time reading, and he knew that reading kept him away from anything else. So he accepted what his wife said: "What's Nadir going to do with his friends other than what he does here? Read."

Nadir was soon standing on the Maks beach, at the end of the Number 1 bus route. Behind him was the Zephyr Casino, closed for some time, and the Magd Sports Club, which was no more than an apartment in a small building, with a room for watching television and a room for playing ping-pong. Near the building was old Amm Ahmad's cigarette kiosk, and facing it was the old railway station, to which no trains came and where no one worked.

The bus wasn't long in coming. It stopped and two men got off, hurrying in the rain and wind. Amm Ahmad saw him standing in front of the Magd Club, under the balcony, and asked him, "Where are you going in this weather, Ustaz Nadir?"

Nadir was looking at the surging, high waves, their crashing noise filling the air, his shoulders hunched against the cold. He answered, "It's an important errand, Amm Ahmad."

"God be with you, son."

He hurried onto the bus. The driver stayed in his seat, but the conductor got off and headed for Amm Ahmad, returning quickly with a bottle of Spatz. He held it up in front of him and said to the driver, "Only iron dents iron." Then he said to Nadir, "Hello, Ustaz. I read in the paper that in Russia they eat ice cream in the dead of winter, and we're just as good as they are."

Nadir smiled, and gave him a penny for the ticket. The conductor said to the driver, "Don't wait. Nobody will come out of his house except for this crazy guy. Let's get going."

Nadir smiled again and the driver started the bus. Nadir began looking at the windows of the old houses, all of them shut, like the windows of his apartment. Soon the bus was passing the low-slung coast guard barracks, also silent, showing no trace of anyone among them. The bus would enter Maks Street, and everything he would see along the way would be silent: the army depots on the right, the slaughterhouse and tanning companies on the left, filling the air with their smell. He would pass the Wardian Secondary School for Girls, and his old school, Tahir Bey Middle School. He would pass the Khafagi Café, where a few customers would appear behind the glass, like ghosts in the darkness. Would Isa Salamawy be there tonight, in the café near his house, rather than going to Ateneos in Raml Station? He told them that he was always in the Khafagi Café in the morning, and in the evening he was always in Ateneos. Would he break the rule tonight because of the rain and the cold? Should Nadir leave the bus and tell him about the summons? No. He would go and finish everything on his own.

The bus left Maks Street and entered the neighborhood of Mina al-Basal, turning into the Street of the Seven Girls and Manshiya. To his surprise, when the bus reached Raml Station he saw that five people had boarded along the way without his noticing. He got off and walked alone to Faraana Street. The rain lightened as he moved along Safiya Zaghlul Street, where almost all the shops were closed. He turned into Sultan Husayn Street, then he went into Faraana Street and stopped in front of the villa that had become the headquarters of the State Security forces. He saw the tall trees surrounding it, the darkness in the lovely streets beside it, the dim light coming from the villa. It was eight-thirty, precisely the time of the appointment.

But now it was ten, and he had not yet been taken to the one who had summoned him. The dim light in the room had not changed, nor had the moaning stopped coming from its unknown source. But a short man appeared before him suddenly without making any noise, and pointed to a door at the end of the lobby. It had been closed the whole time, and no one had entered it or come out. He said, "Please go in."

Nadir rose quickly and went forward, but the short man grasped his arm for a moment and then said, "The best thing is for you to tell the truth so that you come out quickly. You're going to meet Sayyid Bey Abdel Bari, the head of the State Security forces. He's a good man. Don't annoy him."

The short man said this gently, and then disappeared. Nadir didn't pay any attention to where the man went, just as he hadn't noticed where he came from.

Yara's eyes went to Kariman's face, red from the cold. It surprised her and made her smile like a child who had never seen that before. Kariman came in with a blue cap on her head, a blue coat on her body and a sky blue scarf around her neck, so it seemed as if the cold was concentrated completely in her face and her nose, which was flaming red. She said,

"Of course you're surprised that I've come so unexpectedly."

Yara said, smiling, "On the contrary, it makes me happy. I'm just surprised by how beautiful you are."

Kariman smiled and rubbed her hands. "What lovely warmth!" She took off her coat and scarf to put them on the clothes tree, then rubbed her hands again forcefully, and said, "I wish I could have a coffee."

"Nothing easier." Yara went to a small nightstand in a corner and brought out an alcohol burner, a coffee pot, two small cups, a glass of water, and two small jars, one holding coffee and the other sugar.

Kariman said, "I'd like to put coffee things like this in my room, but my mother won't let me."

Yara asked in surprise, "Why?"

"Actually my stepfather tells her that girls shouldn't drink coffee."

Yara gave a short laugh and said, "Crazy!"

Kariman said, "What's more, he says that a girl who drinks coffee may be smoking hashish too."

"He's really, officially crazy."

"Every so often he tells me my clothes are too short and looks at my legs when I'm going out or coming in. Is it okay if smoke a cigarette?"

Yara was briefly embarrassed, then she said, "Of course." She hurried to close the door of the room, which had been slightly ajar.

Kariman took a pack of Cleopatra cigarettes and a Ronson lighter from her bag and lit a cigarette. She inhaled deeply and closed her eyes for a moment, and then blew the smoke out slowly as she opened her eyes again. It seemed as if she was lifting a heavy burden from her chest.

Yara finished preparing the coffee and offered a cup to Kariman; she took it and lifted it to her nose, smelling it, while Yara looked on happily. Kariman asked,

"Why didn't you come to the college today?"

"The weather wasn't inviting."

Kariman thought for a bit, her face lightly veiled in sadness. "I would have liked to stay home, but . . . ." She thought some more, and then said, "My mother went to her work at school, and her husband stayed home, so I went to the college."

Yara reflected a little and then asked, "What's up with your stepfather, Kariman?"

"He harasses me."

"To that extent?"

Kariman nodded and said, "Don't worry. What matters is that students carrying iron chains appeared in the College of Law today and attacked some of the leftist students. They're from Islamist groups."

Yara's face showed her amazement and disbelief, so Kariman continued: "They'll definitely come to our college."

Yara asked, "Are you afraid for Hasan?"

"And for Nadir, of course. Neither one came today. Likely because of the weather."

Yara's confusion increased. Kariman said, "We'll have to be careful the next few days."

Yara wondered if that was really what had made Kariman visit her in this weather. They would all go to the college tomorrow or the next day and learn what happened. But then Kariman said,

"Can I stay with you tonight?"

Yara smiled happily. "Of course."

She hurried to open her wardrobe and took out a winter night-gown. "My clothes will be a little big, but the bed is small and it will warm us both."

Kariman gave her a long look as she took the nightgown from her, and said, "Your eyes are beautiful, honey colored, shining and moist, as if you were about to cry."

Yara laughed. "How can I compare to Kariman the blonde, with her green eyes! Listen to this beautiful music with me, change your clothes, and stretch out next to me on the bed."

Kariman wondered, "Who's the composer?"

"Borodin, but don't ask me who he is. Maybe I'll learn some-thing about him later on. What matters is that the piece is named *Prince Igor*. I've heard it many times before. The good thing about the music station is that it often repeats the same pieces, and you remember them. I love this piece. They always play it at this time of night."

Yara couldn't keep herself from looking at Kariman as she took off her skirt and blouse to put on the nightgown. She smiled, liking the marvelous form of her body. She found herself asking,

"Did you like the film *The Summons*?"

Kariman chuckled and got under the covers with her. She said, "Hasan didn't give me a chance to enjoy the film—he was kissing me the whole time."

Yara laughed her short laugh, delighted. She said, "It's as if the two of them were in it together, Hasan and Nadir. Nadir did the same with me when we were watching the film. But the song is beautiful, and it scared me."

Kariman said, "Naturally the film can't express the depth of the novel. The story isn't about the naiveté of a man or woman from a village facing the city, or about the naiveté of ignorance in the face

15

of knowledge. It's as if it were destiny, as if every man has a hidden summons to an obscure fate."

"The funny thing is that after we came out of the film, Nadir began to explain the myth of the summons in history, from the time of the Greeks. He told me the story of the Sirens, mistresses of seduction. Sailors heard their song on the sea and then they'd leave the ship and throw themselves into the water and not come back. He told me that he saw the film *Ulysses* in a second-run theater years ago, and he saw how Ulysses tried not to respond to the seductive sound. He had the sailors plug their ears and tie him to the mast of the ship with his ears unplugged. He couldn't stay tied when he heard the voices of the Sirens, so he tore off the ropes and would have thrown himself in the sea, if it weren't for the sailors holding him back as the ship was pulling away."

Kariman said, "Those two guys are both crazy."

They laughed, then silence descended on them for a few moments. *Prince Igor* had ended, and after that the music of *The Godfather* filled the room. Yara knew it well, but her face showed her fear, as she remembered Laila Gamal's song in the film, *The Summons.*

> Something from afar is calling me,
> something has happened to me.
> I can't help it, father,
> Father, I can't help it.

Kariman noticed her distraction and asked her, "Where did you go?"

Yara smiled without answering. Kariman continued, "I wish we wouldn't go to sleep, so we could keep on listening to music and talking until morning."

When Nadir entered the room he saw that it was very large, and he saw the head of State Security sitting at a huge desk at one end of it. The man did not look up; he was writing something on a paper before him, and he motioned to Nadir to sit down. He remained absorbed in his writing for several minutes, while Nadir thought about the sound of moaning, uninterrupted here too, and about foreign films about Nazi concentration camps, and about what he had read in the newspapers about prison camps in the time of Gamal Abdel Nasser. He told himself that these things didn't happen in Egypt now. Still, images of torture from the film *Karnak*, shown in theaters since the previous summer, came back to him and took shape before his eyes. For a few moments he thought about Yara. Yara was more beautiful than Suad Hosni, so would they get to her? He pushed himself to think instead about how to apologize to Suad Hosni. He imagined himself meeting her and beginning to apologize to her for having thought that there was anyone more beautiful than she was. He was contemplating her lovely smile, which opened the expanses of the universe to him and filled him with delight. He took great comfort in thinking about anything other than torture and humiliation, hoping to give himself courage.

At last the head of State Security looked up at him, having finished what he was writing, and Nadir nearly laughed aloud. He had never expected this great likeness between the man and Mustafa the barber, where he went for a shave on Maks Street! It was as if he were his twin. He felt reassured; he would treat him as if he were Mustafa the barber, and not at all as Sayyid Bey Abdel Bari. He might also think about meeting the man's wife so he could tell stories about her, like the fabulous stories that Mustafa's customers told about his wife Laila, who was really beautiful. Everyone knew that their stories were all just dreams and that none of them had met her; at most someone might have seen her passing in front of him on the street. But they never stopped telling stories.

"Hello, Si Nadir."

Nadir was confused as he emerged from his imaginings.

"Will you have tea?"

"No thank you, sir."

"Do you work or are you a student?"

"Both, sir. I give private lessons to the kids in my neighborhood, and I'm a student in the Humanities College. I'm helping to support myself."

"Then you are the only one who has any money, among your classmates?"

"I don't understand!"

"I mean, you spend your money on the wall magazines."

Nadir smiled. "The wall magazines don't cost anything. You know, respected sir, that the price of a piece of cardboard is four pennies, no more, and the magazine is one sheet with articles on it. Ball point pens also cost a couple of pennies."

Sayyid Bey Abdel Bari nodded his head and was silent for a bit, and the sound of the moaning returned, louder. It was a woman's voice this time. But Nadir decided to hold himself together as much as he could. Thus he denied the accusation of being a Communist. He said that it wasn't a crime for a man to be a Communist, on the one hand, and that their studying Marxism in the college did not mean that he was a Communist, either. In the Philosophy Department they studied all philosophical, social, and historical theories. If he and his friends disagreed with the politics of President Sadat—especially his new policy of rapprochement between Egypt and Israel and America and abandoning Egypt's genuine ally, the Soviet Union, and its home and natural orbit, the Arab world—that only meant that they were Egyptians who loved their country.

Sayyid Bey Abdel Bari gave him plenty of time to talk, because he wanted to know all the secrets of his soul. He pretended to like what he heard, to lure Nadir into saying more; and Nadir, who never wavered from seeing Sayyid Bey Abdel Bari as Mustafa the barber, answered all the questions thoroughly and fearlessly. He said he didn't know of any secret Communist parties in Egypt, and that he was hearing about that now for the first time, from Sayyid Bey. Bishr Zahran, Hasan Hafiz, and Kariman didn't know anything about that either. They were his friends and he knew everything about them. He tried to joke a little, and said that Bishr Zahran, for example, edited the magazine out of a desire for fame more than as a political act, because Bishr was short. For a moment he was worried that Sayyid Bey Abdel Bari might be short, but the man laughed and Nadir was reassured. He went on to say that Hasan was an artist who wrote plays and short stories, and who was most inclined to the theater of the absurd.

The titles of his plays showed that, *The Eye Walks and the Foot Sees, The Night Sun and the Daylight Moon*, did that have anything to do with Communism? His last short story, published in the last magazine they hung up, called "The Old Anxiety," was about enemies who don't come to a city, so the people there turn into dwarfs. It was inspired by the novel *The Tartar Steppe* by Dino Buzzati. He just added the story of people turning into dwarfs.

Sayyid Bey Abdel Bari's eyes widened in real amazement. He asked, "Is this Dino Buzzati a foreigner?"

"He's an Italian writer."

"Is he with you in the party?"

Nadir was taken aback, and then he felt a desire to laugh, but he contained it. "There isn't any party or anything else, sir. We're angry artists and this Buzzati is an important Italian writer, like Pirandello, for example. His novel is old. It's been translated into Arabic and it's sold on the sidewalks for ten cents. We don't like politics."

Sayyid Bey Abdel Bari gave him a long look, and then said, "And Yara—don't you love her?"

Nadir was disconcerted. The image of Mustafa the barber, which had occupied the face of Sayyid Bey Abdel Bari, disappeared, and another image sprang into its place, the image of the man who tried to rape Suad Hosni in the film *Karnak*. But he was able to conceal his pain and say, "Please, sir, there's no need to talk about Yara."

Sayyid Bey Abdel Bari's eyes widened, as if he had found Nadir's weak point. He said, "Are you afraid for her?"

Nadir closed his eyes and began to feel true terror. Then he said, in a low voice, "Yes."

Several moments passed in silence, during which Nadir noticed Sayyid Bey Abdel Bari looking at him deeply. He looked at the floor so the other man wouldn't see any more of his weakness. He heard him saying, "Fine, we'll leave Yara aside for now. If I asked you if people are free in Egypt, what would you say?"

"No."

The answer came without thinking, and Sayyid Bey Abdel Bari's face showed wrath. Nadir said hurriedly, once again seeing the image of Mustafa the barber on the man's face, "Sorry. Basically I'm an existentialist, that's why I said no."

"What do you mean?"

Nadir took off, speaking like someone who had found a real escape. "Existentialism considers that man is born and dies without having willed that, and between birth and death he lives as others want him to live, so he's not free. Others are hell, and the only freedom is found in suicide."

Sayyid Bey Abdel Bari was the one taken aback this time. Nadir saw that and hurried to continue, taking courage:

"Existentialism produced the movement of the hippies in Europe, for example, and anarchist singers like Juliette Greco. The only meaning of existence is to get out of the usual rut. A man doesn't like to be committed to anything, he doesn't like to belong to anything."

Sayyid Bey Abdel Bari looked distracted, as if he were thinking about something else. Suddenly he pointed to the exit.

"Please."

"I should leave?"

"Naturally. You won't be of any use to us."

Nadir hurried to stand, saying with feeling, "Thank you very much, sir!" He did not know that as he rushed out, Sayyid Bey Abdel Bari was watching him with disgust.

Nadir couldn't believe he was free until the cold air struck him and he saw the raindrops falling in the darkness. He saw Fuad Street in front of him and took off toward it, hurrying along under the balconies to protect himself from the rain. He noticed that the moon was up, far above the clouds that veiled its light. He found himself laughing and calling, "Good for you, Barber Mustafa!"

He would make his way now to Raml Station and take the tram to the apartment, and tell his friends everything. It would be nice if they could go to the Nawal Boîte nightclub tonight, and stay up until morning with Nawal. In the club he would tell her everything that had happened, and they would laugh. He wouldn't tell Yara anything, and he would ask his friends not to tell her anything. Yara was a bird of paradise, and he didn't want to cause her any fear. Nawal's shoulder was big enough for him. She would make things easier to bear and would reassure him.

He really needed to know, today more than any other day, why Nawal the nightclub owner cared about them. After all, they were just Communist kids, as she said, laughing heartily. Would he learn her secret tonight? But no matter how much he hurried on the way it would be late. He would put off going to the Nawal Boîte until another night.

All the stores around him were closed. He wondered why the street was so dark tonight.

He was alone when he turned into Safiya Zaghlul Street; he didn't see anyone in the street and all the stores were closed here, too. He didn't notice the placards for films in the Metro Theater or the Rialto or even the Alhambra or the Strand, at the end of the street. In Raml Station the booksellers had all folded the cloths they spread on the sidewalk and closed their kiosks along the wall. No one there, either. The tram was standing still, lit from within, but no one was heading for it. It looked as if it had been forgotten for a long time. When it moved off with him aboard he was alone. At Azarita Station a man of about forty got on. The surprising thing was that he ignored the whole empty carriage and sat facing Nadir, rubbing his hands from the cold and blowing on them, even though he was wearing a heavy black coat and had a wool scarf around his neck.

"The miknasa winds." The man made the remark, but Nadir did not respond. He was thinking about whether Sayyid Bey Abdel Bari had sent this man after him.

The man said, "It's well named. It sweeps away everything on earth."

Nadir smiled this time. He didn't think the head of the State Security forces would be stupid enough to send someone when Nadir would see no one else.

Soon the tram arrived at the Camp Caesar stop, and quickly he left the tram and went up the little stairs to the station, to find the street empty and the stores closed here as well. The wind grew stronger and papers on the ground began to fly. Water was still pouring into the drains even though the rain had lightened. He turned into one of the lanes, hearing the sound of the waves and met by gusts of wind as he headed for Tanais Street. It wasn't far, no more than twenty meters, then he turned into the street as the wind moved around him. He climbed the stairs of the house and rang the doorbell more than once. The response was long in coming, but then he heard Ahmad Basim's hoarse voice: "Patience, people."

He smiled, and Ahmad opened the door. As usual he was blocking the way with his very tall frame and broad chest. But Ahmad was shocked at the sight of him.

"Come in quickly, you're soaked!"

He went in and saw Hasan Hafiz sitting in the living room along with Bishr Zahran. Ahmad closed the door and turned to him. "You look as if you're a refugee from a catastrophe."

Nadir was surprised at Hasan's quick return from Mansura, where he had gone a week before. He asked,

"You're back, Hasan? You said you were going to spend two weeks there."

They shook hands. But Ahmad seemed to be finishing an earlier conversation. He declared,

"For your information our village women are very beautiful, but the problem is with the panties."

Bishr laughed and Hasan smiled his partial smile. It seemed to Nadir that he wasn't going to be able to tell them what had happened to him, since Ahmad carried on,

"The panties are all made of either rough cotton or hemp."

Nadir found himself almost forgetting his situation. He was surprised at himself since he had come here to tell his story, and he never expected a conversation like this. He found himself laughing with Bishr, while Hasan kept his half smile and Ahmad went on talking:

"Brother, I saw some panties today in the Prestige Store on Saad Zaghlul Street—I mean I saw them in the window—and they were no more than a thread. And what a thread! And for how much? For two whole pounds! I asked the seller, why two pounds? If it was half a penny, maybe. That thing, the merchandise could fall right out of it."

They couldn't stop laughing, and this time Hasan's voice was raised in laughter, too. But Bishr said, "Stop, Ahmad, please. We want to find out why Nadir came in this weather."

Nadir had already decided to cut off Ahmad's talk. He said, "I came straight from State Security."

Silence and shock descended on them. Bishr and Hasan exchanged troubled looks, but Ahmad said,

"I'm going to go in to Saadiya, you stay with State Security. You won't be satisfied until they arrest you all." He moved toward his room.

Nadir knew the names of all the women Ahmad brought to the apartment, and he knew the names of the female students he brought, too. He, Bishr, and Hasan were careful not to be there when the students came, so as not to cause them any embarrassment. He found himself asking doubtfully,

"Who's this Saadiya?"

Bishr answered, "Don't worry, she sells peanuts in Shatbi Station. He surprised us—he brought her and a box of Rabso detergent and said she was going to bathe with it."

Nadir was too astonished to laugh. Ahmad turned back to them before going to his room and said, "Pipe down, if she hears you she might get annoyed and leave." Then he said to Nadir, "I swear she took a bath with the Rabso and came out white as cream. What can I do? I'm tired of dainty women."

He left them quickly, chuckling, and went into his room.

Bishr said to Nadir, "Hasan didn't go to Mansura. He went to a camp in Amiriya through the Student Welfare Office. Naturally there were students from several colleges with him. They trained them in karate, gave them lectures against leftists, and at the end of the week they gave every student ten pounds."

Nadir looked stunned.

Hasan said, "I accepted the offer from the director of the Office in order to learn what's going on around us. Of course I won't go on with them. I'll keep the ten pounds until we go to the Nawal Boîte so we can spend them there—it doesn't make sense for Nawal to pay for us every time. There're hard days ahead, and Egypt is changing without our noticing. All the lectures in the camp were about capitalism and the freedom that awaits Egypt in all things, and against Communism as a comprehensive ideology." The he smiled his partial smile and added, "Sons of whores."

Silence fell over them for a few moments, then Bishr said to Nadir, "Now tell us what happened to you."

Nadir was thinking about whether it was a coincidence that he had been summoned to State Security just as students were being trained to beat up Communists.

Warmth enfolded Yara's room as dawn approached. The rain had fallen silent and the waves had calmed, leaving only the sound of the royal palm fronds moving in the wind. The whole world was sleeping around Yara and Kariman, but they remained awake, Kariman sitting cross-legged on the bed and Yara supporting her back against the headboard. Yara said, her eyes sparkling,

"This is the music of *Dr. Zhivago*; I know this piece, too. I'm going to read the novel soon. Nadir was reading it and talked to me a lot about it." Then she laughed. "The problem is that I'm not used to reading novels and he says this one is huge."

Kariman shrugged her shoulder. "Don't read it."

"I'm afraid he'll be annoyed."

"Then read it."

Yara lifted her voice in her short laugh, delighted, and then said, "I would have liked to see the film with Nadir. It was forbidden in Egypt after the 'setback' with Israel. The government was protesting against Omar Sharif—they said that after the Naksa in 1967 he said something in support of Israel, in Hollywood. When Sadat came to power they showed the film, but I didn't see it; I was in the last year of middle school. A month ago it was in the Fuad

Theater, but I told Nadir I was afraid of a second-run theater, afraid of the audience. I wish I'd gone with him."

Yara's apparent pain surprised Kariman, who leaned over and gave her a kiss, and then said, "You're really sensitive, Yara. How do you live here among us? Nadir is right to compose poetry about you."

Yara's eyes shone and she asked, "Do you want to hear the latest?"

Kariman answered, "Poetry and music, Yara, there's nothing better than that."

Yara put her hand under her pillow and brought out a notebook. Kariman laughed, and Yara said proudly,

"I always put it under my pillow."

She opened the notebook as Kariman smiled. She closed her eyes for a moment, and then began to read:

My spirit yearns for my love's fingertips,
I float above them with my lips,
my heart beating to the sound of my kisses.

Kariman's eyes widened in admiration and surprise, but she said nothing so that Yara would continue.

My love's fingers are the candles of my ether,
a glow like water,
a light like air,
like the light of the Virgin fair
appearing by night
to a monk, alone
in his cell beyond sight
amid the desert stones.

Yara closed her eyes again, and Kariman said, "How lovely!"

Yara said, "Listen to the end," and she returned to reading:

Here in Alexandria
Lovers have wept on the beach;

The waves of the sea have taken all the lost stories of love
And brought them back as sorrows,
In the clouds of autumn.

Here in Alexandria
The waves may take the stories of love
But no forgetfulness enfolds them.

Here in Alexandria
I will not bid her farewell,
The story of my love will not be lost,
Rather all the walls will bear it.
There is resolution in my heart
And courage in my spirit.
Even if all the gods abandon me,
I will take my love with me
And go with the quail
When the winter ends
To countries I know not,
But where I know
That women will receive me,
Singing,
On the roofs of houses,
With men playing guitar in the streets.
The story of my love will remain after me,
A song above Alexandria,
Until I return to her again,
When my story has turned into trees
Filling her sky.

2

THE MORNING WASN'T WARM ENOUGH for Rawayih and Ghada to sit
on the large balcony as they usually did on sunny mornings. Usually
they came home before dawn, exhausted, from the Blue Pearl nightclub. Then they woke up at eleven, bathed, and sat on the balcony,
proudly drinking instant Nescafé (unknown in the country until
recently), mixed with milk. Then they combed their hair.

Today the two women were sitting in the living room of the
second-floor apartment, where they had been living for four years.
They were barely thirty years old, but they looked older. Sometimes
other women would come to live with them, but they soon disappeared. The first floor of the building was an empty apartment; no
one knew why the owner had closed it. The building was surrounded
by a wall a few feet away, but the space inside the wall was just dirt,
with no trace of the flowers and trees that the previous owner must
have intended to plant, to have built it that way. A man in his fifties came every month to collect the rent. The clothes presser Abul
Hasan, who also acted as a rental agent for apartments, said that
the man had bought the house from its Greek owner when he left
Egypt in 1962. In the past the houses in this street had been owned
by Greeks, Syrians, Jews, or well-off Egyptians, who had lived there
themselves. Most of the houses had been built before the revolution
in 1952, or at least during the fifties. Their owners had observed the
building regulations, so the height of the houses was no more than
one and a half times the width of the street. That meant that almost
all of them had no more than three floors, or four, if the house was

on a corner between Tanais Street and one of the lanes leading to the Corniche or to Port Said Street.

When the University of Alexandria was established in the forties it started with only a few colleges, and the students were Alexandrians, with families and homes. The number of colleges increased in the fifties and students began to come from the countryside, so the university built dormitories to house those students, among the farms and trees of the Smouha neighborhood. That was enough then but that situation could not continue, especially after Gamal Abdel Nasser declared in 1961 that tuition would be free. The number of students living away from home increased, and some of the long-time Egyptian owners of the houses—or the new owners who bought them from the foreigners leaving Alexandria because of Nasser's policy of nationalizing factories and foreign banks—began to use the apartments to house students. That's how the students found their way to Tanais Street, and to Tiba Street as well, on the other side of Port Said Street, preferring them to other streets in the city because of their proximity to the most crowded colleges, Humanities, Law, Business, and Education, which were all close together in the same neighborhood. Students from more distant colleges, such as Engineering, Agriculture, Medicine, and Pharmacy, also found their way to these two streets. There they found more freedom than the residents of the dormitories in Smouha had, and the dorms were in any case no longer enough for the students from outside Alexandria.

It was natural that many of the women from the nightclubs along the Corniche, parallel to Tanais Street, would find their way to the apartments, and from there to the students' apartments. The original Alexandrian residents began to flee these two streets, as did the newer residents who had moved into apartments left vacant by the earlier departure of the foreigners. It wasn't hard to leave, for there were many apartments available in Camp Caesar, Sporting, and Cleopatra, whose owners burned incense in the hope that someone would come to live in them. More than anywhere else, Tanais and Tiba Streets became known as a school to learn love and sex.

Tanais Street was more famous than Tiba, and the saying went, "If you want to raise hell, Tanais won't tell." Little by little all the families left the apartments, and nearly all of them became apartments for students or women of the night.

Most of the doormen also disappeared, and the few who were left began to work with the pimps. Some of the clothes pressers, too, would put a curtain behind the ironing board, behind them as they worked; if a client asked him he would lift the curtain, and the client would find two or three women from whom he could choose.

Rawayih and Ghada lived below the apartment which Hasan Hafiz and Ahmad Basim shared with Bishr Zahran and Nadir Saeed. Rawayih was flipping through the pages of a *Playboy* magazine, given to her by one of the nightclub clients, someone who worked on a merchant vessel. She kept staring in amazement and shaking her head, so Ghada said to her, "How long are you going to keep on looking through that magazine?"

"I can't believe that there are magazines like this, magazines that show everything. What would you say if I cut out the pages and hung them on the wall?"

Ghada cried, "You're crazy! That magazine is forbidden, you'll get us into trouble!" Then she laughed. "Give it to the guys upstairs and let them hang the pictures on their walls. At least they're men and it won't hurt them, like us. It'll warm them up more."

They laughed, and Rawayih said, "I'll finish my Nescafé and take the magazine up to them. While I'm there I'll make fun of Ahmad for that woman who's been with him for days."

Ghada said, surprised, "Another woman, not us?"

"I saw her going up with him after sunset in the worst weather. He was taking advantage of the darkness and her dark complexion and thought that no one would see them."

They laughed more. Ghada thought a little and then said, "I don't know why Nadir and Hasan don't respond to us. They sit with us and eat and talk, but they never sleep with us."

"Losers."

Ghada said, "They seem to be in love."

Rawayih looked at her in astonishment. "Love! What does love mean?"

Then she closed the magazine and stood up, to take it up to the next floor; but Ghada said, "Save yourself the trouble and don't go up now. When I was standing on the balcony I saw them all going out to the college."

Rawayih thought for a bit, and seemed annoyed. "And I wanted Nadir to write a letter for me today."

Ghada looked at her skeptically, but she didn't comment.

They were sitting in the large cafeteria, which was both wide and long, and crowded more than usual today because of the rain outside. Nadir, Hasan, Bishr, Kariman, and Yara sat in a group with Isa Salamawy in the center, a tall, thin, elegant man over forty. Isa was a little distracted as they were engaged in side conversations. He was thinking about whether he would come back to study in another college when the coming academic year ended. He had previously finished the colleges of Business and Law, and he couldn't start in a practical college, as he had taken his secondary diploma in the humanities section. The only theoretical college left in Alexandria was the College of Education, and it did not accept external, affiliate students because it had applied lessons in teaching methods. He only had this year and the next left among the students.

He was surprised at himself for thinking about this so early. He also found himself wondering what it meant that his only work in the world was to attract students to Marxist thought, without being affiliated with any secret party, where he would be able put his lessons into practice. He shook his head as if to banish these thoughts, especially since he never knew the fate of the students who had surrounded him in previous years. Sometimes he would meet one of them in the street, always walking with a beautiful girl who seemed to be his fiancée, or with a woman who appeared to be his wife. The former student never looked at him, or took any notice of him, as if he had never met him before, or sat before him listening to his lessons, just as these others were doing now. He wondered why there were never any female students among his disciples. There was Kariman who always seemed inclined to Marxism, but maybe that was just because she was Hasan's girlfriend. And Yara, with innocence shining from her eyes and pouring from her lips when she spoke, was Nadir's girlfriend.

Isa knew there were secret Communist parties in Egypt, and he knew their names—the Egyptian Communist Party, the Communist Workers' Party, the Revolutionary Current, the Eighth of January—but he didn't talk to the students about them. If anyone asked about them he would say that discovering them was a matter for each person, and that he really didn't like to belong to any party. He would only say that these parties had been reconstituted after Sadat came to power. Their leaders were from among the Communists who had joined the Nasserist experiment previously, after they got out of prison in 1964. Isa had come out with them, having been arrested on the last night of 1958, on New Year's Eve. He had not belonged to any Communist party. Simple chance had placed him with a person he didn't know in the Alexandria Café in Manshiya Square. The café had been noisy and crowded, and this dignified person had been sitting alone reading the newspapers, with a free seat in front of him. Isa had asked him if he could share his table to drink his coffee, and the man had agreed. He had met him again only in the Oases Prison, in the new Valley Governorate. It turned out that his name was Nadir Naeem, and he was the leader of the Democratic Movement for the Liberation of the Homeland in Alexandria.

Isa hadn't read anything about Marxism in his youth. He had ended his schooling after receiving his secondary diploma before the revolution and then had gone to work in his father's wood business, which had been nationalized while he was in prison. He came out to find that his father had died of grief, and his mother didn't linger long after him. No one in the family had understood the idea of losing property that they had built by means of long years of work and sweat. Nationalization was carried out for the sake of returning wealth to the people, but they weren't foreigners or thieves. Many Egyptians had lost their assets to nationalization. He especially remembered the Tawil family, who had owned the nearby tannery. They had founded the workshop at the beginning of the nineteenth century in Azarita, then moved it at the end of that century to Maks Street, beyond the Wardian neighborhood, near the slaughterhouse, "the skinner" as people called it. They had exported leather to many countries and supplied the Egyptian market as well. His father and the head of this family had been close friends, so Isa remembered them. Their factories had been nationalized, and just as had happened with his father, the head of the Tawil family had died of grief. In spite of that Isa didn't feel any bitterness about the policy of nationalization. He had become a Marxist.

He learned about Marxism from discussion circles in prison, held after the beatings and torture during the day. It was something that made all the torture and resistance worthwhile, something worth knowing and respecting and later, embracing! His only sister had married and emigrated to Canada after the 1967 defeat, and he had been left alone. He decided to enroll in all possible colleges to spread Marxist thought among the students, after getting a new secondary diploma through home study. All that was left to him of his father's business was a small warehouse on a side street off Qaffal Street in Wardian, but this came to be enough for him. The business could have grown, but he didn't want it to grow. *You're crazy!* He often said that to himself, as he did now. If someone analyzed his personality, what else would he say? At the very least he would judge that he was a *misfit*, as they say in English, not conforming to society. *As long as you know that, why don't you go back to society? Society isn't these students.* He had thought that many times, but still he didn't give up on his choice. He also told himself that there was still hope, that the best days were yet to come. All the great patriots he had seen and loved in prison had paid the price for Marxist thought, and he must spread it. Didn't Marxism bring justice to the world? He didn't need evidence from the Soviet Union or China, for those who had paid the price, and with whom he had paid the price by chance, were not stupid or ignorant. Today he would tell his disciples about Friedrich Engels' *The Origin of the Family, Private Property and the State.*

The voice of Ahmad Adawiya filled the cafeteria from the cassette system, and the waiters in their black pants and white jackets were more active than ever among the students, who sat happily at their tables. Students appeared behind the glass that stretched along the cafeteria walls, moving nimbly or standing and talking cheerfully. The girls lit up the cloudy day with their smiles, laughter, and elegant clothes—knee-length skirts and miniskirts and wool coats. Their hair was flying in the air and they were always putting it back where it belonged with their hands.

The talk at the table turned to what had happened to Nadir with State Security, after Isa finished talking to them about Friedrich Engels' book. He had contented himself with speaking briefly, hoping they would buy the Arabic translation; it was available in the East Bookstore on Safiya Zaghlul Street, which was the one remaining trace of Egyptian-Soviet relations that had not yet been closed.

The story of Nadir and State Security had been a slip of the tongue from Hasan, after he had told Isa about the attempt to mobilize him against leftists. Nadir had not wanted Yara to know about it, and two weeks had passed without her knowing. Now he saw her face clouded, with a trace of fear, and she was swallowing hard. He called Yara "the butterfly gatherer," and he didn't want any fear or sadness to affect her. She couldn't bear this terror—but there was no turning back now. He decided to make them all laugh, intending to make Yara laugh especially, so he told them the story of his conversation with the head of State Security about existentialism, and about how confused Sayyid Bey Abdel Bari had looked, and about how had he resembled Mustafa, the neighborhood barber. They did laugh, Yara and Kariman more than Hasan and Bishr, who already knew the story. Isa took it as an opportunity to talk to them about Marxism's encounter with existentialism, and how that shift had happened through Jean-Paul Sartre, after the Second World War. All the poets, writers, and thinkers of every school, from the Communists to the Surrealists, had participated in resisting Germany's occupation of France, and that's when Sartre's struggle on behalf of committed literature appeared and he had written a book about it.

Hasan said in a low voice, smiling, "Leave us with Nadir's idea of existentialism, it's better for us now. Any talk about committed intellectuals will get us accused of being Communists and thrown in jail, especially as the last wall magazine we hung up a week ago was produced with government money."

They laughed. They knew that the Student Welfare office had recently summoned Bishr Zahran also, and that the young instructor who was the head of the Office had tried to draw Bishr away from what he imagined was the left. Because he knew Bishr was poor, he had given him five pounds in aid, on condition that he not edit any magazine. Bishr had bought paper and pens with the money and had used them to edit three magazines that they had hung up all at once a few days ago, with articles by him, Hasan, Nadir, and Kariman. They had made three large headlines for the magazines: 'Where is Sadat Taking the Country?,' 'Encouraging Islamist Tendencies at the Expense of Freedom,' and 'The Hero of October is the Fighter, Not the Politician.'

Isa said, "Bishr was called to the Student Welfare Office after Nadir was summoned to State Security, so there's an attempt to divide you."

Bishr responded, "Of course, Professor. But we played a good trick on them, Hasan and I. He trained in karate and he got ten pounds, and I didn't train in anything and I got five!"

Kariman and Yara laughed aloud and their happiness spread to Nadir when he saw that Yara was really laughing. She said, "Did you see what the new psychology prof wrote on the cover of his book? He listed all the diplomas he ever received in his life up to getting his doctorate from the University of Oxford. The only one he left out was his middle school diploma."

They were all delighted, Nadir all the more because he saw Yara so cheerful.

Kariman added, "The only thing he missed was writing his mom's name."

At that their laughter rose and filled the air around them, and everyone in the cafeteria looked at them. But they were surprised to see an angry look on Isa's face. With despairing calm, he said, "Don't laugh like that. I've told you before, Communists are always preparing themselves for a long struggle."

They looked at each other, ashamed, and suppressed their mirth. But Yara said in a low, child-like voice, "Besides, laughing for no reason is ill mannered."

Once again they exploded in laughter, and she blushed, ashamed. Silence fell over them for a few moments and then Nadir asked abruptly, "Why haven't you been summoned to State Security before, Ustaz Isa?"

Isa was thrown into confusion, looking everywhere and not answering. Yara whispered to Nadir, "You've embarrassed him."

Isa heard her but he wasn't annoyed at Nadir; Nadir was a poet and it was hard for him to settle down. Hasan was a playwright and short story writer, and he was more settled. But Bishr was the steadiest, the most prepared for the struggle. Silence settled over them again; it seemed as if the session was about to end. Isa said, looking into the distance, "It looks as if the years I spent in prison are enough for them."

A deep silence fell over them this time. Then Yara stood up, saying "I have to go to the library," and hurried off. But she had no sooner gone through the door of the cafeteria than she rushed back, saying, "Help, help! There are students tearing down our magazines!"

Hasan, Kariman, Nadir, and Bishr rushed out. The three magazines had been torn up and thrown on the floor, and three students with small beards were standing on the pieces, each with an iron chain in his hand, while between them a girl in a hijab was still tearing up the remaining pieces of the magazines. No one knew precisely what happened next. In a moment Kariman was being held by the arms by two other students and Nadir yelled to Yara to stay away. He was arguing with one of the students and Hasan and Bishr were doing the same. Many students were running toward them trying to separate them, and they soon succeeded.

Among the students was Muhammad Shukr, the handsome blond student who always wore a blue suit, summer and winter. Everyone liked him for his constant smile, and because he had come up with a wonderful suggestion the previous year, when the Islamic philosophy instructor had been treating them all harshly. He had collected what money he could from every student, and at the beginning of the next lecture he went up to the instructor carrying a large gift, a plaque bearing the ninety-nine beautiful names of God. He presented it to the instructor from the students of the Philosophy Department as an expression of their love for him, and then in a loud voice he recited a line from the poet Ahmad Shawqi:

Stand for the teacher, with the respect he is due,
for a teacher is almost a prophet for you.

Then all the students in the class stood and applauded. After the lecture he went with the instructor to his office and came out flying high, bearing a paper with a list of the most important lessons that would be covered on the exam. The instructor had removed nearly half the books.

Now Muhammad Shukr stood among the scuffling students, shouting that this was unworthy of university students, saying "We're all going to graduate to build our country, not to destroy it, and we have to have minds broad enough to permit freedom of opinion!" He was speaking with great feeling, but some university employees appeared and asked them all to go to the dean's office.

Meanwhile Isa Salamawy had slipped away without getting involved. He went out and walked the short distance along Port Said Street to Suez Canal Street, where he headed for the Corniche. The cold winds met him, and he saw thick clouds over the sea. He would walk to Ateneos to the sound of the wind and the waves. The December qasim winds were over, both the first and second stages, and so only a few days were left before the end of the year. Maybe it would rain on him now. If it rained he would keep on walking and abandon himself to the rain. . . .

Hasan and Kariman walked away together, after the dean of the college had threatened to turn them all over to the Disciplinary

Council if they didn't stop causing trouble. Hasan, Bishr, and Nadir knew better than anyone else that the dean would not do that, since it wouldn't be fair to them.

"What do you say we go sit a while in the largest tea garden on the beach, the Shatbi Casino?"

Kariman didn't answer. She was furious with the two students who had grabbed her arms, even though when she had freed herself she had slapped one of them in the face.

Hasan said, pointing to the sea, "All this lovely fresh air in Alexandria, how come no one notices how magnificent it is?" She still didn't answer. He said, "Forget what happened, Kariman."

She said, "You got them back."

"You did too, you slapped the guy."

"It's not enough."

He took her hand. "It's enough that there's no mark on your face. I . . . "

She smiled. "But you beat them up."

"Let's just look at the sea . . . ."

They had come close to the Casino. The waves were striking the concrete pillars that supported it and they could see the green seaweed floating around them and the moss that had grown on them over time.

They went through the corridor leading to the lovely tea garden over the water. On the inside it was extremely large, with soft chairs and broad tables, glass windows on the sides with views in every direction, and warmth and quiet. In this entire expanse there were only three young couples, each one sitting at a table far from the others. They were all near the windows, while beyond them stretched the blue sea with its surging waves and the distant horizon. Sadness returned to Kariman's face.

Hasan took her hand and said, "Please forget about it while we're here, Kariman. Don't spoil this beautiful view. Anyway the guy did apologize to you."

She replied with feeling, "Did he have any right to grab my arms, him and his idiot friend?"

He said nothing for a while, smiling his half smile and nodding his head. Then, unable to turn her away from the topic, he said, "It's strange. It seems as if the war actually has begun."

She said angrily, "What makes me furious is the position of the dean. What good is it for them to apologize to us? They ought to be turned over to the Disciplinary Council and punished!"

"He's helpless, Kariman. The main security forces in the country do it too, not just the Islamist groups and the Muslim Brothers."

She said sharply, "He was looking at them as if to say, why didn't you finish them off, why did you come back defeated?"

He patted her hand and again tried to change the subject: "Relax, Kariman, you're with me and here's the sea in front of us. What do you say to going to a movie? How about going to see *Barry Lyndon* at the Cinema Royale? It's a great film, with Ryan O'Neil, and the producer is Stanley Kubrick. Of course you know Ryan O'Neil."

"No."

"Oh right, you were too young. I was too, but I saw his most famous film in a second-run theater in Mansura, later on. It's old but it's really famous, *Love Story*."

"I only know the music. I heard it last when I was with Yara. . . ." She was silent for a moment and then said, smiling, "Let's sit here as long as we can. The sea is beautiful, you're right. Don't be mad at me."

He smiled happily. She looked at him deeply, her green eyes wide and a broken smile fluttering on her lips. He took her hand, afraid she would return to the same subject, but instead she said, "I want to travel. I want to go overseas."

"Me too. How about making that our project after we graduate?"

"And writing? Your stories and plays?"

"I'll write over there and be a correspondent for Arabic newspapers and magazines. There are Arabic papers and magazines in Europe, too. Who knows, I might learn the language of the country we go to and write in that language."

She began looking into the distance and dreaming, and he signaled to the young waiter, who hurried over. He ordered a cappuccino for himself and another for Kariman. She seemed far removed from him. He said, "I miss you."

She smiled. "I've been with you since morning, we went into battle together, and you miss me?"

He laughed his partial laugh, always incomplete, like his smile. Then he said, "What do you say to spending the evening in the Nawal Boîte?"

"Me, spend the evening in a nightclub? Do you want my stepfather to kill me?"

"You'll love her."

"Nawal, or the *boîte*?"

This time he actually laughed aloud. "Nawal, of course."

"You men have all the rights in this world."

"Fine, how about if I treat you to dinner at Muhammad Ahmad's?"

She laughed in surprise. "A battle and then only broad beans? That's not fair!"

They both laughed, then he said, "Sandwiches are now two whole pennies, the price has doubled." But she was looking at the sea again. He said, "I'd like to take you into my arms."

"What's holding you back?"

He was at a loss for a moment, then he looked around and stood up, saying, "Then I'll do it right here in the casino."

He took her hands to pull her up as she shied back in surprise, saying, "You're crazy!" But she had stood up, so he pulled her to his breast and quickly kissed her cheek, since she had moved her mouth away from his. He let her go and sat down again, saying with a smile, "A day that began with a battle can end in the police station, no problem."

She bowed her head and put her face in her hands, as if she wanted to hide from the eyes of the customers and the three waiters standing at a distance. She said in a whisper, "We have to leave right away!"

But the warmth that had passed to his chest from hers and her softness were still cradling his spirit, along with the sensation of the kiss on his lips. He said, "Don't be afraid." He looked at the three waiters in the distance and found them looking at them, but not talking.

She said, "I'm really afraid."

"Wait until we drink our cappuccinos."

Silence surrounded them until the waiter arrived, carrying the cappuccinos. He placed everything before them on the table and left.

"Pay the bill and let's go. It's not important to drink it."

"Since you insist, and since you're afraid, I will, even though nobody objected to anything we did. On just one condition—that you come with me now to the apartment. Don't abandon me this time too. Why do you always refuse?"

She was silent for a few moments while he held his breath, waiting. Then she said, carelessly, "Why not? What matters is not to stay out too late."

Bishr Zahran was now sitting between Rawayih and Ghada.

It hadn't taken him long to get to them. Just a few minutes after coming out of the dean's office he had left the others and hurried to the apartment. He was like that, only able to extinguish his wrath with a woman . . . and there was nothing easier.

Quickly he had changed his clothes to winter pajamas. Then he waited for them, having knocked on the door of their apartment on his way up and told them to come up to him. They had made lunch today, a platter of potatoes with meat and rice, and they soon came up, bringing what they had prepared as a gift for the students. They were used to doing that from time to time.

Each one put what she was carrying on the dining table, and then Rawayih said,

"Before anything else, I want you to write a letter for me."

Bishr smiled angrily. "Wait for Nadir, he's the specialist in your letters."

"I want it now. That's the condition."

"All right. To whom?"

"To my boyfriend, of course. Did you forget?"

Ghada was smiling broadly. Bishr said, "Rawayih, I'm Bishr, not Nadir—we don't even look alike, I'm short and he's tall!"

"That doesn't matter."

Feeling his desire becoming more urgent, he said, "Fine. How about we go into my room and take care of business, then come back and eat, and write the letter however you like."

She said, "I have my period."

"Then I'll go in with Ghada."

Ghada said, laughing, "After you write Rawayih's letter."

He struck one hand with the other in despair and said, shaking his head, "God help me." He took a notebook and a pen from the dining table where they usually studied and said, "Dictate, Madam."

Rawayih dictated: "Beloved Ali. I miss you so. I don't know when you're coming back from Syria . . . ."

Bishr stopped writing and looked at her. "I know he's in Libya. I heard you last time when you were dictating the letter to Nadir."

She said, "Be quiet and write."

He looked at Ghada, who was still smiling, and went back to writing. She dictated:

"Sure Syria's pretty, but there's nothing prettier than Egypt. I've seen a lotta pretty women from Syria in Alexandria, but still, there ain't anything prettier than the women of Egypt. Sure, there's blondes with blue and green eyes in Syria, but I can dye my hair yellow, and there ain't anything prettier than black eyes...."

He was writing and nodding his head, letting his left hand wander on her thigh. She removed it off every so often.

"And anyway you're not answering me even though I sent you two letters. My days are sad and lonely without you.... A whole year is a lot . . . ."

"He's been in Syria for a year?"

"Yes."

He yelled in a loud voice, "Fine, then who is in Libya?"

She looked at him angrily and said, "That's it, that's enough. Give me the letter, I'll send it tomorrow. I'm going down to our apartment. You've got the food, bon appétit, but don't forget your friends."

Ghada stood up with her and walked after her, saying, "I've got my period too, just like Rawayih."

Nadir and Yara were sitting in the Petrou Casino in Glim, far away from the college. He said,

"What do you think of this place?"

"It's beautiful, but there's no one else here."

They had ordered two cups of tea from the waiter.

"It's the first time I've come here. It must be empty because of the cold and the winter. But in the summer Naguib Mahfouz usually sits here, and Tawfiq al-Hakim."

She said, smiling, "Oh, I see. Did you meet them here?"

"No. All I wanted was to sit with you some place as far as possible from the college so we would forget what happened today."

The waiter returned and put the tea in front of them, then disappeared from the room entirely.

She said, "I was really afraid for you." She put her hand on his forehead where the mark of the punch showed. He took her hand.

"It's nothing, don't worry."

She smiled. He said, "Once I was sitting in the Sultan Hasan Café and I saw Naguib Mahfouz walking on the sidewalk on the other side of the street. He was walking toward Raml Station on Safiya Zaghlul Street, looking straight ahead as if there were no one else on the street, staring off into space. He was wearing a summer suit. I stood up to look at him, not believing my eyes. He was wearing glasses. I nearly walked after him but I didn't move, I just stood in front of the café watching him until he disappeared, that's all. By the way, have you read the novel *Khan al-Khalili* that I gave you?"

"I read it and I cried when Rushdi died."

He was silent for a bit, then he said, "If I wrote stories like Hasan I would write a novel about the Second World War and one of its heroes would be named Rushdi."

She said, smiling, "And Nawal, too?"

"No, Yara, this time."

She laughed and he went on, "The important thing is to bring him back to life." He paused, and then spoke again. "Who knows, maybe I will write a novel, too, some day . . . ."

She put her hand over his and said, "You write beautiful poetry, my love, and you're going to be more famous than Salah Abdel Sabour and Naguib Mahfouz too."

Her honey-colored eyes shone as she looked at him. He took her hands in his and found himself bringing his face close to hers, as her eyes widened. He came closer and she closed her eyes; he placed his lips on hers and put his left arm around her, while he pressed his right hand on hers. It was a long kiss; when they separated, they found the waiter standing before them. Yara was embarrassed and she went pale as she covered face with her hands and bowed her head in shame and fear. Nadir looked at the waiter in confusion, not knowing what to say. The waiter said,

"I'm sorry, did you call me?"

"No."

"Again, I'm sorry. I thought I heard something."

The waiter retreated until he disappeared from the room once more. Nadir lowered her hands and lifted her face so he could see her, and said,

"What can I do, Yara? I can't resist! You never want to come with me to the apartment. Just once I want a place with no other people."

She looked at the table in shame and said, "I will go with you."

He cried, "Today!"

"No. But very soon."

Isa Salamawy was sitting sadly in Ateneos. He was like other Alexandrians, happy when they felt the cold wind on their faces. But today was different.

His eyes rested on the eastern port where the waves reached the beach despite the distant barrier, and sometimes crashed over the wall of the Corniche. He saw the Citadel of Qaytbay in the distance. A few pedestrians were hurrying along the broad sidewalk below the window, among them two girls wearing the hijab.

He remembered the sheikh's sermon from the nearby mosque the previous Friday, when the voice had come loud from the speaker, filling the air around the mosque and coming into his apartment. "The time has come for us to return to God. We've been victorious and returned Sinai and forced back the Jews, the enemies of God, and I have seen angelic hosts fighting with our soldiers. An unveiled woman is vice on two feet. Cover, cover, before your life is over!"

Isa had seen this slogan written on the walls of many houses in the Wardian neighborhood, and then on some of the walls of the Street of the Seven Girls, before it arrived in Manshiya Square. Now he smiled mockingly. It seemed the sheikh didn't know that Egypt and Israel were engaged in negotiations, between Muslims and Jews, under the protection of "the believing president," Muhammad Anwar al-Sadat.

There weren't many patrons in Ateneos—a few elderly men and women, a young man and woman, and a number of foreign sailors who must be Americans. They were eating, and between the many dishes in front of them there were a lot of bottles of beer. Their voices were indistinct in the distance, speaking English. In front of Isa stood his second bottle of beer. He had not yet ordered lunch. Where was Christo?

Barely had he said that to himself when he saw Christo coming in the distant door. After he entered he stood still, as usual, looking around the room; Isa knew he was looking for him. When he spotted him he hurried over, short, square shaped, wearing the brown suit he always seemed to have on, his camera slung over his shoulder.

Isa noticed that the music flowing around him was Turkish. He knew that because he had asked one of the waiters about it once before. It expanded into the spacious room and left him vaguely anxious.

"*Kalimera*, you lost Communist," Christo called to him as he approached. Isa smiled and stood to shake hands with him. Christo's face was very red, under the thin white beard that surrounded it.

"Have a seat. Tell me about the famous people you photographed today."

"Seif Wanli, the painter. I saw him sitting in As You Like It, on the sidewalk, alone, as usual. He was staring off into the distance and not talking to anyone. His white hair was big, the way it always is. Sometimes I see him wearing glasses and sometimes not. Today there were glasses. My friend, my whole life I've seen Seif Wanli as an old man—how old do you think he is now? Seventy, maybe?"

Isa was surprised at the question. "I don't know when he was born, Christo. But I think at the beginning of the century, about 1906."

"Oof, was anyone even alive, back then?" They shared a big laugh, and Christo began speaking again. "It's possible. I've photographed him a lot before this. He doesn't want the pictures, and I'll sell them some day for a lot of money. Why don't you order me a beer? I'll buy you lunch."

Isa smiled. He signaled to the waiter, calling, "A beer, and the usual lunch."

Christo himself was almost seventy and looked older than Seif Wanli, but he didn't realize his age. He still had hopes in life. He kept a lot of pictures in his studio on Tiba Street—Cavafy, Forster, Durrell, Antoniade, Salfago, Smouha, Zananiri, Shekorel, De Gaulle, Churchill, King Farouk, Omar Sharif, Youssef Chahine, Nadia Lutfi, Shukry Sarhan, Hind Rustum, and others, dozens of pictures that his father had taken before him and others that he had taken later. He often confused them and imagined that he had taken them all, and would not part with them, even though he always talked about selling them someday for a lot of money.

All at once Isa said, "Aren't you going to go to Athens, Christo? There are almost no Greeks other than you left in Alexandria."

"I'm not going, khabibi. I'm an Alexandrian. You know, Isa, last week I visited the grave of Cavafy. I stood there and said…" He recited a short poem in Greek, and then asked Isa, "You know it, khabibi?"

Isa, who didn't know Greek, was embarrassed. But then he said, "Naturally: 'As Much as You Can'." He could say that because Christo had recited it to him before, many times. He had also often talked to him about this same visit before too, and had explained the poem to him in Arabic, so Isa had looked for it among Cavafy's poems in English. There was a little silence and then Isa began to recite the poem....

And if you can't shape your life the way you want
at least try as much as you can
not to degrade it
by too much contact with the world,
by too much activity and talk.

Try not to degrade it by dragging it along,
taking it around and exposing it so often
to the daily silliness
of social events and parties
until it comes to seem a boring hanger-on.

Isa ended the poem and looked at Christo, who said, "I don't know how you can be a Communist and still love Cavafy. Cavafy was very far removed from the world. He liked to be alone." He smiled. "But with his beloved with him . . . ."

Isa laughed. Christo sometimes seemed to have lost his memory, but now he seemed in possession of all his mental powers. It was a rare moment. Christo plunged ahead, speaking with confidence:

"Look, khabibi, I've already taken pictures of all the casinos and nightclubs, all of 'em. They're all going to close, khabibi. Yes, Alexandria's over, pretty soon there's no more Alexandria. Look, look, today I was taking pictures of a boy and girl next to the 'Mermaid' statue. Of course you know the artist who made it."

"Of course, Christo. Fathi Mahmud. But I don't know him personally."

"I know him, I've taken his picture a lot. The point, khabibi, is that a man showed up wearing a white gallabiya, and he had a big black beard. He was wearing a suit jacket over the gallabiya, with sandals on his feet in the worst of the cold, but with socks under them."

46

"He asked you to take his picture."

"No, khabibi, he attacked us and said that taking pictures is *haram*, forbidden!"

Isa was amazed, and looked at him attentively.

"Yes, khabibi, he yelled at the boy and the girl. The boy was afraid but the girl turned out to be more of a man than he was—she said, 'What's it to you, you ass?' She took off her shoe and said really loud, 'Get out of here before I beat you over the head with my shoe!'"

Christo began to laugh happily. Two waiters arrived carrying their lunch and the beer, preceded by the appetizing odor of the food. Christo said, cheerfully,

"Ah, here we go, grilled sea bream and calamari. You're a real Alexandrian, khabibi, even if you are a poor Communist."

They both laughed, and began eating with gusto. Isa thought for a moment about what had happened today in the college—how had it happened so fast? But Christo looked handsome as usual, cheering him, even though he noticed that new wrinkles had crept under his eyes.

Christo said, "Forgive me if I eat and run, khabibi. My brother's leaving for Greece today and the ship sails at eight tonight. I have to sit with him a little. Every day I tell him, don't go to Greece, and he doesn't agree. I have to go tell him again. My daughter wants to go with him too! Does it make sense that my beloved daughter would go and leave me here?"

Isa didn't answer; he listened to it all in silence, as usual. Christo's brother had left Alexandria long before, as had his wife, son, and daughter. There was a girl who worked with him in his studio but she was Egyptian, and her name was Gamila.

In the farthest eastern part of Alexandria the number of houses and apartment buildings was growing; they were built on sandy land in Sidi Bishr and Asafra and Mandara, north and south of the Abu Qir train line. The owners of the wooden cabins and bungalows in Sidi Bishr and even Mandara began to sell the places they had used as summer houses, or else they took them down to build houses and apartments in their place, after they saw the ones rising behind them along the train line. In the south the houses and apartments went up more quickly, far removed from any sort of order.

There were streets that began wide and then narrowed, little lanes branching off them where houses rose randomly, just as had happened and was still happening in "The Mountain" in Dekhela. Here the space was bigger, deep and extensive, although a lot of the land was watery marshes, especially in the south. Along the Corniche at the end of Khalid ibn al-Walid Street, a café appeared that hung up a sign saying "Alcoholic drinks forbidden," and the large Kit Kat Club was sold to become a wedding parlor. President Sadat met with the sovereign of the Kingdom of Saudi Arabia, and Sadat announced, with his broad smile (unmatched on his face except by his expression of violent anger) that they agreed about everything.

A dark young man appeared on the Corniche wearing tight black pants and a black sweater over a white shirt; he was carrying an accordion in his hands and playing it all by himself in the middle of the road, between the few cars, in the wind and rain, not seeming to care about anyone. He moved to the beach between Raml Station and Miami, all alone. Cars and taxis passed him, some of their occupants laughing and some feeling sorry for him.

The Security Council agreed to the participation of the Palestine Liberation Organization in the discussion of a new Israeli aggression against the West Bank and Gaza. The French President Valéry Giscard d'Estaing arrived in Egypt and warmly praised his reception by the Egyptian people. The poet Ahmad Fouad Negm wrote his satiric poem, that Sheikh Imam sang among the intellectuals:

Valéry Giscard d'Estaing
along with his lady
is setting out to do big things
and feed all the hungry.
Oh là là, what a man,
what a perfect gentleman!

The poem went on, and it spread fast among the university students.

Eid al-Adha came and the university students who were away from home went back to their villages for the holiday vacation. Hasan Hafiz and Ahmad Basim did the same, and Nadir and Bishr stayed away from the apartment during the holiday. President Sadat chose the city of Dinshaway for his Eid prayers, praying in the village mosque of Sidi Bishr and meeting some of the descendants of the martyrs of the Dinshaway Incident of 1906. He also addressed a crowded public political conference.

The film *The Liar* began its run in the Cinema Radio in Alexandria, and the first exposition of visual arts was held in the Khafagi Café in Wardian. This café had been a cultural club in the sixties. It had rented the garden across the street from the governorate, and had set up in it a small statue of Gamal Abdel Nasser and a large television set. Now, however, the statue had been removed and the governorate had reclaimed the rented garden from the café, confining it to its space in the apartment building across the street from the garden, on the corner of Qaffal Street and Maks Street. No discussions or gatherings were held there until Yahya Khafagi, the son of the café's owner and a graduate of the College of Fine Arts, set up this exposition as the beginning of a tradition to be repeated every year.

The winner of the Nobel Prize in literature was the Italian poet Eugenio Montale, unknown in Egypt. The prize for peace was won by Andrei Sakharov, the Soviet nuclear scientist and father of the hydrogen bomb, who had become an advocate for peace and tolerance and had come under pressure in the Soviet Union.

At the end of the year in Egypt court-appointed committees began to inspect the financial accounting statements of government employees, with President Sadat first in line, and after him Prime Minister Mamduh Salim, the rest of the ministers, the members of parliament, and the Central Committee of the Socialist Union. Thank heaven all turned out to be in order.

As the battles were starting again in Lebanon, with tanks taking part for the first time in Zgharta and Tripoli, the Communists in

Syria were arrested, and Khalid Bakdash, the leader of the Communist Party there, fled the country. Preparations began for the solar new year.

In the Wataniya Café in Manshiya a man was sitting holding a newspaper and reading the weather forecast. Surprise showed on his face, and he said to the man near him, "I know that the high temperature in Cairo is always higher than it is here in Alexandria. Today, for example, it's 25 degrees centigrade in Cairo and here in Alexandria it's 20 degrees. But how can the low in Cairo be 7 degrees and higher in Alexandria, at 11 degrees? Have they started to lie about the temperature too?"

The second man smiled and said, "No, that's right."

"How?"

The second man smiled again. "There's a geographical phenomenon called 'sea and land breezes.' In the winter the sea keeps the heat in coastal cities during the day and it leaves at night, so the low will be higher there than in cities in the middle of the desert or in the middle of the fields, like Cairo. We studied that when were we kids in middle school, if you remember. 'Sea and land breezes,' that was the title of the lesson."

The first man thought for a bit and said, unconvinced, "Maybe. I was the worst student in geography."

They laughed, then the second man spoke again:

"All that will change in the future. They've begun to empty the city sewers into Lake Maryut and it stinks all along the desert road between Amiriya and Muharram Bey. They'll destroy the lake, and its waters used to act like the sea, in addition to absorbing the hot westerly winds coming from the desert in the summer. The lake would give the winds a little freshness and lower the temperature."

The first man said, "The governorate is always up to something disgusting. They're also still filling the lake with the garbage from the city around Muharram Bey, to make a garden."

The second man said, "Their ignorance, my friend, is huge. The garbage has organic matter from the remains of meat, fish, poultry, and so on. This organic matter will produce insects underground, and they will eat the roots of the trees. The project won't succeed and in the end the place will turn into cafés and restaurants and shops, and we'll have lost the lake."

The first man was silent for a while, thinking about what he had heard. Then he said, "What matters more than that is that we won't find any cheap fish to eat. God damn them all, we've got a bunch of dumb animals in charge of the place!"

They both laughed out loud.

3

THE DAY WAS THE THIRTY-FIRST of December, and tonight would see out the old year. It was a night the city and its residents had prepared for, even though the rain continued and in fact had increased during the day, just as the Christmas winds had become stronger.

The lightning and thunder increased too, and it seemed as if the sky was lighting up in joy at the coming of the new year. Few were those who appeared in the city streets tonight after eight. Most of the houses were closed over a lovely family warmth, and the shops that were still open would soon close their doors. The cars still in the street would reach their safe harbor and the taxis would be few, ending up standing in front of the bars and nightclubs to wait for those who would come out after midnight. They would remain in the streets but they'd be moving slowly, until they halted completely at midnight.

The rain stopped between eight and nine, as if it were giving Alexandrians one last chance to reach their destinations. Then it poured down in torrents, just as Isa Salamawy was emerging from his apartment in Wardian. At almost the same moment Nadir also left his house in Maks, but they would not meet. Isa was going to Ateneos and Nadir was going directly to the Nawal Boîte, ahead of his friends.

In Maks the waves were high, rushing to the beach and striking the base of the old lighthouse from every side, rising all around it, announcing their inability to destroy the foundation of the ancient lighthouse. Their rapid succession on the shore seemed natural, but around the lighthouse it looked as if they were engaged in battle. The tram had stopped moving in Maks Street, because the area between the slaughterhouse and the army storehouses was low and the rain water rose there, beyond the capacity of the drains to absorb it. The bus was also moving slowly in the water, veering to the left and right. At the beginning of the Wardian neighborhood, where the apartment buildings began beyond the Tahir Bey Middle School, the high windows of the old houses were all closed, with light showing behind them. One woman ventured to stand on a balcony in front of the Swedish clock, looking at the rain falling heavily and listening to it strike the ground. She was letting it fall on her head and on the shoulders of the winter robe she wore, crossing her arms over her chest and thinking about her husband, who worked as a cook on a passenger ship and who was spending this night in the Italian port of Genoa.

In the Khafagi Café, where the visual arts exhibit had not yet closed, a dim light appeared behind the front window, along with colored lights that were the paintings themselves. There were no more than five or six people in the café, smoking water pipes; they would leave soon and the café would close its doors. In the Mafruza neighborhood there were small houses of no more than two or three floors, with the exception of the one odd, tall apartment building in the neighborhood, which rose much higher, overlooking the broad corner of Ikhshidi and Maks Streets from the corner balconies. Ikhshidi Street led to the Karantina neighborhood with its improvised buildings and random residents. A little farther along on Maks Street, beyond this building that always drew one's gaze, a man stood on the balcony of his apartment above the Launch Café. He was dressed in a gallabiya and had a long beard but no mustache. He was leaning on the wall, sheltering under the balcony above to protect himself from the rain, and he was looking at the row of little houses facing him. One of them was a small home containing the Mahaba Coptic Association, with an apartment above it. A girl was standing on the apartment balcony, laughing, with a young man, both of them dressed in handsome evening wear. Behind them appeared a younger girl who threw a bottle into the street.

54

The bearded man across from them heard the sound of the bottle as it crashed to the ground and broke, and he heard the older girl's voice as she told her, "Not now, at twelve o'clock," pushing her inside from the balcony as the little girl laughed. The bearded man's face expressed strong indignation; he cursed them inwardly, closed the window, and went inside.

No one appeared in the street after that, in Qabbari and Mina al-Basal, up to the Street of the Seven Girls. That street was lit up more than at any other time, with its lampposts and balconies decorated by strings of little lights hung on the walls. A lot of glass would be thrown here tonight, for even though many of the businesses had changed from restaurants and bars to shops selling electrical appliances, nonetheless the street still honored the rites of this night, like many of the old neighborhoods and their elderly residents. A man emerged from the one remaining bar, facing the Liban police station, laughing and running, with a woman behind him demanding that he stop. She caught up to him and clutched his arm, yelling, "Where're you going? I'm not leaving you tonight!" Her heavy wool shawl fell back, revealing her bare shoulders and chest; her lips were freighted with red lipstick and she had thick makeup on her face. Beating his chest with her hands in affectionate anger, she said, "You've made the weather ruin my makeup, you jerk!" She got into a nearby car with him and they took off. Before the end of the street stood more private cars, with men and women in elegant evening clothes around them. The women were ululating in celebration as they all waited for a bride and groom, who were performing the usual wedding rites of photography in the Cleopatra Studio.

In Manshiya, the square spread out wide beneath the rain. Everything was now closed, and only the lights of the square itself and Muhammad Ali Pasha on his horse still braved the rain. Not many of the balconies were lit up, for many of the apartments in the Italian-style buildings had been abandoned by their residents, who turned them into offices for companies, or lawyers, or shipping agencies, or fabric warehouses. There was silence on the right side of the square. In the distance was the large building of the Socialist Union, the old stock exchange, completely dark. There was more silence on the left side, before the Court of Justice, and in Victory Street, despite its width, where the clothing shops on both sides were shut.

On the right side of the Socialist Union building was Adib Ishaq Street, going to "Sheikh Ali's" bar, the Cape d'Or. It had become known by the name of its new owner, Ali; when he bought it from its Greek owner many years ago he began closing it on Fridays, so the patrons started calling him Sheikh Ali. The Spitfire Bar was in Bursa al-Kadima Street near the East Cinema, which had been demolished to make way for a large apartment building. A man came out of the bar and fired a volley of shots into the sky, then went back in, crying, "There's nothing in the whole world better than Alexandria, you bastards!" On Chamber of Commerce Street the tram was running slowly, almost empty, everything around it silent. On Mina al-Sharqiya Street a person came tottering out of the Black Cat Bar. No sooner had the rain hit him than he went back in, terrified, as if he had never seen rain before. He said, "What's going on? What's with this winter weather?" and all the bar patrons burst out laughing.

Silence encompassed all the neighborhoods of the city, the main streets and many of the side streets as well. But the light from the street lamps was strong, and light showed clearly behind the windows. The people were in their houses or hurrying to them under the balconies, and the few who had opened their shops were closing them. They were all waiting for twelve o'clock, to throw out empty bottles and a few other things they wanted to get rid of as they said goodbye to the old year, hoping for a better one.

Along the sea in Anfushi only the Greek Club and the Yacht Club were open for the evening, and the sound of the music reached Yara in her room, through the closed windows and across the eastern port, in spite of the distance. Her mother and father had left her and had gone to spend the evening with friends of theirs. She had excused herself from going with them because she was pale and exhausted, as happened to her every month for several days, when she had her period. She always had intense pain that she could not imagine anyone else experienced, and she lost a lot of weight, becoming pale as her blood pressure fell. It went on for five days that seemed like years, during which she was likely to faint at the slightest effort. She had told her mother and father that she would study some important lessons tonight, ashamed to speak openly to them about her condition. Of course they knew and did not comment. Her mother had previously taken her to several doctors, and they all said that it was a natural matter that women experienced differently, and that perhaps it would end when she married.

She was thinking about Nadir and what he was doing tonight. She knew that he would spend the evening in the Nawal Boîte, and she wished she could spend an evening there with him sometime. But she asked herself what attracted Nadir and his friends to this nightclub—was it really because the owner liked them, as Nadir said? In the end it was a nightclub filled with drunkards and women with bare shoulders, chests, and legs. The voice of Abdel Halim Hafiz came from the television, singing "Fatet Ganbena," "She Passed Us"; she had left her room to sit in front of the television and follow the New Year celebrations, if only for a while, to take her mind off her pain a little. As she listened with pleasure to Abdel Halim's voice in this song, she found herself thinking about how she had suddenly gone with Nadir to the apartment. Kariman had confided in her that she had gone with Hasan—was that enough to make Yara do the same? She was annoyed for a moment, but then she shook her head happily.

She had been sitting with him in Petrou for the second time, knowing he had chosen it again to get another kiss. He said to her that they should stay away from the farms and trees of Smouha for a while, as there were houses there even if they didn't see them. Many of the houses were in fact empty of their former residents, but they might return for some time at the end of the year. A lot of apartment buildings were now being built there, and there were always building materials in several places, and workers and guards, so the situation was changing in Smouha now. Looking down and entwining her fingers nervously, she had found herself saying,

"There are people here too. The waiter who said nothing last time might not be silent this time."

He replied immediately, "Then come with me to the apartment."

"I will." Her face burned in shame.

When he took her into the room she looked at the small bed, the small wardrobe, and the old desk with neglected books, papers, and notebooks on it. She felt sorry for him in this chaos.

He sat her on the edge of the bed and sat next to her, hurrying to start kissing her.

"Slow down, wait a little. I'm dizzy."

He was flustered, but she said, "Don't be afraid. I'm fine, just giddy. I can't believe I came here with you. Is there anyone else in the other rooms?"

"No, don't worry."

She reached out and took a book from on top of the desk. She found the name of Bishr Zahran in it. She asked, "Is this Bishr's room?"

"His room and mine. The other two are Hasan Hafiz's and Ahmad Basim's. We pay a third of the rent because we don't come often, the way they do. They live here during the term."

"I'm afraid one of them will come back now."

"Don't worry. Hasan is with Kariman and Bishr is in the Wali Café right now. Ahmad always comes home late—I don't know where he goes all day."

She shook her head and said, "I don't like Ahmad Basim. He always looks at girls as sex objects. A lot of my classmates complain about him."

He gave her a long look and then leaned over her face, saying, "Don't spoil the moment I've waited for."

He pulled her toward him and began to kiss her, slowly and sedately, on her lips, her cheeks, and her forehead, then on her neck. She moaned in a low voice, her head began to move, and the sound of her moaning became louder. He thought for a moment that she had had some previous experience, but he told himself that this was born of deprivation and not experience.

Her breath came faster and her body was on fire. He began to undo the buttons of the suit jacket she was wearing, seeming confused and unable to control himself. She began to laugh and shake her head in refusal, and every time he undid a button she buttoned it again. He leaned her back on the bed and she subsided, and in the end he was able to take off her clothes . . . .

Now, in her apartment, Yara was amazed at her quick surrender, despite the refusal she had displayed and her toying with him. She remembered how he had moved his penis over her chastity, and how she had begun to laugh with a hysteria she had not known in herself before, confusing him for a moment. She blushed now as she remembered his quick shudder atop her, as she had clasped her legs together to push him away from the center of her purity, the place that terrified her. . . .

He had done that three times before she dozed, drunk, for a few minutes. When she opened her eyes she grasped his hand and kissed it. He asked her,

"Were you afraid?"

"Of course."

"God condones it between lovers!"

She had looked at him smiling, and then laughed aloud. *Does God really accept this from us?*

Now in her room she began shaking her head, amazed by what Nadir had said. He didn't know that she had suffered great pain, that she had wished he would deflower her but could not say so, because she could not live without her virginity until after she married.

She suddenly thought about where Kariman was spending her night. Was she with her mother and her mother's loathsome husband who claimed to be pious? She felt sad for her, and wished she would visit her unexpectedly as she had before. She heard the apartment doorbell and was unsettled, then amazed. Was it really Kariman? That would be a wonderful coincidence.

She got up and went to the door, and looked through the peephole before she opened it. She saw the face of a huge man who had a very large beard. She hesitated to open the door. She said fearfully, "Who's there?"

"Open up, Sister. There's a letter for you."

A letter, at this time of night? New Year's Eve, and it was after ten o'clock!

She opened the door to the extent allowed by the chain that she latched it with from the inside when she was alone. She saw that the man had huge shoulders, and was holding a sheaf of papers to his chest with his left hand as he drew out one of them with his right hand and handed it to her. He said,

"May God reward you greatly, Sister."

He stepped back to go up to the floor above. She closed the door calmly, in amazement, and stood in the middle of the living room. Shadia was singing "Ah, Asmarani al-lun," "Oh, Dark One"; the songs of Abdel Halim Hafiz had ended while she was lost in her encounter with Nadir. She looked at the foolscap sheet and read it, three sentences printed in a large font so they filled the whole over-sized sheet:

> Cover before your life is over . . . Face the wolves from under cover.
> Prayer! Prayer! Prayer!
> Celebrating the Christian New Year is a custom for infidels.

"Good God, all these people?" exclaimed Ahmad Basim, as they entered the nightclub and stood dazzled, looking at the large hall.

There was dim light throughout, floating cigarette smoke, and colored lighting, with voices jostling above it and below. A large number of young women were moving about tonight, carrying empty trays and trays filled with beer, whiskey, brandy, wine, vodka, and champagne. Their clothes were shorter than ever before, showing more of their thighs. Their backs and shoulders were covered with ample, short-sleeved blouses. The women around the tables with the men displayed shining arms and shoulders, many of them smoking in the dim light, and the aroma of perfume hovered over them all. Bishr said,

"All this flesh tonight!"

Hasan smiled and asked, "Unhappy?"

"Feeling sorry for myself. Those are what you call women!"

They were looking for Nawal, who was not in her usual corner tonight. Ahmad spotted Nadir sitting with her at a distance, on the other side of the hall. He said,

"Of course he had to get here first. It's his night, it seems."

They went over to Nadir and Nawal happily. As he did every time, Hasan bowed and kissed Nawal's hand. She greeted them in English: "*Happy New Year,* boys."

Ahmad and Bishr shook her hand, not kissing it as Hasan had done. He was the one she considered the gentleman among them. Immediately two security guards stood behind them, pulling the chairs away from the large table a little so they could sit down, one after the other. Hasan and Bishr exchanged looks of surprise—they were being treated wonderfully tonight, better than at any other time. Quickly Hayat appeared; she seemed to be assigned to wait on them. She was pushing a small cart prepared in advance, bearing a bottle of champagne, a bottle of whiskey, a number of bottles of beer, and a large quantity of appetizers on the lower tray. On the table were the remains of a bottle of champagne and a few appetizers. Ahmad cried, "All of this for us, tonight?"

Nadir said, laughing, "As you see, I haven't had much to eat or drink. I was saving it for you."

Nawal lit a cigarette. She was wearing a marvelous gown in which she would sing tonight, showing a large part of her chest and shoulders. She had put on a light shawl that revealed her body beneath it, but soon she would remove the shawl. She must. More than a month had passed since the last time they came to her.

Had their meeting the previous year been arranged by fate? It had been a long winter night, and Bishr had been sad because the neighborhood girl he loved had become engaged to another. When Nadir had asked him if she had just left him, suddenly, he said that she had not known that he loved her.

This was the first time that Nadir had heard anything about love from Bishr. He had told Nadir how she lived across from him, how she was as beautiful as the moon, how if she looked out of her window the whole world danced around her. He had been in her house often, because of his friendship with her brother, and because of the friendship between his parents and hers. He had looked at her as a sister, but all at once his feeling of love for her had awakened. He had decided to approach her the proper way, in marriage; but then he thought he couldn't do that until after he graduated. He had decided to propose to her when he was in the final, license year. Then there would be a little time left to work and to establish a household. He had not realized that like him she had grown up and gone to the university, to the College of Medicine, and that her body was bursting out of its childhood form.

It was as the professor of political philosophy had said, that sardonic man they all loved, when their classmate Mufida had asked him about the meaning of 'living space.' He had looked at her and thought for a moment, and then laughed and said, "You are a little kitten in your parents' eyes, but your neighbors and others see things bursting out in you. Two spheres have appeared on your chest and a larger one behind, you hair flies out behind you. At this point someone sees this as his living space that he must take, so he declares his love to you, or comes knocking on your door if he's respectable, or if he's crazy he assaults you. That's what Hitler did with Czechoslovakia when he saw it as living space for Germany, then he did the same with Poland, and then he expanded to all of Europe." Mufida didn't hear the last, political part of what he said; she had fainted among them in the lecture hall.

Bishr said, sorrowfully, "I didn't know that anyone else saw his living space in the girl I loved in silence. Then there she was engaged to a young doctor."

They had been sitting that night on the wall of the Corniche, in the cold. The sea was sighing behind them with a peaceful, lazy sound. Nadir had said to him, "What happened doesn't deserve your grieving, because you didn't go through a real love story with her. It looks as if you're an artist, Bishr, and we didn't know it. Let's walk a little, walking will warm us up."

They hadn't gone far when they found the Nawal Boîte night-club on their left. Its door was lit up, and above it were pictures of the dancer, Alya, and of the musicians, men and women. In front of the door were a security guard and a beautiful woman. Bishr had said, laughing sarcastically, "It's a night that deserves to be spent in a club like this one, the way it happens in Arab films when the hero wants to forget the story of his separation from his beloved. But how can we?"

Nadir said, "It's a good idea. I've got ten pounds and I'm going to spend them all for your sake, it might be enough."

They hadn't hesitated any longer but went into the club. They ate chicken and drank brandy to economize, they watched Alya dance, and they listened to oriental singing. The evening had ended with the check at exactly ten pounds, but Nadir discovered that he only had five pounds with him—he had left the other five with his mother before leaving the house. The ten pounds were his monthly salary for giving a middle-school student lessons in English and Arabic.

They were embarrassed; Bishr had begun to bit his lips in anger. Several guards had surrounded them, while Nawal, the owner of the club, sat at a distance. Their young age had already attracted her attention, and the light clothes they wore, which she wasn't used to seeing among the patrons of the club—just pants, a shirt and a sweater. She was watching what was happening, and signaled to her men to bring them to her.

Before she asked them anything Bishr had said, "Our check is ten pounds, Madam, and we have discovered that we only have five with us. We can each leave you our identification cards until we come back tomorrow with the rest. We're respectable students in the Humanities College."

She had considered them for a moment, trying to suppress the smile that nearly rose to her lips. She said, "You speak with confidence while your friend seems embarrassed and ashamed. Why aren't you like him? Do you have the five pounds and doesn't he have anything?"

He replied, "I'm always broke, he's the one with the five pounds."

She had laughed, and signaled to the men to leave them. She invited them to sit down and they did, exchanging glances. Nawal seemed lost in thought. She asked them, "From Alexandria?"

"Naturally," Bishr answered. "That's why we're not afraid of anyone."

She had smiled and said, "From the Humanities College, you say?"

"The Philosophy Department," Bishr answered.

She had directed her next words to Nadir, whose silence and embarrassment had attracted her. "Why is it that you aren't saying anything?"

Bishr answered her, "Because he's a poet. He's sensitive. He must be sad and confused about what happened."

She contemplated Nadir silently for a few moments. Then she said to Bishr, "Naturally you aren't a poet."

"I'm a politician," he had said, and then was embarrassed, even more so when Nadir looked at him in surprise. But he went on: "Yes, a politician disgusted with the 'believing president' and what he's doing to the country. What do you think now? You can get us into trouble if you want to."

She had laughed aloud and asked, "What's your name?"

"Bishr. Bishr Zahran. And he's Nadir, Nadir Saeed."

She had opened her eyes very wide, as if a distant memory had come to her, but Bishr had gone on talking:

"Nadir Saeed, 'happy,' and as you see there's misery all around us."

She had looked at Nadir, her thoughts apparently still far away. "No misery or anything else. Consider yourselves my guests tonight, and keep the five pounds. But I have one condition."

Bishr burst out, "Madam has but to command!"

"That you come back to us another time. And the invitation is for your friends too, if you have friends." She fell silent, and then said, "And that you promise me, Nadir, that I will hear your poetry someday." Then she added, smiling, "If I like your poetry, everything will be free."

She had reached out to shake hands with them, from her seat. They looked at each other in disbelief, then shook her hand and hurried out. The first thing they had met was the wind, which had grown stronger outside the club. Bishr said, "There's something strange about this woman. When she heard your name her eyes flashed and opened wide, and the same when she found out you're a poet. We'll let time tell us what it is."

Nadir had asked, "Are we really going to come back again?"

"Of course. But you have to be with me—she's comfortable with you. Without you we'll be done for!" They had both laughed.

They had gone back to her another time during the last academic year, and this was the second time this year. They had brought their friends Hasan Hafiz and Ahmad Basim with them and each time Nawal seemed more generous, but she no longer asked Nadir about poetry. She had begun to listen to them talk, and realized that they were leftists of a sort—at least Bishr, Hasan, and Nadir, who had gone last time without Ahmad Basim. She asked them directly, that time, after they had talked a lot and laughed more about Sadat's rapprochement with America and Israel, "Do you oppose Sadat for that reason only?"

Bishr had said, "Also because he opened the door to the economic policy he calls 'the Economic Opening.' It's a capitalist policy opposed to the entire socialist achievement that has become established in Egypt."

Her thoughts wandered away from them, then she smiled and whispered, "Communists?"

They had looked at each other, then Hasan said, "You could say that. But what's most important for us is hope."

*

65

Now Ahmad Basim was following the girls of the club as they moved among the patrons, with obvious desire in his eyes. Suddenly a man stood up with a glass of champagne in his hand and said, "Alexandria was built by Alexander the Mad, and the Alexandrians have turned out to be just as mad!" Many of those seated in the club laughed and some clapped. He went on: "Sayyid Darwish took the hashish, he took it with him to Cairo, and he took hashish from Gabal Naasa too!" More laugher rose. He grasped the arm of the beautiful woman seated next to him and pulled her up. He pointed to her and cried, "The sun has risen, its light glistens, the mighty sun is here!" He abandoned his glass and clasped her to his heart, then he spread out his arms and cried, falling to his chair like someone fainting, "I'm down and I'm done!"

Many people clapped, then some of the men began to call "Nawal! Nawal! Nawal!" But the members of the oriental musical ensemble were starting to come in from behind the curtain in back of the platform, and after them came the dancer, Alya, fluttering like a butterfly between the orchestra and the patrons.

Hands clapped enthusiastically to the eastern music. Unusually for her, Alya was wearing a white dance costume tonight, and her white flesh gleamed in the dim light. Her lightness and quickness made her seem like a real butterfly. Her slenderness distinguished her from the other dancers in Alexandria, who were plumper. She was more like Samia Gamal in her movements. Ibrahim Ahmad appeared, the young singer who was new to Radio Alexandria, and he began to sing "Ya zayid fi-l-halawa," "Most Beautiful One," the song made famous by the Alexandrian singer Ezzat Awad Allah. Alexandrians loved it. Ahmad Basim's eyes were now following Alya, and he whispered to Bishr,

"If only she was a little plumper."

Bishr answered, "You've always been an ass—you don't know beauty when you see it."

Ahmad laughed and did not comment. Nawal asked them, "I met you last year after New Year's Eve. Is this the first time you've come to a *ra's al-sana* celebration in a club?"

Bishr said, "Of course."

Hasan added, smiling his half smile, "It's really *raqs al-sana*, the dance of the year, not the 'head'!"

They all laughed out loud. Nadir said,

"If Isa Salamawy were here and heard you laughing like that he would be very upset."

They laughed again, all but Nawal. She noticed the name and thought a bit, then she asked them, "Who's Isa Salamawy?"

Ahmad said, mockingly, "A good man. A Marxist who's over forty, who likes to spread Marxism among the students. God willing, he'll get them all in a lot of trouble."

Nawal smiled slightly without commenting. She closed her eyes for a few moments, then Bishr said,

"By the way, Hasan has ten pounds. They gave them to him in the Student Welfare Office, after they took him to a camp in Amiriya for a week to train him in karate. It's a political activity under the Student Welfare Office, to form groups of Islamist-leaning young men to oppose Communism." Nawal seemed upset, so he went on, "I mean, they took him to train him to beat up Communists, and at the end of the week of training they gave him ten pounds. He came back and told us, and decided to spend the pounds here and not go back to them." She looked at them, bewildered, so Bishr continued, "Nadir also was summoned to State Security for an interrogation. Tell her what happened, Nadir."

But Nadir said nothing, so Ahmad said, "Is this the right time or place to talk about this, Bishr? And you say I'm an ass!"

They laughed, but she became more thoughtful for several moments. Then she said, "Spend the ten pounds somewhere else. Tonight you're my guests. I'll settle the account with Nadir after the party."

Silence and surprise held them, and Nadir was embarrassed. But Nawal went on: "Do you see those Saudis sitting over there?" They were three men wearing Arab dress. "Usually they go to Cairo."

Bishr said, "The Libyans usually come to Alexandria, but Brother Qadhafi's problems with Sadat have gotten in their way."

Ahmad laughed. "Thank God—they raised the prices of the women!"

Everyone was embarrassed. Nawal smiled slightly and Ahmad said, "I'm sorry, Madam, by God I'm sorry! I don't know why I said that."

Her smile widened and she said, "They offered to buy the club for a hundred thousand pounds. The law doesn't allow them to buy it now, but they have Egyptian agents until a law is issued allowing foreigners to own buildings and land. And it will certainly be issued."

Nadir said in surprise, "That's the price of an apartment building on the Corniche!"

"They want to turn it into a café in which they will forbid alcoholic beverages, or into a wedding parlor."

Bishr looked at the three Saudis. "It's not important that they are drinking alcohol, what's important is that they raise a sign saying 'Alcoholic drinks forbidden.'"

Hasan Hafiz said, "Your public is calling you, Madam."

She noticed that and laughed. Alya had disappeared along with Ahmad Ibrahim, and only the oriental ensemble remained. Nawal stood and removed the light shawl from her shoulders, and her body glowed in the dim light. She left the shawl on her seat and went up to the platform in front of the orchestra amid noisy applause. One of the patrons stood up and called, "Long live Asmahan!"

Nawal began singing Asmahan's song:

I'm in love, I'm in love,
if you tell me, I'm in love
I'll bring you coffee, hot and frothy.
I, I, I, I'm in love!

"Damn you, it's only eleven o'clock—why are you throwing things like that?"

Isa Salamawy said that to himself on Digla Street, the short street leading to Ateneos. He had been walking in a crazy circuit that ended when a bottle thrown from above came close enough to hit his head from behind. The hat he was wearing tonight to protect himself from the rain fell onto the ground when the bottle hit it. He picked it up, not noticing the blood that had appeared in his hair, and hurried into Ateneos, steps away.

He had left the bus before Manshiya Square, having decided to walk through in the streets tonight before getting to Ateneos. Why did he do that? He didn't know, exactly, except that he had wanted to. He had hurried along Salah Salem Street, where all the shops were closed, to Fuad Street. He'd turned left to Nabi Danyal Street and had seen that Cinema Fuad, on his right, was as usual showing two old films. The Arabic one was *The Bathhouse of Malatili* and the foreign one was *The Vikings*. A marvelous feast. The Arabic film oozed with sex, for the ordinary viewer, and with loss, the hidden meaning that the ordinary viewer would miss. He had loved *The Vikings* in the sixties, when he had seen it in a second-run theater, after its first run when he was in prison. Kirk Douglas and Tony Curtis were both in it, as they were also in *Spartacus*, which he had likewise seen in a second-run theater, for the same reason. The little theater must be crowded tonight.

Across from it the Plaza Cinema was also showing two old films, both foreign: *Some Like It Hot* with Marilyn Monroe, Tony Curtis, and Jack Lemmon, and *Irma la Douce*, the daring, enchanting film from the director Billy Wilder. It was enough that Shirley MacLaine and Jack Lemmon were in it. God, why were the second-run theaters so dazzling tonight, even though he had seen all the films after his release from prison, in similar theaters? He had gone on walking, not noticing the rain under the protection of the balconies, and looking at the posters for the films. The Cinema Royale was still showing *Barry Lyndon*. How had he ever missed seeing a film from the great director Stanley Kubrick? He would see it later. Those who went into the nine o'clock showing would only celebrate the new year in the street. He went on walking and scanning the film posters; everything was closed. On the marquee of Cinema Rioux was *Dawn Visitor*, which he had seen a few days before. How had he forgotten to advise his students to see it, when it was a film that exposed the centers of power in the Nasser era? On the marquee of the Amir Cinema was *Dog Day Afternoon*. It also had a great director, Sidney Lumet, and it was enough to say that the lead actor was Al Pacino.

He had hurried into Safiya Zaghlul Street, and smiled at his interest in the movie posters tonight. His attention was caught by the Elite Restaurant which had been surrounded by a wall of wood and glass, so he didn't notice the poster for the Metro Cinema on his right. He walked on thinking about how things had really changed, so he didn't notice the Rialto Cinema poster either, or the Alhambra Cinema, or the Strand after that . . . .

He had realized that he wasn't walking in order to see the movie posters, but that he had wanted to walk alone in old Alexandria, his cherished city, which the Italians more than anyone else had excelled in building. Why hadn't he heard any music coming from the Pastrou-dis Restaurant, when he was near the Amir Cinema? It was impossible that there wouldn't be any celebration there tonight. Maybe he had been too distracted with his thoughts to hear. Yes, he had been looking at the front of the apartment buildings and their beauty, annoyed at the air conditioners that the new renters had planted on their walls, disfiguring them. Anyone who didn't know the history of Alexandria's architecture didn't know the city. He needed to reread the history of the city—that would be his goal in the coming days. If he couldn't defend the city, at least he would see it as if it had not undergone the passage of time. He would tell his students about it as well—he would open a magic cave for them and they would not disappoint him. Even if they didn't become real Marxists, they would know the value of the earth on which they stood. In Greek mythology, the giant Antaeus ambushed, robbed, and killed people, until Hercules faced him. Hercules knew that Antaeus was the son of Gaia, the earth. He did not fight him, he simply rushed him and lifted him off the earth, and Antaeus was scattered into particles of dust. His feet had left the earth, his origin and the strength upon which he stood. He would simplify it for them. Why did the Ittihad Alexandria Soccer Club often go down to defeat when it played against Ahly or Zamalek in Cairo? Because it had left the earth that was the source of its strength. A day should never come when Egyptians would find themselves standing on another earth. But the desert and its sands had begun to creep into it from the Arabian Peninsula.

Yes. These Wahhabi ideas, which were gaining ground now, however small the gain, would later cover all of Egypt's soil and sink into it, and Egyptians would become estranged from their own history. It would be very easy for this subject to be his goal in the coming days. He would take a little time to come back to Alexandria!

In the end he had found himself walking to the garden of the statue of Sa'd Zaghlul. This was where he should have gotten off the bus rather than making this circuit. He had stood like a bewildered child looking at the statue, listening to the sound of the rain as it hit the raincoat he was wearing and the hat on his head. He saw the lights of the Cecil Hotel behind its high window shutters, and the lights of the Metropolitan Hotel too. Really, why didn't he spend a night in one of the hotels? There was an old familiarity in Ateneos . . . . Abruptly he asked Sa'd Zaghlul why he was still looking toward the sea. *Now our country is looking to the east, to the desert of the Arabian Peninsula. Really, can't you turn around, or leave your place, so people can forget the Revolution of 1919?*

He had chosen not to stand there for long, but had returned hurriedly to the tram tracks, to go to Ateneos from Digla Street. There the bottle fell on his head, as if it was giving an ironic answer to his question and his bewilderment.

When he first entered the Crazy Horse Room, where parties were held, he stood staring at the people seated there, filling it in the dim light. How had he deprived himself of all this warmth for the sake of a tour he could have made in daylight on any other day? Never mind. He had arrived at Ateneos, and now he would surely forget his sorrow. Christo was in the distance, so he went to him after giving his hat and coat to one of the waiters. There was a woman with Christo tonight. It couldn't be his wife, who was in Greece—would he call her his wife?

But Christo said, presenting her, "Paula, from Switzerland."

The aroma of various perfumes filled the air in the room, but her perfume was more penetrating, reaching his spirit and surrounding her. Isa bowed low as he took her hand and kissed it. She noticed the small amount of blood on the back of his head, and cried out in alarm, "Blood?"

He didn't notice that she spoke in Arabic. He smiled and sat down. "It's a small thing. A bottle landed on my head in the street, but my hat protected me."

Christo said, "Khabibi, why are you walking in those streets now?" Then he patted his shoulder, saying "There, there."

But the woman had pulled out several tissues from the large box on the edge of the table. She moistened them with wine and said, "Give me your head."

Christo cried, "Alcohol? Right!"

Isa inclined his head and Paula started removing the blood. Isa felt some pain at first, as Paula set about changing the tissues and moistening them with wine every time, until no trace of the blood remained. He was happy, not believing what was happening to him. As Paula was wiping her fingers on Kleenex after finishing her work, Christo suddenly said,

"Mr. Salamawy is an important Communist, Paula. Just like Jacob, God have mercy on him."

Paula smiled and Isa realized that she was Jewish. Since she spoke Arabic he supposed that she had been born and lived her early life in an Arab country, but Christo told him that in fact she was Egyptian: she had been born in Alexandria and had lived her life there, like her ancestors. Her husband Jacob had been put in prison for no reason in 1957. He had been in his forties, working in the cloth trade, and she had been twenty-five and had owned a small shop for beauty products on Nabi Danyal Street. Her husband was tortured with the other Jews who were arrested after the Suez War, but he only spent a month in prison. Afterward he left Egypt completely for Switzerland, with Paula. She was back in Alexandria for the first time after all these years.

Isa looked at her searchingly. "Why didn't you go to Israel?"

She shrugged and replied, "So what's this Israel? I'm an Alexandrian." Then she laughed and continued, "I'm not the only one who did that, who didn't go, nor was my husband Jacob. A lot of Jews did the same."

Suddenly Christo cried, "Where's Mr. Salamawy?"

Isa was very startled. He said, "I'm here next to you, Christo."

Christo slapped his forehead and said, "How strange! I thought I was sitting alone."

Isa and Paula laughed. She raised her glass saying, "Here's to your health, Christo, yours and your Communist friend's . . . ."

They all raised their glasses to each other and clinked them together. Paula took several sips and silence descended on them for a while. Then she said,

"I was overcome with a yearning to visit the places where I grew up, where I worked. Everything's changed. Even my shop, I found that it's a shoe store. Of course our house was on the street of the goldsmiths, al-Sagha Street. I found a very tall apartment building in its place. For a week now I've been walking along the sea, sitting here sometimes, or in the Trianon or Délices, nothing else. I've spent most of my time in the Cecil Hotel, looking out over the sea from the window."

She fell silent for a few moments, but she was smiling. Looking at Isa, she began to intone in a low voice, carried away,

"'Recite the fatiha for Abul Abbas . . . O Alexandria, your people are first class.'" She stopped and asked him, "Isn't that right?"

He answered, also singing, "'Recite the fatiha for our lord Yaqut . . . God willing, our enemies die destitute.'"

They laughed. She looked at Christo. "Say something, Christo."

He was embarrassed. He looked around him, then looked at her and said, "Fine. 'Recite the fatiha for Abul Dardar . . . anyone against us is starting a war.'"

They all laughed loudly.

Lorice had appeared and had been singing for several minutes. She was a young singer who some said was Italian and some said was Swiss, while in fact she had an Egyptian father and European features that she had inherited from her French mother. Behind her was a small band, with a young man named Sami playing the keyboard and a girl named Samia playing the violin. Christo noticed the music and the singing, and said,

"Tonight it's all French. Right. *'Sous le ciel de Paris,'* the song of Yves Montand."

Paula said, laughing, "And of Edith Piaf."

Isa said, "And Juliette Greco. Do you know her?"

Paula laughed, admiring him. In complete silence they gave their attention to Lorice's singing, and to her beautiful voice . . . .

Sous le ciel de Paris
S'envole une chanson, hum, hum
Elle est née d'aujourd'hui
Dans le coeur d'un garçon.

Distracted from them, Paula began to repeat softly,

Under the Paris sky
a song flies,
just today it was born
in the heart of a boy.

She completed the song in Arabic, along with Lorice, who was singing it in French:

Under the Paris sky
the lovers pass by,
building their joy
on the tune they employ.

Isa was surprised by her command of formal as well as of spoken Arabic. She fell silent, and they were carried away by the peaceful song and the sight of the couples who had gotten up to dance quietly, each pair embracing passionately, as if they were meeting after a long separation. As soon as Lorice finished everyone clapped in delight. "Bravo, bravo, bravo!"

Lorice stood laughing happily and bowed to them more than once, but then she pointed to the young man playing the keyboard and said,

"We're close to twelve o'clock now. Sami is going to sing "Sway" for you, by Dean Martin."

Cries of joy and happiness broke out. Sami came forward and took the mike from her while she took his place at the keyboard. As soon as Sami started singing many went back to dancing, moving to the passionate song.

Isa said to Christo, laughing, "Even in France a night like this can't go by without Dean Martin."

Paula laughed. She seemed young to Isa, continually moving her shoulders and repeating the song. He was afraid she would ask him to dance now, as the room was ablaze with the song and the dancers. He might not be able to keep up with her. At that very moment she grasped his hands and wordlessly pulled him after her, taking him out among the dancers. Christo seemed distracted from them.

On stage, Sami was also moving continuously as he sang, in English,

Dance with me, make me sway.
Like a lazy ocean hugs the shore,
Hold me close, sway me more.
Like a flower bending in the breeze,
Bend with me, sway with me.

"Come on. How can it have taken me all this time to hear your poetry?"

Nadir smiled, and said, "Listen to this poem:"

Days to come stand in front of us
like a row of lighted candles—
golden, warm, and vivid candles.

Days gone by fall behind us,
a gloomy line of snuffed-out candles;
the nearest are smoking still,
cold, melted, and bent.

I don't want to look at them: their shape saddens me,
and it saddens me to remember their original light.
I look ahead at my lighted candles.

"I don't want to turn for fear of seeing [them], terrified....

Nadir said no more, and silence descended on the large room in Nawal's apartment, as dawn approached. Around him were many paintings hanging on the walls. Some were copies of Monet, Manet, Renoir, Van Gogh, and Salvador Dali, and others were originals from Seif and Adham Wanli, Mahmud Saeed, Muhammad Nagi, and other Egyptian artists. He had gone to look at them earlier when he came into the apartment and he recognized their signatures, although he was a long way from knowing anything about visual arts. Nawal had changed her dress in her room while he went around looking at the paintings and the stately furniture. She had returned and sat down in front of him, wearing a flowered robe in beautiful colors. Now she seemed to be very touched by the poem.

He said, "What you just heard isn't one of mine. It's a poem by Cavafy."

She looked at him in surprise. Then her thoughts seemed to wander for a bit before she said, "I heard that name one day."

"Do you like the visual arts?"

"You will learn everything about me, but only after I hear your poetry. Why don't you change your clothes?"

He filled his glass with the wine set before him and closed his eyes. He decided he would recite his poetry. Today he would learn what he had yearned to know about her, so he would honor her request, to open the way for her.

What would happen if the sea withdrew
and unknown cities appeared, among them women with
slender bodies,
dancing to the airs of a guitar,
and then the waters returned to cover everything,
to hide the cities and the women
while wonderment remained suspended in the city sky.

"Wait." She said that and stood up, then went to the record player over in the corner of the room. She put on a record of Mozart's music, and returned as the music rose behind her. She sat before him concentrating her gaze on him as if he were a beautiful child.

The woman who visited me in my dream,
the one I woke to find in my place,
cried to me,
"What makes you visit me every night?
And why, when morning comes, do I not find you with me?"

Silence enveloped them again. He seemed hesitant. But this was another woman, not Yara; he did not love her, not yet, even though he was comfortable with her. If she loved him, perhaps he reminded her of something she had lost. He would learn everything tonight, so he should take courage and put things in their place, to see what might happen. He closed his eyes for a moment and then went back to reciting his poetry.

She is Yara, and not another woman.
I only see her gathering butterflies.
She is Yara, and not another woman,
who gathers the strands of lace
and makes with them a cloak
to carry her, to fly with her to the sky.

Before Nawal could speak, as she seemed to want to do, he went on:

She is Yara, and not another woman
who asks me, what is the home country . . .
and why does my father seem
out of tune with society?
Why do he and mother search
for old things,
old films, old furniture, old songs?
Can a man stop in one age and not leave it?
If our life is long, do we no longer have a country that is
     home?
Is it betraying us, as my father says?
My mother believes his words, handing him his coffee in an
     old cup
she has kept for dozens of years.

He stopped speaking and closed his eyes, thinking about how memory had come to his aid with this poem, when he usually did not easily memorize what he wrote. Nawal and the music of Mozart were the reason. Just Nawal, and the warmth of the place, and the gentleness of her spirit.

Her eyelashes were fluttering, trying to hide a tear that had welled up and was about to fall. Wishing to bring her to what he wanted, he said,

"You promised me you would tell me how you came to love visual arts."

"It's a long story, Nadir."

He learned that her husband had been one of the important Communists in Alexandria. His name was Nadir Naeem. He was shaken when he heard that the man's name was also Nadir. Nawal added that she had met him and other Communists because she had loved a doctor who took her to sing for them. She was a nurse who was always singing at work, even during surgery, and there was a doctor who sometimes asked her to sing. She laughed as she said that. She had not known that her beloved Ahmad was a Communist until after she had gone with him several times to Nadir Naeem and the others around him. Naeem was a handsome man of about fifty, and all this furniture and these works of art had been in his apartment in St. Catherine Square. They were all arrested on New Year's Eve, the last night of 1958, after she had sung beautifully for them. They were sent to serve their time in the Oases Prison. As for her, she had been arrested also, and held in the State Security building on Faraana Street. She had been held underground there for many days. Her father got her out, in a strange story. She laughed until she cried happy tears as she told it. Her father had sent a letter to Gamal Abdel Nasser complaining about the arrest of his daughter, and this letter was the reason for her release. Before the arrests Naeem had promised to find a way for her to sing on Radio Alexandria but he had not succeeded— and of course after that she was unsuccessful in finding any opportunity, either in Alexandria or in Cairo.

Originally she was from a poor home in the railway residences along the Mahmudiya Canal, between Karmuz and Kafr Ashri. Her father, Hamza, had strange stories to tell also, as he had been kidnapped by the Allied soldiers during the Second World War, when she was just a child.

After that unforgettable New Year's Eve and what had happened to her, she went on with her work as a nurse for more than five years, in terror, until the Communist prisoners were released. Ahmad did not return to her. Instead the one who sought her out was Nadir Naeem, who looked as if he had aged greatly. He told her that Ahmad had left the country for France and would not return, and then he offered to marry her. Naeem was alone, and he didn't know to whom he would give his apartment with its furnishings and works of art. He was going to leave Egypt and go to the Soviet Union, and no one had a better right to what he owned than she did. It was a strange offer, mixed with her sadness over losing Ahmad forever. She lived a year with Nadir Naeem and he transferred everything to her. She sold the apartment and with that money she bought the nightclub, to sing.

In some embarrassment she said, "Just to sing, just to do what the State Security apparatus had prevented me from doing, even though I sing for wretched drunkards. Now do you know why I liked you all? Maybe you'll learn more later on, too."

She seemed sad, and he was astonished and speechless. But she hurriedly stood up and went to a desk across the room, on which there were a lot of books which he thought must belong to her absent husband. She opened a drawer and returned with an old notebook. He stared at it in surprise.

"This notebook is very old, as you see. It belonged to a poet named Ismat Muftah." He looked confused, so she said, "You won't know him. He was among those who were arrested. I heard his poetry for the first time in Nadir Naeem's apartment. He was tortured and killed in prison."

"How did you get it?"

"He smuggled out his poems by means of Isa Salamawy's sister, who visited them in the Oases after they began allowing visitors."

Greatly surprised, he asked, "Isa Salamawy was with them?"

"Yes. I know him. They allowed family visits during the last two years, as I learned later. Ismat used to write his poetry on cigarette papers, and Isa would give them to his sister. She's the one who wrote down all this poetry, this is her handwriting. Isa gave the notebook to my husband after they got out of prison, and he left it to me. I think the time has come to publish it—what do you think?"

He took the notebook from her without a word. He opened it and began reading, silently,

> Delacroix, who had just finished
> painting "Liberty Leading the People,"
> went running out into the gardens,
> where he saw the woman who had just finished
> making the revolution.
> He wept before her, calling to her to wait,

for he had not yet painted true liberty.
"Who are you, o woman of mystery?"
She said, "I am the one
whose milk was expressed by Goya.
He arose, crazed, to paint 'The Third of May 1808'
and to run in the streets with the bulls.
The bulls knew Goya and made way for him,
and Goya came rejoicing to the edge of the river.
Come, let Goya lead us all in prayer,
come, let Goya lead us all in prayer!"

Nadir stopped reading and seemed very far away. He closed the notebook and studied her for a few moments. Then he said, "You are a very beautiful woman."

Nawal burst out in tears and threw herself into his arms. "I beg you, don't become attached to me! I'm just a passing story, like everyone I've known. Someday I'll leave Egypt—that's another story that I'll tell you about some time. What matters is that we publish this poetry."

He began wiping away her tears with his hand, and found himself kissing her cheeks. She seemed to yield to him completely and he soon found himself kissing her mouth, while she clasped him strongly to her breast, as if she wanted to bring him into her heart. He wanted to stand up with her, but she said, "No, let me stay in your arms."

But he could not. He pulled her up and then carried her into her room.

In bed she seemed like someone who had thirsted for him for a long time. When they had finished and lay naked, he asked, "Why did you wait so long to invite me here?"

She smiled. "You're a Communist and a romantic, Nadir, just like your friends. Communists are always arrested at dawn on this night; that's the legacy of the July Revolution. Look at the light that's beginning to steal into the world—the police must have finished arresting the Communists a little while ago." He looked at her in disbelief, and she continued, "I wanted to make them miss their chance tonight if you were one of their targets, especially since I knew that you had been summoned to State Security for interrogation."

His mind wandered in shock for a few moments, then he said, "But that could still happen tomorrow."

"Then you will have gained a lovely day."

As she leaned over and rested her head on his chest, what she described was indeed taking place. Among those taken to prison in the transport vans that night was Bishr Zahran, who had arrived home before dawn.

4

TWO DAYS AFTER BISHR'S ARREST Nadir, Hasan, and Kariman decided not to meet, neither in the college nor anywhere else. They decided that they would stay away during the days that remained before the vacation. Yara was absent that day and Nadir decided not to contact her. She would certainly figure out that he was afraid for her, now, if she appeared with him anywhere. Hasan went to Mansura while Nadir stayed at home in Maks; each of them thought that if he was arrested it should be at home, so that their families would know from the beginning. Kariman went to the college more than once, since she saw no difference between being arrested at home or in the college. Either way, no one would look for her—and either way, her stepfather would divorce her mother.

Yara was absent from school for a number of days because of her menstrual pain. When she went back it was during the last days before the vacation, and the college was nearly empty of students and professors. She had learned of Bishr's arrest from the newspapers, in the reports about the arrest of Communists, which gave their names. But she couldn't find any way to contact Nadir, who didn't have a telephone in his house. When she called Kariman her stepfather answered and asked her for her name and what she wanted, so she hung up on him in disgust. If only Kariman would visit her at home! But Kariman did not come so she realized that the man had not told her about the call, and she became all the more disgusted with him.

As the days passed, Nadir resisted his desire to call Yara so he could see her. Out of an abundance of caution he also did not go to Nawal in the nightclub, despite the great need he had to see her—she who had taken him to her home to spend New Year's Eve in safety.

It was the fifteenth of January, 1976. At that point two weeks had passed since Bishr's imprisonment, and the midyear vacation began. Nadir went to the Khafagi Café and met Isa Salamawy in the morning. He found him unusually happy, smoking a water pipe. He told him he wasn't meeting any of the friends, and Isa seemed happy and satisfied. Isa in turn confirmed that he should not try to meet Yara, Nawal, or Kariman, these days. He said,

"I learned from the newspapers that those who were arrested from other towns have been divided between the Tura and Qanatir prisons. It's a small number this time, from the Egyptian Communist Party and the Communist Workers' Party only."

Surprised, Nadir said, "I saw Bishr's name among the members of the Communist Workers' Party, but none of us is a member of any secret party."

Isa shook his head dismissively. "That's the incompetence of State Security in Egypt. They arrest innocents, who then meet members of real Communist parties in prison, and then join them after they get out. Even if they were all innocent, they would found a new secret party when they get out."

Nadir seemed very worried. Isa said, "The law decrees that those who are imprisoned must be presented to the court within a month, and two weeks have already gone by. Don't worry, they will be released. The State Security men say they found publications in their possession, and usually the State Security apparatus plants them with them during the prosecutor's investigations. Even if they have recorded conversations and meetings of the real members of secret parties, the lawyers object easily, as it's done without the prosecutor's permission. They usually edit out what's not political from the tapes, and that's also easy to discover."

Isa laughed, and then went on: "This Anwar Sadat is really strange. He gives the accused their legal rights, and then allows the State Security apparatus to trump up charges against them. A day will come in this country when the rulers regret what they're doing to the leftist forces now."

Silence descended on them. Nadir's face still showed his worry. In fact he yearned to see Yara, and struggled to keep himself from calling her. He stood up to leave, having decided to go to Raml Station to wander among the booksellers. Isa said,

"Don't forget what I told you—don't contact anyone, and particularly not Yara. There are no guarantees with this pitiful regime."

Nadir got on the bus thinking about why Isa had singled out Yara this time. He soon found himself calling her from the Raml telephone exchange, and to his surprise she was the one who answered. He had hoped that her father or mother would answer; then he would hang up and tell her later on that he had tried to call her once. But happiness engulfed him and his spirit soared, so that he had to catch his breath before he could speak to her. He would meet Yara, whatever happened. Yara was created by God himself, so human devils could never touch her, never.

Isa did not stay long in the Khafagi Café. Leaving a little while after Nadir, he stood to pay the bill and noticed that the art exhibition was still in place. How had he not asked Nadir to look at the paintings by Alexandria's artists? And how had Nadir not noticed the exhibit around them? He realized then how deeply worried Nadir was, but he did not forgive himself for failing to see that it was important for Nadir to view the exhibit.

He decided to go up to his nearby apartment, to go on with his reading about the history of Alexandrian architecture, so he could turn it into lessons for his disciples, as he had decided previously. But he felt a desire to see the film *Barry Lyndon* in the Cinema Royale. He had seen the poster on New Year's Eve, and he asked himself how he had managed not to see it until now. He would go to the three o'clock showing, then return to continue his readings—his former readings, really, that he wanted to revive.

But that evening he laughed heartily when he realized that he had not seen the film today, either. On the way to the theater from

Fuad Street he had turned on the street ahead of the one he wanted, finding himself standing and looking to his left at a little, half-open door, with laughter coming from inside. He looked up at the sign over the shop and found its place empty, just as it had been for a long time. He was standing in front of the "Coward's Bar," where Christo had taken him many times years before, but which had not come up in conversation with him recently. Why had that happened? He remembered having asked himself this question before, although he had somehow not asked Christo. He answered himself by saying that the owner had left Alexandria, that tall Greek man with a red face held high on a long neck, who wore a long white apron that nearly reached his feet. Was it an act of fate this time too, and would he find Christo here?

As soon as he entered he was astounded by the small size of the place. How had he not noticed that before? Six people were sitting there. Every time he had come before there were six or seven people there. So the place was just as it had been, not having gotten any smaller or larger. Those sitting there were poor, as before. The owner of the bar was behind the marble counter, on which there were a few glasses and a few bottles of whiskey, wine, and brandy. Behind him were shelves of bottles stretching to the ceiling, as before. The man had not left Alexandria, and Isa told himself, smiling, that he would have to stay a long time before all these bottles were finished!

"Welcome, khabibi." The owner said that, and Isa remembered his name: Matiakis. Isa saw him smile; Matiakis remembered him, too.

He sat at an empty table and Matiakis emerged from behind the counter, carrying a small bottle of brandy and a glass, which he put before him. He opened the bottle with the opener in his hand, but he did not pour anything. It was just as before: his clients were the ones who poured. Isa poured himself a glass. Matiakis returned to the counter and from behind it, from low shelves below it that no one could see, he took a plate of Greek salad, a plate of fried fish, and a plate of potatoes mashed with parsley. He returned and put them all in front of Isa, who had not ordered them. Matiakis was just the same.

He said, "Anything else, khabibi?"

"No thank you, khawaga."

After he answered, Isa began looking at the happy faces of the people sitting there. Isa was not surprised when a young man came in the door and stood there nervously for a moment. Matiakis shouted,

"Out, khabibi, there's no alcohol, none at all."

The young man became more nervous. He looked poor, despite his bell-bottom pants and his long hair and sideburns.

He said, "I'm twenty-two, khawaga."

"Where's your ID?"

The six patrons scattered in their seats were laughing, and Isa was smiling. The young man pulled a wallet from the back pocket of his pants and took out his ID, handing it to Matiakis.

The bar owner looked at it and said, "Born in fifty-six, that means twenty years old. Not possible, out!" He returned the ID to the young man, who took it angrily, and turned around to go out. When he reached out to open the door, Matiakis cried, "Wait!"

He came out from behind the counter, then opened the door and looked left and right along the street. The patrons were laughing. They knew that he would allow the young man to sit down, even though he was not yet twenty-one, the legal age to consume alcohol. He only appeared to be afraid, during this regular routine; that's why he had become known as "the coward," and the bar became "The Coward's Bar."

"All right then, stand here. No sit on chair." He motioned to the counter, so the young man stood there. Matiakis poured him a glass of rum. The man looked at him in surprise and said, "I want a beer."

"No, no. A beer is too much. Rum. One glass. Come on, hurry up and drink, I don't need trouble."

The man took the glass, embarrassed, and began to sip slowly. Matiakis said, "Come on, khabibi! There are no more Greeks in Alexandria, no more foreigners. There's no consulate to protect people the way there used to be." He looked at the patrons and said, "What's this twenty-one, I don't get it. It's a big injustice!"

They all roared with laughter, and Isa smiled. One of the patrons said, "The problem, khawaga, is that the 'believing president' said 'an Islamic state,' even though he drinks alcohol and everybody knows it."

The Coward said, "You no talk about Sadat, please. Also Sadat no drink alcohol. Khashish maybe."

Everybody laughed, and Isa joined in heartily. He thanked the chance that had placed him in front of this bar today. Really, why had he stopped coming, when it contained the true spirit of the people!

Another person said, "The whole country smokes hashish. Egypt has always loved hashish. It's colonialism that caused alcohol drinking."

The patrons laughed more, and Isa thought about the man's words. Had Egypt really known hashish before alcohol? Of course not, Egyptians had known alcohol since the time of the pharaohs. But this was not the right place to explain that to them. He would watch and be surprised and happy. He would have a real Egyptian afternoon.

The first man replied, "I heard that the government has imported alcoholic drinks without alcohol, made in European factories especially for Saudi Arabia and the Gulf states. The Egyptian government wanted to keep up with them."

They laughed. The young man had finished the glass of rum and asked for another. Matiakis told him, "That's all, khabibi, just one glass. Come on, give me a quarter of a pound."

The man paid the quarter pound and went out, annoyed. But at the door he smiled and nodded before he disappeared. The Coward went out after him and leaned out of the door, looking left and right in the street. He returned amid their laughter and said, "What's this alcoholic drinks without alcohol? That's not possible!"

The second man said, "Now that they've made alcoholic drinks without alcohol, they'll make meat without cholesterol, and milk without fat, and carbohydrate-free bread."

They stared at him, amazed, and he continued, "And in order to protect people from temptation, they will make women without sexual organs."

At that, everyone gave in to laughter, and the Coward's smile grew still broader. But as soon as the laughter died down, Matiakis clapped his hands. "That's all, that's all. I'm going to close the bar. A break till nine tonight. Come on, get going!"

He clapped his hands again, apparently serious. They exchanged glances; it seemed as if they never rebelled against him. He began collecting both empty glasses and full ones from in front of everyone, along with empty bottles and those that had not been opened, and they in turn took money out of their pockets to pay him. But a man came in the door, wearing a yellow raincoat with a black scarf over it and carrying a short bamboo cane. He looked as if he was in the secret police. The Coward suddenly said, "Never mind, you no go. There's no break or anything. What'll you have, khabibi?"

The informer said, "You know."

Matiakis hurried to put a glass of wine on the marble counter. He said to him, "Sit here in front of me, khabibi, because there's some really nice mullet. Drink your wine, it'll warm you up, it's on me, too."

They began to smile and laugh silently. Isa chose this moment to leave. He didn't want his experience at the bar to be sullied by the presence of an informer.

Daylight had begun to slip away from the sky as night slowly advanced. Isa walked to where he had been heading and stood in front of the Cinema Royale, where the audience for the three o'clock showing had not yet emerged and the six-thirty audience had not yet gathered at the door. How he loved this neighborhood—the Muhammad Ali Theater, the Cavafy Museum, the Greek Patriarchate with its huge bell lying useless on the ground. Actually, who had put this bell here, and why? He had never learned the answer to that question. In the background, too, was the restaurant Chez Gaby along with fine leather shops everywhere. In the small surrounding streets there were a few cafés. The faces of their patrons were relaxed and pleased.

He looked at the façade of the theater and didn't see any pictures of Ryan O'Neil. So the film had finished its run. He closed his eyes for a moment, feeling some sadness but no regret. He had laughed today as he had not laughed for a long time!

Before him now were pictures of *Funny Girl*, with Barbra Streisand and Omar Sharif. How beautiful were the foreign films being shown in Egypt these days! This film would need a whole day dedicated to it alone, just so that he could enjoy Barbra Streisand, as well as the star of the east that shone in the west. Now he would go to Ateneos, especially since he had not eaten any of what the Coward had offered him, and had drunk only two glasses. In Ateneos he would look out over what was left of the middle class, which was going to be trampled underfoot by the parasitic class of new money men in the period of "The Opening" inaugurated by the believing leader!

He held her hands and kissed them, as they sat next to each other on the edge of the bed. He said,

"Forgive me. Every day that passed was like a thousand days. I was determined not to call you, I was afraid for you, but I couldn't wait."

She drew his head to her chest and said, "Two weeks have gone by since Bishr was put in prison. Don't worry; if they had wanted to put you in prison too they wouldn't have waited. Besides, I'm ready for anything for your sake."

"I love you, Yara. I can't imagine the world away from you."

She began to pat his back, feeling as if he was really a child. She said, "You're really wonderful, Nadir. By God I'm not afraid! I was very worried about you. There's no telephone in your house so I couldn't call and check on you. Why don't you get a telephone?"

He smiled. "We'll apply to the utility, that's easy. But the phone will arrive ten years later."

She laughed. After a moment she said, "Listen, a funny thing happened to me on New Year's Eve."

She told him the story of the man who gave her the pamphlet urging the hijab, and calling for a ban on celebrating the Christian new year. He looked at her in shock for moment, then he said, "Are they organized to that extent? Who allows them to do that if not the regime?"

She said, "I was really afraid that night. I was afraid he would come back to me every night after that, but thank God he didn't come. I spent the night with music and reading your poems. I've memorized them all, do you want to hear them?"

Nadir smiled and brought his lips close to her, kissing her on the cheek. He whispered, "I know them all. I'm the poet, or have you forgotten?"

She laughed, then brought her lips to him to be kissed. An hour passed as they floated in a world beyond, a world of pleasure. His hands passed over her entire body, as if they wanted to leave their imprint on every part of it as they bore into her. She felt herself withdrawing, going far away, to a place where there was nothing around her and she didn't know the way back. His lips moved too, with the gentleness of an ascetic who felt that there was nothing in the world but Yara, that he would never find anything else. A feeling of transcendence spread within him, that place where the sense of the body ended and a man became completely spirit, annihilated in the divine spirit. Should he tell her about that now? Instead he gave himself over to the transcendence, eagerly taking the divine blessings that God had placed in Yara's crystalline body, as if it were a cradle for adoration and devotion.

When he finished and lay down on his back next to her on the narrow bed, she seemed calm, as if she had not yet returned from the world beyond. He saw that her eyes were closed and said anxiously, "Yara . . .".

She did not answer. He spoke her name again, concerned, and again she did not answer. The third time she opened her eyes and smiled a little. Like a child, she answered, "Yes?"

"Where did you go?"

"I don't know." Then she smiled. "Didn't you feel anything?" He didn't answer. She said, "I fainted, I swear, I fainted away."

They both laughed, and he embraced her, kissing her quickly. She pinched his chest and tickled him, and he laughed more. She remembered that he became very sensitive after sex; she had real-ized that the time before. So she went on pinching him quickly in several places and he couldn't help himself, laughing and trying to keep her hands away from him. At last he succeeded and threw him-self on her again, kissing her, and she subsided.

She said, "That's enough for today." He sat up beside her and took her in his arms. Suddenly she said, "You never told me how your New Year's Eve was at the Nawal Boîte?"

He looked at her calmly. "I've forgotten . . . I don't remember anything that happened. There's no one in the world for me but Yara."

He embraced her again for several minutes; they did nothing but remain in each other's arms. Then she put her hands on his shoulders and said, "I'm late, I have to go now."

"It's not ten yet."

"At ten o'clock I'll be home. I told them I was going to meet Kariman and then come back."

He thought a bit and said, "I wish you had told them you were going to spend the night with Kariman."

She looked at him in amazement, her eyes shining. "Imagine! That's an idea. Maybe I'll do that next time."

He embraced her again, kissing her. After several kisses on her lips, she said, "Let me keep my word to them so I can go out again."

They both laughed. He said, "Fine. Shall I come with you to Raml station? It's cold out and the streets are empty. I'm afraid for you."

"Don't worry, the tram's nearby."

She put on her clothes and said goodbye at the door of the apart-ment, kissing him quickly. "What will you do, all alone, tonight?"

He said confidently, "I'll write some poetry."

She kissed him again and went out. He stood there for a few moments, until she left the stairway, then he closed the door. He wanted to watch her from the balcony, but he remained where he was, looking at everything around him in the apartment. It seemed as if he was seeing it all for the first time. He jumped into the air, disbelieving and happy.

*

Bishr Zahran stood among a number of prisoners, his eyes bold and challenging. There were many people present in court, some of them coming up to the defendants' cage to shake hands with the prisoners, and most of them looking worried. The lawyers were in the first row in their black robes, laughing and talking. It was the first time Bishr had seen the lawyers known for taking the cases of Communists: Nabil al-Hilali, Abdallah al-Zoghbi, and Zaki Murad. Their names were also among the accused in many cases, especially Hilali and Murad. They had all volunteered to defend the accused; in fact they were all leftists. Around them were a few younger lawyers, one of whom had come with Bishr to the prosecutor's office.

None of Bishr's family was in the courtroom. His father had visited him once in prison and he had not told him the date of the court session to prevent him from coming from Alexandria again. But Kariman's voice suddenly filled the courtroom, calling, "Bishr!" He looked toward the wide doorway of the courtroom where the sound was coming from and saw Kariman coming toward him happily, waving her arms. Bishr's eyes widened in surprise—he didn't believe it. But it *was* Kariman, with her blond hair, her green eyes, her pale face, and the blue coat she often wore in the winter. It was Kariman and no one else, otherwise this joy would not have sprung up in his spirit and filled the air of the room. It even seemed to him that everyone around him was happy and expecting good news.

She nearly left the ground as she hurried toward his embrace, stopped by the solid iron bars in front of him.

"I can't believe it," he said as he put his hands between the bars and she took them.

"Believe it, Bishr. I came especially to see you."

He wanted to look at his companions and ask them, "Do you see how beautiful she is? Does any of you know anyone so beautiful?"

But Kariman said, "The case is a bust, you're all going to be declared innocent. Hasan sends you his greetings. He would have liked to come from Mansura," she laughed, " but he told me on the phone, 'Let Bishr see you alone so he knows how blessed I am. Who knows, maybe he'll change and love someone.'"

Bishr smiled, and once again his face showed his amazement. Truly, how was it possible that he not fallen in love with one of the girls around him in the university up till now? He smiled. "You're great, Kariman!"

She said happily, "Yara also encouraged me to come. She told me to go to the session and come back and tell her about everything in Cairo. She told me not to come back without Bishr beside me."

They laughed together.

The three judges entered along with the court usher, who cried, "The court is in session!"

It didn't take long. The judge confined himself to the prosecution's claims, condemning everyone for working secretly to overthrow the regime, and to the lawyers' pleading, which was very short. None of lawyers took longer than ten minutes, and only the three important lawyers spoke. The judge adjourned the session for the ruling. Neither he nor the members of the court on his left and right asked any of the accused anything.

The judges returned to the courtroom more quickly than anyone expected; everyone was released from the courthouse. Hands exploded in applause and shouts of "Long live the Egyptians' struggle!" and "Long live the struggle of the working class!" rang out in the room. The prisoners kissed each other and Kariman hurried to Bishr, saying,

"Alexandria is waiting for you, my friend."

An hour later they were on broad Port Said Street. Bishr had not seen anything of Cairo before. The police van had brought him from Alexandria at dawn and by the time it was light he was entering the door of the Khayriya Qanatir Prison. When they had brought him to the prosecutor's office he hadn't seen anything either, since only the walls of the buildings were visible from the small, high windows in the van. Now he stood on the street, hesitating.

Kariman said, laughing, "Are you afraid to cross the street?"

He answered, "There's a lot of traffic—trams and busses and a lot of trucks and all these people!"

She said, "I was afraid too yesterday, when I got to Ramses Square. But I went out to the Square at the Husayn Mosque. It was a lovely evening."

"You came yesterday? Where did you stay?"

"You'll hear about everything. Give me your hand." She reached out and grasped his hand and said, laughing, "I'm taller than you are. Okay then, it's as if you're my son."

He laughed, but he changed the position of his hand so he was holding hers. As they crossed the street he said, "Don't be afraid."

On the other side he asked, "But how will we get to Ramses Square?"

She called out, "Taxi!" and a taxi that was passing in front of them stopped.

He said, "The taxis really are black, the way we see them in the movies."

She laughed, and told the driver, "Ramses Square."

Bishr whispered to her, "I don't have any money with me." He remembered that he had had five pounds with him which his mother had given him the night he was arrested, and that he had put them in the "canteen" of the prison, since it was forbidden to keep money in the cells. He hadn't spent any of it, and he hadn't taken it before going to court since he had not expected to be released. The excellent judge had released them from the courthouse and that was wonderful, but he had lost his five pounds. Well, there were others who were still waiting for their cases to come up, and they ought to be able to take advantage of his money.

Kariman laughed and answered, "I have some money. But where's your suitcase?"

He smiled. "I left everything behind me in the prison, pajamas, underwear, shirt, and pants. It's not a problem."

This time the driver heard what he said. "Thank God you've come out safely, sir. Would anyone who knows a pretty girl like this leave her and go to prison?"

Kariman and Bishr were surprised for a moment, then they burst out laughing. The driver said, "But you're not wearing prison clothes, sir?"

Bishr replied, "I was a different kind of prisoner, I mean, political." Silence enveloped them until they arrived at Ramses Square.

Bishr stood looking at the great expanse of the square, the high iron overpass around it that spoiled its beauty, the ceaseless movement of the people, the bus stop, the vendors spread out everywhere, and the spaces for drivers offering trips outside of Cairo, whose voices rose everywhere over the travelers. The statue of Ramses II seemed unconcerned with all of this, as it stood challenging time. Abruptly he said,

"Kariman, be frank with me, what made you come to Cairo?"

She smiled. "You'll find out everything when we stop to rest in Tanta."

They heard a voice calling, "Alexandria, Alexandria!" in front of the line of Peugeots, and they headed for it.

In Tanta, where the cars stopped for the travelers to rest, Kariman said nothing that would explain her sudden visit to Cairo. She bought two packages of Cleopatra cigarettes; she gave him one and then invited him to lunch. They ate sandwiches of meat that cost a whole pound, and she gave him four pounds more, saying with a laugh, "You pay the driver his fare in Alexandria, three pounds. You're the man. Keep the other pound with you until you get home. That way the ten pounds I had when I came yesterday will be spent completely."

He looked at her in unending amazement. What was happening to him today?

She said, "Tell me a little about life in prison." He continued looking at her for a moment. She asked, "Do you want to forget?"

He replied, "Who can forget? In any case it's not like what we see in the movies. There were good young men there with me, and I met real militants for the first time. I'll tell you everything in detail later on, right now let me enjoy this wide world around me."

At home, in the presence of his mother and father, Bishr forgot about what he had wanted to know concerning Kariman and her trip to see him. He was distracted by the reproachful look that seemed set in his father's eyes since his visit to him in prison, even though he never reprimanded him, and by the pain and reproach in his mother's eyes. His sister's joy did not make him forget his mother's and father's eyes. They all wanted to turn him away from politics, but no one said that to him. His mother celebrated his return with a wonderful meal of duck and rice, and he ate with a real appetite. She took him to his room and he saw that the bed was just as it had been; no one had even straightened the cover, which was still in the corner of the bed, just as he had left it when the State Security officer and the soldiers took him away.

His mother said to him, in a weak, constricted voice, "The bed is just as it was. No one has slept in it."

He took her in his arms, kissing her forehead and patting her back, tears almost pouring from his eyes. "Don't be sad, Mother. I owe you an apology."

She lifted her eyes to him, pleading, and said, "Does that mean it's over?"

He nodded his head in agreement without speaking. She said, "May God light your way, Bishr."

He stretched out on the bed, not to sleep but just to feel the warmth of the mattress, remembering the mattresses they had been given in prison, which were no more than two inches thick. What second-rate factory made prison mattresses? And as for the blankets, they were old surplus army blankets that were sold in second-hand markets. Cold had penetrated his body from every direction, just as it had for the other ten who shared the prison block with him. It wasn't a small block; it could have held ten more. That's why the cold was greater, because of the emptiness. The families of his companions from Cairo visited them nearly every day, distributing themselves over the days of the week, and those who came brought enough food for everyone. There was plenty of food, in fact, but in the end it was still a prison. It was a prison in spite of the wonderful nightly lectures given to them by Comrade Khalil whom he had just met, that thin Nubian whose weight was probably less than

110 pounds. How had he forgotten Khalil today? He should have visited him in Cairo before coming back with Kariman. Khalil had gotten out after twenty days, the charges dropped by the prosecutor, so the last ten days were long and boring, even though his companions were also very well educated. Why was it that they all seemed more educated to him than the men from Alexandria? Cairo really was the city of great expertise. All the banned books were smuggled to Hagg Madbouli's bookstore in Sulayman Pasha Square—that's what Khalil had told him once, with a laugh. If you lived in Cairo all you had to do was visit Old Man Madbouli and ask for the banned books. He would look at you for a moment, trying to understand your spirit; then when he was reassured about you, he would tell one of the workers behind the counter, "Take him to the storeroom." When you came out with the books he would know from another look at you that you were broke, so he would tell one of his workers, "Set up a credit page for him." Hagg Madbouli was an old Communist.

He really should have visited Khalil. He knew the address of his house in Cairo, and he also knew that he sat in a café called Ali Baba in Tahrir Square, but he couldn't visit him along with Kariman. Still, why hadn't Khalil come to the court session with the others? Maybe he had gone to Nubia for a time after getting out. In any case there were many days ahead, and he would certainly go to Cairo one day to see Khalil and to buy the banned books from Old Man Madbouli.

Bishr went to sleep as dawn streaked the sky, but despite his obvious exhaustion he woke by himself at nine the next morning. His mother heard him coming out of his room. He said,

"Forgive me, Mama. I've missed seeing Alexandria."

"It's winter outside."

"I won't be late. I'll be back by three at the latest to have lunch with you. Don't worry."

It was Friday, and tomorrow classes would begin for the second half of the academic year. Hasan would surely have come back to the apartment today, and Ahmad Basim, and maybe he would find Nadir there too. In fact he was thinking about Rawayih and Ghada. He must extinguish the fire of his rancor in someone, as he usually did.

On his way to Tanais Street he bought a copy of the newspaper *Al-Ahram*. He found the report of the prisoners' release on an interior page, in a small font, with no names listed. He left the paper on the seat of the tram, and got off at Camp Caesar. The rain was light but the wind was strong, and the space around him was wide and open. The people he saw hurrying in the streets seemed happy to him. He turned into Tanais Street and found it empty, as usual, stretching before him with no one on either side. But the houses were still in their places, silent, as if they were waiting for him. He hurried up the stairs. He didn't want to knock on the door of Rawayih's and Ghada's apartment; they must be sleeping now, after a long night. Thursday was always the longest night in the nightclubs. They would wake up in a little while. They must.

He turned the key softly in the door to the apartment, to surprise Hasan and Ahmad, whom he expected to have come back from their towns. But he saw no one in front of him and heard no sound. He went in, surprised. Then he turned around and found Khalil sitting across the room, smiling.

"Khalil! In the name of God, the merciful and compassionate!" cried Bishr. He stood still, dazed. Khalil's childlike smile, lighter than air, filled the space around him. Then Khalil stood up, and each clasped the other to his breast.

"Thank God for your safe arrival, comrade," said Khalil. "What do you think of this surprise?" He sat down and Bishr sat in front of him, still amazed. He said,

"It's the best surprise! But how did you get in?"

"You'll learn everything. Do you want to talk here or somewhere else?" Bishr seemed confused, so Khalil said, "Don't worry, they won't arrest us again in a hurry." He laughed. "Every year in January the State Security bureaucracy shuts down."

Bishr laughed. "You're the guest, so you're the one to decide whether we should stay here or go out."

Khalil said, "What about the Wali Café?"

Bishr smiled. "You know it?"

"I know all the cafés in Alexandria, from the Khafagi Café in Wardian to the Abdel Karim Café in Sidi Gabir."

Bishr laughed. "I don't believe that I'm seeing you so soon, and here in Alexandria! The prison block really was a prison without you, Khalil." Khalil smiled, then Bishr said abruptly, "Listen, let's stay here, that would be better. The apartment is empty and it doesn't look as if anyone will be here today, since they didn't come in yesterday. We can be comfortable talking here."

Bishr stood up, heading to the kitchen to make two cups of tea. He returned shortly and sat in front of Khalil, who gave him a long look, and then said,

"I could have brought up the subject in prison, but I put it off until I was certain of my choice."

Bishr looked confused, and Khalil continued:

"You're not a member of the Communist Workers' Party or of any other party. They took you unjustly, just because you have an opinion about the politics of the regime and the ruler. But your education, your strength, and your beautiful spirit would make you a cadre in any party. I've already mobilized Kariman in a secret party."

Bishr was stunned. He said, "Kariman? How did you meet her?"

"Through Hasan."

"Hasan's been mobilized too?"

"Yes, but he's discreet and doesn't say much. That happened about two weeks before New Year's Eve. By the way, he's the one who gave me the key, when I visited him in Mansura yesterday. Don't ask me how Hasan was mobilized, that way you won't know the names of all the members." He laughed, and added, "And so that you don't feel that Kariman spent her own money on you, and feel the shame of an eastern man, we are the ones who gave her ten pounds to make the trip and bring you back. We knew about the innocent verdict."

Bishr couldn't believe what he was hearing, continuing to smile in amazement. He said, "But why didn't Hasan come to me in Cairo?

He could have come back to Alexandria with me too, since classes will begin tomorrow."

"Kariman was the one who insisted on traveling. She had been dreaming of visiting Cairo and spending an evening in the Husayn area. One of our female comrades took her on a tour of the Gamaliya neighborhood there, and she slept at her place. She came back with you, and with a small number of copies of our secret publication in her bag." Bishr could barely take it all in. Khalil explained, "She's from Alexandria and they wouldn't monitor her in Cairo."

Then Khalil laughed. "By the way, there was an informer with us in the cell." Bishr looked shocked. "Do you remember the young lawyer who was there with us in the prosecutor's office the first time, who kept coming to us in prison? The one who kept coming to see me, especially?"

"Yes."

"He was the informer, a lawyer mobilized for State Security. I learned that and confronted him, so he didn't come any more. I didn't tell you. What matters, comrade, is that we need someone to do what Kariman did on a regular basis. Once every three months, for example, he will transport many copies of our secret publication. Not just five or six copies, like Kariman brought—those were just for all of you. We want someone who'll bring enough for all the party members in the area."

"What area?" asked Bishr.

Khalil smiled and said, "Alexandria, I mean."

They were silent for a few moments until Khalil said, "You might be suitable, Bishr, if you agreed to join the party."

"The Communist Workers' Party?"

"No, the Egyptian Communist Party. I'm not in the Workers' Party, did you forget?"

Bishr hit his forehead with his hand, laughing, and then said, "That's the one they accused me of belonging to."

"That's better for you and for us. They'll never find you among the comrades in the Workers' Party."

Bishr seemed to like what Khalil was saying as he thought about it. Khalil asked, "Do you need time to think?"

"No, I'm completely convinced. But I'm thinking about someone who would be better than me for the task of traveling and bringing back secret papers. Do you know anything about Nadir?"

"The poet?"

"Yes. Have you met him too?"

"No, but I have him in mind after what I heard about him from Hasan and Kariman."

"Nobody will suspect Nadir if he travels between Cairo and Alexandria, because he's a poet who can talk publicly any place about going to Cairo to offer his poetry to literary magazines, and coming back to Alexandria is natural because it's his home."

Khalil gave him a nice smile; he seemed pleased with Bishr. "You're going to be a distinguished cadre in the party, Comrade 'Amir.'"

Bishr was startled. "Amir? A 'prince' all at once?"

"That's your movement name from now on."

They laughed, and Khalil asked, "What's the easiest way to approach Nadir?"

Bishr said, "Leave that to me." Then he looked up. "I'm hungry, aren't you?"

Khalil said, "I'm going to Wali Café. Kariman's waiting for me there. She's going to treat me to fish in Azarita, at Houda Dongol."

Bishr laughed. "You know Houda Dongol too? Hey, man, you're more of an Alexandrian than I am!"

Khalil stood up, smiling. He seemed thin compared to Bishr although they were about the same height. He said, "I'll leave you now. It's best that we three not meet in a public place, and I might not come here again." He extended his hand to Bishr, still smiling, and said, "The student section of the party has now gained some comrades who are out of the ordinary."

Bishr felt pride, but then there was a knock on the door. Khalil was startled, but Bishr said, "Don't worry, that's Rawayih's and Ghada's knock. They live below us, and they never use the bell. It's best if everything seems natural."

He opened the door, and Rawayih's voice met him:

"Si Bishr at last! Where've you been, you lout, during the whole vacation?" She noticed Khalil and said, "Oh, mama! Who's this dark, handsome guy?" Ghada was smiling without speaking.

Khalil stepped between them on his way out, saying, "I'm going now, I'm late." As soon as he passed them he looked back and smiled, saying to Bishr, "You didn't ask me why I waited for you here, and how I was sure you would come." He motioned to Ghada and Rawayih. "We were sure, Hasan and I, that you would leave your house and come to your darlings." He laughed and went quickly down the stairs.

Ghada said to Bishr, who stood there smiling, "Didn't you miss us, you rascal?"

Opening his arms, he said, "And how! But don't either of you tell me she has her period or wants to write a letter!"

They laughed. Rawayih opened her arms and he embraced her. Suddenly the sound of the call to Friday prayers reached them from the distant mosque, so she said, "Wait till the call to prayers is over, you maniac! It's a sin!"

Did Zeus really cover the distance between Greece and Tyre to kidnap beautiful Europa, the daughter of the ruler of the city? Zeus was bored by his life with Hera on Mt. Olympus, and—as usual when he was bored—he was looking at humans on earth, choosing a beautiful woman. This time it was Europa, who was always on the beach, and always joyful. The ruler's bulls were also always on the beach; since they were all black, Zeus came down to the beach in the form of a white bull, who stood out among the others and attracted fair-skinned Europa. As soon as she approached he threw himself on his back, and loving fun, she began to caress his chest as he laughed submissively. When she was comfortable with him, he stood up and asked her to get on his back. The merry girl climbed up and he went down into the water with her, ignoring her plea to return to the beach. He took her to the island of Crete, where he resumed his form as the Lord of Lords and had intercourse with her. She accepted him and he had three sons from her. Who can refuse the wishes of the gods? Afterward Europa settled on the continent that bears her name, the continent that came to Alexandria with the Greeks and the Romans—Alexandria, which in Greek myths was called "the island behind the sea of darkness" before it was known as Alexandria. The great artist Fathi Mahmud embodied this story in a statue, raising white sails behind Zeus and Europa, and making the entire statue white like them, Zeus having taken the form of a white bull. Everything was white, suggesting the light coming from on high over the Mediterranean, the same light that Alexandria would radiate over the world for many centuries.

During the war between Rome and Alexandria, were the Ptolemaic soldiers really able to reflect the rays of the sun from a mirror on the lighthouse of Alexandria, and then focus them on the Roman ships and burn them? What a city Alexandria had been in the ancient world, its people famous for cock fighting, for wine drinking, and for making fun of their rulers! Diocletian stood before its walls for six months, unable to break through, and when he did enter the city he killed eighty thousand Egyptians in his war against Christianity. Thus its people consider the day of his ascension to the throne of Rome the beginning of the Coptic calendar, in opposition to the Gregorian calendar; they gave up Roman time for their own true time, and named their months after the old Egyptian gods. They announced the Egyptian Era, in opposition to the Roman Era, and did not give the months Christian names. Egypt had for a long time been bigger than any one religion, and the people knew it. It was a refuge for all religions, and Alexandria was at its heart.

These thoughts chased after each other in Isa's head as he stood before the statue, "The Bride of the Sea." He didn't believe that the "Cavalryman's Statue," previously "Pompey's Pillar," had really been erected by Alexandrians in commemoration of Diocletian, who inaugurated the Era of the Martyrs. He must have been the one who erected it and wrote that on it, in the way of all tyrannical rulers.

Isa did not spend his evenings in nightclubs, but today he stood here in sadness, because three important clubs were closing. No one knew whether the buildings would be changed into wedding parlors, or whether they would be destroyed so that tall, ugly buildings would rise in their place along the sea, screening the city from the sea air. The Kit Kat was already finished, and now he had heard that the Hollywood Nightclub would close its doors, as well as the Atiyat Husayn and the Côte d'Azur. Isa was not addicted to alcohol, but he was annoyed that people would not be free, that all outlets for joy would be shut for the sake of one day of reckoning, when God would pardon everyone, as long as their sins did not affect others. A time would come when the people of Alexandria would only be able to pour out their troubles into the sea. Could the sea bear all the pain of humanity? Waves would stop rising along the wall of the Corniche, weighed down by feebleness. These buildings, empty in the winter while they waited for the vacationers of the summer season, would have men and women in them crying all year long!

He was hunched over against the cold, standing alone in the darkness, taking advantage of a break in the rain. Behind him was the Silsila promontory, still off limits to the public, and there were no lovers sitting on the Corniche wall. He was the only madman out tonight. He had walked a little and then turned back, after getting to Shatbi and seeing the Atiyat Husayn nightclub was closed.

Isa had not gone to the college up to now, two weeks after the beginning of classes. He had gone back to The Coward's bar three times, then decided to go back to his earlier ways and to return to Ateneos; he longed to hear the voices of Lorice, Sami, and Samia. Now, as soon as he entered the Crazy Horse Room, he saw that those seated there were dressed in their finest clothes, and above and around them swirled the aroma of perfume, causing the breast to open and spirits to soar. The crowd tonight looked more like New Year's Eve, even though they were in the last days of February. He saw Christo and Paula at a distance, and looked at them in amazement. Was Paula still in Alexandria? When he got to them Christo stood up to shake his hand, calling, "Why're you late? We didn't want to open the bottle of champagne before you came."

Isa was surprised—they didn't have any appointment, they hadn't made any appointments for a long time. For some time now they had been meeting without setting the time. But in fact there was an unopened bottle of champagne in front of them, and a few appetizers. He extended his hand to Paula and she got up, as women usually did not, and kissed him on the cheek as if they were old friends. As soon as Isa sat down Christo said,

"I'm going to open the bottle."

He opened the champagne bottle with a loud pop, and the champagne bubbled up so fast that some of it was nearly lost, as Paula laughed at his aggressive approach. But he was able to catch much of that in a small glass. The flow from the bottle subsided, and he filled a second and third glass, then raised his glass, crying, "To Paula's health, so she will remember us in Switzerland and come back to us again."

Isa looked at Paula. "Are you really going to leave?"

"Tomorrow," she replied.

"Didn't you like Alexandria?"

She pointed to her heart and said, "Alexandria has been here for a long time, what I've seen now isn't important. To your health!" She raised her glass to him.

Christo said, "There's a really good film at the Metro Cinema, a film with Melina Mercouri."

Isa was startled and raised his eyebrows. Paula asked, "Don't you like Melina Mercouri?"

Isa replied, "Who doesn't like her?" She smiled at him, pleased. He asked, "What film is it, Christo?"

"*Phaedra.*"

Isa's face showed skepticism. He looked at Paula and she realized what he was thinking: this was an old film from the sixties, it couldn't be showing in the Metro Cinema now. Christo's mind seemed to wander away from them, so Isa said to her,

"I wish you would stay with us a little longer. We should have met more often. Maybe if I had gone around Alexandria with you, you would have had a better trip."

She replied, "There's nothing left but the memory. I visited the places where I lived and worked. They've changed a lot. But I stood looking at them as if they were still the way they were. I chose not to bring pain on myself."

She seemed very moved, in fact, and unable to hide her pain. Christo came back to them, saying in a loud voice,

"Melina is very strong. Like Hera, Zeus's wife. Right, Isa?"

Isa said, smiling, "That's right, Christo."

Silence enveloped them. Isa wanted to engage Christo, so he said, "Christo, do you remember the Auxiliary Territorial Service?"

Christo answered in confusion, "What's that, what's that? What does that mean? Have I forgotten English?"

Isa laughed. "The ATSA, Christo. The girls of the land troops of the British Army. Tell us about the girl you used to love, one of the ATSA girls, during the Second World War."

Christo smiled and his eyes opened wide, shining. He said, "Khabibi, you're a dear Communist, reminding me of good times. It's too bad, the English were crazy. Rommel got to al-Alamein and they were afraid he would take Alexandria. They took the lovely ATSA girls and hid them in Aswan."

Isa and Paula laughed. Isa said, "Naturally you were angry with the English, that's why you fought them with the Egyptians in Port Said."

"No, khabibi. I love Egypt. Alexandria, actually—Cairo is crazy. If anyone attacks Egypt, I'll fight him. Right, Paula?"

"Right, Christo." She smiled and lifted her glass, saluting him.

Greek music was filling the room from hidden speakers. Suddenly it changed and became faster; it lost its Greek spirit and sounded American. Many in the crowd began to move, as did Paula, who began to shimmy her shoulders as she looked at Isa. He was afraid she would ask him to dance to these fast rhythms, but she smiled and did not. A young man got up with a girl who was wearing a short dress with a wide skirt, who twirled around him like a butterfly. He was carrying her and turning with her like a real ballet dancer, and shouts of admiration rose continually. He let her turn fast around him, going away from her but holding her hand; then he let go and went farther away, and in a moment she twirled back to him, very fast. He lifted her up high and the small black panties she was wearing under her dress showed, so everyone shouted and applauded. The girl smiled and blushed, her face nearly on fire, and then went on dancing with him to the slower beat on which the music ended. Then they went back to their place, he kissing her cheek and putting his arm around her as they made their way among the tables, while the audience continued to applaud.

Christo abruptly asked Isa, "Khabibi. You're a cultured Communist, do you know what the name of that dance is?"

Isa answered immediately, "I don't know exactly, but it's from an old Gene Kelly film. I don't remember its name now."

Paula applauded. "Bravo, bravo! The film is *Singing in the Rain.*"

Isa smiled, elated. Christo said, "A world without dance would be really awful, right, Paula?"

"Right, Christo. To your health!" She raised her glass to him again.

Lorice and her troupe appeared, and the audience applauded. She stood greeting them, with Sami, the young accordion player behind her, playing random soft tunes in preparation for the singing. Samia was doing the same with the violin.

Isa remembered his surprise when he came in. "Tonight is really strange, and the crowd is unusual. The last time it was crowded here was a month ago, the night of Epiphany. Is there some new occasion that I don't know about?"

Paula shrugged her shoulder, smiling, but Christo said, "There is an occasion, khabibi. All these people are here to say goodbye to Paula. Yes. I told them…".

"Habibi, my dear." Paula leaned over to give him a kiss. He lifted his face to her, and then his mind wandered away from them again.

"Christo's great," said Isa. Paula nodded and fluttered her eyelashes, admiring him.

Lorice was wearing a long white dress tonight, and Samia was wearing one that was almost the same. The music was swaying, and shouts of pleasure rose.

"I will not regret anything," said Paula, emotionally. Then her mind wandered away from Isa and Christo, who began looking at Lorice in wonder. Lorice was singing Edith Piaf's song:

Non, rien de rien,
Non, je ne regrette rien,
Ni le bien qu'on m'a fait, ni le mal,
Tout ça m'est bien égal . . .

No, no nothing at all,
I don't regret a thing,
Not the good, not the evil I've seen,
To me it's all the same thing.

Paula continued repeating the meaning of the song in Arabic, in time with Lorice, emotionally at times and cheerfully at other times, until she said, laughing,

Because my life and my joy
Begin today,
With you.

Paula pointed to Isa, who beamed. The audience applauded loudly, some whistling noisily, as Lorice stood happily before them. She motioned to Sami and Samia, who in turn greeted the audience. Then she called,

"What do you think of Demis Roussos?"

Everyone present clapped loudly, and some shouted in pleasure. She said, "An Alexandrian, like us."

She motioned to Sami, who came up and took her place while the audience again clapped noisily and she took his place to play. He began to sing "Far Away" in his plaintive voice, imitating Demis Roussos in the way he extended the end of the words, as if he were chanting in endless space and embodying remoteness itself. All kept silent, happy and delighted by Sami's beautiful voice.

There's a lucky man who'll take you far away,
Far away, so very, very far away,
He will come someday,
To another land he'll take you far away,
Far away, so very, very far away.

The applause was loud. Isa began nodding his head, this time translating the song for Paula, even though he was sure she must know English, since she knew French and had lived in Alexandria.

. . . This will come, they say.
Nobody knows who will share
Your love pure and fair,
But in your eyes I can see
That someone will be me.

When the song ended Isa had completely forgotten Christo and everyone else around him, focusing his eyes solely on Paula, this lady in her forties who had come from another land. She said,

"It's really lovely."

"The song?"

"The whole evening."

Christo put in, "I told you, this evening is a celebration of Paula."

Lorice had come back to sing, and Sami had returned to his place behind the keyboard. Samia stood near Lorice, both of them resplendently beautiful in their dresses. Fast music rose from the keyboard and everyone shouted happily. Many of the men and women, young and old, rose and began moving toward the wide space between the small stage and the tables.

"Dancing!" cried Paula happily as she stood up. Isa's enthusiasm had been kindled, so he stood up with her as soon as she extended her hand to him, feeling power spreading inside him as it had on New Year's Eve when they had listened to Dean Martin's "Sway." This time it was the group ABBA.

The music began on a calm beat and Lorice and Samia began singing. Everyone moved around them as if they had a long-standing date to dance.

Love me or leave me,
Make your choice but believe me,
I love you,
I do, I do, I do, I do,
I can't conceal it. Don't you see? Can't you feel it?
Don't you too?
I do, I do, I do, I do.

There was a long pause, as the music, the singing, and the dancing stopped for a moment. Then it all resumed, joyfully.

Oh, I've been dreaming through my lonely past,
Now I just made it, I found you at last.
So come on now, let's try it, I love you, can't deny it,
'Cos it's true,
I do, I do, I do, I do.

The evening passed like magic. Laughter and shouts filled the air as the people left, saluting each other as if they were friends. Each man emerged with his beloved beside him, enclosing her with his arm, happiness on her face and joy on his.

After Isa, Paula, and Christo passed through the door, they stood on the sidewalk facing the Corniche. Silence enfolded them amid the voices of those coming out and the sound of their cars as they began to move. The sound of the sea rose above all the other sounds. Paula suddenly seemed very far away.

Christo said to Isa, "Khabibi Musa, we'll have to have a lovely evening like this for you."

Isa realized that Christo was calling him "Musa" and he looked at him in astonishment, but Paula burst out laughing and said,

"No problem, Isa is a prophet and Musa is a prophet, and everyone who has a prophet blesses him. That's right—I still remember a lot of things."

Isa looked at her in admiration, but he noticed tears welling in her eyes as she said in a low voice, her mind far away, "The sound of the sea is very beautiful." She was silent for a moment, and then went on, "Unfortunately I have to leave tomorrow."

Isa found himself asking her, "How did you get into Egypt? I know that all the Jews who left signed declarations saying they would not return."

She was embarrassed for a few moments, then said in a whisper, "I wasn't among them. All of us, the whole family left illegally."

She hugged Isa and kissed him on his cheeks, as he kissed hers. She said, "I would have liked to spend a longer time with you. I haven't spoken with anyone enough during this visit; maybe you are the one who could have listened to my old stories, just as you told me. I don't know how it is that we never met after our first meeting, and tomorrow . . . departure."

She left him and hurried toward the nearby Cecil Hotel. Christo cried, startled,

"She went away and left me!"

He hurried after her, looking as if he was rolling along the ground because of his short stature.

Isa stood looking after them for a few moments. A taxi suddenly stopped in front of him and the driver asked,

"Are you waiting for someone, sir?"

Distracted, Isa said, "Yes."

The driver left him and went on. He remained alone, listening to the sound of the ancient sea.

Many events occurred in Egypt and in the world. Agatha Christie had died in January, after the number of her books in circulation worldwide had reached one billion. In Egypt the master of the praise poets also died, the head of the school producing the most beautiful religious supplications, the shaikh Sayyid al Naqshabandi;

and Ali Amin joined them in death, who with his twin Mustafa Amin had found the newspaper *Al-Akhbar* in the forties. Husayn Sidqi also passed away—the actor and producer, whose films included *The Shores of Love, The Unknown Lover, Khalid ibn al-Walid*, and others—as did the famous actor Lee J. Cobb and the Italian producer Visconti.

President Sadat made trips to Abu Dhabi, Bahrain, Qatar, and Kuwait. He announced that Moscow would not supply Egypt with spare parts for MiG jets and the opposition considered it a fabrication, as everyone knew that he was the one turning away from Russia and throwing himself into the arms of America every day. The petroleum minister announced that Egypt would begin using natural gas in homes for the first time, in the neighborhoods of Maadi, Masr al-Gidida, and Helwan.

The film *Karnak* was still the talk of the newspapers, which were also preoccupied with the trial of the officer Muhammad Safwat al-Rubi and two of his colleagues for the torture of prisoners under Nasser. The articles concentrated especially on Safwat al-Rubi as a colossal example of savagery. They said he had a unique talent for torturing prisoners and extracting confessions from them. They recounted how he had joined the army with the rank of private, and how Nasser had accorded him the rank of lieutenant, after he'd traveled to East Germany as part of a delegation of Egyptian officers to be trained in the arts of torture.

A young man in the Sidi Bishr neighborhood tried to kill his sister after he saw her walking with a man. Qadhafi threw many Egyptian workers out of Libya because of his rejection of Sadat's rapprochement with America, and Sadat nicknamed him "the crazy kid from Libya." Kamal Jumblatt, the leader of the Druze in Lebanon, said that the war there had reached the point of no return. In Egypt 2100 prisoners were freed on the occasion of the noble prophet's birthday, and a new government was formed, with Mamduh Salim as prime minister. In Cairo, Yusuf Wahbi's theater showed the play *The World of Ali Baba.*

Sadat canceled the mutual defense pact with the Soviet Union, and his vice president, Hosni Mubarak, announced his pride in what

China was offering Egypt and in the doubling of the trade between the two countries, with new imports of clothing, tobacco, and textiles from China, which appeared in the working-class markets and increased traffic in them.

The Smouha neighborhood was subdivided. It had been filled with gardens and scattered free-standing homes, most of whose foreign owners had deserted them in the sixties. The Egyptian owners who remained also sold out, so it became a residential area. The neighborhoods of Maamura and Muntaza, south of the Abu Qir railway line, also began uprooting their guava, citrus, pomegranate, and other trees to divide the agricultural land and sell it as land for building. The filling of Lake Maryut was extended and now reached Ras al-Sauda and Abis; likewise to the west, a large area was filled in for the expansion of petroleum refineries. Along the sea the number of private clubs increased, and new clubs appeared for the armed forces, for judges, and for lawyers.

The young man who played the accordion along the Corniche appeared less and less and then disappeared, and it was said that he had died, but then he turned up again. A new apartment building south of Sidi Bishr collapsed; it was seven floors high in a narrow lane, and it hit the houses around it as it fell. Rescue workers toiled throughout the night to pull people from the rubble. They had trouble getting in cranes to lift the debris, so the rescue proceeded by hand, with people helping the workers, and at that point it seemed like an impossible task. Then in the middle of the night car horns were heard in the distance, accompanying a bride and groom. They stopped because of the crowds in front of them and everyone got out, including the bride and the groom, who learned what had happened and ran forward through the people, shouting. They stopped in front of the remains of the building in which their apartment and their furniture had been. The bride fell down in a faint, her white dress stained with mud and dirt, while the poor groom collapsed, sitting on the ground in his blue suit, weeping with his hands over his face. It was a painful sight for everyone.

5

THE BEAUTIFUL VOICE OF MUHAMMAD Kandil was coming from the cassette player in one corner of the living room, as Nadir, Bishr, and Hasan sat around the large dining table. Before them were sheets of poster board and colored pens; tonight they would finish the last three magazines they would hang up this year.

The young men from the Islamic Group had stopped attacking their magazines after their initial assault, and they in turn had hung up only one magazine after that, while the Islamic Group and the Muslim Brothers had hung up five magazines in various places around the college. On many walls, at widely spaced intervals, they hung paper signs bearing Hadith sayings of the prophet or Hadith sayings pronounced by God himself, not in the Quran; students would stop in front of them for a while, and then move on without comment. There was always a student with a short beard and no mustache standing in front of the magazine, debating what was written with the other students who stood there. They often grumbled about talking with "uncovered" female students (as they termed them), and consequently not many of the female students stood in front of their magazines. The hijab was not yet widespread among the students of the college, and those who wore it were no more than thirty or forty out of the very large number of girls in the college.

Jeans had spread all over Egypt, including in the colleges, and were worn by young men and women alike. Many of the girls wore a short tank top over the jeans which sometimes revealed a very small area of the belly, or of the undershirt below the tank top. Many of the girls who wore jeans and tank tops also wore short jackets, which they did not close in front. Thus the jacket did not cover this small area of the belly, if the girl talked and gestured with her hands, for example. There were also some among them where this area appeared whether or not they talked and gestured, because of the shortness of the top. The students from the Islamic Group and Muslim Brothers looked at them in disgust. The miniskirt fashion was still common among the girls as well.

Hasan, Bishr, and Nadir were not happy tonight. While Hasan did not show his misery and retained his small smile, Bishr and Nadir were very angry for him. The administration of the Culture of Freedom Palace had accepted a one-act play of his and had contracted with him to produce it a month before—but today when he'd gone to meet the young director proposed by the Palace, they had informed him that the play had been refused. Why? He had found no answer. They had presented the play to the censors and they had agreed, and he had received ten pounds as an advance on the price of the play, which they had bought from him for fifty pounds. They had specified that the rest of the money was to be paid in two stages, twenty pounds after the end of rehearsals and twenty pounds after the staging of the play. He had not even thinking about money at all—he had been overwhelmingly happy that a play of his would be seen by an audience, even if it was the small audience in the Culture of Freedom Palace.

After they had finished with one entire magazine, Bishr said, "So what do you think? The headlines alone are enough to shake up the country." He began to read them aloud in delight: "Removal of Censorship over Books, Journalism, and the Arts." "Social Controls over the 'Economic Opening' Policy." "Release of Political Prisoners."

Then suddenly he said to Hasan, as if remembering something he had forgotten. "Wasn't there a clause in the contract that you would receive the rest of your fee if they withdrew from producing the play?"

Hasan thought a moment and said, "No. On the contrary. There was a clause saying that it was within the rights of the Culture Palace to cancel the contract at any time without providing any reason."

Bishr said, sarcastically, "These are servile contracts you won't find anywhere else in the world, I can tell you!"

At that Hasan smiled his small smile. "Naturally, you have a lot of experience with contracts!"

They laughed, and Nadir said, "Somebody like Hasan would agree to any conditions. You don't know, Bishr, the joy of a writer when he sees his work presented to an audience."

Hasan said, scoffing, "Obviously the refusal came from State Security. Forget about it, I've forgotten it. Let's stay with the magazines for now. But why aren't the students from the Islamic Group and the Muslim Brothers attacking our magazines any more? Is that also on the instructions of State Security?"

Bishr said, "Maybe they're getting ready for something bigger."

They heard the key in the door and knew that it was Ahmad Basim. He came in and stopped, smiling at them in surprise. He went up to the magazines and looked at the one that was finished and spread out on the table, reading the headlines in silence. Then he said, "Very nice. And even though there's no use, I'm happy with the story about removing censorship, and dear God let it happen for movies in particular. I'd like to see Suheir Ramzi naked, and oh wow, if it were Mervat Amin—and if God blessed me it would be Suad Hosni!"

Nadir said, smiling, "Go into your room, Ahmad, and let us work. Why are you alone tonight?"

"Today is a holiday, according to the schedule." During recent weeks he had made a schedule with the names of the female students who came to the apartment with him and their set times, so that if one of three roommates was there, the roommate would stay in his room. That way the girl would not see him and feel embarrassed, and then not come again. There were three girls from the Philosophy Department among them and two from Archaeology, which he said had the most beautiful girls in the college despite its name. The department was like a secret room; no one on the third floor noticed it except someone who appreciated beauty.

Suddenly Ahmad asked them, with surprise in his voice, "Have you seen Muhammad Shukr lately…?"

They exchanged glances, also looking surprised. Muhammad Shukr was the handsome student who had stood between them and the students of the Islamic Group and whom everyone liked, but he wasn't part of their group.

Ahmad continued, "I saw him today going into the Trianon. Guess who was with him?"

Nadir replied, "That doesn't matter to anyone, Ahmad. You, for example, have ten girls, not one."

"No, this is the most important girl in the department. Fawqiya, Fawziya's twin, the daughter of the former minister." They looked at each other in disbelief. Ahmad went on, "Now those are girls! He's smart, that Muhammad Shukr. I have to know how he was able to do that. The daughter of a minister, damn!"

He laughed, and Bishr said, tensely, "Sure, okay, fine. Go to your room and let us work." The voice of Muhammad Kandil was singing,

Your eyes are black, but I say they aren't
So others will not find you,
To protect you from their envy and spite.
I'm even jealous of you, for you . . . .

Ahmad listened for a moment, and then he laughed. "And on top of everything, 'Your Eyes are Black' when not one of you loves anyone with black eyes. You're losers even in choosing your songs!"

Suddenly they heard a knock on the door, and they all looked at each other. Ahmad said, "It must be Ghada and Rawayih . . .".

Nadir replied, "But they work at night."

Ahmad said, "Then it's State Security. It's a black night, not black eyes. Even so I'll open the door. I mean, State Security when it's not even nine o'clock?"

He turned and opened the door, and Rawayih and Ghada appeared, each of them wearing a lovely evening dress under a coat. Right away Rawayih said, "What do you think of this surprise? We feel like spending the evening with you, for once, so we've come in our evening clothes. We feel like talking to you, talking a lot, without any ill manners."

Hasan and Nadir smiled and Bishr laughed with Ahmad, who said, "Do you have a day off too?"

Ghada replied, "Yes, there's an unexpected holiday at the night-club. We decided to spend the evening with you. We want to feel like we're a real family."

They had sat down without waiting to be asked. Rawayih said, "Also, this time it's Ghada who wants someone to write a letter for her."

Ahmad said, laughing, "Didn't I tell you it's a black night?"

Ghada said, "No, Ahmad. The black one is that girl of yours who sells peanuts. I really have to talk to these guys."

Bishr collected the magazines, though for a moment he seemed to be grinding his teeth in frustration. He got up to sit near them and said, "Come on, Nadir, Hasan. We won't disappoint them."

Nadir and Hasan realized that Bishr had decided to extinguish his fury in one of them, as usual. They smiled and sat down, and Ahmad came over too.

Ghada said, "If it's a bother for any of you to write the let-ter then it's not important, I'll manage. What you need to know is that the one I want to write to isn't in Libya or Syria, like it is with Rawayih. He's in Saudi Arabia."

They looked at each other in surprise. Ahmad chuckled and said, "Naturally, Arab nationalism."

Ghada replied, "You be quiet, Si Ahmad! I don't know what you're talking about. This is a very important person, whose name is Sheikh Zaalan."

Zaalan, "angry". . . ? They shook with laughter. Ghada briefly looked upset, then she said, "You don't believe me. Fine, he married me, what do you think of that?"

They fell into a stunned silence. She said, "I met him in the nightclub a week ago. He's very rich. He's really an Egyptian who's been living in Saudi Arabia for twenty years. He came on vacation, and he wanted to buy the club."

Bishr, Hasan, and Nadir looked even more surprised, while Ahmad was hiding his laugher by putting his hand over his mouth. Rawayih said, "The bey who owns the club agreed. Sheikh Zaalan said that all this immorality in Egypt has to stop."

Bishr asked her, "How do you know that?"

"Everyone who works at the club is talking about it. But listen to Ghada—tell them, Ghada."

They looked at her in silence while Ghada said to Rawayih, "No, you tell them. I'm too embarrassed."

Rawayih said, "Okay. He gave Ghada two hundred riyals and a night in the Metropole Hotel."

"The Metropole!" Ahmad laughed. "And nobody arrested the two of you?"

Ghada replied, "The law doesn't forbid foreigners from bringing in women, only Egyptians."

Bishr nodded and said sadly, "And it doesn't forbid rich Egyptians either."

Ghada said, "He didn't sleep with me the way you think. He married me and then slept with me."

Rawayih added, "Don't be surprised. He married her and divorced her on the same night."

Bishr, Hasan, and Nadir looked even more astonished, while Ahmad was smiling and holding himself back from laughing. Ghada said, "In the hotel room he gave me a hundred riyals before I took off my clothes, and asked me to sit in front of him. He took my hand and said, 'I hereby marry myself to you for the marriage settlement specified between us, the delayed portion of which is one hundred riyals,' and he asked me to do the same, so I said what he said. I was terrified."

Ahmad laughed loudly and said, "Terrified of marrying a millionaire? This guy must be a millionaire."

Ghada replied, "Naturally, I was terrified that he would not divorce me and would go away and leave me. Then what would I do? Who would listen to me if I complained, and me without a single official document?"

"It would be as if you never got married."

"Everything is simple for you, Si Ahmad. But our Lord sees us—I mean, after that I would be sinning against our Lord and against my husband. Our Lord grants pardon, but what about my husband?"

Ahmad nodded his head and said in amusement, "That's right. Go on."

She said, "That's all. After he slept with me he divorced me and gave me a hundred riyals. I left the room without his noticing, he had gone to sleep."

A deep silence descended on them for some moments. Nadir, Bishr, and Hasan were all looking at the floor, heads bowed. Rawayih suddenly burst into tears. "It's all over. He bought the club and closed it and left town. We don't know what he'll do with it when he comes back. For sure it won't be a nightclub any more, and now we're out of a job."

Ahmad stood up and extended his hand to Ghada, saying, "Come with me, Ghada. I'll marry you too, but for half a pound in advance and half a pound in the delayed payment, and our sin will be on the neck of Sheikh Zaalan."

She stood up. "No, forget about marrying. I'll go with you because I'm upset."

Hasan and Nadir looked at each other in pain, and then looked at Bishr. All at once he got up and said, "Come with me, Rawayih. You shouldn't be crying either."

Nadir and Hasan were left alone in the living room. Hasan said, distractedly, "What are we going do, when the world is changing around us like this?"

Nadir said, "I don't think I'll stay here tonight."

"Where will you go? It's really windy out."

"I don't know."

Ahmad Basim was amazed by Ghada as they made love. She seemed to be giving him all her emotions, as if she had never had sex before. She cried out, moaned, and embraced him strongly with her arms and legs, biting his chest and arms and shoulders, moving ceaselessly.

He knew of course that she had years of experience, but she was not acting. He sensed that she felt that these moments were like the very last thing she wanted out of life. He fell back next to her, spent and disbelieving, and she startled him by suddenly bursting into tears, as she lay on her back beside him. Moved by some genuine sympathy for her, he put his arm under her head and drew her to him, so her head was on his chest.

"Don't cry, Ghada. The closing of the nightclub isn't the end of the world, there are a lot of clubs."

She didn't answer. Her mind seemed to have wandered, but she began calmly kissing the thick hair on his chest, in quiet ecstasy. All at once he said,

"You and Rawayih have been here with us for a long time, but I don't even know if you are from Alexandria or not."

She said, "You forget. I'm from Suez and Rawayih is from Ismailiya. We've told you that before."

"That's right, how did I forget? I meant, why did you leave Suez and Ismailiya? Why don't you go back there?"

She moved away from him and lay down on her back again, wiping away her tears with her hand and saying, "Do you think anyone still remembers us there?"

Silence settled over him as she told him how most of the residents of the area had been forced to leave after the defeat of 1967. They scattered to several towns, and her family's lot had been a village school in Qalyubia Province, which had become a camp to shelter people forced out of Suez and Ismailiya. There she met Rawayih. About ten people slept in each classroom; all the rooms had been emptied of their desks, which had been replaced by sponge mattresses instead. Many sexual assaults happened at night, and sexual harassment was constant. There was only one bathroom in the school. She and Rawayih had fled that hell, and the reason was that each of them had lost her virginity to a man who had later disappeared from the place. The same man had done that to most of the girls, sometimes by force when people were sleeping and sometimes tempting them with marriage, even though he was living among them with his wife and little daughter. Like Ghada and Rawayih, a lot of the girls fled to Cairo and Alexandria, where they were swept up by the nightclubs and hidden brothels. The two had arrived in Alexandria in 1968 and completely lost contact with their families, and their families had not looked for them. "Thank God they didn't, otherwise our fate would have been death," as she put it. Naturally it was impossible for either of them to go back to her town after the October War. Egypt had been victorious, but in the end the two of them had been defeated.

She fell silent, lost in thought. Then she said, "Even if I went back and swore to my family that I'm pure they wouldn't believe me. If only because of this." She pointed to the top of her leg, where he saw the track of a long wound that nearly encircled the thigh. He didn't know how he could have missed it during the few times he had slept with her before, when she hadn't been as fully engaged with him as she was today. She had always been stiff, as if she was performing a task that had been imposed on her. If she cried out and moaned that was to hurry his desire, so he would ejaculate and she would be done with him. It would have been possible for him to see the wound before, but during those times he also had cared more about ridding himself of his desire than about satisfying her; maybe that's why he hadn't noticed the scar. Amazed at himself, he asked her, "What's this?"

"A wound, don't you see?"

"Yes, but how did it happen?"

"Don't you know?"

"No. I never noticed it before, and I never asked you."

"And here you are a client of mine who's into women! Listen, mister."

She told him that the road along the Corniche was divided up into areas among the girls, or rather among the pimps. Every pimp was responsible for the women in his area, and if any of them left him he would put a mark on her that made her unfit to work after that, or at least that would reduce her value.

He looked at her in amazement. How was it that he was hearing this for the first time, when he knew so many women?

She said, "Don't be surprised. Thank God he didn't touch my face. He wounded me here and said it was a warning. The son of a whore chose the highest part of my thigh and ran his razor over it while his helpers were holding me down and I was screaming."

He almost laughed, but her voice dropped and she said, "The truth is he loved me. That's why he chose a place where the wound wouldn't keep me from working."

He asked sarcastically, "A pimp who loves?"

"He was different that way."

"What did you do, for him to do that to you?"

"I worked for one day in another area. The truth is that I was in love with the other pimp. But what could I do when the club I worked in is in the area that belongs to the guy who loved me when I didn't love him?"

"Okay, but how did the first one find out?"

"The second one told him. My darling wanted to get his goat. Anyway it's all over now. The first one went to Cairo and the second one, the one I loved, he was killed in the fields of Smouha. They found his body and it was written up in the newspapers. Didn't you read something in the papers a couple of years ago about . . . ."

He cut her off saying, "Okay, enough, enough." He was really upset.

"Don't let it bother you, it's just that one thing led to another while we were talking. Now we have a pimp in our area who's a lightweight, a young guy who's not quite right. Forgive my language, but I feel like he's a faggot. Yes, he really is like that." He laughed this time, and she continued, "He always has a girl with him who's as beautiful as the moon, she never leaves him. She's eighteen. He takes her around to houses and lets us do what we want."

Surprised, he said, "Eighteen years old?"

"Do you want me to bring her to you here?"

He cried, "No, please! This is a respectable place, just for studying."

She laughed, and seemed to have put what happened out of her mind. She said, "You're a devil, you've made me confess a lot to you," hitting him gently on his chest.

He smiled and looked at her a moment, then asked her abruptly, "Seriously, as God is your witness, is the story of Sheikh Zaalan true?"

"By God it's true."

"Okay, and is a marriage like that permissible religiously?"

She shrugged her shoulder. "You're educated and you would know. Naturally I believed him and thought, my sin is on him. Personally I think he's a bastard and he's lying to our Lord God. If somebody does something wrong it's better not to lie to our Lord, don't you think?"

He thought for moment and then he said, "Yes. You're right." But he was thinking about something else: Lying is the best way to get along in life. All at once he felt happy, having discovered something he hadn't realized before.

It was midnight, and the sound of the wind outside was loud in Yara's room. A thin line of smoke rose in the air from the cigarettes Kariman was smoking.

Kariman was stretched out on the bed wearing Yara's winter nightgown, which Yara had started to call "Kariman's nightgown." Yara was sitting behind her desk, explaining to her what she was reading from their Islamic Philosophy book, or talking it over with her. She had noticed how preoccupied Kariman had been ever since she had arrived two hours before. Now she stood up and left the desk for the bed, where Kariman moved over a little so she could stretch out next to her.

Yara asked her, "What's on your mind tonight? I don't think you've heard a word I've said. Has anything bad happened between you and Hasan?"

Kariman replied, smiling, "If only the whole world were like Hasan. He's still smiling, even after the Culture of Freedom Palace refused to put on his play after they had agreed to do it."

"We were all angry, but there will definitely be other opportunities, and they will definitely be better."

Kariman smiled. "I went to the apartment with him."

Yara said, laughing in surprise, "Damn you! But lower your voice. You went a second time?"

"And a third and a fourth, I swear."

Yara was silent, thinking about whether she would confess to her that she had also gone with Nadir.

Kariman closed her eyes, seeing Hasan as he placed his hand on one breast and then moved it to the other, as she bit her lower lip and moaned softly. Then he descended to her belly and to the blond pubic hair below, moving over it slowly, as if he was savoring its silken touch. Then he reached the center of her chastity, and she opened her legs cautiously, saying "Be careful" as she let herself go in pleasure, unable to stop herself. She clasped him in her arms and held him to her breast as he kissed her forcefully and her body trembled. She shook her head at Yara and said, smiling, "Damn you, Yara, you've brought it all back to me!"

Yara laughed. "For sure I've brought back something good."

Kariman lit another cigarette, blew out the smoke, and said, "Hasan looks at my body and regrets not being a visual artist so he could draw me."

Disturbed, Yara asked, "Draw you in a painting?"

"Yes."

"And display it so people would see it?"

"Why not? Don't artists do that?"

"With models, not with the ones they love."

"With the ones they love too, by God."

"In Europe, maybe. In our country it would be a scandal."

Yara was silent as Kariman's face showed her irritation. "How long will our country stay so backward? The worst of it is that it's begun to go backward all over again."

"Personally, I can't accept that whether we're in Europe or in Egypt." Yara laughed. "The beauty of love is in concealment. The beloved isn't merchandise displayed for sale."

Kariman shook her head, unconvinced. Now she was sitting on the bed leaning her back against the wall, looking at Yara, who was now resting against the headboard. She said, "Every time Hasan seems to me like someone who's lost while he feels my body. I asked him once why he closes his eyes, and he said that for lovers sex is like the Sufi stations, ending with the station of annihilation. Orgasm is a state like the state of annihilation."

Yara put her hand over Kariman's mouth and looked fearfully at the closed door. Then she said in a whisper, "That's what Nadir says."

She blushed, her face on fire. She remembered that she had not told Kariman before that she had gone with Nadir, and she blushed in shame. Kariman looked at her in surprise, her facing glowing with joy. She said,

"I've gotten a confession out of you."

Yara replied, "Damn it, yes. I couldn't hide it, you've reminded me of everything. Nadir feels my body as if he were in a temple."

"In the end Hasan always curses virginity. He makes a face and says that the orgasm isn't in its natural place."

Yara was embarrassed, and asked, "What does that mean?"

"Frankly, I'm thinking about letting him enter the temple."

"Don't do that, Kariman!" Yara was very disturbed.

"I want it more than he does."

Yara moved from the bed to the desk and said, "Come over here on the chair. Let's just study, please."

Kariman laughed and moved over to the desk. They looked at each other in silence. Yara seemed very distant, but then she said,

"It really would be wonderful for your beloved to make a painting of you."

"So you agree?"

"It would be wonderful to look from the painting at the people while they were looking at me."

Kariman laughed, but then Yara moved her hand over her chest and said in irritation, "Why doesn't the wind die down tonight? It sounds terrible."

"It's been blowing with no letup for two days. It's the awwa wind, dear."

Yara nodded. "Right, 'the awwa blast, it's the last,' it's over. Let's study and see it out with Hallaj."

Suddenly the sound of Arab music rose from the radio. They looked at each other in surprise and Yara said, "The station broadcasts are interfering with each other. It must be because of the wind."

Kariman cried, "Wow, it's Abdel Halim Hafiz! It's the best thing the awwa wind has done."

Abdel Halim was singing:

Look within the flower bouquet,
To see the most beautiful eyes and cheeks,
Lovely, and gathered in open display.
Color and scent and dew from the Lord we seek.

Yara got up, running her hand over her body. "To tell the truth I have to have a coffee, after everything we said."

She started making the coffee as she heard Abdel Halim's calm, gentle voice lilting,

I have trouble with other men,
Oh Lord of perfection and of beauty.
Let me be your slave, alone,
And serve not money or hierarchy.

Yara noticed that tears were welling up in Kariman's eyes. She asked, "What is it, Kariman? Has Abdel Halim made you anxious? We still have at least a month and a half before the vacation at the end of the school year. That means you can meet Hasan just as you like. But me, my brother's come back from his sea voyage and will spend the next three or four months with us, making me account for every minute I'm late coming home."

"Will he prevent you from going out alone?"

"He won't prevent me, but he'll be everywhere in Alexandria, maybe even in the apartment on Tanais Street, at any moment."

"Is he that strict?"

"He lives his life however he wants, like any other man. They enjoy every pleasure, and then declare that we have to be pure."

Kariman nodded sadly. She said, "In the end he's your brother. But me, it looks like I'll kill my stepfather one of these days."

"Is he still harassing you?"

"I threatened that I would tell my mother and he laughed in my face. I threatened that I would go to the mosque where he prays and tell everybody, and he said nobody would believe a brazen, unveiled girl."

Tears appeared in her eyes again. She told Yara how she had heard him the day before telling her mother that he had a groom for her. She had gone into their room suddenly and heard him say that. As soon as he saw her he went out, on the pretext of praying in the mosque. There was a picture of the groom in her mother's hand, and her mother gave it to her, asking her not to refuse before she looked at it and met him. Her mother was really beaten down, and nobody in her family would stand up for her.

As soon as Kariman took the picture she threw it on the floor without looking at it. From the floor the picture showed the face of a man who was at least fifty years old, with broad shoulders and a thick beard, wearing a gallabiya. Fifty years old, imagine! Kariman said that she had nearly stepped on the picture but restrained herself, and began crying on her mother's breast. She told her mother to ask her husband to divorce her. She always heard him insulting her, and anyway she worked and had a salary that would be enough for her without him. But her mother said that obedience to a husband was part of obedience to God.

Yara was stunned as she listened to this. Kariman told her, "He's brainwashed my mother completely."

The coffee had boiled over in its pot without Yara noticing, and it had put out the flame below it. She noticed now, when she smelled the odor of the coffee beans in the room. She said,

"May it be for the best, oh God make it be for the best!"

Suddenly the broadcast channel changed and the radio got much louder. They stared at each other and then broke out in laughter, as the voice of Tina Charles burst out of the radio, singing, *Dance, little lady, dance!*

Yara couldn't keep herself from crying out happily, "Oh God, I love this song! Hurray for the awwa wind!"

Kariman was laughing softly. Yara left the desk and took her hand, saying,

"Get up, c'mon, get up and dance! You have to forget everything and listen to Tina Charles!"

"But the coffee!"

"I'll make some more after the song."

Kariman stood up, not believing how Yara was acting. As always, she seemed like an innocent child to her. She began to dance with her, calmly, to the rhythm of the song:

> *Someone taught me*
> *How to dance last night.*
> *What a mover he was!*
> *And someone taught me*
> *How to do it right.*
> *What a groover he was!*

Yara laughed and said, "Where's the guy who'll teach me to dance now?" and Kariman laughed too.

> *He taught me all the*
> *Steps to do the rock 'n' roll.*
> *I found my sense of rhythm*
> *But I lost my self-control*
> *When he said,*
> *Dance, little lady, dance!*

Yara reached out to raise the volume of the radio, to Kariman's surprise. She said,

"Your mom and dad are sleeping!"

Yara replied, nodding and laughing, "It doesn't matter, for once we'll get what's ours!"

Kariman's pleasure increased, and she laughed heartily.

You know you've only
Got one chance,
Dance, dance, dance!

Yara shouted, "Dance, dance, dance!" and Kariman danced with her, enjoying it thoroughly.

When Nadir went into the nightclub he saw Nawal in her usual place. She also saw him, and her eyes lit up.

When he got to her she did not stand up and embrace him, as she would have liked; she was afraid that if she did that, she would not let him go. Instead she greeted him with a handshake where she sat, and then said,

"You've stayed away from me for a long time, Nadir."

He looked around him and then whispered, "We were worried after Bishr was arrested."

There was a lot of noise around him, and the dancer, Alya, was sparkling as usual. His eyes sent a message to Nawal, and she agreed without answering aloud. He was asking, Can we leave this place? She patted his hand. "Half an hour more, and we'll go to my place." Then she looked at him deeply. "How I've wanted to listen to you . . . ."

A full hour passed, during which he was silent. She sensed his anxiety, but the audience wanted her to sing. They called for her loudly more than once, so she got up and sang a song of Nagaat al-Saghira:

My love for him appeared when he first came along.
God, how long had I been dreaming of his love, how long!

In the dim light she was looking far to her left, where Nadir was sitting. Then the audience demanded that she repeat the song, which she seemed to be singing with deep sincerity.

When I first looked into his eyes,
'My long nights are ending!' I cried.
Heaven protect him and defend!
I've known what awaits me in the end,
And what gives my heart a song,
Since he first came along.

Then she fixed her gaze on Nadir, this time letting it linger:

From my fear for him I cannot sleep,
My lashes pave his path as I weep.
He called and his love held me in thrall,
Why? For I answered love's call,
And I held him in my heart, oh how long,
Since he first came along.

The noisy crowd would not let her go her until she sang the song one more time. This time they went crazy at the end, because when she sang, "A window to love I opened wide," she motioned to her breast as if she were tearing off her clothes and baring it. The room exploded in applause, whistles and cries. Then when she sang, "'The world below is blooming!' I cried," she motioned vaguely to her body below her belly, and the applause, whistles, and cries became more tumultuous. Some of the women closed their eyes in shame and others smiled in surprise.

At the end she hurried to Nadir, took him by the hand, and rushed out. Everyone who saw her do that was surprised, and some of them laughed. At the door of the club the high wind blew out her skirts; she extended her hand to hold down her long gown and said, "I wish I could walk along the sea with you in the wind. I'm really elated tonight and really crazy. You saw what I did with the audience! It's the first time in my life I've done that. I wanted to, just once, because I'm so happy with you." The sea before them was loud. She said, "Unfortunately I can't. Let's go." She got into her Fiat and he got in next to her.

Later, in the apartment, she seemed calmer and less emotional. She had changed into a beautiful nightgown, and when she came back to the living room she said again,

"You've stayed away from me for a long time, Nadir."

He gave her the same answer: "We were worried after Bishr was arrested."

"I thought you had all forgotten me."

"Maybe everyone else can forget you, Madam Nawal, but I cannot."

"Call me just 'Nawal' and I'll believe you."

"I really was afraid to come see you. I didn't want to cause you any trouble."

She looked at him, then smiled and said, "We didn't have anything to drink or eat in the club, what do you say to having something now?"

Before he could say anything she stood up and headed to the kitchen. After a few minutes she returned with a small cart bearing dishes of cheese, honey, yogurt, and bread. She put them on the dining table and invited him to sit. As soon as he did she left him and returned quickly with a bottle of wine and two glasses; she opened the wine and filled the glasses. She saw him giving her a long look and said, "Did you come with me just to see me?"

"I missed you a lot."

"I'll hear some new poetry. Don't you dare tell me that you haven't written anything."

"I wrote a little."

She sighed and looked pleased. They began to eat slowly, in silence. All at once he said, "There's something else that made me afraid to come to you." She looked up, uncomprehending, and he went on, "I've joined the Egyptian Communist Party."

She stopped eating and looked at him in amazement. "Are there parties in Egypt now?"

"It's a secret party."

She was embarrassed momentarily, and he was more embarrassed. He should never have told her, but he couldn't back out now. She said,

"Why did you tell me that?"

"I don't really know. Anyway I'm sorry if I've embarrassed you."

She smiled broadly and said, "I'm not embarrassed. On the contrary, you're taking me back to good times in the past, as I told you. But it's a secret party as you said, so how can you tell me about it?"

"Because I have confidence in you."

"I know, but watch yourself, so that I don't go through the same story again and end up losing you." She paused. "But I learned a long time ago that the Communist parties dissolved themselves after their members were released from prison in 1964."

"More than one of them began to reorganize, years ago."

"Then the charges against the people they arrest every year are true?"

"Not all of them, naturally. But a lot of them are in parties. Communism is a ready-made charge for the State Security apparatus, you taught me that."

She smiled, wordlessly, and he fell silent in turn. They finished eating and returned to where they had been sitting. She brought the rest of the cheese, the bottle of wine, and the glasses and put them down in front of them. She sat beside him this time and put her arm around him and said,

"Nothing has made me happier than the fact that you remembered me tonight, Nadir, even though I know I won't stay in Egypt much longer."

"You said that before, and you said you would explain it to me later. Will I find out tonight?"

She said, smiling, "First tell me about your friends, Bishr and Hasan. I learned of Bishr's arrest from the newspapers, but I don't have a telephone number for any of you, so I couldn't call . . . and of course I don't know where you and your family live. I would have liked to offer to help."

"Bishr was released after a month, thank God. After that we all joined in the secret work."

She laughed. "You're revealing your friends' secrets to me too?"

He smiled, amazed at himself. "As for Hasan, unfortunately they refused his play at the Culture of Freedom Palace after they had contracted for it."

"The place on Fuad Street at the intersection of Sherif Pasha?"

"Precisely."

"Why did they refuse it? Was there some artistic flaw, or was it censorship?"

"They agreed to it artistically and the Censorship Office agreed, then when they started rehearsing everything stopped. It must have been on instructions from the State Security apparatus. We realized that, we know they've got eyes everywhere. Even though it's an absurdist play named *The Eighth Heaven*. They use the theater of the absurd to accuse us and they don't know that it's rejected in the Soviet Union. I swear, Beckett and Ionesco are banned writers in the Soviet Union!"

She looked at him in admiration and smiled, even though she did not know the theater of the absurd that he was talking about, or the two writers he mentioned. Destiny always brought educated people to her.

"By the way, what have you done about Ismat Muftah's poetry collection?"

She answered, "I took it to Hagg al-Ramli, the bookseller in Raml station. He told me to bring him the consent of the Censorship Office first. He asked me about Ismat Muftah, who he was, and I told him. He said the censors would never agree. I told him Ismat had died, but he said that no one dies for State Security."

"That's strange. Even though he sells Isa Salamawy's book?"

She laughed. "I saw it there, *The Meaning of the Communist Manifesto*. I asked him how he could sell that book and not help me to publish a collection of poetry, and he said, 'The author of this one is alive and got permission from the censors himself, and published it at his own expense. I didn't publish it, and nobody buys it. The author's crazy.' I laughed. He doesn't know that I know Isa."

Nadir thought for a moment and said, "It's strange that Isa got permission from the censors, isn't it?"

She realized what he meant and said in all seriousness, even though her voice remained low, "Don't ever think that Isa has any sort of connection with State Security. Isa is a very good man. They must not take him seriously, even though sometimes he finds people he can convince of what he says, like you and your friends."

"Anyway we don't see much of him these days, and we haven't told him about the secret party. Maybe they're really letting him do what he does so they can find new people to accuse, without his knowledge."

She laughed, her voice no longer lowered. She raised her glass to him and said, "You haven't toasted me tonight."

He raised his glass and kissed her on the cheek. He said,

"Near al-Ramli's book display there's Amm al-Sayyid. I borrow expensive books from him to read and pay him a small amount. I can ask him, maybe he would suggest a publisher for the collection."

"Don't bother. Hagg al-Ramli told me something useful. He said to find a way to publish it in Beirut. He liked the collection a lot. But I'm thinking I won't publish it, I'll give it to you instead before I leave, for you to publish. For now it belongs to me alone, and it's better that no one else share in it."

Then she stood up and said, "How is it that we haven't listened to any music? How could I forget?" She turned to the old record player and put on a record of Turkish music. "This is wonderful music, I bought it when I visited Istanbul."

"You've gone to Turkey too?"

"Once."

The peaceful sound of the music rose in the room. It had a touch of sadness, which was quickly reflected on Nadir's face, leaving him briefly preoccupied. After she returned to her place next to him he said, "You still haven't told me anything about your leaving

Egypt. Don't blame me for asking, it's just that this music is like a sad farewell."

She took a deep breath and closed her eyes for a moment. "I'll tell you everything."

She put her head on his chest and told him how her first visit to Paris had been at the invitation of a Greek friend who had left Alexandria with her family in 1965. That first visit had been just five years ago, and she had become devoted to visiting Paris every year.

"You were looking for your lost lover."

Her head still on his chest, she answered, "Perhaps. But when I got there, I asked myself, what's the sense of adding the last chapter to a novel that's over? I plunged into Paris, I can never get enough of it." She lifted her eyes to him with an expression of childish joy. "But something else happened that had never happened to me before in my whole life."

He was silent, perplexed, so she went on speaking. "There was a young man during the Second World War. He was in high school and I was a child, maybe five or six years old. His father worked on the railroad with my father. He had a love story we heard about later, with a Christian girl from Ghayt al-Aynab. His family lived with our families in the railway residences where poor people lived along the Mahmudiya Canal, between Karmuz and Kafr Ashri. Do you know them?"

"No."

"Do you know Ghayt al-Aynab?"

He laughed. "Of course, it's all drugs now, it's outstripped Gabal Naasa. But I haven't been there."

She laughed and continued, "As I was saying, after the Second World War Rushdi—that was his name—left and went to France. After that his family left the residences in a hurry and we didn't hear any more about them, even though we still knew about his story. People would tell it often, marveling over how Rushdi had loved a girl when he was young, and a Christian too, and how their love story had ended because of the difference of religion. The girl's name was Camelia. Of course I only knew her name because they would say it when they told the story. They said that she became a nun in a convent in Upper Egypt a long time ago. We children never forgot Rushdi. He didn't say much and he always had a book he was reading, on the roof of the house or on the bank of the Mahmudiya Canal."

He asked in surprise, "He left Egypt and she became a nun?"

"That's what the grown-ups said in front of us."

"It's a strange story."

She hit him gently on the chest. "Listen to the rest, to my story of when I was in Paris."

He hugged her, feeling as if she really was a child, despite her years. He said, "Don't tell me you met him there!"

"I did meet him there."

He sat back a little and looked in her eyes as she smiled broadly. Smiling in turn, he said, "No, you're a better storyteller than Yusuf al-Sibaie! No, by God, not Yusuf al-Sibaie, not even Muhammad Abdel Halim Abdallah could make up a story this melodramatic. Maybe Hasan al-Imam, the producer who makes melodramas, could make a movie of it."

She began beating on his chest while he laughed. She said, "Listen to me! You asked me, let me tell you, and then believe me."

He hugged her to him. "Please finish, my lady."

"God knows I don't believe it myself. Back to the story. We were having dinner in a Greek restaurant in the Raspail neighborhood, a restaurant where Georges Moustaki was singing. He's a Greek too, an émigré from Alexandria. We saw a man of about fifty who looked like an Egyptian, sitting alone. As soon as Irini saw him, my Greek friend, she went over to him and shook his hand. He seemed happy to see her, and they talked, and she pointed to me. He seemed pleased, and looked at me and raised his hand in greeting. Then Irini surprised me by coming back and asking that we join him. He had been her professor at the Sorbonne, where she finished her education."

She fell silent. She looked as if she was remembering and picturing everything that had happened after that. He prompted her. "What then?"

"I'll finish the story. It looks as if I won't hear any poetry tonight."

She spoke unhurriedly, as if she really had forgotten her desire to listen to poetry. The man learned that she owned a nightclub in Alexandria, and he smiled. He learned that she knew some of the Communists who were arrested at the end of 1958 and nodded his head as if he knew the story. When he asked her what neighborhood she came from in Alexandria and she told him, his eyes widened in surprise. He smiled and said, "Can anyone who comes from there know about Communism?" He was really amazed. She asked him if he knew the place and he said "Somewhat," and then said nothing more for the rest of the evening. They ate and drank and listened to Georges Moustaki, and then they left.

But destiny willed that she would meet him again, also with Irini, in a Moroccan restaurant on Rue St. Germain (she had come to know a lot of the features of Paris, now). She decided to return his previous invitation, since he had refused to let them pay anything the last time. They laughed at the coincidence, and as they were eating, he said, "You asked me before if I knew the place where you grew up and I said 'Somewhat.'"

She didn't answer, but looked at him in surprise.

"I'm from there too."

She had learned from Irini the last time they had sat together that his name was Monsieur Rushdi al-Masri, and that he was well known in Paris as a professor of comparative literature. Nawal was delighted that he was from the place where she had been born, and she asked him to tell her how she had never seen him there. He promised to tell her later on, but she asked God in her heart to let her learn everything about him on this visit, not another. She might come another time and not find him. Her desire to know was clear on her face; who was he really? He gave her his telephone number and told her to call him when she came back to Paris again.

He did not know that she was going to stay another week, and she did not know that they would run into him again by chance three days later, in a restaurant in the Odéon. This time she laughed happily, and he also said that destiny was arranging odd meetings for them. They did not discuss anything in particular, but she kept looking at him in admiration, to the point that he was embarrassed by it—she noticed his embarrassment more than once. She decided she had to meet him alone, telling herself that she should try for it. She called him that night and he agreed, perfectly easily, and arranged to meet her in a café in Saint Michel. So she would meet him by herself, just as she wanted.

It was summer, and light filled the world. People looked like moving rainbows because of the colors of their clothing, and the women's bare skin reflected the light everywhere. Everything was cheerful, even the waiters who passed quickly and agilely in the café and among the many seats spread out on the broad sidewalk. She now realized that his real name was Rushdi Abdel Ghani, because she had remembered the whole story, and she looked at him in disbelief. The story had been told as truth, but those who heard it took it for a myth, pure imagination. She said to him in great amazement, "You're Rushdi who loved the Christian girl Camelia," and he nodded, smiling. He said that he had married another woman here in Paris and that he had a son and daughter who were working and studying in the university now. Unfortunately he had lost touch with his family. He didn't know how that had happened, as he had been sending them money up until recently. He had not seen his mother and father again after he left Alexandria, since he had never gone back to Egypt, and after their deaths the correspondence between him and his brothers and sisters had diminished until it stopped completely.

He smiled and said, "Did you all know my story and retell it?"

"Naturally—who doesn't know the story, in that place?"

She in turn told him in detail about the doctor, Ahmad, whom she had loved, who took her to the Communists for the first time, and how she had liked them, and what had happened after that. She told him how she married their leader after he got out of prison, and how he gave her everything he owned and went to the Soviet Union, and died there.

When he asked her about her name she told him Nawal Hamza, and he began to think deeply. He said he remembered a kind, friendly man among the railway workers whose name was Hamza; he had been kidnapped by the English in the Second World War. She laughed and told him that he was her father. They both laughed a lot that day.

They did not meet again after that until a year later, and now they met every year.

For a moment Nadir thought that she was like Rawayih, telling imaginary stories or stories that she wished had happened. Maybe the nightclub trade left no room for the heart, except in the imagination. But he sighed and said,

"It really is a strange tale."

She was enthusiastic. "If I leave Alexandria I'm going to live in Paris. I'm thinking about buying a small café there, or a small nightclub."

"But that must be very expensive."

"Definitely. But the ones who are offering to buy the club from me to turn it into a wedding parlor are offering fabulous sums that increase every day." She laughed. "One of them is person named Sheikh Zaalan, people call him '*angry* over the existence of the clubs.' He says that openly to everyone around him. He's thinking about buying the movie houses too, especially in the poor neighborhoods."

He was startled. "What's with Sheikh Zaalan and me today?"

"Do you know him?"

"Of course not. But I heard about him today from Rawayih and Ghada, the two who live below us and work in a nightclub. But I hadn't heard anything about buying movie houses before this."

She paused for a moment, and then said, "If they could they would close every place where people enjoy themselves. There's somebody pushing all this, and financing it."

Streaks of dawn were becoming visible through the windows, and the sound of the wind was relentless. He seemed frozen in place.

After a few moments she said, "I still have the feeling that you came to me because of something else. Is there a problem between you and Yara? Are you worried because you're going to go to Cairo after graduation, the way you said? Did you tell her, maybe, and is she against the idea?"

He shook his head. Then he stood up and took her hand, and she stood up in front of him. He took her in his arms and she said, "We didn't listen to any poetry."

He kissed her, softly. "Right now I don't see anything but you, I'm not thinking of anything else."

He gave her a long kiss, then moved toward her room with her. He asked himself if he had become like Bishr Zahran, who fled to a woman when the world closed in on him. Or did he really love her without knowing it?

They were sitting around Isa Salamawy in the college cafeteria, happy because the academic year was ending. They only had one exam left, Psychology, with the professor they were always making jokes about. He was the one who inscribed the covers of his four books with every degree he had ever gotten, and they had also discovered that in reality the four books were just two—he had made two new books out of chapters from the first two, rearranging them and giving them new titles.

None of them was concerned right now about being separated during the vacation. There was an air of exams and of dawning summer, so they had all thrown off their heavy clothes, and the girls' arms gleamed.

The students who had exams that afternoon were scattered in the gardens, in front of the Abbadi Lecture Hall and near the tennis courts, reviewing what they had prepared for the exam. Some were sitting in the cafeteria, studying in silence.

Isa had often stayed away from the lectures during recent weeks, plunging into his study of the history of Alexandria and its architecture. He had put into practice his plan of talking to them about the ancient city and its historical situation more than about Marxism. Today he planned to add realistic examples to his talk of history.

He asked, "Since the last subject is easy, what do you say to a series of tours to get to know the real Alexandria?"

They looked at each other, nearly laughing. What tours, when they would only meet one more time before the end of the term? Yara couldn't keep herself from laughing so she hid her mouth with her hand and suppressed the sound.

Hasan was planning to take Kariman to the apartment. Yara seemed exhausted, and she had made her excuses to Nadir. When he asked her why she was so exhausted she said that it was staying up late and studying; he didn't know that it was her cursed period. Bishr asked him,

"What exactly do you mean, Ustaz Isa? You've talked to us before about the history of Alexandria and advised us about books to read. What do you mean by tours of the city when we live in it?"

Once more they almost laughed. He said, "I mean visiting the Greco-Roman Museum, for example, or Pompey's Pillar, or a lot of the archaeological monuments that nobody really knows. Most important is visiting the cemetery." Silence descended upon them as they exchanged glances, so he went on. "The Shatbi Cemetery is a historical treasure—it preserves a history of Alexandria that maybe no one even imagines. I'm thinking of going there today. It's one now, and it closes at six."

No one answered. Outside the window they saw the handsome Muhammad Shukr, the one Ahmad Basim had told them he had seen going into the Trianon with Fawqiya, the minister's daughter. He was walking with her and smiling, smoothing his thin blond hair with his hand. Her long hair flowed down her back, and she was wearing a gorgeous dress. They all saw the couple at the same time; Hasan commented, with his small smile,

"Muhammad really does love Fawqiya!"

Isa said, "Didn't you know that?" They looked at him in surprise and he continued, "I know that and I'm not here very often."

Bishr said, "We only see her coming or going with her twin Fawziya. Their driver waits for them at the gate of the college. They rarely speak to anybody."

Kariman shook her head. "Stop talking about other people and listen to Ustaz Isa." She turned to him and said, "Forgive me, Ustaz, but I'm superstitious about visiting cemeteries, especially during exams."

They laughed except for Isa, who always seemed serious. She added, "Have you seen the new clothing store for veiled women in Safiya Zaghlul Street?"

They looked at each other in surprise. Yara asked, "What does 'clothing for veiled women' mean?"

Bishr said, "I've seen it. It started out as a shoe store; the Beriony Shop. It's the first store to change to this business, but soon that'll be an everyday occurrence. Why aren't there any rich Marxists, Ustaz Isa, who could expand the nightclubs or increase the number of movie theaters or open clothing shops for working-class people?"

Yara's loud laugh attracted their attention, and she was embarrassed. She said, "I'm sorry, I don't know what veiled women's clothes are, so how would I know about working-class clothes? I'm really sorry." She turned to Isa. "I'm really exhausted, Ustaz. I can't go with you to the cemetery."

Nadir said with a smile, "I can go with you another day, Ustaz Isa."

Hasan said, "Me too. Today I need a deep sleep." He looked meaningfully at Kariman, and Yara smiled when she noticed.

Bishr said, "I'll go with you, Ustaz Isa. I feel good today and the dead are sure to bring me down, and that's what I need."

They laughed. Only Hasan and Nadir knew what he meant; he would finish with the cemetery and visit the apartment, where he would meet Rawayih and Ghada. He only needed them when he was angry and upset.

Bishr walked to the cemetery with Isa, who walked ahead of him. Bishr wasn't surprised at his long steps since he was tall compared to Bishr, but he was surprised by how fast he went. Why in the world was the man hurrying as if he were going to Paradise when he was really going to death? Bishr smiled and nearly laughed. They entered by the first gate they came to, the gate of the Orthodox Copts. Isa stood between two graves and began to speak:

"Before you see many of the important names contained in the earth of Alexandria, you should know that the large number of sections in the cemetery is one important sign of Alexandria's cosmopolitan nature. The large number of its nationalities, religions, and sects shows it too."

Bishr was looking at a small number of beautiful women dressed in black. Their faces expressed sadness and silence, but their complexions spoke of prosperity and beauty.

Isa said, "This is the cemetery of the Orthodox Copts, and we'll go to the cemeteries of the Greek Orthodox, the Armenian Orthodox, the Syriac Catholics, the Armenian Catholics, the Latin Catholics, the Jewish cemetery, and the Anglican one. See how many there are? And the most important is the cemetery of the free thinkers, the ones who didn't belong to any sect or religion."

Bishr said, "My whole life I thought this was a cemetery for Egyptian Copts only."

Isa smiled. "From the beginning of the tram tracks up to Gamal Abdel Nasser Street there's an area where the dead declare Alexandria's internationalism!"

The number of people decreased as they moved away from the Orthodox Coptic cemetery until they saw no one. In the middle of the Greek Orthodox cemetery Isa said, "Did you notice that there's no one here but the guard, the gardener, and the dogs?"

Bishr noticed, his eyes widening. "Naturally there are almost no Greeks in Alexandria, but what are all these dogs doing here?"

Isa smiled. "Almost the only Greek left is my dear friend Christo. As for the dogs, they're part of any cemetery in Egypt. Don't be afraid of them."

Isa moved on with Bishr, the dogs surrounding them, from the Greek Orthodox to the Catholics. Here Isa stopped for a long time before a small grave of white marble next to two other small graves. The writing on them was in Greek, and all Bishr learned from it was the dates of birth and death. As Isa stood there, Bishr noticed two statues, one on each side, apparently of the god Apollo and of Aphrodite. In fact there were a lot of statues that attracted Bishr's attention: Greek statues in poses of love, or flight, or strength; statues of Mary and the Messiah; many statues in many places.

All at once he asked, "Who are they?" meaning, who was in the tombs where Isa stood. Isa didn't answer at first, looking dazed. Then he said, "Persa."

Bishr said nothing. He didn't know anyone famous by that name. But then Isa continued, "It looks as if I'll be like Christo."

Bishr looked at him in silence, not knowing Christo or Persa. Isa went on, "Persa is still alive. These are the graves of her father, her mother, and her older sister; she's in Greece now. I met her in 1966 in Ateneos, with Christo. She was young and beautiful, and Christo couldn't keep up with her in dancing. I danced with her. I went out with her three times, then she left for Greece before I could tell her that I loved her."

Bishr did not comment. He walked beside Isa, who was also silent for several minutes, saying to himself: Romantics are of two kinds, Isa, one kind that tries to change the world and another whose life turns into a melodrama. You refuse to acknowledge the second and cling to the first, while every beautiful thing slips between your fingers.

Bishr sensed the solemnity of the moment. Isa must be sad now, he thought, so he remained silent until they stopped in front of the grave of Cavafy. They stood there a long time, while Bishr wondered how it had happened that he had never read anything of Cavafy's up to now, when he was the poet whose name was always linked to the city. Suddenly Isa's liveliness returned and he took Bishr to the grave of Antoniadis, owner of the famous garden and palace that bore his name in the Nuzha neighborhood. Then he took him to the graves of Salvagos, Anastasi, Costa, Bianchi, Glymonopoulo, Averoff, Zervoudakis, and other notables and businessmen of Alexandria whose names could still be seen in the sky above the city, where they had left them on shops, or schools, or hospitals, or in the memory of old people. The names were still there despite what had happened to their factories and businesses during the nationalization in the time of Nasser, to them and to others like the owner of the Green Salon or the Brazilian Coffee Shop. It had happened even though the Greeks were in a city they had made in the first place. They didn't feel as if they were an expatriate community in Egypt; they felt as if they were more Egyptian than anyone else. Nasser had promised them that nationalization would not affect them, but he had broken his promise. That's how Isa was telling the story, but then he corrected himself as a true Marxist. "That's what happened to the Egyptians, too, and we accepted it, there was no injustice for anyone. But the point is that the city accommodated all nationalities and religions. That's how Alexander built it. Do you know what happened while he was standing among his engineers as they showed him their plan for the city?"

"No."

"They couldn't find any lime for the engineer Dinocrates to draw the lines of the city on the ground, so he drew the plan for him with seeds. No sooner had he finished than birds swooped down from the sky and began eating the seeds." Bishr laughed and Isa went on: "It seems that Alexander took it as a bad omen, but one of his men said, 'It's not a bad omen, my lord, but a good omen: this city will be for all the men in the world.'"

Bishr stood dejected, thinking about this fact and how it had been true for many centuries. He asked himself what had happened to Alexandria, and what was happening to it now.

Since all the names on the gravestones were in Greek, he decided that Isa might come here often, since it was easy for him to find the graves he wanted. He walked with him silently, admiring the delightful Greek statues and the statues of the Virgin Mary and of the Messiah. Isa paused again in front of the graves of the English Protestants. Here the names were in English, and he was surprised that the families of some of the dead had insisted on writing that the person had died in the Raml neighborhood. When Isa took him to the Commonwealth cemetery, Bishr was amazed by its expanse, its cleanliness, and the harmony of its trees and grass. Isa told him that most of those buried there were victims of the Second World War, and that these graves and those of the Allies at al-Alamein were still cared for by the Commonwealth states, so they were clean and beautiful. They wandered through the graves of the Armenians, both of them standing silently, as neither knew Armenian. It seemed to Bishr that Isa had not visited them before.

Isa was showing signs of fatigue, so Bishr said, with a smile, "That's enough for today. We've walked a lot and there's no telling what the dogs will do with us later on."

Isa smiled. "Let's just quickly go to the Jewish cemetery."

"Why not?"

But the cemetery guard told them that visiting was forbidden without a permit. It was a protective measure taken by the Jewish community, and the permit could be obtained from them.

Bishr smiled ironically. "And where is this Jewish community?"

Isa shook his head and they left, making their way through the gate and then to nearby Alexander the Great Street, at the corner. Isa suddenly stopped and took Bishr's hand, saying, "We forgot the graves of the Latins and the free thinkers!"

"We'll come to them another day."

Isa smiled. "In any case it's an outing. Whenever you're in a bad mood then come here, to learn the grandeur of this city."

Bishr did not look convinced, especially since he too was beginning to feel fatigued from the walk. But in fact his mind was filled with amazement and pleasure, completely contrary to what he had expected. He had seen the graves of great men from every sect and nationality, some of whom he had known by name and many of whom he had not known. Why ever had he expected to be overcome with chagrin? Even if his city never knew great men again, it was enough that it had known all of these.

Isa said, "A day will come when I take you to the old Shatbi Cemetery, and to the Roman graves in the Ras al-Souda area. I'll even look at the Muslims' graves in Kom al-Shuqafa, near a great archaeological site. It's as if they're announcing to the world that in the history of Alexandria, nationalities and religions cannot be separated from one another."

Bishr had never thought about this before, even though he had walked more than once in the funeral of a relative or neighbor to bury him in the Amud al-Sawari Cemetery. Only now did he realize that the talk of death had gone on for longer than it should have; he felt as if his teeth were about to chatter, and a salty taste was rising in the back of his throat.

He would go to the apartment, then, and smother his anger in Rawayih or Ghada. Now!

6

THE TEMPERATURE IN ALEXANDRIA REACHED 85 degrees Fahrenheit, sometimes rising or falling by a degree, while in Cairo it was always over 95 degrees. As usual in the summer the country experienced waves of high humidity, especially in Alexandria, where the beaches were filled with summer visitors. They felt it when they left the beach, even just to cross the street. Khalid ibn al-Walid Street—where the restaurants and cafés that had been closed during the winter were open again—was filled with them. Peddlers filled the sidewalks and sometimes went down into the street itself.

The case of the man the newspapers had dubbed "the torture murderer," Safwat al-Rubi, and of his two comrades was still before the military court, filling the pages of the daily newspapers and the weekly magazines. The Cinema Rioux in Alexandria showed the film *Two Legs in the Mud* starring Poussi. Talk had begun that the state was considering launching a subway project in Cairo. A man killed two women in one hour; he strangled the first in order to rob her, and smashed the head of the second against a wall, after raping her.

Nadir was not able to meet Yara until the day the examination results appeared. He had tried to call her twice but no one had answered the telephone, and he had fallen into despair. Then he ran into her on the day the results came out, a month after the end of the exams. They all passed with a grade of "good" except for Yara, who had achieved a grade of "very good." That made Nadir leap in the air in the courtyard of the college, and he nearly kissed her in front of all the students who had come to see their results. To his surprise he saw that the wall newspapers they had hung up a month before were still in place, as were the newspapers of the students from the Islamic Group and the Muslim Brothers. Only a few of the edges had come loose. When he told her that he had called her twice and no one had answered, she laughed like a happy child.

"Did you forget? We spend most summer days in the Stanley Beach cabin."

How in the world had he forgotten that, when he knew it from the year before? He said sadly,

"And of course there's no telephone in the Stanley cabin."

"You called the house when we were in the cabin. You must have called during the day. At night we're always at home."

"The main thing is that I found you today, sweetheart. I want to celebrate our success with you, let's go."

She was looking around, perplexed. "Why hasn't Kariman come?"

"Did you plan to meet?"

"No, but I thought she would come, to find out the results."

"Then she must be going to come tomorrow, or the next day. Or maybe she's come already."

"I would have liked to see her. She's disappeared too."

He was looking at the effect of the sun on her face, her neck, and her bare arms. She looked to him like a mulatto, the tan enhancing her beauty. Walking beside him as they left the college, she said happily,

"Why don't you come to Stanley Beach some time?"

"And see you in your bathing suit."

She laughed. "You'll see me and all the girls." She stopped and took his hand, looking into his eyes. "Can you imagine? Women have started going into the water in pants and a long dress, of course with a swim cap on their heads. And the men are also wearing long shorts that go to the knees that they call 'lawful shorts.'" Nadir laughed. "There are only a few of them so far. But never mind that, how are we going to celebrate? I have to go back to my family, they're waiting for the results."

He looked at his watch. "It's one o'clock now. I'll take you out to lunch at Ateneos, and at 3:30 we'll go to the Metro Cinema to see the new Youssef Chahine film, *Return of the Prodigal Son*."

"I can have lunch with you, but let's put off the movie for another date."

"It's a really good film and I'm afraid it won't be showing for long."

"Why? A film of Youssef Chahine ought to show for, say, three weeks."

"His films are hard for ordinary audiences. With God's help it might show for a week."

She laughed. "All right, then. I've missed you, Nadir, sweetheart, a lot." She emphasized the last words, opening her eyes wide and smiling.

Ateneos was extremely crowded. They sat at a table far from the entrance, and she said, "This is the first time I've come to Ateneos. Wow, it's really beautiful!" She began to look at the Greek reliefs that formed a circle on the walls below the ceiling. "They're Greek myths, right?"

He smiled. "They're beautiful women who remind us of the gods of beauty and who sing and dance and make music. As you see, there are also a few statues here and there and pictures of Zeus, Hercules, and Apollo, for those who know them. All of the ones on the walls and under the ceiling, it's as if they're circling over the heads of the people seated below in celebration. The women are like butterflies and they're all happy, even though they're fixed on the wall."

"You must come to Ateneos a lot, then."

"This is the first time. But that's what Isa Salamawy told me about the place. There's also the Crazy Horse Room for evening parties, but I haven't gone there yet."

She said, regretfully, "Isa is a cultural encyclopedia. Why doesn't he write a book and put what he knows in it?"

"He has a little book. Its title is *The Meaning of the Communist Manifesto*."

She shrugged, smiling. "I've never heard of it. He hasn't told us about it even though he sits with us."

He smiled, gesturing. "Look at the antique chandelier and the chairs and all the collectors' items and statues in the corners. Even the unusual Italian floor tiling. All of that is the work of the old Greek owner, Constantine Ateneos, who opened it in 1900. The site was a vacant lot owned by an Italian Jew; Constantine convinced him that he would build an apartment building on it and in return he would get the first floor to open a pastry shop and café. Ateneos died and in 1970 his wife Catina sold it to the owner of the Nassar Restaurant— you know it, of course, the one on the sea. Nassar kept everything in Ateneos, as you can see. Do you know what 'Ateneos' means?"

"The name of the owner, as you said." She was puzzled.

"Yes, but it also means 'Athenian.' It should be pronounced 'a-*thee*-nee-us,' not 'a-*tee*-nee-us,' as we say."

She smiled. "Right, like we say 'an A-lex-an-da-*raa*-nian.'"

He laughed and clasped her hands on top of the table for a few moments. They looked at each other passionately in silence until the waiter came with lunch, which he began to put on the table while she looked on in amazement. After the waiter left she asked Nadir, "Do you have enough money with you? This is a lot, fish and calamari and a lot of salads!"

"Don't worry, I have ten whole pounds. It'll be enough for lunch and the movie and the ice cream we'll have during intermission, too."

Time passed quickly for them, as it does for people in love. They went to the Metro Cinema for the 3:30 showing. The number of patrons in the theater was not large but they kept shouting all during the film, because the characters' dialog and the change of scenes were both rapid and no one could settle on the sense or the picture. Like them Yara was unable to comprehend the film or understand the meaning, but she made an effort to put up with it. Nadir was pleased with his ability to understand it. He was preparing himself to talk to her about it at length later on, since he was sure that she would ask him about it.

Many of the scenes in the film were interesting, but the young Lebanese singer Majida al-Rumi, previously unknown to movie audiences, was something beautiful, innocent, and pure for Nadir and for Yara as well. Her operatic voice was new to the audience, and they in turn were yelling along with her, spoiling the song. Yara was extremely annoyed with the audience, who were keeping her from understanding the film. Nadir largely succeeded in identifying with the film and in separating himself from what was happening around him, but the effort exhausted his mind and spirit.

The film ended and the lights came up, and of the small audience only a few individuals were left. He said angrily, "We should see this film alone without any of the audience, but how?"

She took his hand to soothe him, even though she was more frustrated than he was, both with the rhythm of the film and with the audience. She said, "Majida al-Rumi's voice is very lovely. You know, I heard all the songs, and especially the last one, in spite of the audience."

But he asked, "How will I see you?"

"Call me on Fridays, any time during the day. We usually don't go the cabin on Friday because of the crowds on the beach."

"Will you be the one who answers?"

"Call at one in the afternoon. My father will be praying in the Mursi Abul Abbas Mosque and my mother will be busy in the kitchen."

"And your brother?"

"That one never stays home." She laughed, then she began repeating Majida al-Rumi's song:

Some mornings I wake with grief in my heart.
I look beyond the door, and yearning pulls me apart.
What I bought has been sold, what I found I could not hold,
The one I met has gone away, it's too late now, today.
Then again I say, the birds still are singing,
The bees still are winging, children's laughter still is ringing,
Even though not all have a song in their heart.

He looked at her in great admiration. "You've memorized the song! How could you, in spite of all that racket?"

"Pure genius, my friend! And after all, it wouldn't make sense not to get anything out of the film."

"The song is all about hope, that's what matters."

"Of course I would have liked to hear it in better circumstances." She looked at her watch. "Oh! I'm really late. I'll have to take a taxi."

The humidity was high on Safiya Zaghlul Street. The Elite Restaurant on their right was now enclosed by a wall of wood and glass that did not show those behind it; previously the patrons had been visible to those passing on the street as they ate and drank coffee or beer. He chose not to say anything to her since she had not noticed. She got into the taxi and he stood looking after her, not believing his day. He walked on happily, taking his time.

In Raml Station he stood watching the crowds around the ice cream and popcorn vendors, the shoe shiners who sat on the sidewalk, the ceaseless movement of people to and from the tram, the other sidewalk with the As You Like It café and the Fayoumi pastry shop, the booksellers and the central telephone exchange behind them. Then he headed for Amm al-Sayyid, asking himself how it was that he didn't walk with his beloved in the streets, just as he liked, and at any time, and how it was that he didn't see her every day. He stopped in front of Amm al-Sayyid, who noticed his preoccupied expression and asked him, "What's wrong, Ustaz Nadir? You seem unhappy."

"On the contrary, today I'm very happy! What do you have that's new?"

Amm al-Sayyid reached for a little collection of poetry, saying, "This is a new collection by Amal Donqol, it came in from Beirut." He gave him the collection, *The Coming Promise*. Nadir hugged it to his chest joyfully and took out the money to pay.

Amm al-Sayyid said, "You can borrow it. Read it and return it."

But Nadir smiled and said, "Amal Donqol is not to lend, he stays here," pointing to his heart. Then he walked on happily, forgetting all his earlier questions.

*

In Lebanon the Tell al-Zaatar Palestinian refugee camp fell after a great massacre carried out by the right-wing Lebanese Phalangist Party, along with Syrian forces; the Palestinian Liberation Organization laid the blame for it entirely on the Syrians. More than three thousand Palestinians were victims of the massacre, in an operation of mass annihilation that was unprecedented in the Arab world. Not even in Palestine in 1948 had the extermination reached this number. The operation was carried out after food, water, and electricity had been cut off from the camp and it had been besieged, making things easier for the Phalangist Party militias and the Syrian army. They finished off the Palestinian fighters entrenched in the camp and the residents, in their entirety. The few residents who did survive had been eating the flesh of the dead, from fighters, dogs, and cats, to keep from dying of hunger.

In Egypt two justices of the appeals court, judges, were discovered in a mental hospital where they had been placed during the previous era by the State Security apparatus. President Sadat was continuing his travels, visiting Qatar and Kuwait followed by Amman, Saudi Arabia, and Ceylon. Relations between Libya and Egypt became more strained, because it was discovered that a group loyal to the Libyan regime was planning a series of explosions in Egypt. In Damascus there was an explosion in the officers' club, and a Syrian organization opposed to the ruling party claimed responsibility for it.

In Alexandria itinerant vendors occupied all the sidewalks of Cairo Station Square (Martyrs' Square), and large areas of the streets in the heart of the square, selling used clothing made in China from synthetic fibers, imported fruit, and cheap frozen fish. The crowds around the vendors were poor people from impoverished neighborhoods near and far, Ragheb Pasha, Emary, Karmuz, Erfan, and Bowalino. On the ground the remains of leaves, bags, food, and garbage began to pile up and expand, and no one picked up any of it. Now no one cleaned the square, no one cleaned the streets of Alexandria.

In Maks, where Nadir lived, Bishr arrived in the early morning. He knocked on the door of Nadir's apartment and his mother opened it and saw Bishr before her, short and dark. She hadn't seen him before so she stood there in surprise; her confusion was contagious and he stammered as he asked for Nadir. She hurried to his room and woke him up. Bishr refused to come into the house, it was better to talk by the sea, he said. Then he went downstairs where Nadir joined him without delay.

Nadir's mother saw him changing his clothes and rushing out without even going into the bathroom or drinking a cup of tea, and she said to herself, "I hope everything's okay, dear God let it be all right." Then she busied herself with drinking a cup of tea with milk and listening to the radio. She loved the voice of Fuad al-Muhandis in the program "A Quick Word." When he raised his voice and bellowed she felt as if he was pushing someone in front of him. She also liked the program "Light News" presented by Gamalat al-Ziyadi, with her friendly voice, and after that she liked to listen to the morning songs. They usually featured singers who were unknown but whose voices did not lack beauty, like Kamal Hosni.

As soon as Nadir joined him in the street, Bishr said "Thank God I didn't ask directions from anyone. I found you on my own, I remembered your address from when you mentioned it to us once a couple of years ago."

They passed through the street and the train station where no trains came and the small Corniche, where an area was taken up by fishmongers. The vendors used the sidewalk to set up tables holding fish of all kinds: bluefish, silver sea bream, striped mullet, grey mullet, white sea bream, and grouper, along with some shrimp, sardines, sand smelts, octopus, and sea turtles. A few cars stood before them while the owners shopped, and men and women came from the neighborhood and from other nearby neighborhoods, such as Wadi al-Qamar, Wardian, and Dekhela. Barefoot children loitered among the tables, searching for small, overlooked fish; they gathered them in tin boxes, and the fishmongers let them do it. Some of the children moved under the nets stretched out high over the sand, with a few strands of sea plants hanging from many of them. That's where the feluccas were resting after their return from fishing trips, and where the children also gathered fish that had fallen or been overlooked, even jumping into the feluccas to look for them. The smell of fish was light in the air, almost unnoticed, an indication of how fresh all the fish was. As Bishr surveyed the scene and compared the fish here to the fish on display in the Bacos Market near where he lived, he felt as if the fish they sold over there was trash fish. All at once he said, "People are strange. They haven't left anything on land or in the air or in the sea that they don't eat."

Nadir laughed. "Did you come to me early in the morning to give me this bit of wisdom?"

"It's the first time I've seen something like this. Let's watch a little and then I'll talk to you."

Nadir walked among the fishmongers with him so Bishr could explore. Some of them greeted him, and he also spoke to them. Amm Gabir, the most renowned fisherman in that area, spied them from where he sat on the other sidewalk, where his boys had placed a small old wooden table in front of him with a cup of tea on it. He called to Nadir, who smiled and went to shake his hand with Bishr behind him.

But Amm Gabir said, "So, your friend here looks like he's educated, like you. I said to myself, I have to do my duty." He ordered one of his boys to gather a gift of fish in a plastic bag, while Nadir asked him not to do that, they had a lot of fish that his father had bought yesterday. But the man laughed and said, "Actually it's that your friend is short, and he reminded me of my father." Bishr was embarrassed but Amm Gabir spoke to him directly: "Don't be upset, Ustaz. My father had me and my brothers and we're all tall, even so."

The boy brought the plastic bag containing the fish and Amm Gabir offered it to Nadir, saying, "Don't be embarrassed, you have to give this fine friend of yours a breakfast of our fish." He called to his boy and asked, "Did you put in a mullet, boy?"

"Yes, boss."

"And a sea bream?"

"Yes, boss."

"And a bogue?"

"Yes, boss. Everything Ustaz Nadir's father gets, 'cause I know what he gets."

Amm Gabir proudly told Bishr, "It's a small fish, but you'll bless me for it."

Nadir took the sack and walked with Bishr along the other sidewalk, approaching the Casino Zephyrion. He said, "How about I leave you for a few minutes and give the fish to my mother to make us breakfast for when we get back?"

"No, let's talk first. We won't take long."

They sat in front of the Zephyrion Restaurant that had been closed for years, on the Corniche wall. Nadir pointed to the restaurant.

"Artists used to come here to the Zephyrion Restaurant to eat, like Abdel Halim Hafiz and Omar Sharif . . . ."

Bishr spoke directly. "Khalil wants you to go to Cairo the day after tomorrow."

Surprised, Nadir asked, "Did you see him?"

"He met Hasan in Mansura."

"How did you find out from Hasan? By telephone?"

"What telephone? You're crazy, phones are always under surveillance! Hasan's been in Alexandria for two days, and he visited me at home."

Nadir smiled. "Great, I've missed Hasan. I'll be able to see him today, then."

"No, it's better if you don't see him." Bishr didn't wait for him to answer. "Come on, let's go to your lady mother to break our fast with the small fish from tall Amm Gabir."

Nadir laughed aloud.

Before Hasan returned to Alexandria he telephoned Kariman and made a date to meet her at the Wali Café, and after he visited Bishr he went to meet her. She had arrived before him, and as soon as she stood to shake his hand he saw that she was pale and sad. He felt afraid.

"What is it, Kariman, are you sick?"

Her hands shook and she stammered. They sat down and a deep sadness came over her. He said,

"Let's leave here, that would be better, so we can be comfortable talking."

She nodded in agreement, tears glistening in her green eyes. As soon as they were on the street waiting for a taxi he put his arm around her, hugging her to his side, and she responded as if she had been seeking this affection. They didn't speak during the short ride to Tanais Street. When they went into the apartment she sat on one of the chairs and he sat next to her. She turned her face to him and he saw her eyes bathed in tears again. He wiped the tears from her cheeks with his fingers and said,

"These pearls shouldn't fall from their place."

He began kissing her cheeks, slowly, then her forehead and her lips, as she said nothing. He took off her clothes and she stood, surrendering, allowing him to do it. He took her to the bed in his room, and still she said nothing. He placed her on her back and began moving his hands over her body, yearning for her, but she burst into tears. He had hoped he could take her far away from any sadness. He lay down beside her, looking at her, and said,

"What's wrong, Kariman? What happened while I was gone? Was I wrong to be gone so long?"

She broke down, crying harder. Then she sat up in a heap, putting her arms on her knees with her head between them. She lifted her face to him and he began wiping away her tears again, with his hand. He asked in real fear,

"What is it, sweetheart? Please tell me."

She extended her left arm in front of him, and he saw the mark of a deep wound on her wrist. In shock, he asked,

"What's this?"

She burst out crying again. "I tried to commit suicide."

He felt shock and confusion. He gathered her into his arms, rocking her, in pain for her sake. He said,

"Your stepfather, again?"

Weeping, she answered, "He took advantage of my mother being in the hospital to give birth. He came into my room when I was asleep. He wanted to rape me."

He shouted, "The dirty bastard! He went that far!"

She nodded in terror. "I had put a knife under my pillow, I was expecting it. But instead of stabbing him with it I slashed my wrist."

She threw herself into his arms, weeping. He was stunned, and felt as if he was bound to explode in his anger against this stepfather of hers. Moments passed. When she stopped sobbing he asked her,

"Who saved you?"

"He did. He yelled and bound up my wrist while I was lying where I fell on the floor. He jumped up and called an ambulance. He made out a report saying that he had come home and found me trying to commit suicide and he saved me."

Hasan was determined and resolute. "This man has to be killed, he has to disappear from this world. And I'm going to do it."

"And lose your life for a dog? What would happen to me, after that?"

He couldn't keep himself from crying. But soon he stopped, and asked,

"Why didn't you tell the police everything?"

"You don't know the position my mother is in. She's alone and he's brainwashed her—she no longer believes anyone else. My mother has started wearing the face veil, she's almost the first one in Alexandria to wear it. And now he's had a baby with her." She wept as she went on, "We have to leave Egypt, Hasan."

He took her in his arms again. "We will leave, sweetheart. Egypt has left us, now, left her history, and she will be gone for many years. I see her now riding a camel in the desert with a group of outlaws. Yes, outlaws! But there will be retribution for the one who pushed her on that road. President Sadat, the one who opened the door to all of this."

They were not able to make love.

Hasan started his way to Mansura that night from the Sidi Gabir station. Before he left her he said, "I'm thinking about transferring to the Humanities College in Cairo, and about you transferring with me. We'll get married there and look for work, we have to find work while we study. That will save you, too."

She smiled. "There's a year left, sweetheart. Don't worry. Forgive me if I spoiled your day. I couldn't wait for you to come so I could cry on your shoulder. Don't be afraid for me. Now he knows what I can do to him, I think he'll give me a long truce."

Hasan took her in his arms in the darkness and kissed her, then got into the car that would take him to Tanta; from there he would take another car to Mansura.

She stood in the wide open space, amid the darkness untouched by the distant streetlamps. She felt as if she were the daughter of the sky whom God had just now placed on earth, and no one would be able to harm her.

The next day Nadir arrived in Cairo, and emerged from the train station to see Ramses Square before him for the first time. He was jolted by the scene and stood still, instantly thinking about going back to Alexandria. He didn't believe his eyes, and he could feel the beating of his heart. All this expanse and all these people and all these cars and this raised iron overpass that enclosed the square, a huge overpass that added to the grim appearance of the place, which didn't have a single tree! The sky was broad, the sunlight was strong, and the intense heat burned his face and arms, since he was wearing pants and a short-sleeved shirt. He could feel it entering his body. Many people stood under the roof of the metro station waiting for the arrival of the train that traveled above ground. Around and among them moved people selling Coca-Cola, Pepsi, and other cold drinks from pails, and most of the people standing there were drinking these carbonated beverages. On his right were restaurants for broad beans, and couscous, and rice pudding, and falafel, and potatoes; they were all displaying their wares before him in the shop windows, while most of the food was being sold by the peddlers who stood in the square. The statue of Ramses stood silently holding his crown high, looking forward confidently, unconcerned with his surroundings, as sprays of water from the fountain in the base below him extended only a small distance. If Ramses only knew what was happening around him! Nadir shook his head and decided he would hold in his spirit this sudden longing to return to Alexandria, after Cairo had frightened him like this, but first he would complete his trip. He would rethink the matter of moving here to work after graduation.

It was now two in the afternoon, and his appointment with the girl who would give him the Party magazines and publications was for seven, in the Cleopatra Casino restaurant in Zamalek. He would see Zamalek, about which he had heard so much in movies, and he would see the Aquarium Grotto Garden, but on another visit. Now he had to go to the *Vanguard* magazine in the building of the *al-Ahram* newspaper. Here was Galaa Street as Bishr had told him, repeating everything Hasan had passed on to him from Khalil, who had given the directions.

He plunged into the crowd of pedestrians on the sidewalk, the aroma of food from the shops and peddlers wafting over him as he walked. He said to himself that this was an excellent place for infection, looking at the tall piles of falafel rising before him in every shop. In Alexandria they ate it hot, and the seller didn't fry more than what the customers ordered. On his way he didn't find any pedestrians who respected the traffic signals. On the street corners in Alexandria girls from the high schools and colleges now volunteered to direct traffic. It was a nice accomplishment for the governor, who had started out by destroying Lake Maryut! In fact it was an old accomplishment, from the sixties, that had reappeared. The beautiful girls all wore short gray skirts and white blouses with sleeves, and on the head of each was a gray cap bearing the emblem of the traffic division. Who in this world wouldn't obey beautiful girls?

He arrived at the *al-Ahram* building and stood thinking in front of the broad, stately glass door. This was the new building of the venerable newspaper, erected a short time before when Mohamed Hassanein Heikal had been the editor, and it was truly a fitting building for the newspaper. The security guard told him how to reach the office of the *Vanguard* magazine's literary critic, a man whose writing he had previously read and liked.

The door of the office was open so Nadir went in, finding the important critic before him, behind a broad desk. Around him were books on the floor, books on shelves on the wall, and books in several cases; there were also a lot of books and folders on the desk. The critic was wearing thick glasses. He raised his head and asked, "Yes?"

"Are you Ustaz Farouk Abdel Qadir, sir?" he asked nervously, but the critic said, "Who else would it be? Have a seat, why are you standing?"

Nadir sat down and opened the *Rose al-Yusuf* magazine he had with him and took out two sheets of paper on which a poem of his was written. He said in embarrassment,

"I'm a poet from Alexandria. My name is Nadir Saeed. This is a poem I hope will have the luck of being published in the magazine."

The critic stared at him, his eyes widening in surprise as he took the paper from him. He asked,

"Have you published anything before?"

"This is the first time. I never tried . . . ."

"The first time, and you want to publish in *The Vanguard*?"

Nadir was thrown into confusion. What could he say to him? That he was a Marxist and that this magazine was the most fitting for him, because it was the magazine of Marxists in politics and of new directions in literature, that he knew the names of all its writers and read them? Or should he say he was in a secret Communist party? He said nothing, and was surprised to see the critic put his papers into a folder on his right. Abdel Qadir stood up and said, "The best thing would be for you to come with me to the Café Riche. I'll buy you a beer and we can talk in comfort."

Nadir felt some comfort and some pride, and forgot his idea that the critic might read the poem and tell him what he thought of it right away. The critic left the office and Nadir went out behind him. In Galaa Street the critic stopped a taxi and got in next to the driver while Nadir sat in the back, silent since the critic said nothing. The taxi moved off and on their left a metro train was moving to its last stop at the Nile Corniche. When the taxi turned to go into Tahrir Square Nadir saw a large building on his right, and the critic said, "That's the Egyptian Museum. Other than that I won't tell you anything."

He smiled, surprised at the man's manner of speaking. The square appeared before him; the taxi would circle it to go into Talaat Harb Street. He asked,

"This is Tahrir Square, right?"

"Naturally." The critic answered him in surprise.

Nadir was overwhelmed by the size of the square, He saw the Hilton Hotel on his right in the distance, and in front of him were many standing buses and a crowd of people. He saw the government office building, the Mugamma of Tahrir, as the taxi turned into the square; he recognized it from what he had read about Cairo in the newspapers. He also saw the stone "cake" or traffic circle on his left as the taxi approached the entrance to Talaat Harb Street, a cake that Amal Donqol had made a symbol of the Revolution that no one could forget. He cried enthusiastically, "This round stone base is the 'stone cake,' right?"

"Yes, sir. But Amal was referring to the demonstrators who surrounded it. The base has its own story. Long ago it was supposed to be the base of a statue of Khedive Ismail. He died before the statue was erected. After the death of Abdel Nasser they covered it with marble to be the base of a statue of him. Sadat stopped the project."

Nadir thought about why Amal Donqol had called it a stone cake. Was it because it was round or because those who came to it savored the taste of freedom? Maybe the latter, since this place had witnessed a long history of national protests.

But he was surprised by the high iron overpass that surrounded the square. He exclaimed, "An overpass here too! It spoils it."

The critic replied, "Asses, may they keep away from you. Our rulers are asses who spoil everything."

They alighted in front of the Café Riche, where tables and chairs were placed in a small passageway. On the left there was a little cigarette stand whose owner was inside it, only his face appearing. The critic pointed to the people sitting at the large table just beyond the sidewalk and asked, as he paid the taxi driver, "Have you ever seen them?"

"No."

"Come on."

He went up to them and sat down, saying as he pointed them out, "Amal Donqol, Naguib Surur, Sulaiman Fayyad. You know them, of course?"

Nadir was mortified. These were the authors whose writing he was mad about. He said nothing and the critic said, "Pull up a chair and sit with us." Nadir sat down, unable to speak. The critic introduced him, "Nadir Saeed, a poet from Alexandria."

No one answered. Naguib Surur seemed preoccupied with looking at the street, and Amal Donqol gave a little smile that showed his large teeth. But Sulaiman Fayyad said, "Welcome. I used to be a teacher long ago in the Abbasiya Secondary School in Alexandria."

The waiter came; he was over fifty, and he rattled the silver coins in his pocket. The important critic ordered two bottles of beer. There was more than one empty bottle on the table in front of them, along with three other bottles from which they filled their glasses. Suddenly Naguib Surur's smile broadened and his eyes flashed; a girl was hurrying past them, dressed in a miniskirt and a blouse that revealed her arms, a purse hanging from her shoulder and her long hair flying out behind her. "A filly!" he cried in enthusiastic admiration.

Nadir wondered at him and his gazes. The waiter came back with the beer, which he put before him and the critic. He placed two glasses in front of them and then stood rattling the metal coins in his pocket, and Naguib Surur burst out angrily, "Whenever you come over you stand there rattling coins. Do we owe you money? Do us a favor and go away, do your work somewhere else!"

The waiter withdrew, raising his eyebrows. "Right away, Naguib Bey, I apologize."

Sulaiman Fayyad whispered, "It's just a habit of his, Naguib. I've told you a hundred times."

"No, he only does that in front of us. He knows we're broke. Every time he gets his money twice over.... Fuck."

Nadir was astounded at what he was hearing. It was something he had never expected to hear from important writers he loved.

Amal smiled, showing his teeth: "In a while Felfel will come, Naguib, and relieve you of Malik."

From that Nadir learned the names of the current waiter and the absent one. But Naguib's eye had fallen on another beautiful girl passing in front of them. "A gazelle!" he smiled.

The important critic said to Nadir, "Naguib Surur is just like that. Drink up and don't worry about it, you'll get used to it."

But Naguib looked sharply at the critic. "What was that, you little mama's boy? What'd you mean, 'Naguib Surur is just like that'? Oh, 'cause Sadat's Lutfi al-Khuli appointed you at *al-Ahram*!"

Nadir's amazement verged on real horror. Silence settled over them all. But Naguib smiled and said to Nadir,

"I'm sorry, don't be upset." Then, angry again, "Do you have bloody bastards for critics in Alexandria the way we do here?"

Nadir was even more horrified, and he blushed. Amal Donqol shook his head while Sulaiman Fayyad smiled more broadly, as if what was happening was normal. But shock and silence settled over Nadir, and the critic rose, saying to him, "Let's go sit inside, we'll be able to talk more easily." He picked up the beer and the glass. Nadir stood up in confusion but then he did likewise, following him to the interior section of the café.

There he saw a number of large photographs of writers and artists who had passed away, and he realized immediately that they had been among the customers of the venerable café. He started looking at them, and then drew closer, passing before them all in amazement. The pictures did not differ from those he had previously seen of some of them in newspapers, but here their eyes expressed contentment and tranquility. There was a veil of calm over their faces even though their lives had been filled with storms. Al-Aqqad, who had gone through major intellectual and political battles. Blind Taha Hussein, who had seen what the sighted did not in the past, the present, and the future. Naguib al-Rihani, Anwar Wagdi, Husayn Riyad, artists who had filled the lives of Egyptians with delight. With them were the handsome Suleiman Naguib as well as Stefan Rosty, who monopolized the viewer's attention whenever he appeared.

The two directors Mahmud and Ezzeldin Zulfiqar. God, how had the world gotten along without these treasures? Nadir went to stand in front of others, pictures of important poets. Salih Gawdet, whose songs he loved without liking his position regarding the left. Kamal al-Shinnawi, who wrote songs only the heavens could hold. The novelist Abbas Ahmad, author of the beautiful novel, *The Town*. Umm Kulthum—he couldn't believe she was gone, for here she was sitting in the picture, leaning back in her seat with a serenity she transmitted to all who saw her. And others, many others. He decided he would take time to look at them when he came again.

He returned to the important critic, who seemed to be completely preoccupied as he drank his beer. Contrary to what Nadir expected, there was no long conversation between them. The critic did not ask him about his poetry, for example, or when he began to write it, or what he read, or which poets he liked; the critic was alone with his beer. Then he invited him to lunch also, telling him to try the *escalope Riche*. He ordered another beer, but Nadir stopped at one. He asked the critic how to get to Zamalek, and he told him that the street behind them was Huda Shaarawi, at the end of which was the Ministry of Endowments. Next to that was a stop for the number 13 bus, which would take him to Zamalek. Nadir left at about five. How had all that time passed in silence? Nadir had no idea.

He asked the conductor about the way to the Casino Cleopatra, and he told him to get off at Hasan Sabri Street, near the building where Abdel Halim Hafiz lived. He would walk in the street in front of it, finding the second turnoff to the Nile, and there he would find the Casino. Nadir was happy when he got off near Abdel Halim Hafiz's house, and he began to stroll a little in the streets of Zamalek, without straying far so he wouldn't lose his way. He admired the trees and the old buildings. The people he saw were splendidly dressed, and although there weren't many women in the streets, the ones he saw were beautiful. At five minutes after seven he entered the Casino, which stretched lengthwise along the Nile. There were only eight customers seated at four tables, each pair made up of a young man and a girl. There was one girl sitting alone at a distance at whose feet he saw a leather bag, so he thought she was the one he was to meet. He went forward a little toward her and saw the *Rose al-Yusuf* magazine also on the table, so he smiled as he put down the magazine he had been carrying in front of him.

"Hani," he said, using his movement name.

"Wafaa," she smiled.

He sat down. He was attracted by her beauty; she had a dark complexion, green eyes, a round face, and firm, full lips. Her thick, black hair hung down her back and over her shoulders. Were all the girls in the Party this beautiful?

He asked, "May I take the bag?"

She smiled. "Wait a little, so it doesn't look as if you only came for that."

He realized his foolishness, but he was still cheerful. He was going to sit with her for some time. Zamalek, the Nile, and a real mulatto girl who was splendidly beautiful, in Cairo!

She said, "Order something for us from the waiter, you're the man. But it's my treat."

He smiled and ordered ice cream for them both. He learned that she liked Alexandria but that she had never gone there, because her father liked vacationing at Ras al-Bar. He told her that one day she would come to Alexandria, she had to, and the city would be delighted with her. She laughed and blushed in embarrassment, and covered her mouth with her hand. He found himself saying, "It's funny how two people can meet without knowing anything about each other except their movement names. It's like being in a movie."

She laughed again. Clearly she always covered her mouth with her hand when she laughed, even though her beautiful teeth were gleaming white. She said she was a student in the College of Languages and lived in Maadi and that she would not say any more than that, so he told her that he was a student in the College of Humanities and lived in Maks and would not say any more, either. They both smiled. He asked her how to get to Ramses from there, and she said the best way was to take a taxi; she would get off in Tahrir, and he could continue to Ramses.

They left the restaurant. She picked up the bag and allowed him to take it from her. In the taxi she sat in front while he was in back with the bag. She got out in Tahrir Square, and he felt how beautiful she was, and how beautiful the day had been. It was 9:30; they had sat talking for a long time without noticing, chatting about life, culture, and learning.

On the 10:30 train he told himself that Cairo really was best for him as a writer, not Alexandria. What he had seen today of its major writers didn't mean anything else. They were strange, nonconformists, therefore they were real writers. I'm strange, so I exist. Naguib Surur, who wrote shocking plays, was like that, and so was Amal Donqol, author of timeless poems. So was Sulaiman Fayyad, who looked older, and who wrote splendid stories and novels, and so was Farouk Abdel Qadir, the author of articles of criticism shaded with the politics of total refusal. He forgot his previous thought of not leaving Alexandria. Carrying the bag, he had lost all his fear.

The bag contained fifty copies of the magazine *The Victory*, the secret publication of the Party, and twenty copies of the magazine *Egyptian Writing*, which came out in Beirut, as he had learned from Bishr and from Wafaa. *The Victory* had no more than sixteen pages, but *Egyptian Writing* was a real magazine, with more than a hundred pages. Still the bag was not large and did not attract attention. He would treat it as if it were a suitcase of clothes. In fact he put it on the shelf above him in the air-conditioned train, and was careful not to doze off during the four stops the train made, so that no one who got off at that station would mistakenly take it, or steal it, who knew?

He was overcome by fear only in the Sidi Gabir station. Wherever would he go now, with what he was carrying? Should he go home, to Maks? He rejected that idea, since his little brother might fiddle with the bag, and he was in the first year of middle school and could read. Maybe the police had been following him all day. This time he would go the apartment on Tanais Street. It was after midnight, and none of his roommates would be there. Hasan must have left Alexandria, and even if he was there, he was a comrade.

He would climb the stairs quietly so Rawayih and Ghada wouldn't hear him, if they weren't in the nightclub . . . .

He went up the stairs slowly, without a sound. He turned the key gently in the lock and went in, breathing a sigh of relief. He put the bag in front of him on the dining table and sat down in front of it. However had he made it to Alexandria? But quickly he picked up the case and put it under the bed in his room. He opened the window overlooking the street; no one was there, now. He would take off his clothes and smoke a cigarette on the bed, reviewing the whole day. But no sooner had he put on his pajamas than the bell to the apartment rang.

He froze. That was the bell. Rawayih and Ghada knocked on the door, they didn't ring the bell. Bishr had the key and so did Hasan, if he were here. Nadir took his time, and the bell rang again, and then again. . . .

He went out to the living room and stood looking at the door. Then he heard Rawayih's voice: "Open up, Si Bishr. We heard your footsteps."

He sighed in relief and opened the door. As soon as they saw him they exclaimed, "Si Nadir! We apologize, we thought you were Bishr."

"It doesn't matter, please come in."

They were wearing summery nightgowns that showed their arms and a large part of their chests. It occurred to him immediately that they might be a refuge for him from his fear, if only for a time.

The sat before him and then said nothing, for several long moments. He expected that one of them would ask him to write a letter for her, especially as they hadn't seen him or any of his roommates for a long time, but then Rawayih said sadly, "Sheikh Zaalan has bought the other club, the one we worked in."

Ghada added, "That was a month ago. We couldn't find work in any other club, so we went to work in a new café on the sea that doesn't serve alcohol. We decided to repent, since everybody was saying that. But the owner harasses us every night, after the café closes."

He looked at them with real sympathy. "Why don't you work in the café during the day?"

"He refuses. He says that the customers who come at night like female waiters, and of course you know that café customers aren't like cabaret customers, I mean, the tips are pennies. We accepted it, and thought that maybe our fate is to live a clean life."

Rawayih showed more emotion that Ghada. Tears began to well in her eyes as she said, "Can you help us? Talk to Madam Nawal, the owner of the Nawal Boîte, ask if we can work for her. She's a respectable lady and known all over Egypt. I know she likes you, you're all always saying that about her."

He smiled. "That's easy, but what matters is that she not sell her club too."

They smiled, but then Rawayih said, bewildered, "We never learned any other profession. We've accepted clean living but nobody gives us the chance. If it's got to be sin then let it be with real customers, and not with the café owner, and for free." She was silent for a bit, looking at the floor, and then added, "God forgive us."

They stood to go but he said, "Wait, spend the night with me here."

"With you, Si Nadir? We know you're in love!"

"I don't mean anything, sleep in another room. I need company with me in the apartment, I'm not used to sleeping alone in this place."

In the morning he woke around ten, and found them sitting on two chairs in front of the bed. They were wearing house dresses and each had her hand on her cheek, looking at him. He opened his eyes and said in surprise, from the bed, "What happened?"

"Nothing. We've made breakfast for you. We were afraid to wake you up, since it seems you're really tired."

He smiled, amazed by their delicacy. He got up and went to the bathroom, and then saw a lovely breakfast on the dining table: boiled eggs, soft white cheese, sharp hard cheese, honey, jam, and bread. "All this?" he wondered.

Rawayih answered, "We went downstairs and bathed and changed our clothes, and brought up breakfast. What do you think of it?"

He kissed each of them on the cheek, not believing what had happened. He remembered also that during the time they had lived there the two woment had often prepared food for them at their own expense. They said, "The apartment is really dirty. Do you mind if we clean it, if you're going out?" He nodded, agreeing.

An hour later he had eaten breakfast, bathed, and shaved. He picked up the case and went out, leaving them in the living room. He made his way to the Annah Café in Anfushi, carrying the same issue of *Rose al-Yusuf*. He would find an organization official there carrying that same issue. To his surprise the person he found sitting in the interior of the café with that issue in front of him was Bishr Zahran. He stopped in confusion, so Bishr said, "Come on over, Hani."

He was even more surprised. Bishr stood up and extended his hand, introducing himself as if he didn't know him: "Amir."

"Your movement name?" he blurted.

Bishr looked around him anxiously. "Shut up, damn you."

Nadir sat down, bewildered. After a few minutes he asked Bishr why he had chosen this distant café, and he told him that the customers there were all fishermen, with no intellectuals, artists, or students who would know them and have a lot of questions about the case and what was in it. Well, why didn't he take the bag from him in the apartment, for example? Bishr said that this was better—no one would expect them to meet here.

Nadir was having a hard time keeping himself from laughing; finally he left the bag and went off. When he was well away he laughed heartily, not believing what had happened. Two friends talking with their movement names, madness!

The world witnessed many events, as did Alexandria. Nadir began to meet Yara every other week in the apartment on Tanais Street, and his spirit opened to writing poetry. He learned from the security guard who stood in front of the Nawal Boîte nightclub that Nawal was in Paris and would return in October; it was a long vacation, this time. When September came the numbers of summer vacationers in the city diminished. The wind ran free in Khalid ibn al-Walid Street after the vacationers left and the shops closed, and it seemed like real devastation. The number of microphones broadcasting the call to prayer increased in the poor neighborhoods of Alexandria, and unregulated housing extended to areas no one expected, such as Hannauxville in Agami and between there and Bitash. Whenever anyone built a house without a permit from the quarter, against building regulations, he would put a little Friday mosque on the first floor—in reality not a Friday mosque but a small chapel—and the doorman would give the call to prayer even if there were no residents there. The authorities were helpless to inflict any punishment on them, because Sadat had issued a law exempting houses and apartment buildings with Friday mosques below them from any building violations. At the same time he kept on clamoring in his speeches for a stop to the fighting in Lebanon, although the fighting did not stop. Isa Salamawy was still going around Alexandria perfecting his knowledge of the art of Italian architecture. The Concordia Cinema on Chamber of Commerce Street was destroyed to make way for a large apartment building. Mao Tse Tung died, the man who was the leader of the Chinese Communist Party, the founder of Communist China, and the instigator of what was known everywhere as the Cultural Revolution in 1966. The Cultural Revolution was never mentioned when Isa spoke with his students, because he considered Mao Tse Tung and his ideas a deviation from Leninist Marxism.

The month of Ramadan began along with September and the beaches were nearly empty, except for a small number of vacationers, usually sitting under umbrellas. A few girls still went into the water in bathing suits, Alexandrians or visitors from Cairo who preferred to avoid the crowds of July and August. Many were seen having the iftar meal on the beach. They put out plastic tables with the food on them and sat around them on chairs also made of plastic, which had now become numerous on the beaches.

During Nadir's last meeting with Yara in the apartment she said with a smile, "Summer's over and you didn't come to Stanley or see me in my bathing suit."

She was naked beside him. He smiled. "I told you I always go to Maks Beach."

She said with a chuckle, "I don't believe you. How can it be a beach when everyone who goes there is a carriage driver washing off the horses and donkeys?"

"That's what it's become, but long ago it was a beach for relaxation and for therapy too. There were foreigners in Alexandria; I was little, but I remember that. Even the wooden cabins that are in Maks now used to belong to Greeks, and others. They sold them for the land rights, and then they left the city."

"Don't you go to any other beach, sometimes?"

"Sometimes I go with my friends to Agami and we sit on the public beach, because Bianchi has become a private beach."

She cried, "Bianchi! That's the most beautiful beach. There are artists there too. Abdel Halim Hafiz and Fatin Hamama and even Salih Salim the soccer player."

"How do you know? Did you go there?"

"My brother tells me about it." She laughed. "And of course there are a lot of bikinis there."

He smiled. "I go to that beach via the water, because they've put a rope barrier between it and the public beach. I walk among the bikinis when the girls are sleeping. Can you imagine, the women stretch out on their bellies and unhook the bra strap from behind so the sun will reach the place of that thin line."

She laughed and poked his chest. "So you know everything! That's why you didn't come to Stanley."

He grinned and took her in his arms, kissing her reverently. He said, "I dream of a day when I'll have the power to fly away with you in the sky, to go around the world with you. We would see the white snow on the mountains, we would see the trees in the forests, and birds we don't know, and rivers and falls and seas. . . ."

She laughed and said, "I dream of a day when we'll have a home that everyone knows is ours alone and where no one comes uninvited."

7

KARIMAN SAT WAITING TO GO in. The appointment was for eight in the evening and it was already almost nine. As usual when they summoned someone, they left him prey to his anxious thoughts and apprehensions, so that when he went in and faced the official he would not know what to expect. It was a cheap, well-worn tactic known to everyone who dealt with them. That's what she told herself as she smoked continuously, taking the package of cigarettes and the lighter out of her purse and putting them back. After three cigarettes in a row she put the package and the lighter on the small table in front of her. The seats were leather, it was true, but cold seeped from the floor tiles into her legs, even though it was the last day of September and winter had not yet arrived. She heard the sound of women screaming, without being able to tell where it came from; it rose in volume at times and at others subsided into moaning. It must be the sounds that Nadir had told them about. Even though there was an ashtray on the table in front of her, she threw the cigarette butts on the floor and stamped them out with her shoes.

Suddenly a young man with a dark complexion emerged from a door she had not seen, coming toward her and motioning for her to go in. At that moment she was overcome by a feeling of tranquility, even though she was about to meet the head of the State Security apparatus, Sayyid Bey Abdel Bari, famed throughout the city. What mattered was that she was going in and her wait was over, whatever happened. They had summoned Nadir before, but Bishr was the one they had arrested.

She gently pushed the door open, without knocking. She did not notice the size of the room, only the man sitting at some distance, behind his large desk. She remembered what Nadir had said about how he looked like the barber in Maks; she hadn't seen that barber before, but she saw that the man's face looked unexpectedly kind. He said,

"Welcome, Miss Kariman." He stood and extended his hand. He genuinely seemed to admire her, perhaps because she was wearing a handsome suit.

She did not shake his hand. Instead she sat down, suddenly nervous, and asked, "Please, could you stop the sound of the screaming that I've been hearing since I arrived?"

He seemed unconcerned, withdrawing his hand quickly as if he had never extended it, and sat down. "What screaming?"

She said sharply, "The women's screams."

"I don't hear a thing."

"I hear it. Please stop it, if you want me to answer your questions." Suddenly she was struck by amazement, realizing that the sound had been cut off while she was speaking. He said, smiling, "I don't know what you're talking about. I really don't hear a thing."

She shook her head, having understood something: someone was listening to their conversation. All at once she felt as if she were about to go crazy, and she had to hide that with as much strength as she could muster.

Almost in a whisper, he said, "Miss Kariman, are you suffering from something? From a mental condition, I mean?"

She pressed her lips together and looked at him, stating calmly, "I'm fine, and at your disposal. Please ask your questions."

He shook his head, feigning surprise. He reached over the desk and took from it several postcard-sized pictures, extracting one from among them and giving it to her. She took it and looked at it, as he said, "Without doubt you know her."

"Of course. It's Yara, my friend and classmate."

"Splendid! She's also our friend."

She looked at him in disdain, understanding the trap that was being laid for her. Before she said anything he continued, "She's going to graduate this year, and so are you. She will be appointed as an assistant in the Philosophy Department. What do you think of that?" She looked at him indifferently and he went on: "Becoming an assistant is the ideal path toward a doctorate and becoming a professor afterward. Of course you know that." Again she did not answer. He said, "You'll be disappointed, and you'll ask me how two assistants could be appointed in a single philosophy department. That's our business. We will choose another university for you, maybe the University of Tanta, which is new, or Cairo." He fell silent for a moment, looking at her searchingly. Then he said, "Personally, I would prefer the University of Cairo for you, or even Asyut, since there are problems between you and your mother's husband."

At that she closed her eyes in pain, feeling very angry. The dark young man she had seen before came in carrying a large glass of lemonade. He put it down in front of her and then went out. Sayyid Bey Abdel Bari ignored her for a few moments, leafing through some papers in front of him and reading them. Her chest rose and fell in anger, and she was exerting great effort not to allow any tears to fall. He said,

"Drink your lemonade, don't be upset. We know everything, not just about you but about all the students. Your stepfather is in the Islamic Group, the Gama‘a, and you're a Communist, so of course there are problems between you." He lowered his voice and said, smiling, "And then too, you're very beautiful, and those people love beautiful girls."

"Please!" she said angrily.

He said quickly, "Nadir was here too, last year, and refused to cooperate with us. Of course you know that. He didn't refuse flatly, so we'll leave him for a little while. We didn't call in Bishr because he won't cooperate, he'll continue as he is. Maybe if we arrest him another time he'll be easier. Hasan, just because he's your boyfriend, we'll call him in someday without arresting him. What's important is for you to cooperate with us." He stood up and came around the desk. "We're not opposed to love, by the way. That's the way things are with Nadir and Yara. But we will help you to a happy ending."

She looked at him ironically, and with unexpected courage she said, "Sir, you are talking to me about very strange things! What love, and what assistantship? I can believe you when you say that my stepfather is a member of the Gama'a Islamiya, but not about anything else."

In a very calm voice he asked, "Fine. And Khalil?"

She was confused. He went on: "Khalil is his movement name. He's a literary critic and a translator whose name is Asim Bahgat, isn't that so?"

She kept her composure and said, "I don't know anyone by the name of Khalil or Asim Bahgat."

At that his face showed fury. He returned to his seat and was silent for several long moments, then he smiled and changed the subject:

"You really are very beautiful, Miss Kariman, I can't sit still in your presence. I can't bear the thought that this beauty could be exposed to ill treatment the way Suad Hosni was, for example. You must have seen the film."

She shook her head. "That was in the days of Gamal Abdel Nasser. President Sadat has forbidden torture."

He laughed so loudly that she was momentarily terrified. Then he reached for a small, velvet-covered box on his right, took out a piece of chocolate, and offered it to her. She looked at him with confidence and took it, as he took another piece and put it in his mouth.

"Since you took the chocolate, there's still hope. It's true that President Sadat has forbidden torture, but who can guarantee how long that will last? The officers in the prisons are still officers, and State Security is still State Security. Will you permit me to ask a question?"

"You ask and speak as you wish, sir."

"Do you know the secret slogan of the Communist movement?"

She shrugged. "Not even the public one."

He said, "The slogan, madam—no offense—is 'Chat, then the cherry.'" She was clearly shaken, so he went on, "You're obviously naive. Chat with the girl about joining the party, then pluck her cherry."

She raised her voice: "If you please!"

He put his head in his hand and said, mocking her,

"I'm sorry. But would you like me to tell you how many beautiful girls have been deceived?"

All at once she was unable to control her tears. "If you please! For shame."

He handed her a tissue from a box in front of him and said, "Dry your tears. It's true that the world has changed, Kariman, but time can turn back."

Great courage suddenly came over her, after she dried her tears. She said, "I won't be afraid, and you, sir, won't make me afraid, and you won't get anything out of me."

"I'm opening a path of honor for you, Miss Kariman. At the least I'll relieve you of your stepfather."

"He's an insignificant man who doesn't matter to me at all. You can throw him on any trash heap. Or is he working with you, is he the one who led you to me?"

"He will work with us sooner or later, but you are what matters. Don't answer yes or no now; you can leave and think it over at leisure, we aren't in a hurry. I hope you won't try to commit suicide again." Before she could answer he said, smiling, "Goodbye, Miss Kariman."

She stood up quickly and he said, "In two days the new school year will begin, and three months later comes the beginning of January. Give my greetings to Ahmad Fouad Negm."

She moved to leave. She realized that he was alluding to the poet's famous song, "When the Good News Comes in January Every Year," where he talks about the repeated arrests of Communists every January.

She emerged from the rear door of the building to find herself in Faraana Street, surrounded by darkness, the weak light of the street lamps, and a cold but refreshing breeze. She took a deep breath, and walked resolutely away.

Bishr said to them proudly, "That's what I told you, too. That's absolutely correct. We're at the end of October."

It was around five in the afternoon. They knew that Ahmad Basim would come home late, as happened frequently now. He would go out in the evening with prayer beads in his hand, having put on a white gallabiya with a white kuffiyeh on his head, and not return until very late. They had learned that he would be late if he went out in a gallabiya. He now spoke to them very little, telling them that the best thing in the world was for a man to know his Lord. He did not oppose them in what they were doing, or discuss it with them. The schedule of women and girls was as it had been except for their number; now there were only three, who came on three different days of the week. He put on a gallabiya on those days too, but without leaving the apartment. His beard had also grown longer than before. All of this had happened without preamble. When the year-end vacation was over, he had returned to the apartment in a new state.

The pages of the magazines were spread out on the dining table, and they were waiting for Yara and Kariman to come. Now there was no longer any reason for shame, since each of them knew that the other came with her boyfriend, and the two lovers knew. Bishr knew also but he acted as if he didn't know, and anyway they all trusted him. He was the one responsible for contacting the Party, or at least the one who connected the regional official with Nadir, who was going to leave once again to collect new issues of the Party magazines.

The bell rang, and Hasan and Nadir smiled. Bishr looked at them, pleased, and then whispered, "This is a meeting for work. Don't anyone ask me to leave."

Hasan smiled his half smile, and Nadir grinned as he opened the door. When he saw the two his heart raced, beating in joy. He shook their hands without kissing Yara, although that was hard for him. How he would like to give her a real kiss! She looked more beautiful today than ever before.

Yara had learned of what had happened to Kariman in the State Security investigations, and she had decided to respond to it by being with them everywhere. Nadir didn't like it. She knew that they were editing a new magazine, and she had decided not to limit herself to giving Nadir her articles for it, but also to produce it with them, just as Kariman would do. This was the only answer to State Security. "I won't let them drive a wedge between us!" she said, with determination and innocence beyond anything Nadir had expected.

Now Bishr said, "Since Yara is true to her word and has decided to go into battle with us, no one can defeat us!" Then he motioned to Nadir to follow him into another room, and as soon as they went in, he asked him,

"Does Yara know that you are in a secret party?"

"No. I'm really afraid for her."

"Don't be afraid, she's more courageous than us all. Don't think about her innocence; she knows what she wants and how to make sacrifices. What do you say to taking her into the Party with us?"

"No, please, not now. What Yara's doing is a simple, spontaneous reaction to hearing from Kariman what the chief investigator said about her. Yara's not made for political work, Bishr."

Bishr shook his head and said sadly, "It's true that she's more delicate than a butterfly. Come on, let's go back."

They went back to the living room and sat with the others at the table. Bishr immediately said, "Yara, I want to speak frankly with you. Your presence with us here or anywhere means that you are our comrade in the Party."

Nadir shot him a look filled with fury and said, warningly, "Bishr, I beg of you!"

But Bishr answered, "Nadir, I beg of you! Yara has to know everything. She should not be liable for any action for which she hasn't accepted responsibility."

Yara blushed and looked very confused, so Bishr said to her, "My dear Yara, we are members of a secret Communist party." Nadir ground his teeth in fury as Bishr continued, "The name of it is the Egyptian Communist Party."

Hasan said, "Bishr is right, Nadir."

Nadir didn't answer; he looked down, still furious. Bishr said, "If they arrest us that will implicate you, because you're always with us, and we're inseparable from you."

Yara smiled and then looked lovingly at Nadir. "I felt that instinctively. I'm with you in everything."

Silence descended on them and they seemed surprised, looking at each other in disbelief. Bishr said, "Then Nadir will tell you about the Party and its goals later on, and give you some printed matter about it. From now on your movement name will be 'Fatin,' though of course you won't use it among us, since we know each other." He looked at Nadir, smiling, as if he didn't want him to mention the day they had met in the Annah Café, when Bishr had used movement names. "But you will if you contact others from different cells, outside our student cell in the Humanities College. Our cell still only has the four of us, Hasan, Kariman, Nadir, and me. And now we are five."

But Yara said, smiling, "Fatin Hamama! Then Nadir should be Omar Sharif."

They laughed aloud, as Nadir's fury turned into confusion and acceptance. He looked at her as if he were apologizing for what had happened. She said, "Don't worry about me, dear, I'm stronger than you think. I can take responsibility along with you, anywhere."

They went on for two hours, during which they put in place a plan to contact other students, both in their college and in others as well. They decided that Nadir should join the literary club at the Culture of Freedom Palace in order to recruit other writers, and Hasan also should start going back to the theater group at the Palace with the same goal, and forget about what had happened with his play. They decided to read and discuss four books every month, here or anywhere else they might choose. "We want to shake the throne of the 'believing president,'" said Bishr, amid their laughter. They decided to tear down any of the posters they could that called for the hijab, removing them from the walls of Alexandria, and to erase the slogans written on the walls that called for it too. Since the long discussion had taken so much time they decided to finish writing the magazines three days later. Nadir would get Yara's articles from her, and Hasan would do the same with Kariman. That wasn't what the girls wanted, but there was no call for them to come here every time, just for the weekly meeting.

All at once Nadir said, "I'll bring you some poems from a poet no one knows, who was killed in the Oases Prison in the sixties, under torture."

Yara closed her eyes, moved by what she heard. Hasan asked, "How did you find out about that?"

"Nawal has an old notebook with all of his poems in it."

Bishr laughed, "Nawal Boîte! What's she got to do with it? Was she in prison without our knowing about it?"

Nadir answered, "She was in an old Communist cell too." They all stared at him in surprise. He said, "It's a long story that I'll tell you someday."

Bishr exclaimed, "Oh my god! Is that why we love her?"

"Precisely."

Hasan said, with his small smile, "A Communist and a nightclub owner! Strange."

Bishr mused, "We haven't gone to see her for a long time."

Nadir noticed that Kariman was looking at Yara, who seemed suddenly thoughtful. He took Yara's hand and kissed it, saying "There's no one in my life but Yara."

But Hasan said abruptly, "We have to find a way to get Ahmad out of the apartment! He shouldn't go on living with us. I don't like the way he grows his beard or his constant silence or the prayer beads in his hand. Something in him has changed."

Bishr said, "What you don't know about him is that he has become a regular in the evening religious classes at the Qa'id Ibrahim Mosque. I don't know what's going on there."

Nadir laughed, and couldn't keep himself from commenting sarcastically, "Religious classes? Last week he brought home a woman wearing the hijab!"

Silence fell. Nadir was ashamed, and Yara was embarrassed. She stood up and said, "I'm really late."

Kariman stood up and left with her, but she looked back at them with a smile, shaking her head as if she were scolding them and warning them.

*

In the college cafeteria today Isa Salamawy wasn't interested in listening to them talk about anything. It was cold outside and a light rain was falling, and they were all in fall clothing. He was talking to them about Manshiya Square.

At the beginning of the nineteenth century the large square had been a sandy area, where Bedouins came from the outskirts of the city to sell their sheep and other products. People began to think about creating the square after Muhammad Ali took power in Egypt. Its name changed a lot, from Army Square, to Muhammad Ali Square, to the Square of the Consuls, to Tahrir Square. In the beginning commercial caravansaries and markets grew up there. Then the Italian architect Mancini created a design for the square and foreign consulates rose around it, like the Greek, the French, and the Belgian consulates, as well as insurance companies, banks, cafés, restaurants, and offices. There were also shops for jewelry and clothing belonging to international houses, French for the most part. And there were also churches, like the Evangelical Church, the Scottish Church, the Greek Orthodox Church, the Maronite, the Armenian, and the Church of St. Mark, designed in 1831 by the British architect James William Wild, and built in nine years.

Isa made an effort to remember the names of the foreign architects, but he found himself forgetting a lot of them. Nonetheless he went on talking to the group about the old stock exchange, which had now become the headquarters of the Egyptian Socialist Union, the single political party of the regime. Nasser used to give his speeches from its balcony, and in 1954 there was an attempt to assassinate him during one of them, undertaken by the Muslim Brothers. Isa said that it had been one of the largest stock exchanges in the world, with a library containing over eighty thousand books. The walks in front of it were filled with foreign moneychangers, Armenians and Jews, and the cafés teemed with traders speculating in the market. The square was also filled with the perfume of beautiful women, as worldwide fashion passed in the streets and around the statue of Muhammad Ali. This last was carved by a French artist and raised on its marble pedestal (also designed by a French artist) between

1871 and 1873, during the period of Ismail Pasha. And when the French consulate was erected in 1909, the Square of the French Gardens was created in front of it, where the trees (now neglected) were the image of well-ordered French gardens. The names of many financiers and distinguished men, Egyptians and foreigners, were familiar in the square, names like Aghion, Menashe, Sursock, Rolo and Bughus Nubar, Rally, Salfago, and Benaki.

The post office was also there, which had been destroyed in the English attack on Alexandria in 1882 and rebuilt afterward. Many of those people had moved to other houses or apartment buildings with the extension of the Raml tram line, but the buildings remained, which Italian architects more than anyone else had participated in designing and building. The place where the statue of the Unknown Soldier now stood, together with the monument to him, was designed originally for the statue of Ismail Pasha. He would look toward the sea, just like the statue of Sa'd Zaghlul in Raml Station; they looked to the Mediterranean Sea beyond which lay Europe, and not to the Arabian Peninsula, from which came Wahhabi men and their ideas, to eject Egypt from its natural history as a place that was the gift of the Nile. No one knew where the Free Officers of the July Revolution had put the statue of Ismail Pasha. It was said that it was thrown into one of the storehouses attached to the Antoniadis Palace.

Yara suddenly interrupted him with a question:

"Speaking of that, what's going on with all this clamor for a 'return to Islam'? Sometimes I wonder, were we unbelievers without knowing it?" They laughed, and Isa smiled. She went on: "What's amazing is that there isn't one single new mosque as beautiful as the old ones. I live in Anfushi, and there are mosques all around me— Abul Abbas, al-Busiri, Sidi al-Adawi, al-Shorbagy, the Terbana Friday Mosque, and others too. Speaking of which, that Terbana Friday Mosque is really beautiful, Ustaz Isa, it's an architectural gem. Do you know anything about it?"

Isa let out a long sigh. "Of course. It's in the Turki neighborhood that stood between the eastern and western ports. Naturally that means that the neighborhood is older than Manshiya Square. It extends between Manshiya, Gumruk, Sayyala, and Anfushi, and it has inns and markets you're familiar with. The mosque goes back to a Moroccan trader named Ibrahim Terbana who built it in the seventeenth century, maybe in 1684. Like a lot of other North African and European traders, Ibrahim Terbana had an inn in Faransa Street in the heart of the Turki neighborhood. This mosque and the Shorbagy Mosque are among the most important remnants of the Ottoman period." He took another deep breath and continued: "This discussion of mosques needs a day to itself. There's the Attarin Friday Mosque that used to be called Jami al-Juyushi, referring to Badr al-Din al-Jamali al-Fatimi, commander of the armies. Then there's the Jami al-Turtushi in the Bab al-Akhdar area of Gumruk, named for Abu Bakr al-Turtushi who's buried there, and who came to Egypt from Andalus. He was a Maliki legal scholar (and by the way, the Maliki School is the dominant one in the west). He died in 520 A.H., so around a thousand years ago!"

They exchanged glances, surprised by this religious knowledge that Isa had suddenly produced. Was he really talking to them about Alexandria or had something changed in his spirit? Especially as he went on talking about a lot of mosques, al-Shatbi, Abul Abbas, Sidi al-Qabbari, Sidi Gabir, and al-Qa'id Ibrahim, until he came to the Ahmad Yahya Pasha Mosque in Zizinia. They learned a lot about their founders, and about the architects had who built them, especially the Italians.

Kariman exclaimed in surprise, "The Italians built mosques too?"

He answered, "The Abul Abbas Jami, the Qa'id Ibrahim Jami, Sidi Tamraz, the Muhammad Karim Jami—all were built by Italian architects. In all of them Western classicism is paired with Islamic ornamentation." He laughed. "Just the way they built the cinemas, the Metro Cinema and the Cinema Royale, and the way they built Hannaux in St. Catherine's Square—you don't know that Hannaux used to be a center for beauty! Just the way they built the hospitals too, the Fevers Hospital, the Hospital of the

Jewish Community, the Malika Nazli Hospital, and others. As for the banks, you only have to visit the Bank of Egypt or the al-Ahly Bank to see how the Islamic spirit combines with the European spirit in their construction."

Bishr said with a laugh, "Ustaz Isa, Alexandria is very large. I'm afraid you're going to start talking about all its apartment buildings and individual houses, too!"

They laughed, and Isa joined them. He said, "It's obvious that you want to leave. Me too, I want to have lunch at Ateneos. You're all invited."

Hasan looked at Kariman, wanting to take her to the apartment; she looked down. He said, "It's a lovely invitation, but I'll have to excuse myself."

Yara said, "Me too. I'm going to spend the rest of the day in the college library, finishing the paper they assigned us on Muhammad Abduh."

Bishr had an appointment with one of the comrades from the party, at the spinning and weaving factory in Karmuz. He said, "Unfortunately I also have to excuse myself."

Isa said hurriedly, "Don't refuse, Nadir! I especially want you with me today. Please don't refuse."

Nadir said nothing and seemed to agree. But Yara said, enthusiastically, "Wait! Just one question, Ustaz Isa? Who built the Cecil Hotel, do you remember? I went into it once and thought it was really beautiful."

"The Italian architect Loria built it in 1928. By the way, you'll find the name Loria often in Italian architecture. I don't know his full name, only "G. A. Loria." That name came up a lot in my reading in connection with the Italian Hospital, the Hospital of the Jewish Community, and the Bank of Egypt, as I said."

Hasan smiled and said, "Fine. And what about the Hotel Metropole? I see a lot of women sitting behind the glass there when I'm walking in Sa'd Zaghlul Street."

Kariman poked Hasan's arm and Isa laughed out loud, this time, to their great surprise. He said, "An Italian architect built that one too; I think his name was Corrado Pergolesi. It's older than the Cecil since it was built in 1890. . . ."

Bishr shook his head. "Sometimes those Italian names are hard."

They smiled, and Isa hurried on. "That's true. We've become used to English, but the Muntaza Palace and the Haramlik were built by Verrucci, the Italian Consulate in Raml Station was built by Enrico Bovio, and the al-Ahly Bank was built by Paraskevas . . .".

Hasan was startled. "Who?"

Isa spelled it for them: "P-a-r-a-s-k-e-v-a-s. At the same time, there are easy names, too, like Loria, the one I mentioned, and Kasili, who built the Don Bosco School. Do you know it?"

Nadir answered, "Who doesn't know it, Ustaz? I pass it on the tram whenever I go from Maks to Cairo Station."

Abruptly Kariman stood up. She stretched and yawned, then smiled and said, "One last thing: Raml Station."

They all stood up as Isa smiled and said, "Lasciac designed it and built it."

Bishr cried, "So didn't the Egyptians do anything at all?"

"They were all Egyptians. It was the era of cosmopolitanism and Egypt was part of it, and Alexandria in particular was a world city. That era ended with the Suez War in 1956. But there were also Egyptian contractors, by the way, like the company that belonged to the engineer Muhammad Awad Bey, al-Abd and Mukhtar Ibrahim, Ali Labib Gabr, and Ali Sabit. But before we separate, are you going to visit the Greco-Roman Museum with me?"

Hasan said, "Before we separate, please answer my question— why does nobody except old ladies sit behind the glass windows of the Metropole?"

Isa laughed and shook his head. He really seemed happy today. "You're determined to upset Kariman!" They laughed, and he added, "I wish you really would visit the Greek Museum with me next week."

They all said, "Definitely." Hasan added, "And now we're going to spread out in Alexandria to look at everything you told us about."

Yara said, laughing, "We'll all cry, God willing!"

They left him with Nadir. Isa walked at an easy pace, not believing that they had put up with him all this time. He thought about how he had given them a lot of information and how he still had ten times more to give; but he hadn't said anything about the art of architecture itself, its features and its styles. He told himself that was hard, now. The important thing was that the city wake up in the souls of its people. They must waken it for the people they knew, they must dedicate their wall magazines to that next time. He would suggest that to them later.

He didn't know that as soon as he and Nadir left, Bishr stopped the others and said to Hasan, "Next month, three new wall magazines, all dedicated to the glory of Alexandria!"

"God is great!" shouted Yara, and they all set off laughing in the light rain.

Isa stopped a bit at Amm al-Sayyid, the bookseller in the Raml station, on their way to Ateneos. Isa asked him about his book, *The Meaning of the Communist Manifesto*. Amm al-Sayyid gave him his accustomed smile and said, "We finally sold a copy, thank God. Would you like to take the money?"

Isa answered, embarrassed, "No. When you sell some more."

Isa was hesitant in speaking to Hagg al-Ramli, at the next counter. Hagg al-Ramli always seemed serious. He said, "Ustaz Isa, you should take the copies of your book and sell them to the used book shops in Attarin. You'll get a piaster per copy, and that's better than leaving them here. Believe me, we've had your book for more than a year."

Isa looked more embarrassed, especially since Nadir was with him, smiling awkwardly. The book didn't cost much, only ten piasters, but no one bought it and Isa still hoped it would sell.

Walking to Ateneos with Nadir, he said, "I won't ever give up on selling the book!" Nadir answered only with a smile. Suddenly Isa said cheerfully, "You're going to have two surprises with me today! The first is Christo, almost the last Greek in the city. He's a first-rate photographer, with a treasure trove of pictures of Alexandria. And then, my dear poet, you're going to see Nawal."

Astonishment showed on Nadir's face, then joy. Had Isa set up this meeting, or had Nawal arranged it? It wasn't accidental because he had insisted on Nadir coming with him, but he had also addressed the invitation to everyone. Maybe he was expecting their excuses and wanted the invitation to seem natural. Nadir's smile widened. As soon as they climbed the stairs of Ateneos one of the waiters said to Isa, with a smile,

"Madam Nawal is waiting for you, in here."

He pointed to small room to the left of the entryway that was called the Alexander Room. They went in and Nadir saw Nawal at the head of a table; on her right was a window overlooking the eastern port, like all the windows of Ateneos, and on her left was an empty chair. Christo sat in front of her, having put his camera on another table behind him. Nawal stood up to shake hands with them but Christo did not. He grumbled, "You're really late!"

Nawal took Nadir in an embrace and kissed his cheeks. He was embarrassed but submitted, and couldn't keep himself from taking her hand and kissing it. She motioned for him to sit next to her, while Isa sat next to Christo. He immediately pointed to the window and exclaimed, "Is there any view as beautiful as this one in the whole world? The castles of the Ptolemys and the Romans are under these waters. From here they ruled the world. . . ."

Christo surprised them by asking Nadir, "Who are you, sir? Are you Madam Nawal's brother?"

Isa smiled: "Nadir is a cultured university student, a friend, and a poet."

"All of that? Well, it's possible."

Nawal laughed and Nadir smiled. There was a bottle of red wine on the table and two full glasses. Isa lifted the bottle and looked at the label and at the details on it, and then said,

"How I used to wish to travel to Bordeaux! All of France is an old dream I haven't made come true. I envy you, Nawal. But have you ever gone to Bordeaux?"

"I've visited Bordeaux and La Rochelle too, with Irini, my Greek friend." She laughed and then went on with sudden enthusiasm, "I visited Bordeaux on the day that the Beaujolais wine appeared. There were signs on all the walls announcing the arrival of the Beaujolais. That was the first time I had ever heard of that wine. The posters were everywhere, '*Le Beaujolais nouveau est arrivé*,' 'the new Beaujolais is here.' I asked about it and Irini said that it was like a holiday dedicated to Beaujolais: on the evening of the third Thursday of that month, and it was November, all the restaurants and cafés serve this wine. It was the evening of that day. Don't ask me why that day, or why in the evening, I have no information about that. Anyway we had dinner in a Turkish restaurant, where the seats were cushions on the floor—it was more like a big tent. There was an Algerian dancing girl performing a dance from the mountains. People were drinking Beaujolais as if it was water. We ate Turkish kebabs and meatballs and labneh and everything Turkish, and we left in the middle of the night. We saw a scene you would never expect to see in France, men peeing on the walls of houses right in the streets from the effects of what they had drunk, unable to control themselves, and it was a really cold night. In the morning Irini saw a headline in *Le Monde* that read, 'Two million bottles of wine were opened in France last night.'"

Christo cried, "You drank two million bottles of wine, you and your friend?"

They looked at him in surprise for a moment, then they laughed aloud. Nawal said,

"She and I only drank one million."

They laughed again, and Isa poured wine for himself and for Nadir.

Nadir's desire for Nawal filled his breast, as if meeting her meant overcoming obstacles, even though he was the one who didn't go to visit her. Two waiters came in carrying their meal and another bottle of wine; Nawal had obviously ordered everything. Delicious dishes of fish and appetizers filled the table, and lovely aromas rose from them. Christo said,

"I've visited Paris a lot. Every year I go and buy pictures from the salesmen along the River Seine, to sell here in Alexandria. Beautiful pictures of old-time films and beauty queens and actors, and old transportation, carts and tram cars and trains from the old days."

Nawal said with a laugh, "I'm the one who buys them, I give them to him every year. Christo here is something else. . . ."

Isa said, "Okay, Christo. Photograph us, maybe you can sell the picture someday."

Christo got up and took a large number of pictures of them with his old camera. Nadir was surprised by Nawal putting her arm on his shoulder in a lot of them; happiness filled his breast and his spirit. Then Christo sat down to eat and Nawal said,

"Christo told me a strange story about something that happened to him today. Tell them, Christo."

As they began to eat, he asked, "What story's that? I don't remember."

"The story of the people who nearly beat you up."

He suddenly seemed to remember. "Oh! I was in Faransa Street. Look, Faransa Street is all jewelers, so that means that everyone who walks there has money on him because he's going to buy gold. I found a guy there holding a little kid and slapping him, a kid who worked for him. He was asking him, 'Why're you insulting religion?' People were saying, 'Enough, Boss, enough, mister.' He was an ass of a boss and it was no use, he was beating the boy. I told him, 'Why're you beating him? All of Alexandria insults religion.' The boss looked at me, and people laughed. I said, 'In fact everybody who lives in a port insults religion, it's a habit, it's not unbelief. They're just like that. It's because towns on the sea have lots of religions in them, so insulting a religion is easier than asking 'What's your name?' or 'What do you do?'"

Isa looked pleased by Christo's sudden ability to analyze the situation. Nawal laughed and Nadir smiled in surprise. Christo went on:

"I said to the boss, 'That means if I say to you that your religion's a bastard I don't really mean it. Anyway, boss, you're not an Alexandrian . . . .'"

Isa asked, "What did they do to you?"

"He said to me, 'What's your family's religion?' People laughed and pulled me away. I said 'The same as your family's, you ass,' and I went away." They laughter loudly and he went on: "Frankly I was afraid the guy with the sonofabitch religion was going to come after me and beat me up."

They laughed again, then began eating in silence. Nadir couldn't stop shaking his head in amazement. Then Christo said,

"It's over, there's no more Elite." They looked up and he said, "I don't know if Christina sold it or what. I saw it with wood walls and dark glass all around it, so you can't see anyone sitting there, eating or drinking."

Isa said, "It's been that way since around the beginning of last year, but Christina hasn't sold it, sometimes I see her there. No one sits on the sidewalk to drink a beer, now, or any alcohol, not in Raml Station, not in Calithea, not in L'Aiglon and not here in Ateneos. People only sit outside to drink coffee."

Christo said angrily, "So it's over, there's no more kharam?"

But the food was appetizing and they fell silent again for several minutes, occupied with eating and drinking until Nawal said, "Christo, I only see you once or twice every year, in the summer. Can you spend New Year's Eve with us this year?"

"Maybe. Every year I come here, to Ateneos. But I miss the folk dancing."

They laughed again. In fact they laughed a lot, the sound emerging from the room, which Nawal seemed to have reserved for them alone. They were laughing as they left. Nadir no longer cared how Isa had arranged this meeting with Nawal.

On the sidewalk, Isa said, "I'll take Christo and leave you two."

As he got into her Fiat, Nadir asked himself if Nawal was going to take him someplace else now. To her apartment, maybe?

She said, "Of course you're wondering how this meeting came about. Isa visited me and I set it up with him. I decided to do it since you don't visit me any more. Don't tell me what kept you from coming. I've really missed you, and I've found you. I'm really happy today."

"I'm happy too! It's been a beautiful day. In the morning Isa told us about the beauty of Alexandria and its history and its architecture, and now I've spent three hours with you."

It was almost five and dusk was stealing over the city. She asked, "Where do you want me to take you? To your house in Maks?"

He was momentarily embarrassed. That would mean their encounter was over. He said, "To Tanais Street."

She smiled. "Is something lovelier waiting for you there? Yara, for example?"

He shook his head, smiling. "No, there's nothing lovelier than you today." He reached out and took her right hand and kissed it. "It seems as if you wanted to tell me something important."

"There are a lot of things I want to tell you, Nadir, a lot. But for now let me invite you to come to the nightclub with your friends on New Year's Eve. It's just a few weeks from now, and it will be a night like no other."

The Corniche was almost empty of cars and pedestrians. Black clouds filled the sky and the rain strengthened. The car moved unhurriedly to Tanais Street, which seemed completely empty. Near the house he motioned for her to stop. She asked,

"Do you live here?"

"Yes."

"Do you like Tanais Street?"

He laughed. "That's also a long story."

"No, I know everything about this great street."

He was embarrassed momentarily, but he didn't want to leave the car. She took his hand in hers, as the rain intensified and the sound of it falling on the car grew louder. Rain covered the windows on every side, coming down in wave upon wave. The lights stealing from behind the windows of the houses could not overcome the gloom that settled on the city with the nightfall and the dark, thickening clouds.

"It's as if I was in Paris."

Saying that, she leaned over to kiss him on the mouth. They fell into a long kiss, and he could not keep his hands from grasping her breasts, and moving to her belly and her thighs. He whispered,

"Come up to the apartment with me."

"No, let's stay here."

"The car isn't big enough," he whispered. Then he was panting and moving his lips over her neck, and she was also gasping and moaning. She said,

"It's something I never did in Paris, let me do it here."

His hand encircled her shoulders while the other found its way under her dress between her thighs, as his kisses covered her face, neck, and breasts. She clasped him to her, kissing him, her hand between his legs. When she sensed that he could no longer control himself, she moved away a little. She looked at him with shining eyes, her breath rapid and her lips parted. She whispered:

"This is enough. When I was in Paris I wished you were with me. In fact I dreamed that you were doing this with me there, at night, just as we are now." He came closer and she blocked his hands from her breasts, saying with a smile, "Don't forget that we're in Egypt. If anyone saw us they would arrest us and accuse us of public indecency."

He whispered, "There's no one in the street."

"I've made my dream come true. Now, farewell!" She laughed, "And don't tell me that anyone who lives in Tanais Street is deprived of women!"

He left her, circling in front of the car to go into the small door to the building that was always left open. She moved away in the car as he slowly climbed the stairs and turned the key in the door, hoping that he wouldn't find anyone there. But no sooner did he open the door than he saw Ahmad Basim sitting at the dining table with Rawayih and Ghada, with the remains of food in front of them. Ahmad saw him and stood up, taking his prayer beads from the table to go to his room. He said, "Here's Nadir. Tell him."

Nadir was no longer surprised at finding Ahmad in a gallabiya. That was the way he was, now. But why did he insist on keeping the prayer beads in his hand even at home?

Rawayih said, "It's over, we've found out that Madam Nawal is going to sell the club. We were so happy, we couldn't believe we got to work for her."

He looked at them in amazement that quickly turned into anger. Was this encounter his farewell to Nawal? But that couldn't be true when she had asked him and his friends to spend New Year's Eve with her.

Rawayih said, "Sit with us a moment. We'll tell you who's going to buy the club."

He didn't answer. Ghada said, "We just want you to help us understand. We know that the reason for buying the clubs and turning them into wedding parlors is because they're forbidden in religion, haram. Okay, but are movies haram too?" He smiled, and she continued: "The man Madam Nawal is negotiating with for the nightclub, they say he's bought a theater named the Nile Cinema in Karmuz that he's going to turn into a factory, and a theater in Ragheb called the Republic that he's going to turn into an apartment building."

He found nothing to say, and simply shrugged. But Ahmad came back out of his room, exclaiming, "And the Coronation Cinema in Anfushi and the Qays and Layla in Bacos and the Cleopatra in Farahda and the theaters in Raml Station, the East, the Rex, the Alhambra, the Park, the Majestic, and the Ritz! All of them will be destroyed someday, so seek guidance while you can!"

He retreated to his room once more, leaving Nadir shocked and furious. Where had Ahmad gotten all this information? Did his beard really have anything to do with what was happening in the city—and had he transformed himself in order to gain something? Time would tell what was hidden from him now.

The last weeks of the year witnessed a political opening in Egypt, since the political groupings within the Arab Socialist Union, the state's sole political organization, were transformed into parties. The socialists, despite their different tendencies and phases, had a political party bearing the name of the National Progressive Unionist Party. Some people jokingly referred to it as "Tutu," shortening the name to its initials, though of course "Tutu" is a nickname for children, as well as the name prisoners give to a little alcohol burner they make in prison. The Labor Party appeared, and the Egyptian Socialist Party, and Nasserist Party. Parliamentary elections were held and the results were certified as free from tampering for the first time in the modern history of Egypt. Jimmy Carter had been elected to the presidency of the United States of America, and Sayyid Mar'i was elected as speaker of the Egyptian parliament by a vast majority. New names appeared in the political firmament in Alexandria, like the young Abul Izz al-Hariri, the Labor representative from Karmuz, and the Nasserist Kamal Ahmad from the Attarin electoral district. Abul Izz al-Hariri was known in Marxist circles. The name of the Alexandrian prosecutor, Justice Mahmud al-Qadi, also gained prominence.

The winter coastal winds blew in regular succession, heading into the new year. The Metro Cinema was showing the film *The Sinners* with Suheir Ramzi, which by the standards of Egyptian films went to the extreme in the sex scenes. This reflected the daring of its young producer, Saeed Marzuk, who had other wonderful Egyptian films to his credit, such as *My Wife and the Dog* and *Fear*. Since the plot of the film was based on a criminal investigation into the murder of the main female character in the film, it revealed the sexual relations between her and the new men of money and politics in society, as well as the enormous scale of corruption. The film became the unending topic of the newspapers, whether they attacked it or praised it. The names of the actors—Adel Emam, Hussein Fahmy, Zubayda Tharwat, Samir Ghanem, and Kamal al-Shinnawi—came to be associated with this film alone, even though they played many other roles in their careers, and even though the careers of some of them, such as Kamal al-Shinnawi, were very long.

President Sadat inaugurated a poultry project that would produce seven million chickens a year. The Zamalek Theater in Cairo showed the play *Ali Bey Mazhar* by Muhammad Subhi. The first Islamic center in Guinea was erected according to Egyptian architectural designs, which Sadat gave to the people of Guinea. The conversation among the secret Communist parties was about what would happen now that the leftists had a public party. Some of them expected that the secret parties would now be dissolved. Bishr, Nadir, Hasan, Kariman, and Yara prepared three new magazines with pictures and articles about Alexandrian architecture and its history, a development that confused the students of the Islamic groups and the Muslim Brothers. The magazines attracted large numbers of students who stood in front of them, surprised and pleased with the pictures that had been collected from old magazines and newspapers, and with the commentary below them. And a week before the end of the year Ahmad Basim came into the apartment with Muhammad Shukr, whom they greeted with happy surprise. Ahmad told them, "I found Muhammad Shukr in the street looking for a place to live, and I told him to live with us."

They learned from Muhammad that the owner of the apartment he was living in on Tiba Street had asked him and the others with him to vacate the place by the end of the year. His roommates had all found places to live in other apartments on that street among friends of theirs, but he hadn't found anything there so he had come looking for something on Tanais Street, where Ahmad had run into him. They were happy to have him live with them. He could stay with Ahmad in his room, or in any other room. After he went into the room with Ahmad, Nadir, Hasan, and Bishr said to each other, "We were thinking about how to get rid of Ahmad, and now we have two others living with us!" But what they knew of Muhammad Shukr and how all the students loved him made them welcome him among them. They wondered if Ahmad had really met him by chance or if he had wanted to find out about his love story with Fawqiya, the minister's daughter, and maybe to get to her sister Fawziya by way of him. Ahmad had become a puzzle for them now; but even if they were certain that he was in contact with the Islamic groups and the Muslim Brothers, Muhammad Shukr couldn't be like that.

What happened in fact was that Muhammad spread a lot of cheer in the apartment, as the voice of Abdel Halim Hafiz was always coming from his room, from his personal cassette player, always singing songs of love and passion. Ahmad did not object. In fact it got so that Ahmad only came to the apartment every day to sleep, and when he did Muhammad would go to Hasan's room to study with him, bringing his little cassette player. He didn't notice that they had a cassette player he could have used for the tapes he loved. It seemed as if the tapes and his personal player were a single unit, and that made them laugh.

New Year's Eve came. Muhammad excused himself from going with them to the Nawal Boîte; he would spend the evening alone, listening to recorded songs. Of course Ahmad excused himself from going this year, and they didn't know where he would spend his evening. Even though it was New Year's Eve Kariman decided to stay home, so that if they arrested her it would be from her house. Yara had better luck this year since she wasn't having menstrual cramps as she had the year before, so her mother and father took her with them to their friends. She was only thinking about when she would be able to spend New Year's Eve with Nadir and whether that day would ever come, just as Kariman was thinking about Hasan.

Nadir, Hasan, and Bishr went to the Nawal Boîte, and there they found Isa Salamawy. They sat with Nawal, listening to the music:

Our boats have come to rest on the shore of the sea of love,
The night has brought us together with the ones we love.
Our boats have come to rest on the shore of the sea of
love....

The singer was young Ibrahim Ahmad, singing the song of Karim Mahmud, as the dancer Alya moved lightly around him and among the audience that filled the hall tonight, while the winter carried on outside. Isa was sitting among them but he was thinking about not having made the same circuit as last year. Instead he had come directly to the Nawal Boîte at ten o'clock, where he now sat among the others.

As usual, Nawal was wearing an evening dress that bared her shoulders, as she gracefully smoked a cigarette in a long holder. The dim light in the room made the women's bare flesh gleam, and the club girls were circulating among the tables with the orders, placing them in front of the guests and removing what they had used. People were still coming in. Rawayih and Ghada were among the girls, smiling at them from afar as they stood behind the guests. They were waiting for someone to ask them to sit with him, the way the other club women had been asked.

Bishr was very happy, talking about the new magazines they had hung up with pictures of the great buildings of Alexandria and its monumental ruins. Isa was filled with pride. He said,

"But we haven't gone to the Greco-Roman Museum yet. I've put off visiting it so you can come with me. And by the way, there are a lot of crumbling monuments in Alexandria that I haven't talked to you about. I've told you more about the present."

Hasan smiled his usual small half smile and said, "We will do it all, Ustaz Isa. But now let's listen to this beautiful song that I haven't heard before."

The sea of passion has water sweeter than sugar,
One who loves and tastes it falls as in a stupor.
If you visit our home you'll wish and pray,
You'll rejoice with us, and enjoy your love, on that day,
Longing has brought us together with the ones we love.

Affected by the words of the song, Nadir was reaching under the table to take Nawal's hand and press it, as she seemed distant from them. Suddenly Isa said to her, "Christo apologizes to you for not coming." She looked up in surprise, so he added, "He told me two days ago in Ateneos that he was used to that place." He laughed, "And he no longer likes folk dancing."

She laughed in turn. "Even though he told us when we were together that he missed folk dancing! Anyway he remembered my invitation, so he's of sound mind. Why do you think he isn't?"

Isa smiled. "I consider him of sound mind in everything he says, because the best way to face what's happening around us is madness!"

The lovely Hayat was placing bottles of wine and dishes of food before them. As usual, Bishr could not take his eyes off her legs. Nadir asked, "Will Nana sing tonight? I see her picture outside a lot of nightclubs now."

Nawal answered, "She became known here, and tonight she asked my permission not to come. She's going to sing in the Palestine Hotel. Of course I didn't prevent her from going. In fact you're only going to hear me, tonight."

Bishr and Hasan cried together, "Allaah! That's wonderful!"

Nadir looked at her, then took her hand and kissed it. "Would that we never heard anyone else as long as we live!"

Bishr asked her, "Have Rawayih and Ghada started working here?"

Nawal answered, "They're nice girls. They came to me and said that they live with you, and that they had asked Nadir to help them get jobs here."

Nadir said, "That's true, and I forgot to ask you."

"I like them. They're rather pretty and they have experience. I told them that Nadir really had told me about them—I didn't want to disappoint them."

Bishr was surprised. "They never told me!"

Hasan said, "Maybe they were afraid you would jinx them, Bishr. Please, Sitt Nawal, take care of them!"

They laughed. Many of the guests were applauding the singer, Ibrahim Ahmad, and some of the women had left their places to dance with Alya. Nawal noticed Nadir looking thoughtfully at the food, so she said, "Did you read the sign in front of the club?"

"I read it—an Alexandrian night."

She said, "Every kind of food tonight is from Alexandria, the fish, the seafood, the quail, the kebabs, the liver, the sweets—they're all things Alexandria has known over its history. Turkish food, Italian food, Greek food, Levantine food, and French food, like everyone who lived here and left their mark."

Isa struck his forehead. "How did I forget to tell you about the restaurants of Alexandria? Some have disappeared, like the

Restaurant des Fouls et Foules ('Beans and Crowds'), and the Union Restaurant that was near Sheikh Ali. It counted Abdel Halim Hafiz and Umm Kulthum among its customers—there were always two seats reserved for them—and Churchill and Roosevelt visited it too. And the May Fair Inn in Stanley on the sea, it was like a carved wooden gem, and Kleenzo Restaurant, it's closed now and they say it's been sold. And there are restaurants and bars and pastry shops that are still here, like Ateneos of course, and the Hamos Greek bakery that Dimitri Hamos opened on Faransa Street in the Turki neighborhood in 1900—now its name is Alexandra Hamos, and it's owned by Dimitri's grandsons, and it's on Omar Lutfi Street in Little Sporting. And of course San Giovanni, founded in 1939, and the Swiss Beaurivage that was bought by the Salama family, where they made a lot of Arab films."

Nawal said with a laugh, "Isa won't be still tonight, it's as if he's saying goodbye to Alexandria. My dear, we won't say goodbye to her ever!"

Isa laughed. "I'm sorry, I forgot myself. It's better to talk in the college. I'll tell you about Pastroudis, the Trianon, Monaco, Asteria, Chez Gaby, San Stefano, Délices, Zephyrion, the Seagull, Santa Lucia, and the Greek Club. . . ."

All at once Nawal burst into tears. They all stared at her, confused and worried. She said to Isa, "Why are you doing that? I'm leaving soon and I've been hiding the time of my departure from you all, hiding it from myself. Why are you making me say goodbye to the city?"

The oriental ensemble was playing a musical interlude now, without singing or dancing. Isa was very embarrassed. He took her hand and kissed it. "I'm sorry, I'm really sorry. I should have been paying attention to the singing and dancing tonight. Forgive me, everyone! I've been reading so much these last few months. I feel as if Alexandria is slipping through our fingers.... I'm really sorry."

He took Nawal's hand again, and then embraced her and kissed her. She got up to go to her dressing room, nearby. Hayat had been watching for that, and she hurried after her. Nadir looked reproachfully at Isa, who said, "Please forgive me, Nadir, forgive me, everyone."

The voices of the crowd rose, loudly demanding that Nawal sing, whistling and applauding. Nawal had not returned, and time crept by, passing in boredom. It was ten or twenty minutes but it seemed like an age to Nadir, with the image of Nawal before his eyes, with tears on her cheeks as she hurried away. After a while the patrons of the club stopped calling out, and the music rose.

Then Nawal appeared, coming back in a different, more beautiful evening dress, red this time instead of green, with her makeup repaired. She went straight to the platform and stood there, while applause and whistles filled the air. Then she went over to the ensemble and whispered something to them, and swaying music soon filled the air. Everyone knew it was by Sayyid Darwish:

I've loved and it's over, so why all this blame?
They want me to say I wish my love never came.

The applause was loud, but she did not stop. She raised her voice, crooning,

As long as I don't mind that now my love is gone,
Let anyone who likes talk on and on and on.

The applause rose again. Nawal paused while the music went on; then she continued, finishing the song with a cheerful cadence:

I and my sweetheart, yes, there's nothing like our love,
Yes, yes, yes! It's more than any dream from above.

The applause returned, and men and women exchanged quick kisses in joy.

Nawal immediately began another song. The music flowed and the crowd clapped and laughed and lifted their glasses. Hasan,

Nadir, and Bishr were amazed, and all together they asked Isa, "What's going on?" He was smiling happily.

He told them, "It's the hashish addicts' song." They were even more surprised, and he added, "It's also called 'Those Who Create.'"

Nadir said, "I've heard it, I don't know it at all."

Bishr said, laughing, "If it's about hashish and addicts, it's definitely by Sayyid Darwish! Let's listen."

They all laughed, and Hasan said, mocking him, "Everybody but you knows it. It's a real Alexandrian song!"

Nawal began amid the laughter of the audience:

Ah, how lovely are those who create!
Their kindness and their knowledge are great.
Oh Lord, please give us a night that glows.

The audience could no longer control their laughter. Nawal paused for a few moments, then continued with a theatrical imitation of hashish smokers, which delighted everyone.

It's that those drugs, when they're in control,
Your friend over here will yearn with his soul
For a little hashish, tashish, bararish!

She stopped again to give the audience a chance to laugh and applaud once more.

Just ask someone who knows how it goes,
An old addict like me who takes hits every day,
Fifty or sixty, with more on the way!
Ha, ha, ha, you're welcome to stay.
Put your trust in him, believe the Lord and Creator,
Who said, "Be! A hash pipe for every taster!"

Then in a calm tone, as if she were proclaiming an eternal truth,

We wouldn't take millions for the sweet breath it blows

The laughter exploded, the rhythm of the music quickened, and she hurried the next words:

But God protect us from the gov-gov-gov'ment,
It makes unjust arrests in an instant.
Whenever they hear a mosquito buzz,
You look up and all you see are the fuzz,
Flying express, no stops on the way!

This time the laughter lasted even longer.

See, it's like this, since we're poor folk,
Who cannot read or write a stroke
You look down on what we do.
But long live the tricks we play on you!
Excuse my language, but my fine mustache
On even a dog or goat would add panache!
"Hey, rumbler!" you call, and with no delay
I'll roll up my sleeves and be on my way,
A son of Egypt isn't afraid to play!
Ha, ha, ha, you're welcome, my friend,
Show us the toughest bey or pasha,
The ones who are always saying "gotcha!"
And blaming the hash smokers, that *they* offend—
They're blowing smoke, my boy, let's not pretend!
I'll tell you the truth when we meet someday,
How our dear country has gone astray,
Forbidding us, pretty pipe, from kissing you,
Go on, get out, I'm divorcing you!
Since Egypt wants everyone sober today.

Nawal stood laughing, her breath coming fast and her chest rising and falling, while the audience clamored in happiness and applauded for a long time. She called to them, "Tonight it's all Sayyid Darwish, how's that?"

They all called, "Long live Sayyid Darwish, Sayyid Darwish!"

So she sang "Light-hearted and proud, with a flick of an eyelash," and the hall danced, filled again with joy. Then, "It rose, how lovely is its light," and calm reigned; and when she sang "I loved and saw that others love," all was strangely peaceful, as if they were all lovers and romantics.

Nawal sang ten songs by Sayyid Darwish, and her fatigue showed. Nadir was wondering, why in the world all these songs of Sayyid Darwish tonight? Nawal really was going to leave Alexandria, very soon, it couldn't mean anything else. She had said it, but he'd always hoped she would not leave the city. But now she was leaving the last pulse of her spirit in it, now she was proclaiming to the city her love for it, and for him too, since she looked his way often as she sang.

One of the musicians got up and whispered something in her ear, and she nodded. It was a few minutes before twelve o'clock, when all the lights would go out. She began singing again:

Come to visit me every year,
Don't dare forget me and disappear!

She had barely finished when the lights went out. A moment later they came back up, but Nawal was nowhere to be seen. She had left in the moment of darkness, hurrying to her car and to her house, to finish her weeping alone.

8

THERE WERE NO ARRESTS AMONG the Communists on New Year's Eve that year. It was amazing. Some said that that this was in keeping with the new political spirit, after permission had been granted to establish parties.

Mamduh Salim became the prime minister and Nadir went to Cairo again to bring back the new issues of the Party magazines. He went to the *Vanguard* offices to meet the important critic, as he considered Farouk Abdel Qadir, but he did not find him. He still didn't know if his poem was going to be published or not. This time he knew the way to Zamalek, but as before he had time, since the appointment was once again for seven in the evening.

He went hesitantly to the Café Riche, overcome with something like fear. Was it really possible that he would meet those writers and sit among them again, Naguib Surur, Amal Donqol, Sulaiman Fayyad, and Farouk Abdel Qadir? This time he had to have more courage, he had to talk. They couldn't really be the way they had seemed to him before.

He went to the café hoping that he would run into Farouk Abdel Qadir and learn the fate of his poem, but he did not find him or anyone. He sat alone for a time in the interior section, looking at the pictures of the artists who had departed this life and who used to sit here in the café.

There were a lot of foreigners around him, most of them young, beautiful girls in winter clothing whose perfume filled the air. He saw the waiter, Malik, moving about and continuously rattling the change in his pocket; he remembered Naguib Surur and smiled. He saw the dark Nubian waiter, Felfel, and noticed the enduring expression of kindness on his face, that reminded him of Khalil. He realized that it was a kindness engraved on the faces of all Nubians. He sat in the outside section for an hour and then spent another hour here; feeling bored, he decided to leave the café and walk around downtown. Then he thought that he could go to Madbouli's Bookstore for the first time; he knew it was nearby, in Talaat Harb Square.

He reached it and found a display of books and newspapers in front of the store. He also found Hagg Madbouli in his gallabiya, arranging some of the books—yes, he must be the one wearing the country gallabiya. Nadir stopped, embarrassed. Would he really ask him for books banned in Egypt? But what were the titles of the banned books he wanted? He didn't know. Hagg Madbouli noticed his embarrassment and glanced at him, but then looked away, apparently unconcerned. Nadir found himself asking about any new books. The man looked at him, his eyes widening in mild surprise, and said, "Any books?" Nadir looked more embarrassed. Madbouli asked, "Political, for example, or literary?"

He hesitated, and then said, "Political and literary."

Madbouli gave him a thoughtful look that Nadir didn't understand. Then he called one of his employees and asked him to take Nadir to the storeroom behind the building entrance, telling him to show him the latest arrivals from Beirut.

Nadir was very happy as he followed the young employee, who left him in a storeroom filled with books on all sides and on the floor. He spent an entire half hour there and came out bearing just two books, *Bare Feet* by Tahir Abdel Hakim, which told the story of the Communists in the Oases Prison, and Aragon's book of poetry, *Elsa's Eyes*. He presented them hesitantly to Hagg Madbouli, and he looked at him and said,

"Fifteen pounds."

Nadir flushed with embarrassment. He wondered if books were this expensive in Cairo.

Hagg Madbouli said, "You don't have enough?"

"I only have five pounds."

"Fine, give me five pounds, and when you come again, pay the ten."

Then Hagg Madbouli called one of his employees and told him to take his name and open a page for him in the credit register.

In fact Nadir had eight pounds with him, but he wanted to keep three for his return and to pay for what he would order in the Cleopatra Casino when he met Wafaa. Before he dictated his name to the employee, he told Hagg Madbouli,

"But I might be away for a month or more. I'm from Alexandria."

The old man was arranging some of the books on the display, and said without looking at him, "It doesn't matter. Come any time."

Nadir paid the five pounds and walked away, disbelieving. He would never forget Hagg Madbouli's favor to him.

He started walking in Talaat Harb Street and then in Qasr al-Nil, amazed at the elegance of the shops and the people. Then he returned to Café Riche, not to go in but rather to go through the passageway as he had before. He would go into Huda Shaarawi Street and then take the bus to Zamalek, where he could walk under the trees a little until it was time for the appointment.

At the end of the passage he found a café bearing a sign proclaiming it as The Garden Café; there were no more than three people sitting out front of it on the walkway. But at the end of the passage he also found Amal Donqol alone, drinking a cup of coffee. He stopped, and Amal Donqol smiled as soon as he saw him. So he remembered him!

"Hello, Nadir."

Nadir was very surprised—he even remembered his name! Amal Donqol asked him, "Do you know how to play backgammon?"

"Sure," he said eagerly.

"Have a seat and play with me. Do you have time?"

"Of course."

He sat down, and Amal asked him about the books he was carrying, so he showed him what he had bought. Amal looked at them and returned them without comment. That really confused Nadir, but he asked him, "Why didn't Ustaz Farouk Abdel Qadir come today?"

Amal gestured, smiling, and asked, "Are you a poet?"

Nadir was cheered, and said enthusiastically, "Yes, I write prose poems."

But Amal did not comment. He only said, "Be careful, or I'll beat you."

Nadir was embarrassed, and wondered for a moment why Amal did not respond to what he said. Didn't he like prose poems? But Amal was playing seriously, and that turned Nadir's thoughts to the game. They played three times, very quickly, and Amal won every time. He stood up and said, "I'm going to The Depot to have a beer. Do you want to come?"

"Unfortunately, I'm tied up."

Amal shook his hand and went up the passage. Nadir stood for a moment, thinking about how strange it was that they had spent this time playing backgammon, not talking about literature or anything else. He thought, this Cairo is strange! Then he hurried to the bus stop to meet Wafaa in the Casino.

Wafaa's beautiful smile was enough to make him forget everything; he realized that he was eager to sit with her for as long as possible. But as soon as he shook her hand and sat down she said hurriedly, "We have to leave now."

"Why?"

"Cairo is very tense these days. The government decided yesterday to remove its support from a lot of rationed goods. That's in response to the demands of the International Monetary Fund, and the demands of the American banker—he's a former government official and he's Sadat's economic consultant."

"Does Sadat have an American consultant?

"Rockefeller. Don't you know him?"

He shook his head. She said,

"Then let's go. I've had something to drink, and I'll pay for it and we'll go." At the door of the tea room she said, "I'll take a taxi alone, this time. We shouldn't be seen together." She hailed a passing cab and got in quickly, waving farewell as she rode off.

She left him surprised and upset, taking her smile from him. The space around him shrank, and he realized that night had come and that he was standing in darkness, despite the streetlamps. All he could do was hail another taxi.

In the train he shook his head in wonder, trying to forget this whole day that had ended so depressingly. The best part of it had been playing backgammon wordlessly with Amal Donqol. He suddenly smiled and thought about this "Depot" where he had gone to have a beer. He must learn more about it, next time.

Three days passed, and then on Monday, January 17, the morning papers carried the decision to raise the prices of many commodities. This single decision raised the price of the corn that poor people ate, of sugar, oil, tea, clarified butter, butter, margarine, meats, cigarettes of all kinds, gas for stoves, cotton, wool, and synthetic textiles, all in order to save 170 million pounds in the national budget. Home rents were also raised, in order to encourage investors to build, as were the taxes on automobiles, fees for customs and fiscal stamps, and the price of cooking gas and gasoline. Everyone in Egypt began talking angrily with everyone else, in homes and factories and schools and universities.

The wind was strong, although the rain over Alexandria had stopped. The sound of the wind came to occupy every corner of the sky, and everything went faster, private cars, public transportation, trams, and people in the streets. It seemed as if everything in the city was getting into a fight with some invisible enemy. Bishr, Nadir, Hasan, Yara, and Kariman were in the cafeteria, meeting briefly with Isa Salamawy. He had been intending to remind them of their promise to go with him to the Greco-Roman Museum, which they had not yet done, but he did not bring that up. He seemed calm while they raged around him over these reforms. He was speaking sagely, saying that this was to be expected from a political regime that thought that America held all the keys to solving the problem of the Middle East. Wasn't Sadat constantly saying that 99 percent of the solution was in America's hands? It was completely natural that this regime would submit to the instructions of the World Bank. Bishr was extremely angry, saying "How can we remain silent over this? We must act!"

Meanwhile the students moving outside the cafeteria in front of them seemed oblivious. Even the students from the Islamic Group and the Muslim Brothers were standing in front of their own magazines and were not discussing these reforms with anyone. Instead they were talking about articles in their magazines on the Muslim Brothers' history of torture, or the legal thought of Ibn Taymiya, or dissolute dancehalls, or the unbelievers' film entitled *The Sinners*, or the blasphemous system of interest-paying banks and the importance of Islamic investment companies. Those companies offered fabulous profits that could reach 20 percent a month; their ads filled the pages of newspapers, and people were flocking to them. They were also talking about a Hadith attributed to the noble prophet which said that "It is better for a man to fornicate with his mother next to the wall of the Kaaba than to take interest from banks." Some students read that and were astounded, and then turned away.

This Hadith was the object of Bishr's sarcasm. As soon as he heard about it he went out to see it for himself, and then he asked the bearded student standing in front of the magazine if there had been banks at the time of the prophet. The young man stared at him furiously, and shouted, "What's it to you?" Bishr walked away in disbelief.

He sat with his friends and told them about this, and they were astonished. They got up and left the cafeteria one after the other to read it, and then came back laughing. Isa, who had not moved from his place, told them, "Unfortunately I read this Hadith in an ad for one of the Islamic investment companies on the front page of a newspaper."

Kariman said, "Forget this nonsense. What are we going to do about these economic reforms?"

Hasan responded calmly, in a whisper, "We really have to do something."

Nadir added, "We have to contact the leftists in the other colleges."

Kariman said, "Let's write a declaration condemning these reforms and make copies of it, and then pass it out to people in the streets."

Isa told them, "You can do all of that, but talking here in the college is dangerous. Find some other place."

It seemed to them that he wanted to leave, but they saw that what he said was sound. Bishr got up and said, "Then let's leave the college now."

He shook hands with Isa in farewell and so did the others. As soon as they were outside of the college in Port Said Street, Nadir said, "I don't think there's any reason for Kariman and Yara to come to the apartment with us. We'll do as Kariman said and meet here tomorrow."

Hasan agreed: "That's my opinion too. No one knows what might happen to us today."

Bishr added, "Naturally I expect the Interior Ministry to take pre-emptive measures and arrest us all." He extended his hand decisively. "Goodbye, Yara, goodbye, Kariman. We'll see you tomorrow."

They made their way to the apartment, where they had not spent much time lately. They finished writing the declaration in an hour; Muhammad Shukr had not come back yet, nor had Ahmad Basim, who would come back late, as usual. Bishr and Nadir each decided to go home that night, so that they would not be arrested in one place. Hasan stayed in the apartment, and remarked with a smile, "What I'm afraid of is that they really will take pre-emptive measures and arrest Ahmad and Muhammad with me."

Bishr and Nadir laughed, and left him. Bishr took with him one copy of the declaration they had written and Nadir took another. They agreed that each one would make a large number of copies, and that they would distribute them the next morning in the college.

The next morning they arrived at the college about ten to find all the students outside their lecture halls. They were in the court-yard in front of the Abbadi Hall, or in the cafeteria, or at the tennis courts, or at the entrance to the college, or in the halls between the classrooms for the departments of Arabic, English, and French on one side and those for history, archaeology, geography, and sociology on the other. They found Hasan, Kariman, and Yara among the crowds. Kariman and Yara took many copies of the declaration from the hundreds that Bishr and Nadir had made, and they all started distributing them among the students:

> We, the students of the Humanities College of the University of Alexandria, acting on behalf of all the students of Egypt, hereby denounce and reject the recent economic reforms declared by the regime of President Sadat, reforms which confirm with utmost clarity its subservience to the American regime and to savage worldwide capitalism; which deliver a heavy blow to the socialist societal gains previously achieved for the poorest classes; which confirm the state's renunciation of its role in maintaining social justice among all classes of the people; and which open wide the gate to illegitimate gains for new, predatory capitalism, which has come to Egypt as a wild plant and which has taken control of the funds of banks and of taxpayers alike. We demand of President Sadat and of his prime minister that they resign from their positions and open the door for the first time in Egypt to elections in which people may choose their president from among more than one candidate, ending the era of referenda for a single president, a practice which has created a new pharaoh in Egypt since the Revolution of July, 1952.

In a few minutes the declaration was in the hands of many students, but what inflamed them was the news that the students of the College of Engineering had gone out into Gamal Abdel Nasser Street in roaring throngs, and the news that enormous crowds of workers from the Alexandria shipyards in Wardian now filled Maks Street. How did they hear that? No one knew. The truth was that the shipyard workers had marched out at nine o'clock, after angry conversations in every shop in the company. They plunged headlong out of the gates, carrying some young men on their shoulders and shouting in protest against the economic reforms: "It's not enough we're dressed in threads, now they're coming for our bread! Hey you government, it's a crime, we have to buy our meat on time! Down with Anwar, down with Sadat!"

On their way they picked up the workers from the Bata Shoe Company, and when they drew near to the Mina al-Basal neighborhood they gathered the workers from the cotton gins and the freight companies. Far to their rear were the workers from the oil, chemical, and cement companies, who had also come from Maks, and on the way the students from Wardian High School and Tahir Bey Middle School joined them. Everyone was heading for Manshiya Square by way of the Street of the Seven Girls, and their shouts shook the sky. From Gumruk came the workers from the freight companies there and the longshoremen, going to Manshiya by way of Bahariya Street and Victory Street. From far in the east came the workers of the copper companies in Sidi Gabir and of Al-Nasr Company, the maker of automobile chassis, catching up with the workers from the Egypt Spinning and Weaving Company coming from Bacos, all of them moving along Gamal Abdel Nasser Street. From Karmuz and Ragheb in the south came the oil, soap, spinning, and weaving workers, on their way to Martyrs' Square—Cairo Station Square—by way of Nabi Danyal Street, to Raml Station, and to Manshiya afterward, the largest square in Alexandria.

Cloth banners appeared with slogans and drawings of Sadat, with an X over his face or in his underwear. No one knew how the slogans had been written and the drawings made so quickly, or when they had been prepared.

"Hey ruler of ours in Ras al-Tin, in the name of all that's pure and clean, justice and religion can't be seen! Here he's dressed in the latest style, we live ten to a room in a pile! Tell the one who sleeps in Abidin, the workers are sleeping hungry and lean!"

The students of the Humanities College poured noisily into Port Said Street, meeting the students of the colleges of law, business, and education, and made their way toward the Corniche.

Nadir and Yara saw Fawqiya and her sister Fawziya standing at a distance from the crowds with Muhammad Shukr, whose fine blond hair was blowing in the wind and who couldn't stop smiling. It was clear that Fawqiya did not want him to participate in the demonstration, and he was smiling and trying to convince her not to be afraid on his account. In the end he shook her hand and her sister's in farewell and ran to the crowds. Nadir saw an expression of fear mixed with anger on Fawqiya's face.

The problem was how Nadir, Hasan, Bishr, Kariman, and Yara could stay together. After a while no one remembered anyone else. Yara stayed close to Kariman, who was suddenly lifted onto the shoulders of two young men she didn't know, shouting "Workers and students in defiance against the capitalist alliance! Zionists are on my shores, the secret police are at my door!" Elsewhere Bishr ended up on Hasan's shoulders, while Hasan couldn't stop smiling, and then he was atop someone else when Hasan tired, calling loudly, "Thieves of the 'Economic Opening,' the people are hungry, they're not coping! You eat chicken and drink your whiskey, the people are so hungry they're dizzy!" From afar they heard more slogans: "Hey America, grab your loot, soon we'll make you feel our boot!" Then shouts rose in a violent cadence from different places, "From left and right and all around, we're gonna bring that Mamduh down!" referring, of course, to the prime minister, Mamduh Salim.

Nadir was trying to stay close to Yara, but he wasn't able to. At the end of the Street of the Seven Girls the smoke of white phosphorus bombs rose in the sky, to scare the advancing crowds of workers. It was clear that a number of soldiers from Central Security were standing there, newly arrived. The first wave of soldiers advanced against the demonstrators near Tarikh Bridge. It failed to stop them and the demonstrators moved beyond them, even throwing some of the soldiers into the Mahmudiya Canal under the bridge, so the rest pulled back and only reappeared at the end of the Street of the Seven Girls.

Then after the phosphorus bombs came a succession of tear gas grenades, but the crowds pushed into the street along the square, where the businessmen had closed their shops and the owners of carts had covered their wares. They circled around from the end of the street to the entrance of the square by Victory Street, where the shops were also closed. Demonstrators coming from the other side did the same, many of them going into St. Catherine's Square and coming out into Manshiya Square behind the soldiers. In Martyrs' Square, the soldiers from Central Security could not hold out long against the crowds so they dispersed, and the crowds made their way to Raml Station and Manshiya. Tear gas grenades were still being thrown at them and they were throwing them back at the soldiers. They also managed to tear up some paving stones, break them into smaller pieces, and hurl them down on the enemy. Here too the businessmen had closed their shops and the street vendors had disappeared. The square was empty and the crowds crossed it, going to Nabi Danyal Street, then Fuad Street and Salah Salem Street on their way to Manshiya.

The protestors coming from this direction expected resistance from the Central Security soldiers in front of the Sherif police station, but they were surprised to find no one opposing them. It was as if the police station was empty, even though it was not closed but stood open before them. They did not stop in front of it or attack it but continued along Salah Salem Street, where all the shops were also closed.

The crowds coming from the Corniche were made up of large numbers of male and female students, as were the crowds coming from the colleges of engineering, agriculture, medicine, and pharmacy. When one young man among them shouted "Here he's dressed in the latest style, we live ten to a room in a pile!" and many people repeated it after him, one of the girls commented wryly, "But here we are, dressed in the latest style. I swear, we're more beautiful than Jehan al-Sadat!" Her friend laughed, but then another chant arose: "Who's this Sayyid Mar'i charmer, he's the one who robs the farmer," and the girl said "Okay, then!" to her friend, and they both laughed.

Ahmad Basim was walking silently in the throng, as if he was thinking about something else. More than once he collided with a female student in the crowd; he would apologize and go on walking, strangely distracted. Chance brought him next to Muhammad Shukr, who said,

"All my life I've seen student demonstrations in films, but this is the first time I've seen a real one. I wonder how it will end?"

Ahmad replied, "I think classes will be suspended. I'll wait a little and then leave town."

"Where to? The demonstrations are all over Egypt."

"I don't think they'll be in Desouk, let alone in my village. The people there are living in the Middle Ages."

All the cafés along the Corniche had closed their doors, as well as the shops in the area stretching from Sidi Gabir to Manshiya, with the exception of a few small shops in lanes and side streets. Columns of Central Security forces massed again, no one knew how, in an attempt to block the demonstrators. They failed to stop the students on Gamal Abdel Nasser Street, since they went around the Shallalat Gardens to Sultan Husayn Street, heading for Manshiya and Raml Station. The security forces had disappeared from Manshiya itself, but they reappeared in heavy concentrations coming from Victory Street and the Street of the Seven Girls, which the demonstrators had bypassed. Tear gas grenades rained down on the crowds. Many of them had dispersed into side streets, but they quickly returned to pull up paving stones with those who had stayed engaged in the clashes. They hurled the stones at the security forces, who once more scattered.

Tens of thousands of students filled Manshiya Square, chanting with their classmates; "Parliament is squash and melon, freedom has become a felon! Hey Sadat, God's your judge too, we can't take this life with you! We demand free government, our life now is punishment!" Two students appeared carrying a large banner with a picture of Jehan al-Sadat in a dancing girl's costume, and everyone who saw it laughed or leapt in the air, not believing what they saw.

At last the square seemed to have surrendered completely to the students and the workers. It was well into afternoon when chance suddenly brought Nadir, Hasan, Bishr, Kariman, Yara, and Muhammad Shukr together; they stood laughing, not believing they had met. Bishr said, "Has anyone seen Ahmad Basim?"

Muhammad answered, "I saw him. He said that classes will be suspended, then he disappeared. I think he's going back to his town."

Hasan asked him, "What about you, Muhammad? Will you leave town?"

"I'm amazed by everything I've seen! I feel like I'm in the movies. I'll stay till the end."

The calls rose around them ceaselessly. "Hey Mamduh, keep your dogs at bay, we won't forget what they did today! Tell the one who sleeps in Abidin, the workers are sleeping hungry and lean!"

The fear on Yara's face was obvious as she looked at Nadir, weeping from the effects of the tear gas and coughing hard. She said, "Come on, let's find a lane in Manshiya. Surely we'll be able to buy something to eat and drink."

He said, "I won't leave them."

Kariman said, "Me neither, this is the best day of my life! And speaking of that, where're the Islamist students?"

Bishr said, "Way over there. It's that small group with a black flag that says 'There is no god but God.' They aren't repeating any of the slogans."

Yara said, "Anyone who sees how angry they are in the college would think they've become the majority in town. But they're just an insignificant number!"

Bishr answered, "This isn't the time to discuss it. You have to go home, Yara, and you too, Kariman."

"I'm with you! We'll all spend the night in the square, and I'll be the last girl to leave. But it's better for Yara to go home. Nobody will miss me." Yara gave her a hug and a kiss. Kariman said, "I've gotten used to it, Yara. I won't be sad if I die."

They looked at her in compassion. Hasan said, "I wish you would take Yara home, Nadir, really."

Nadir looked at her, hoping she would agree. Instead, she said, "I'll take Kariman with me."

Before Kariman could say anything, Bishr cut in: "We men are ordering you two to leave. The battle has not yet begun, and when it does we won't be able to defend you. We'll have to concentrate on pushing back the attack that will surely come."

He had no sooner finished speaking than vans of Central Security forces appeared, coming the wrong way up Ahmad 'Urabi Street, the right way up Salah Salem Street, and also coming from the Corniche. Enormous numbers of soldiers emerged from the vans, well away from the square.

The demonstrators divided into two groups. One attacked the soldiers coming from the Corniche and the area around the French Gardens became a real battlefield, smoke from the bombs rising from it to fill the sky. Another group confronted the attack coming from Muhammad Ali square. Live ammunition flew and several students fell, hastily carried off by their appalled colleagues into the side streets. But the students did not retreat, and finally they were able to push the soldiers back and to drive them along the Corniche. No one knew how it happened but fires broke out in some of the closed cafés, as the soldiers retreated hurriedly and the demonstrators went on pelting them with rocks. On the other side the demonstrators attacked the security forces around the statue of Muhammad Ali, driving them into the small lanes. Fires spread in some of the shops, such as the Egyptian Industries Sales, Muhammad Yusuf Sweets, and the Pyramid Clothing Store. A young man with a full face and a square body appeared among the students, shouting ringing slogans which they repeated after him. He wasn't far from Bishr and Nadir, and Bishr said proudly, "That's Taymur Malwani, leader of the struggle in the College of Engineering."

Voices came from the other direction, calling for an attack on the Socialist Union building. One of those calling for it was being carried on the shoulders of other students, and Bishr said, "And that's Hosni Abdel Rahim, also from the College of Engineering. Fuck Sadat and fuck his government! We're gonna beat 'em!"

The students plunged into the Socialist Union building, the old stock exchange, that architectural treasure. They were able to beat down the doors, then they ran into the upper floors and the hall-ways, and it wasn't long before tongues of flame appeared at the top. The students pulled back a long way into the square, beyond the statue of Muhammd Ali, and stood watching the fire in amazement.

Yara said, not believing her eyes, "That's wrong, it's a historic building."

Kariman was next to her. She said, "The fires won't stop tonight. There's some unknown hand behind this."

Muhammad Shukr was standing near them, and he said, "You really have to go home to be safe tonight."

Yara looked at Kariman. "Come with me, please, don't let me go home alone."

All at once Hasan appeared, very tense, and said, "A lot of girls are leaving the square now, you have to go home. We've told you before."

Yara took Kariman by the hand and left, leading her away until they got to Faransa Street. All the jewelry shops were closed, and everyone standing there was looking at the two girls in surprise. A lot of them were young men standing in front of the shops to guard them.

Nadir, Bishr, Hasan, and Muhammad were together now, in the midst of the shouting throngs. Crowds were still arriving, and con-tinuing to march along the Corniche toward Shatbi and Sidi Gabir, pursuing the security forces. Even after the soldiers had retreated they were still running after them, trying to push them as far back as possible. It all happened spontaneously, without forethought.

The squares belonged to the demonstrators overnight, Man-shiya, Raml Station, and Martyrs' Square at Cairo Station. They sat in circles, happily singing songs by Sheikh Imam or reciting poems by El Abnoudy, Salah Jahin, and Fuad Haddad. A light rain fell on the city, and then quickly strengthened. Some people sought refuge in the side streets, while others held out. The rain washed away the odor of smoke, cleansing the earth and the sky. The people who had gone into the side streets sat in the cafés that were open, following the events of this critical day on television, and listening to the lies of the government about infiltrators and Communists who wanted to destroy the country.

News came of fires breaking out in Cairo and along al-Haram Street in Giza, but none of the students or workers believed that their comrades in Cairo had set them. Everyone realized immediately that the Interior Ministry had released the thieves and thugs they had been holding in police stations in order to do those things. No one believed that the burned vehicles, buses, and trams in Cairo were the work of the demonstrators.

Those who left the cafés went back to the square. Manshiya became a center of freedom. Many of the students and workers brought back what they were able to buy in the broad-bean shops and the bakeries in the side streets and divided it among the others. The fire in the Socialist Union building was still going on, though many of the fires in the cafés along the Corniche had gone out. News came of fires in some of the closed nightclubs. Bishr said, sarcastically, "To ensure absolutely that they'll be sold."

Hasan smiled while Nadir was preoccupied by the thought that it might be true.

Muhammad said, "Aren't we going to go back to the apartment to rest?"

Bishr said, "I've read about the Paris Commune. Now we're in the Alexandria Commune!"

Nadir smiled. They were sitting on the pavement, exhausted, while around them hundreds of others sat or stood or moved around. No one knew how the night passed, in singing and poetry, without anyone weakening. In the early hours of the morning the Central Security forces launched another attack, but it was repulsed like the one the day before. The nearby government hospital was filled with the injured.

Around noon they learned that President Sadat had canceled all the economic reforms. They rejoiced, shouting "God is great!" and "There is no god but God!" and dancing in joy. They also learned that the army was heading into the squares and the streets, and that a curfew had been imposed, beginning at four in the afternoon.

Neither Yara nor Kariman got much sleep that night. At first they had stayed in the living room with Yara's mother, father, and brother, in front of the television. Kariman had held her peace when Yara's brother Fuad cursed the demonstrators and insulted them, exerting great effort not to respond. Yara had sensed what she was feeling; she was also very angry with him but was not letting that show. She'd asked Kariman to go to her room with her and listen to the news on the radio and she had agreed, to get away from this brother and his talk. They were both exhausted, and by about one o'clock they could no longer stay up. In the morning Kariman left the house, promising Yara that she would go directly back to her house. Instead she went to Manshiya Square to meet her friends, and stayed with them until the news of the curfew was broadcast and everyone began thinking about leaving.

Bishr said, "The believing president has pulled back from his reforms, so we've won. We can leave the square now."

Hasan decided to take Kariman as close as possible to her house, far away in Mandara. There would be no public transportation now, and people were leaving the squares in groups on their way to their houses. Bishr and Muhammad were going to the apartment, walking along the Corniche with many others. The sea on their left was still angry, the waves ceaselessly hitting the beach with violence, striking the breakwater and splashing above it. On their right were the closed cafés, most of them burned out or showing some traces of fire.

Bishr said, "It would be best for you to leave town, Muhammad. Hasan is going to take Kariman home and then leave directly for Mansura. As you know, Nadir's house is in Maks, and Ahmad Basim saved time and left yesterday, as he told you."

"Aren't you coming to the apartment?"

"I live in Bacos. I'll leave you and go to Gamal Abdel Nasser Street and walk until I get there."

Muhammad smiled. "I'll tell you a secret. Classes have been suspended, as you see. I'll stay in the apartment so I can meet Fawqiya in the coming days when we won't have anything else to do."

"But your family at home must be worried about you."

"I'll call them tonight. I already tried to phone them from a few of the shops in the side streets near Manshiya, but all the lines were down. Tomorrow I'll find a way to reassure them. I'm hoping to see Fawqiya a lot before classes start up again."

Bishr nearly told him that the police might come to the apartment that night, but having decided to make his way home, he began thinking about himself. He was thinking that if he was arrested it would be from his house, the way it happened before. Absorbed in his thoughts, he said nothing.

Muhammad arrived at the apartment alone and exhausted, when it was almost three-thirty in the afternoon. He discovered that there was nothing to eat in the apartment, and that he was very hungry. He wouldn't be able to go out to buy anything, since the half hour before the curfew wasn't enough to walk around and find a store open in the side streets.

He took off the blue suit jacket that he often wore in the college, and his tie, and stretched out on the bed thinking about what to do. But he fell into a deep sleep. He woke up about ten o'clock at night to knocking on the door. He didn't know where he was, exactly, and it took him a few minutes to realize where he was in space and time. He had gone to unknown regions in his sleep.

He turned on the light and went out to the living room, finding the lights on there. He realized that he had turned them on needlessly when he came in.

Frightened, he asked, "Who is it?"

Rawayih's voice answered: "Open up, Si Bishr."

He was surprised for a moment. Was his voice like Bishr's, which was always hoarse? Then he realized that it was because of all the shouting with the others during the protests, yesterday and today. In fact he did feel some inflammation in his throat. He knew that Rawayih and Ghada lived in the apartment on the floor below, but he hadn't happened to speak to them before. Should he open the door for them? Who knew, he might find some food with them, and he was hungrier than ever.

He opened the door. Rawayih and Ghada were wearing housecoats. He heard the sound of the rain and noticed that it had become heavy. Rawayih said, "*Youououou*, damn me, you're Si Muhammad!"

He smiled, and they came in and sat down, without asking permission. Ghada asked, "Where are Si Bishr and Si Nadir and Si Hasan and Si Ahmad?"

"They've gone home."

Rawayih asked, "Why are you still here? Aren't you from the country?"

He smiled. "It's just the way it happened."

Rawayih asked, "What happened in town? The TV says that the army's in the streets."

"That's right."

"So this curfew, what does that mean? We only have enough food for one day."

He said, "The curfew is only until morning." He began to feel hunger pains and put his hand on his belly. Ghada said, "You look hungry."

"Very hungry!" He said it without thinking.

She said, "Just a minute. We'll go down and bring up some food. As long as the curfew is only until morning."

Rawayih said, "It would be best if you came down with us, to watch TV and eat. What do you say? As long as you're alone."

He thought for a moment and then said, "Why not? I'll change my clothes, since I slept in them, and put on pajamas."

"We'll wait here so you don't go back on your word!"

He smiled. Then he changed into pajamas and went down with them. In their apartment he began to eat with a real appetite. They sat watching him in amazement, talking continually.

"We'll go back to working in the café again."

"The nightclubs have closed and most of them were burned."

"Sadat is the reason, may he answer to God!"

"He has a great life and he's letting people go hungry."

"But Jehan is really beautiful, it's a shame for her to be insulted and ridiculed."

"Still, she should have told him, 'You should be ashamed!'"

"The way things are going it looks as if we'll have to leave Alexandria and go back to our towns."

"I wonder if we could?"

He was listening without answering, hearing in their words stories about each of them that he didn't know.

"Damn Sheikh Zaalan! He married me and divorced me. He could have given me a delayed dowry portion that would have left me comfortable."

"Even the club owned by Madam Nawal, that respectable lady, was burned down."

"Can you imagine that Alexandria will spend a single night without singing and dancing and fun?"

"Alexandria Radio, may they answer to God, broadcast everything that happened. What made you turn it on today, Ghada, and for the whole day?"

"My fate and fortune. The TV only had Cairo news, so I thought I should know what happened in Alexandria. I wanted reassurance."

"Anyway we would have found out, either way. Don't worry, we have a Lord whose name is Generous."

Muhammad remained silent for a long time, smiling, even after he had eaten and had tea with them. Ghada said suddenly, "Tell me, Si Muhammad! You're really handsome, blond and blue-eyed. Are you from Syria?"

He laughed. "Why?"

"Because Rawayih loved somebody from Syria who looked exactly like you. That's why she's been sitting and staring at you this whole time."

He laughed again. "I'm an Egyptian, son of an Egyptian."

Just then the television started broadcasting the play *School for Troublemakers*, and the two women burst out laughing. Rawayih said, "Younes Shalaby is great!"

Ghada answered, "And Adel Emam and Saeed Salih."

Rawayih said, "And Ahmad Zaki too. Poor thing, what a pity his mother works as a maid for the headmaster."

Then they fell silent, to follow the comedy. As soon as it ended Muhammad stood up to leave, thanking them. Rawayih gave him a sack with three oranges in it, saying,

"Take it with you so if you get hungry you'll have something to eat. I've been thinking, there's no curfew tomorrow until afternoon, so we'll buy something else."

He felt gratitude and affection for them. For a moment he thought about not going upstairs and staying with them, but he quickly changed his mind when he remembered Fawqiya. He went up to the apartment and sat thinking about whether staying here had been the right thing to do. The mournful sound of the dawn call to prayer came to him from afar. How beautiful the dawn was, when everything was silent! But the doorbell rang long and loudly, disturbing him. It was a detachment of police led by an officer from the State Security apparatus.

9

Surreptitiously, Yara took the newspapers her brother had bought. She used to take them naturally, but now she thought he might ask her why she was taking such an interest in the papers. For two days she read the news of the detentions and the names of the detainees. They were names she had never heard before but she read them carefully, contemplating them, because some sense of terror weighed heavily on her heart. Nadir had not called and she didn't know how to reach him; no one answered her calls to Kariman, nor did Kariman call her. Hundreds had been detained, both men and women. They were distributed among the Citadel, Tura, Abu Zaabal, Qanatir, and Istinaf prisons, charged with inciting demonstrations and attempting to overthrow the regime. She read the names thinking, "Oh Lord, let Nadir's name not be among them, not Bishr or Hasan or Kariman!" She read each name twice, to make sure it did not belong to any of them:

Abdel Qadir Shuhayb; Rushdi Abul Hasan; Muhammad Izzat Amir; Muhammad al-Shadhili; Kemal Khalil; Muhammad Hani al-Husayni; Aryan Nasif; Amir Salim; Ahmad Bahaa Eddin Shaaban, with the word "fugitive" in front of the name; Shibl al-Sayyid Salim; Zuhdi al-Adawi; Salah Isa; Nadia Mahmud; Abdel Hakim Taymur al-Malwani—she remembered that she had seen him, loudly shouting slogans. Samir Abdel Baqi; Shuhrat al-Alim; Randa Abdel Ghaffar; Farouk Nasif; Qutb Hamza; Shawqiya al-Kurdi; Magda Muhammad Adli; Samiha Ahmad al-Kafrawi; Farouk Radwan; Hamdi Eid; Usama Khalil; Ikram Yusuf Khalil; Musaad al-Tarabili; Ibrahim Fahmi; Husayn Abdel Razzak; Muhammd Rafiq al-Kurdi; Magid Sakrana.

She stopped to catch her breath and then went on reading the names: Zayn al-Abidin Fuad; Aatif Abdel Gawad; Abdel Khaliq Farouk Husayn; Shawqi al-Kurdi; Radwan al-Kashif; Samir Ghattas; Husni Abdel Rahim—she had seen him, she remembered. Salwa Milad; Hamad Nasr; Zaki Murad; Mubarak Abduh Fadl; Muhammad Ali al-Zahhar; Muhammad Shukr; Nabil Atris; Imad Atris; Bishr Zahran; Nadir Saeed; Hasan Hafiz; Kariman Ali.

She collapsed in shock, unable to continue reading.

It had now been three days since the demonstrations were dispersed, and she knew that all the charges were being directed against the four secret Communist parties: the Egyptian Communist Party, the Revolutionary Current, the Communist Workers' Party, and the Eighth of January Party, in addition to members of the Tagammu Party and its leaders. All the talk in the newspapers and on television was about the foreign plot that had been carried out by domestic elements. For three days she went on reading the names of the accused, both the fugitives and those who had been arrested:

Michel Kamel; Muhammad Yusuf al-Gindi; Abdel Mun'im al-Qassas; Mahmud Amin al-Alim; Abdel Mun'im Talima; Ahmad Fouad Negm; Rafaat al-Saeed; Nabil al-Hilali; Ezzeldin Naguib; Baraa al-Khatib; Abduh Jubayr; Salah Zaki.

All those arrested were writers, artists, and literary figures, the heart and soul of the nation—how could they be corrupt? There were one hundred and thirty people accused of belonging to the Egyptian Communist Party, ninety-one accused of belonging to the Revolutionary Current, and many others accused of belonging to the Egyptian Workers' Party and the Eighth of January Party. She had read articles in the newspapers by many of them, she had read books written by some of them, and she had seen drawings by others in the papers.

She read the paper several times a day, repeating the names and seeing her friends' names among them. She wept, and tried hard to conceal any trace of her weeping.

Every time she reread the lists she hoped she would not find Nadir, Hasan, Bishr, Kariman, and Muhammad Shukr among them. She had been shocked to find Muhammad's name on the list, when he had only moved in with them less than a month before. How could they consider him like the rest of them, when he loved Fawqiya, the daughter of the previous minister? If only he had listened to Fawqiya and not gone to the demonstration! She didn't know that what had happened to him had happened to many others also, such as the lawyer Zarif Abdallah, who had been living in Paris for nine years and whose name appeared on the indictment even though he was out of the country and working for the United Nations. The name of Ahmad Rifa'i also appeared, when he had been living and working in Yemen for three years. The biggest joke was that they had gone to arrest Dr. Mahmud al-Qawisni, an old leftist who had died a week before the demonstrations, and had gone also to arrest army conscripts who had not left their units for a long time. Nor did she know that six days later the bell of her own apartment was going to ring, loud and long, at dawn.

She was asleep when the bell woke her; she was distraught and remained in her room. Everyone in the house was confused, her father, her mother, and her brother. They came out of their rooms and stood in the living room, looking at each other in shock. Her brother Fuad yelled angrily,

"Who is it?"

The even answer came from behind the door. "Police."

They looked at each other, stunned.

Her mother asked her father, "What does that mean?"

Her father seemed incapable of understanding. Fuad yelled at his mother, "Go and put on a robe!" She was standing in a winter nightgown which revealed nothing of her body. Nevertheless it was still a nightgown.

Yara was listening from behind the door of her room, bewildered and afraid. Her mother hurriedly went into her room and emerged wearing a robe and carrying another for her husband to put on over his pajamas. He put it on the dining table, in a daze.

Fuad opened the door and found before him a young officer with piercing eyes, wearing civilian clothes and displaying his identification with his rank in State Security. Beside him stood a young officer with the rank of lieutenant, in uniform; he did not display anything, and Fuad realized that he was from the secret police. Behind them on the stairs stood a number of soldiers and intelligence personnel, the soldiers carrying small machine guns. The officer in civilian clothes said, "Captain Abdel Salim Samih from State Security. May I come in?"

Before anyone could say a word the soldiers and intelligence officers had come in and taken up positions all over the large room. Fuad protested, "I'm also an officer, in the merchant marine. What you're doing is against the law. Do you have a warrant from the district attorney's office, sir?"

The State Security officer smiled and pointed to the soldiers and intelligence officers, saying, "Search everywhere." Then, addressing Fuad, he said, "We don't have time, Mr. Officer. You can object in the district attorney's office, if you can find anyone to listen to your objections."

The secret police officer scowled. "Resistance is not in your best interests."

At that, Fuad felt chagrined. Being an officer in the merchant marine was useless, since it was not one of the Egyptian armed forces. If he had been in the Egyptian army, it would have been another matter.

His mother pointed to Yara's room and said, "Just a minute, please. Don't go in there, I beg you. My daughter's sleeping. I'll go wake her up first."

The State Security officer said, "Miss Yara?" They looked at him in surprise. With an ironic smile he said, "We've come because of her. Please, madam, go wake her up, because we're going to search the room."

Yara's mother went into her room in a daze. She didn't know that Yara had been standing behind the door, confused and terrified, listening to the entire exchange. The State Security officer said to her father,

"Your daughter, sir, is in a Communist organization. Your daughter is among those who urged the people to demonstrate."

Her father took a step backward and fell into one of the chairs, astonished.

Fuad's face also showed his profound amazement. He softened his tone and said to the officer, "Fine, but please search without damaging anything in the house. I know my sister isn't involved in anything."

The officer nodded. "Certainly." Then he said to his men, "Careful, keep it under control, for the sake of Mr. Officer."

Yara came out of her room with her mother. She was extremely pale and was wearing a robe over her nightgown. As soon as he saw her the State Security officer said,

"Hello, Miss Yara. I'd like you to change your clothes, please, since you'll be coming with us as soon as we've finished the search."

Yara's father seemed overwhelmed by sadness, and her mother collapsed next to him. All at once Yara pulled herself together, saying, "You won't find anything. You've chosen the wrong place, sir."

Fuad was again astonished, this time by the strength shown by his innocent, naive sister, as he had always considered her. But then he thought of something else, and hurried to his room to make a phone call. Two of the secret police were there, searching, and when he lifted the receiver he found the line dead. The State Security officer had cut the main phone line in the living room, so all of the telephones in the other rooms were also disconnected.

Yara sat down next to her father and said, "Don't worry, Papa, don't worry, Mama. I'm not involved in anything, not in anything."

No sooner had she said that than one of the two secret police officers who had gone into her room came out, holding aloft a number of copies of the *Victory*, published by the Egyptian Communist

Party, and more copies of the publication *The People's Struggle*, from the same party. He said, "We found these magazines, sir."

Yara stood up and moved to take them from his hand, shouting, "You planted those in my room, you dogs!"

Her father, mother, and brother froze in astonishment, more at Yara than at the magazines. The secret police officer turned to her angrily, but the State Security officer motioned to him to stay where he was and commanded him sharply "Don't move!"

He looked at Yara, apparently affected by her beauty. He said to her father, "Your daughter really shouldn't be ill-treated, sir, but this is our work."

Silence settled over them all, as the search continued with great care in every part of the large apartment. They even ran their hands over wallpaper that had been on the walls for many years, on the chance of finding something between it and the wall. Yara said, mocking them, "You won't find anything other than what you brought with you."

The officer replied, also mocking, "Go get dressed and pack a small suitcase with a change of clothes. You'll need it."

She went resolutely into her room. Her father asked, from where he sat in bewilderment, "Where are you taking my daughter?"

"Maybe the Hadra Prison, until she's brought before the district attorney tomorrow. Maybe al-Qanatir in Qalyubiya. I didn't have to tell you that, but Miss Yara is really not cut out for ill treatment."

They left with Yara as her mother's tears struggled to escape; she was an aristocratic woman who did not want to appear weak in front of them. As she left Yara seemed possessed of a strength that none of her family had expected of her.

As soon as they were out of the apartment Fuad shouted at his father, "Are you happy with what your daughter's done?"

His father didn't answer; his mother said, angrily, "Reconnect the telephone line they cut and call Ragi Bey instead of talking nonsense!"

She ran into Yara's room to try to catch a glimpse of her daughter in the street from the balcony. She was met by peaceful dawn light coming into the world from afar, by the sound of the waves that had died down, as if the sea were at rest, and by a light rain. Below the house in the street was a private car, a Volkswagen; she saw Yara getting into the back seat while the State Security officer sat in front. The Volkswagen had no back door, so there was no chance for anyone in back to flee. She also saw several Jeeps carrying the intelligence officers, the soldiers, and the secret police officer. They all sped off down the empty street toward Manshiya.

Yara spent the rest of the night in the security headquarters. There were no other Communists with her. One of the senior officers put her in his office for that night and the whole of the following day, until she was presented to the district attorney in the evening. The call her brother had made to Ragi Bey, the former sea captain, had had its effect. He was a man with old and strong relationships with all the influential people in Alexandria, and he reassured them fully.

In fact in the morning the family was surprised by a call from Sayyid Bey Abdel Bari himself, head of State Security, apologizing for what had happened. He had not known anything about Yara, he told them. Naturally they did not know that he knew everything about her, and that he had arranged all of this. Nonetheless it seemed that Ragi Bey had contacted an important person from outside the province of Alexandria. Sayyid Bey told them that Yara could only be released by the district attorney, and that they would not present to him any of the documentss they had found in her possession. At the same time he warned them against letting her go back to her friends, whom he named—Nadir, Hasan, Bishr, and Kariman—who were now all in prison.

Yara was released from the custody of the district attorney that evening.

Thus the return home was easy, in spite of Yara's pallor and the pain that showed on her face. As soon as she sat in the living room she burst out crying, and said,

"I did the same thing Kariman did and now she's in prison, I saw her name in the papers, and I've been released. How come? It's unjust!"

Her family was surprised, and her brother Fuad yelled at her,

"You're upset because your friend is a Communist? You deserve to be killed! You're a failure and so are your friends."

She did not look up at him for several minutes. Then she stood up calmly and walked quickly into the kitchen, shouting, "I'll kill myself and leave you in peace!"

Her mother yelled, "Fuad, your sister!"

Fuad didn't budge. His father was the one who ran to the kitchen to grab her right hand, holding the knife, before she could cut her left wrist with it. Then he yelled, "Help me!"

It wasn't because Yara had cut her veins, but because she had fainted and fallen to the floor.

All through the night
I wake and weep, loving you,
For with your first sight
My spirit flies back to me.
Days and years melt into you,
Then my flute wakes you gently.
As long as this world holds you and me,
To hell with my parents and my family!
Where would I go, when before me I see you?

Bishr, Hasan, Nadir, Kariman, and Muhammad Shukr all spent five months in prison. They listened to many songs sung by their comrades, but each of them, wherever he was held, was especially affected by the songs of Sayyid Darwish. There was always someone repeating this particular song, which they all knew was from a lover to his beloved. They would sing along, mournfully in the first section, then laughing during the second part as optimism took hold and they felt relaxed and hopeful.

They had been distributed in different prisons far from each other, as if that had been arranged ahead of time by State Security: Bishr was in the Istinaf Prison, Hasan in Tura, Nadir in Qanatir, Muhammad in Abu Zaabal, and Kariman in the Qanatir Women's Prison.

Even though Bishr had been in prison once before, this time he was with people he had not known previously, and the prison was filthy beyond imagination. The Istinaf prison, which he had once read was a clean prison under the royal regime, had held politicians and opposition figures before, among them President Sadat himself.

Each one of them had an experience that he would be able to tell others about some day. They never met, even when they were transported in vans to the prosecutor's headquarters, as their scheduled appearances were all different. But they heard news of each other from their comrades.

Each time they came before the prosecution some of them would expect to be released, but the prosecution always extended their imprisonment. Muhammad suffered the most pain and grief. Every time he would tell them that he was not involved in politics, that he had moved into the apartment with Bishr, Hasan, and Nadir by chance about three weeks before everything happened, and that the one who had encouraged him to move in was his classmate Ahmad Basim, who had not been arrested and whom they could ask. But the prosecutor's office always decided to continue holding him.

For the first time, Muhammad saw the Communists holding seminars in the evening and singing the songs of poets he did not know about, except for Salah Jahin and Abdel Rahman El Abnoudy. Even though he had never before heard of Ahmad Fouad Negm, Zayn al-Abidin Fuad, or Naguib Shihab al-Din, he knew that Zayn al-Abidin Fuad was among them in another prison, and that Ahmad Fouad Negm had been a fugitive for a long time. Those in the prison block with him would go to sleep in the middle of the night while he would remain wakeful, thinking about whether he would ever return to Fawqiya again.

There wasn't much difference in what each of them experienced. The windows of the blocks were very high, the glass panes fixed in the wall and not made to open. A faint light came from behind them but no air. The prison food was bad and they didn't eat it, except for the bread, which was good. This seemed strange to everyone except Bishr, who had experienced it before. They knew that the Agency of Prisons had bakeries, with a bakery in every large prison except for Istinaf and Abu Zaabal, where bread was sent from other prisons. As for the broad beans, the weevils swimming in them were visible to the eye. After the visits from the prisoners' families were organized the prison administration no longer distributed anything but bread to them, since they received food from the outside.

The experienced political prisoners quickly became close to those incarcerated for crimes, so every block soon had chess and cards to kill time, provided by those on the criminal side in exchange for cigarettes. The families of the political prisoners, especially those from Cairo, brought large quantities of food and cigarettes, more than enough for them. The cigarettes in particular were a means to make friends with the criminals, who also supplied them with small alcohol burners, officially banned in the prisons, with which to make tea or coffee. Families also smuggled newspapers to them: they folded them and put them in plastic bags and then put the bags under rice in a pot. It was a simple matter to cook the rice in one pot, allow it to cool, and then turn it over into another pot with the plastic bag containing the newspaper on the bottom. The newspapers were always the subject of much ridicule; *Rose al-Yusuf* was the only one they all read avidly.

Bishr was punished more than once, since he was always calling for a hunger strike, and did not hesitate to shout at the warden when he came to discuss ending it. The punishment was sometimes to exclude him from the prisoners who were allowed out in the sun, and sometimes solitary confinement, once for ten whole days.

Hasan Hafiz seemed fine, always smiling when he spoke, believing that things were only temporary and would pass. Once when one of his comrades asked him about the secret behind his smile and he answered, "We're now in 1977." The other man seemed not to understand, so Hasan went on, "So, 1,977 years have passed since the birth of Christ, and there will be another 1,977 yet to come, so why shouldn't I smile?"

His comrade was amazed, but he too began to smile all the time, like Hasan. He'd laugh and say to his comrades, "Watch out, there're 1,977 years waiting for us," and they would all laugh.

There were doctors among them, and in time the prison hospital and clinic began to make use of them. And from their visits to the public prosecutor's office they all learned, in every prison, that Khalil was still a fugitive, along with a few others.

Hasan asked his family members who visited him for a notebook and pencils. The prison administration confiscated them, but then he got better supplies from the criminal prisoners. Nadir did the same and experienced the same confiscation, but he was also able to get supplies from the criminals.

Hasan wrote several stories, in which endless night was a main character; Nadir wrote various poems that he didn't show to anyone. He often memorized what he wrote despite his lack of talent for memorization. During the night when everyone around him was sleeping he would sit leaning his back against the cold wall, reciting his poems to himself, memorizing them. He begged his father and mother not to come again, after their first visit. The trip from Alexandria exhausted them, and they could only visit after getting permission from the district attorney. The truth was that he didn't want to suffer from the sight of his mother's tears, although she did her best to hide them. Bishr and Hasan each did the same with their mothers and fathers.

Muhammad Shukr was met with blame and reproach from his father, but members of his family continued to visit him, and he continued to wait for one visit that did not take place. He wrote several letters to Fawqiya, explaining his innocence on all charges. He didn't want to give them to any of his family to mail, because they might not do it. He found it easier to do what his companions suggested and send them through the criminal prisoners. He kept wondering in amazement how they could allow the criminal prisoners to send letters and not allow the political prisoners to do the same. He learned that it was not allowed for the criminals, either, but they knew how to smuggle them out.

The cold gnawed their bones, because of the large size of the prison blocks, because of the thin mattresses, and because of the old covers that amounted to no more than one worn-out blanket for every prisoner. The drumbeats that sometimes sounded at night attracted the attention of Hasan, Nadir, Muhammad, and every first-time prisoner. They occurred in all the prisons where they had been placed. They learned that these were celebrations held on the occasion of the marriage of an old convict, who was strong and influential, to a new prisoner who was weak and helpless. They saw these "prison wives" in the yard, walking in the sun in front of the blocks, wearing feminine nightgowns that bared their arms and chests. They would put on heavy lipstick and talk like whores.

Innocent Muhammad Shukr was waiting for an answer to his letters to Fawqiya, but he did not receive anything. He told himself that perhaps that was because she thought that letters from her would be opened in the warden's office before they ever got to him, and that the authorities would know what was said and who sent them. He never noticed that no letter ever reached any prisoner by mail. He retreated into silence, turning away from all the prisoners' intellectual activities. He could always be seen sitting far away beside the wall and lamenting his state, stunned by what had happened to him.

Hasan knew that Kariman had been imprisoned and did not expect a visit from her. He would smile and say cynically that she was better off this way than she would have been with her stepfather. He knew he was trying to keep himself from suffering at the thought of her in prison.

Among the recurring scenes in nearly every prison was a criminal convict walking during recreation with his lips sewn together with thread so that he could not speak. The next day he'd appear with his nose sewn shut, and on the third day he'd be walking with his eyelids sewn shut so that he couldn't see. The new prisoners learned that this was a form of protest used by some of the criminals.

The criminals did not know about hunger strikes, one of the means used by political prisoners to obtain their rights. They all used hunger strikes to get the right to visits from behind a wire mesh, at any time and without prior permission from the prosecution. Muhammad Shukr never went on a hunger strike; Bishr participated conscientiously with his comrades, and Hasan and Nadir went on strike to try it. All of them dreamed of huge round loaves of bread, growing on the ground in place of the sand until they filled the desert. They told their comrades about this strange dream, only to find that the others had also had the same dream.

When they were due at the prosecutor's headquarters, they shouted from the transport vans with the old political prisoners, "Down, down with the lying president!" And they sang the song of Sheikh Imam, written by Zayn al-Abidin Fuad:

Gather the lovers in the Citadel Prison,
Gather the lovers in Bab al-Khalq,
The sun is a song rising from the cells
And Egypt is a song spread over Bab al-Khalq.
Gather the lovers together in the cell,
No matter the oppression, no matter how long,
No matter that the beatings come strong,
Who can keep Egypt in prison for long?

Each time they would return with disappointment in their eyes.

In spite of all the good food sent to them by the families of their jailed comrades from Cairo, helped by some of the Communist parties and by some opposition politicians, they still all lost a great deal of weight.

Life on the outside was not remote from them, because of the smuggled newspapers, but they still couldn't believe that life was continuing in a way that was the complete opposite of the great uprising they had wanted. Everything they saw written about the confessions of some of the accused, who admitted to having planned all the destruction even before the price increases were announced, was a lie. Distributed among the prisons as they were they knew that only one or two people had confessed to that, and it was clear that they were agents acting on behalf of State Security. The prosecutor general's statements about seizing publications praising destruction were lies; but as to Sadat's decision to sentence to hard labor anyone who set up a secret organization opposed to the regime, be it civil or military, that was true. The man was tightening his grip on the country, after calling the uprising "an intifada of thieves." They knew that the real thieves had been let out of jail on the evening of the eighteenth by the police themselves, to plunder, steal, and burn. The man who was tightening his grip also gave hard labor to anyone who schemed or participated in any mass communication or occupation that threatened the public order, and public order meant submitting to the state without opposition.

Thus the nightly prison seminars satirized everything, including the futile measures Sadat signed in public and submitted to a referendum, which would of course result in a win of 99%, as had been true for every referendum held since the revolution of July 1952. Sadat repeated his attacks on the Communists, who had infiltrated the newspapers. They laughed at that, because no journalist was appointed without the knowledge of the government. Besides, the Communists were now all either in prison or out of the country. When Parliament decided to convert the public companies that were operating at a loss into private stock companies, they realized that the era of selling off public-sector companies had begun, and that the companies would be sold to men of the regime and its financiers. A policy of pressuring public-sector companies to show a loss had also begun, and an era of parasitic capitalism that pounced on the people's money was taking off in force. It was a capitalism that had no history, serving only the men of the regime.

The prisoners didn't care about any of the news items concerning the differences with Libya, neither the prohibition of Egyptians from entering Libya nor the execution of an operative reporting to Libyan intelligence who had put two bombs in the Mugamma government offices in Cairo. They thought that that might also have been an operation carried out by Egyptian intelligence; the truth was lost between a crazy president in Libya and a crazy president in Egypt.

The Palestinian poet Rashid Husayn was assassinated on February first that year, in New York, where unknown persons set his home on fire. He had been working as a correspondent for a Palestinian news agency. The death of Abdel Halim Hafiz on

Wednesday, March 30, was an occasion of great sadness, even if some of them considered his songs, like those of Umm Kulthum, a kind of opiate for the people. Still many were truly grieved, and most of all Muhammad Shukr, who wept, to the surprise of everyone in the prison block. Nadir also shed tears, but he hid them. In the Qanatir Women's Prison many women around Kariman wept, screamed, and slapped their faces, while she wept in silence. The news of Abdel Halim's funeral stayed in the papers for days, shock lessening to a lifted eyebrow as they became accustomed to it. The same month the poet Muhammad Ali Ahmad died. He had written the songs "As Much as Desire" for Abdel Halim Hafiz, "If You Have Forgotten, I'll Remind You" for Huda Sultan, and "Between Water and Two Shores" for Muhammad Kandil, the most beautiful songs there were about Alexandria; but Abdel Halim's death preoccupied everyone.

Meanwhile Sadat was still making gains from the continuing court cases about torture undertaken by men of the previous regime, Shams Badran, Nasser's minister of defense, and his aides. Badran's trial had begun in April, and he was accused in several serious cases of torture. The prisoners laughed a lot when a Libyan pilot defected to Cairo with his plane, and they laughed about what Qadhafi said, screaming that he was surrounded by traitors in Libya and that the noose was waiting for anyone connected in any way with the incident.

Finally, at the end of May, the Egyptian authorities settled on a decision to indict one hundred and seventy-six people on the charge of participating in the January uprising, and to release one hundred and seventy-seven others, who were not included in the indictment. Among the latter were Nadir, Bishr, Hasan, Muhammad, and Kariman.

Close to five months had passed. Those who had later appointments at the prosecutor's office learned the names of those who had been set free that morning, but they were all released from the prisons at night. Since they were coming from different prisons each of them made his own way back, alone. Hasan thought he might meet one of them in Ramses Station in Cairo; they all thought that. But they did not come across one another.

On the morning of the next day Hasan stood in the courtyard of the college, in front of the Abbadi Lecture Hall. They had learned of the examination schedule from the newspapers, and this was the day before the last exam. Hasan had not gone to meet any of his classmates since he and his comrades had all failed this year; the prison administration had not given them any chance to study or to take any exams. But Hasan's spirit was filled with delight because he was going to meet Kariman. Here she was, coming to the same place in front of the Abbadi Hall, but he couldn't believe what he saw: her green eyes were all that remained of her. Her white face, always radiant with health, was now pale and sallow, with small pimples, and she had lost a great deal of weight. But she was still Kariman, his beloved, who still made his heart beat faster. He did not see what had happened to him, the weight he had lost, and how his small smile that was never full had become smaller.

There were deep blue circles around Kariman's eyes, and she was smoking greedily where she stood. A few students passed by her, reading papers they held. They were the ones who had exams during the afternoon and who had come early to review one last time; those with morning exams had not yet finished them. Why had she come, when she hadn't studied or taken an exam, and had failed this year, like the others? It must be that she expected to see him.

She saw him and froze in place, tears springing to her eyes. He ran to her and took her hands, kissing them wordlessly. Then he put his arm around her with no fear of anyone, and walked with her to the cafeteria. He said,

"I knew I would find you here! I heard about your release from the soldier in the prosecutor's office. Also about the release of Bishr, Nadir, and Muhammad Shukr. I imagine they'll come here too."

She looked at him as if in reproach. Why ever would the others come? She had come expecting to find him. Then she remembered that Nadir might come to see Yara, and Muhammad might come to see Fawqiya, and Bishr might come because he was the craziest of them all.

"Why didn't you go to Mansura?" she asked sadly.

He took her hand. "I would have died if I hadn't seen you today."

Her mind wandered away from him for a moment. She seemed deeply sad, as she lit one cigarette from another. He asked, "Did you have any problem with your family?"

Shaking her head derisively, she said, "The problems aren't new, but this time they're different. My stepfather has married another woman and she's now living in my room."

He was astonished. "Another woman!"

"Yes. She wears a veil over her face and my mother has started wearing one too. The two of them sit around him and bring him whatever he wants, perfectly happy."

"That's crazy!"

She made a small noise of despair. "And you, where will you stay?" Hasan asked.

"He told me, 'There's no place for you here, go to the infidel Communists!'"

"And your mother?"

"She simply said, 'You're the reason.'"

He seemed deeply alarmed. "Where did you spend the night, then?"

"Sleeping on the couch in the living room. He wants it that way so he can always see me wherever he's going."

Tears returned to her eyes. He reached out to brush them away with his fingers, but she began to dry them with a small handkerchief, and pushed his fingers away.

"Don't cry, Kariman. We'll figure it all out."

Through the cafeteria glass he saw Muhammad Shukr, who was emaciated, coming to the courtyard in front of the Abbadi Lecture Hall. A few male and female students appeared, coming from the upper floors where the exams were held, looking happy and comparing their answers.

Hasan called, "Muhammad!" He nearly got up to go to him, but Fawqiya and her sister appeared at the same moment. He said to Kariman, "Fawqiya! God preserve us."

Kariman witnessed the scene with him from the cafeteria, without hearing the short conversation. Fawqiya hurried away from Muhammad after saying something to him that seemed harsh, from the movements of her hands and her lips, and her sister hurried after her. Muhammad stood in confusion and dismay as the passing students stared at him, some with sympathy and others smiling.

Kariman said sadly, "Fawqiya has left him and the love story has ended." Then she went on, "Poor Muhammad! He's kind and lovable, and he had nothing to do with it. He was imprisoned unjustly."

Hasan stood. "I'm going to go get him."

He left her and went out. When he called his name, Muhammad looked up at him in bewilderment, while Hasan came up to him and embraced him, kissing his cheeks and patting him on the back. Muhammad showed no emotion at meeting Hasan, standing passively, broken and sad over what Fawqiya had said.

At that moment Hasan saw Yara coming to the same courtyard in front of the Abbadi Lecture Hall.

"But this isn't Yara!" That's what Kariman thought, as she sat in the cafeteria. "She's paler than we are." She hurried out to greet her. "This isn't Yara's body and this isn't her complexion! She's lost nearly half her bodyweight." Hasan was also looking at her in a daze, without Yara seeing him. Before he could call to her Kariman had shouted, "Yara!"

Yara looked in the direction of the voice and saw Kariman. She froze and stared at her, with her chest rising and falling before Kariman's eyes. No sooner did Yara take a step toward her than a man appeared next to her, around forty years old, wearing an elegant gray suit. He took her hand and led her away, while Kariman stood motionless in dismay. This man was not her brother Fuad; Kariman had seen him before at Yara's house.

Behind Kariman stood Hasan and Muhammad, who had also noticed the situation; Hasan was following it in great amazement, while Muhammad was starting to comprehend what was happening around him. But after she had walked a few steps with the man Yara stopped and leaned on his arm, then staggered, gasped deeply, and nearly fell to the ground. The man caught her in his arms and carried her hurriedly into the cafeteria, placing her on a chair. A number of students came behind him; one brought another chair and the man lifted Yara's legs onto it. One of the girls brought out a little bottle of cologne and began to sprinkle some of it on Yara's face.

Outside Kariman was leaning on the wall of Abbadi Hall, crying with her face to the wall. Hasan and Muhammad went into the cafeteria and stood at a little distance, watching the scene in disbelief.

Yara came to. A waiter brought her a glass of water, from which she took one sip, refusing the rest. She stood up carefully and then began walking slowly, the elegant man in his forties supporting her waist against his right arm and holding her left hand in his right hand, in front of her. As soon as he went out through the door with her, Hasan and Muhammad sat down in a daze. Kariman came to sit next to them, in a state of near collapse.

Hasan said, as if he were talking to himself, "What's happened while we've been gone!"

"Thank God for your safe return."

They looked in the direction of the voice. It was a classmate of theirs named Fayza, known in the department for her talkativeness. They looked at her in silence and she said, "Poor Yara! For three months she's been fainting a lot during the lectures, for no reason. Every day she loses more weight, and she no longer talks to anyone. She should be happy, since she's gotten married."

Muhammad put his head in his hand and looked down at the table, while Hasan lifted his eyes to the fan that hung from the cafeteria ceiling. Kariman once more burst into tears.

When Nadir emerged from the door of the prison, the first thing he thought of was Yara. He would arrive in Alexandria in the middle of the night. Like the others he knew that the exams had begun, and he didn't think they were over yet. He would spend the rest of the night with his father, mother, and little brother, but before too long they would let him sleep. Yara's face, which had been suspended in space before him in prison, and which had gone before him all the way home, would be before him in his room also.

His mother and father enveloped him in joy and his little brother in delight, even though his mother shed a few tears from time to time. Whenever they asked him about anything he seemed happy, as if he had not been in prison; his happiness came from the fact that he would see Yara in the morning. He did not call her by telephone because he wanted her to see him before her suddenly. The world would be his once more! He would tell Nawal everything, and he would tell Yara everything good.

His family left him to sleep at the dawn call to prayer, and he did sleep, from fatigue. To his surprise he woke up at eight, after only four hours, as if he had slept for an age. He smiled because he had not dreamed of anything, as if his mind was at rest and all his trouble had left him. He made his mother happy by eating the whole platter of fish she had made, to get his weight back, as she said. He kissed her hands and dashed out of the house.

It was nine o'clock. He would get to the college at ten, and if there were exams Yara would have gone in and would come out at twelve, and if her exam was in the afternoon he would wait until she arrived. It never crossed his mind that there might not be any exams that day.

He was sitting in the number 1 bus, restless in his seat as if he wanted to arrive ahead of it. He suddenly noticed that he had come to the middle of the great open space in the Maks neighborhood; light was pouring down on it as if on that neighborhood alone, after it had been in deep darkness. He smiled. Here he was seeing nature reveal itself to him in supreme beauty, the beauty which had sent poetry flowing through him before and which would always make it flow.

He remembered how the prison warden had taken from him everything he had written. He had been naive, showing his papers as he was being processed for release from prison. He was holding them in his hand and had not put them in his suitcase, holding on to them so that even if everything else was lost on the way, his poems would not be lost. He smiled in mockery; even if they had been in the suitcase the warden would have found them, since he searched it. He had taken them and took no notice of Nadir's anger, not listening as Nadir told him that what he had written there was his own poetry. But Nadir had not insisted, either. He had memorized most of them alone at night, thinking of Yara, whose love had taken possession of his heart and was locked inside. He would recite them to her as she stood with her face before his eyes, filling the space above him in the prison block. It surprised him that he was not thinking of Nawal, even though he had told his comrades a lot about Ismat Muftah; he had recited to them some of his poetry, discovering that it had settled in his memory since he had read it with Nawal. It must be that Nawal was the filly he was sure of. All this worry for Yara was caused by true love.

He felt afraid, and nearly stood up to get off the bus and call Yara by telephone. But he had drawn near to the Khafagi Café, and the bus was slowing down as it came to the stop. To his surprise he saw Isa Salamawy sitting outside the door of the café, on the sun-filled walk, smoking a water pipe and paging through a newspaper. So there were no exams this morning, and he had time to spend with him. He would certainly hear a lot about Yara from him.

He got off at the bus stop, which was separated from the café only by the width of Qaffal Street. He covered the few steps in a hurry, calling, "Ustaz Isa!"

Isa looked up and saw him. He seemed not to believe it. He abandoned the paper and the water pipe and opened his arms to him, patting him on the back in real joy.

"Thank God for your safe return, you hero! I've missed you!" Isa looked him over from top to bottom. "*Yaa*, you've lost a lot of weight."

Nadir smiled and said, "Weren't you ever in prison, Ustaz Isa? But why are you sitting here, aren't there any exams this morning?"

Isa was embarrassed for a moment. He said, "Sit down and talk, tell me how things were in prison."

Nadir forgot his question about the exams. He thought they must in fact be in the afternoon, or maybe tomorrow rather than today, since Isa was sitting here now. He sat down, as happy as a child, and said, "That's a long story, Ustaz. Maybe I'll write about those days, some time. But it wasn't like what happened to you in the Oases, in any case. You tell me about how you are, about Yara. Can you imagine, I don't want to call her on the telephone because her face is in front of me night and day. It's in front of me right now, in the air over Maks Street. I'm dying to see her, Ustaz!"

Isa was silent, not answering. He gathered up the newspaper he had been paging through and put it between them on the table. He called the waiter, asking for tea with milk for Nadir, and said, "Surely you haven't had breakfast. It's nine-thirty."

Nadir said happily, "My mother made me a platter of fish and I ate it all. It reminded me of the good old days. I'll have tea without milk. Anyway let me hear about you. I want to hear everything, Ustaz."

Isa seemed flustered for a moment; then he smiled and said, "Nawal has unfortunately left Alexandria."

Nadir was surprised and his eyes widened. He hadn't even asked about her, but the disheartening news really hurt him. Isa continued, "You know she was preparing for that for some time, before the January uprising. The club was burned in the intifada, so she sold it and left for Paris."

Nadir did not answer. For the first time, he felt something for Nawal. He really had lost something lovely. He felt despondency pressing in on him, but Isa went on talking.

"It was hard for her to wait for you. When the club burned she said that this was the moment fate had decreed for her. She sold it to a businessman, nobody knows where he got the money. He said he's going to change it into an American skyscraper. The club is still closed."

In pain, Nadir said, "How I would have liked to see her, to say goodbye!"

Isa asked abruptly, "Did you love her, Nadir?"

He was silent for a few moments. Then he answered, "I don't know. I know very well that I love Yara, Yara's face is what goes before me. But I'd be lying to you if I said I never loved Nawal."

"She loved you. She found in you something that took her back to her old friends."

"I know that. I felt sorry for her at times, but I could really relax with her, and grow stronger."

"That Egyptian professor she met in Paris changed her life, especially since he's from the same place where she was born and raised. A meeting only fate could arrange! He's married, though, so I think that she went to live close to her true love, the one who left her after he got out of prison."

"I remember that she told me that he was married there, too."

"Even so. There are lovers who are satisfied with the scent of the place where their loved one has passed. Old Arabic poetry is all like that. Dr. Rushdi is only an excuse for her to move to the sphere of her first love."

Isa said that with an ironic smile, and Nadir felt some anger. Then he remembered his earlier question: "Why aren't you telling me about Yara, Ustaz?"

But Isa responded, "In any case Nawal left you a letter with me. My house is near here, I can go and get it for you, or you can come with me. You've never come to my house." The waiter had returned and put a glass of tea and a glass of water in front of Nadir. Isa went on: "What surprised me is that Ahmad, this first love of hers, was an exemplary person in prison. Everyone loved him. How often he talked about Nawal and his yearning for her, and how he'd entangled her in their Communist cell because he loved her voice and he loved her. But as soon as he got out he left Egypt entirely, as if he had been talking about a fantasy woman. By the way, she took the collection of Ismat Muftah's poetry with her. She said she would find a way to publish it outside the country. She apologized for not leaving it for you."

They were both silent for a while, and Nadir seemed lost in thought. Isa pointed to the tea. "Drink your tea."

"I will."

"Don't worry. Yara is all right."

Nadir said, "Then I'll see her today. Or maybe tomorrow, since there aren't any exams today."

Isa said nothing for a moment. Then he said, "The exams are in the morning, and today is the subject before the last. Today it's modern logic."

Nadir was thoroughly confused. He gave a small smile of disbelief, and then his face showed total bewilderment. He looked at Isa with the question he wanted to ask not coming out of his mouth. In fact he didn't know what he wanted to ask, now. He was completely at a loss.

Isa said, "I decided to fail this year, so I only went to one exam at the beginning. Yes. If I went to the exams I would pass, and I would lose you next year. You will all be repeating the final year and I would be out of the college. And anyway I won't find another theoretical college to enroll in."

Nadir did not taste his tea. He stood up, confused and very tense, and said, "I have to catch Yara."

He rushed off with no more words and with no farewell. He didn't think about the letter to him from Nawal, that Isa had. He didn't have time.

Hasan, Kariman, and Bishr sat in silence in the Wali Café. Hasan had called Bishr by telephone and he had joined them there. Kariman's grief made Hasan feel powerless.

Bishr was surprised by Kariman, and what she had come to; he seemed embarrassed. Hasan wanted to talk, but found nothing to say except for what had happened to Muhammad Shukr in front of them in the college, with Fawqiya. What surprised Hasan and Kariman was that they saw that Bishr was fatter. He seemed to sense their thoughts from their surprised looks at him, and said with a smile, "I used to eat everything, out of fury." But they did not laugh.

Bishr said, "The problem isn't how Muhammad's story ended, the problem is that it's a real farce. He lives with us for three weeks and ends up in prison for six months."

Hasan shook his head. "A tragedy, rather."

Bishr said, "He loved the daughter of a former minister, and for her and her family he'll always be a former prisoner, now."

Hasan said, tensely, "Muhammad and Fawqiya, God preserve us. But what are we going to do about Nadir?"

Bishr had not yet heard anything about Yara, so Hasan told him what they had seen. He seemed really grieved. He struck his forehead with his hand several times and said, "I can't believe it!"

A small tear escaped from Kariman's eye. She said, "I know Yara better than all of you. Yara will die."

Silence descended on them.

Kariman began to dry her tears with a small handkerchief. But Bishr suddenly asked Hasan, "Where did you spend the night? I expected you would go to Mansura from prison."

Hasan was briefly embarrassed, then he said, "I went to the apartment and found it locked up. Ahmad Basim left it to the owner, who took our things to Rawayih and Ghada's apartment, and then closed it. In the beginning of July he's going to make it into a summer rental."

"Then you saw Rawayih and Ghada."

Hasan nodded, and said, "I thought they would be working in the club, but when I went up to the apartment I saw a light coming from under their door. So I went down and asked them why there was a lock on the door of our apartment, and they told me what happened. I learned from them that Muhammad had been there before me and had found out what happened too. He left his things with them, and said he would come to get them some day when he finds a new place. I did the same, but I didn't know where to go in middle of the night, so I stayed the night in their apartment. They let me have a room to myself."

Kariman hung her head, despair showing on her face. Hasan took her hand and said, "I didn't have any other choice, sweetheart. I never went near them. Bishr knows that I never went near them before. You know that, too." Then addressing Bishr, he said, "They told me that Nawal sold the club, and that she gave each of them a nice lump sum, just because they're friends of ours. They're going to leave the apartment in a month and move south, down to Nuzha, as they said. They've rented a small shop there"—and here he smiled mockingly—"where they're going to sell clothes for veiled women."

Kariman's hand could not stop trembling, so she lit another cigarette. Hasan said, "Kariman, sweetheart, why all these cigarettes? At least you're not losing me. I'm with you, Kariman, and we'll make it through everything. Think of Nadir and what happened to him and thank God that we're together. Please, sweetheart, stop smoking, at least like this."

All at once Bishr said, "Let's change the subject. Do you have any news of Khalil?"

Hasan answered, "We don't have any news, except that he's still a fugitive."

Bishr said, "Then I'm going to go to Cairo. I know how to get in touch with one of the members of the party's central committee. We have to discuss how we're going to return to work, work is what will save us from all this pain. We'll also have to arrange some large task for Nadir, who's going to suffer a lot when he finds out what happened to Yara. Work will help him forget."

Kariman said, numbly, "We shouldn't let Nadir find out the truth without us around him. I'm afraid for him."

Bishr answered, "I know his house, I'll go there tonight."

Hasan said, "I'm afraid he'll be like us and go to the college. Maybe he's already found out everything." Then he stood up and said, "The time has come to go back to Mansura. While I'm there I'll think about what we can do together, Kariman."

Bishr knew nothing of what had happened in Kariman's house, so he didn't know what to say. He didn't want to ask them anything, to spare them pain.

Nadir stood far away on the sidewalk of the Corniche, looking at the high, closed window of Yara's apartment. Behind him the fishing nets were raised on wooden stands, spread out to the sun and air. On the sand and in the water there were small feluccas that had returned in the morning and emptied their load of fish. Farther out in the water were larger, motorized fishing boats, rising and falling on the orderly, calm waves, their shadows spreading and receding on the water. A few children had gone down to the water in their underwear, coming out onto the sandy beach and running after each other, throwing sand and laughing. Many people sat around Nadir on the low, wide wall of the Corniche. In front of them were vendors of grilled corn, seafood, sweet Italian wafers, and other popular sweets, as well as several ice cream carts. Nadir was unaware of it all. He heard only the sound of the calm waves behind him, not even feeling the refreshing breeze on his back. The window high in the building did not open. Only the fronds of the royal palm between the two streams of cars in the street moved in the wind, as the cars rushed by in both directions.

Nadir spent more than three hours in that place of his. He would walk to the right or left at times, then come back to sit in his spot, which no one had occupied. It was as if everyone knew that he was waiting for the window to open and for his sweetheart to look out of it. Those who sat around him or passed before him changed, while he remained, or rose and returned. He stayed until night came.

The light behind the window came on, but it did not open. He left his place, tired, and walked in the direction of Manshiya, then Raml Station. He kept on walking on the sidewalk below the buildings, in front of the people sitting outside the cafés, in greater numbers than before. Summer was really here and people were fleeing their houses. Except Yara. He passed Ateneos, L'Aiglon, and the Kotta Theater in Azarita, and he passed the Atiyat Husayn club, which was closed! He passed throught the Shatbi neighborhood and came to Sidi Gabir. Most of the clubs here had signs hung on them saying, "Closed for improvements." Getting ready for the summer, maybe. Nonetheless, many of them were still there. He asked himself where he was really going.

He arrived at the Nawal Boîte and found evidence of the fire still visible in the black soot on the walls. The heavy wooden door was closed, with two iron beams fixed over it in the shape of an X, making sure of the closure. The big sign was no longer lit up, but the name "Nawal Boîte" was clear in the darkness. He realized that he had come here to meet Nawal. Yes. She was the one who could have listened to him today. But he turned back. He still couldn't believe what he had heard when he got to the college.

He had arrived after Hasan, Kariman, Muhammad Shukr, and Yara had left, and he had learned from the waiter in the cafeteria that his friends had been there. When he asked who, he replied, smiling, "All the ones who were with you in prison," and he added a blessing, "God will give you good fortune, kids."

Nadir learned from him what had happened to Yara, and that they were saying that the man with her was her husband. He was the one who had carried her into the cafeteria. Then he told him, "I don't believe he's her husband because he's a lot older. But he seems respectable." Then he said he was sorry, like someone who knew the whole story. "That's the way of the world, Ustaz Nadir. Take care of yourself."

He had covered the distance between the college and Yara's house completely unaware of the time. Was it minutes or hours? He didn't know. He didn't even remember if he had run there or taken a taxi or walked, grieving. He had eaten nothing until now. Everyone around him was laughing and talking and rushing about. They wore summer clothing, announcing their joy at the open air around them, and they opened their mouths and lungs and eyes to the sea air. They didn't know he was sad. When he reached the Silsila promontory, which no one was allowed to enter as it was still a military area, he looked at those seated on the Corniche wall or walking on the sidewalk in front of him, young men and girls. The young men surrounded the girls, eating peanuts or ice cream or cracking open libb seeds. Several vendors of iced drinks walked among them, carrying pails of fizzy drinks and knocking the metal opener on the side of the pails.

He sat at a distance, looking at the Bride of the Sea statue. Had Europa really been worth the trip Zeus had made for her from atop

Mount Olympus? She must have been. That's what Isa had said to them. Yes. Women were an alluring temptation, even for the gods, all the more so if they were like Europa or Yara. Yes. Otherwise the day wouldn't have passed with him searching for certainty about her. Months wouldn't have passed with her face always before his eyes in his prison cell. He didn't possess Zeus's power of disguise to win her. Yara. Europa. Yara. Yara was more delicate. Yara . . . Lara. Lara whom Dr. Zhivago loved. Oh my God, why had the novel leapt into his mind? Was he in the snows of Russia, walking between its distant towns? Rage choked him; he must not give in to the thought that Yara was lost forever. Everything he had heard today was a lie. He had to insist that Isa tell him something. But Isa had been maneuvering not to talk about Yara. So what he had heard from the waiter was true.

He called her on the telephone several times. The idea that he would see her and she would suddenly see him had slipped out of his mind; now he wanted to hear her voice. No one answered. Maybe they were at Stanley Beach as they were last summer. Yes, that happened last year. That was the reason, then. Yara was there, waiting for him. And the exams weren't over yet, so she would come the day after tomorrow for the last subject. He would go to her again in the college. How could he have forgotten about that all day long and during the evening? He wanted to be more optimistic, so he bought an ear of corn and began eating it slowly as he walked, lost in thought. All at once he felt he couldn't go on eating; he left half the ear on the wall of the Corniche and walked on. Once more he had come to Anfushi, when a little while before he had decided to be optimistic!

He found his place free, just as it had been! The number of people was increasing, and the lights of the Corniche dispelled the darkness. The waves were more nervous, noisier. The lights of the Greek Club and the Yacht Club behind him pierced the darkness over the sea. The window of Yara's apartment was still closed, light still showing behind it. The number of people began to decrease. A long time passed. There were very few feluccas on the sand, now;

most of their owners had taken them out to fish. It was the same with the motorboats, which had been numerous during the day. No children were playing in the darkness. There was just one man, a huge black man, swimming in the water. How could the man see in the dark? Little by little Nadir was left alone.

"Beloved."

She extended her hands to him and he reached out to her. She pulled him up and took him in her embrace. Yara was wearing a white wedding dress that showed her chest; she opened it for him to hide his head in it, and closed the buttons of the dress over him as he moved his hand over her back. Then he lay down with her on the sand and began kissing her hands. He opened her dress entirely from in front and began moving his lips on her body until he reached her face. It wasn't there.

He shuddered, and nearly fell off the wall of the Corniche onto the sand behind him. He had fallen asleep as he sat there, and dreams had taken him in the blink of an eye. He had seen Yara's face suspended before him in the prison cell and on his way home, but now he did not see it in front of him. Even in dreams it had disappeared, and he could see only her body.

The first rays of dawn penetrated the sky, and the call to prayer rose from the Mursi Abul Abbas Mosque. Men began to come out of the side streets and onto the Corniche, singly, preoccupied, as if they were coming from old, historical streets, from a town he didn't know. The waves of the sea calmed and their sound subsided; he almost thought the sea had lost its breath. How had he forgotten himself like this? What must be happening in his house now, with his family? How would his father and mother and little brother take this absence of his, when he was just back from prison?

The feluccas began to sail back to the beach with the morning. There were more people in the street, as he walked toward the Ras al-Tin Palace. He turned into Bahariya Street and walked along the tram line, in an area that he knew teemed with shops specializing in marine work. The number of people around him increased as he walked. He saw the old houses in Kom al-Nadura, where women appeared on the balconies. Rope, hardware, and canvas shops were opening their doors, and voices greeted the day with prayers and invocations. He covered a great distance while the world was waking up around him, young and strong, and he was walking distractedly, feeling as if he were in an ancient Alexandria that men did not yet know.

He came to the Mina al-Basal neighborhood and stopped at the intersection of the Street of the Seven Girls with Khedive Street and Maks Street. He found a tram coming from Manshiya, so he got on; it would take him to Maks. Today was Yara's day off and tomorrow was the exam. He would go to her tomorrow. He really should not have spent the day and the night in emptiness and deprivation.

As soon as his mother opened the door she found him in front of her, nearly falling down from fatigue.

"Son!"

She took him in her arms and he sat in the nearest chair. His brother rushed out of his room, and as soon as he saw him he stopped in the doorway, crying and saying,

"Mama's been crying all night and Papa went to work without ever having slept."

Then he came to him, and Nadir took him in his arms, patting his back and kissing him. He said to his mother,

"Forgive me, Mama. I spent the night out with Bishr by the sea in Manshiya. I hadn't seen him for six months."

She answered, wiping away her tears, "Why are you lying to me, Nadir? Bishr was here yesterday, in the evening. He came to ask about you."

He was very embarrassed, and was silent for several moments. Then he said, wearily,

"I'll tell you everything later. Now I want to sleep."

She said calmly, "Bishr told me everything. Let her live her life, son. Our Lord is powerful—he can bring someone better to you."

He burst into tears and put his head on her breast. "What did I do for God to take away the most beautiful thing he ever gave me?"

10

IT WAS A SUMMER WHEN the world opened more broadly before him than it ever had, but he didn't see anyone around him or in front him. Why had God created him alone amid all this emptiness and want? Nadir felt that even when he was on a crowded bus.

He had gone to the college on the last day of the exams, with a plan in his mind and in his heart the certainty that he would meet Yara. He paced in front of the Abbadi Lecture Hall, not going into the cafeteria so he would not miss the opportunity of meeting her. Everyone who came out early stared at him, young men and women, his classmates. He shut his eyes so no one would talk to him.

Then Yara came out. It was Yara and no one else. Yara alone was now the center of the world before him. All the buildings around him fell away, all the people flew into the air, and here she was with her eyes shining in a smile. He had to reach her before she whirled away in the air with the birds and the butterflies. But a man passed him, a man in his forties whom Nadir had never seen before. He came from behind him and reached her first, putting his arms around her and saying, "Come here, sweetheart. The exam is over, thank God."

The man hurried away with her, passing Nadir. He didn't notice anyone, and she walked with him, not looking back. He said "Take your time" when she slowed down, no longer able to keep up with him.

Yara would fall down in a faint, now. That's what he knew about her, and that's why his breath was coming raggedly, out of fear for her. But she held the hand of the elegant man in his forties and leaned on him as she walked. Nadir stood there not knowing what to do. Should he call out to her?

She was heading toward the left with the man, toward the exit gate of the college. He had to hold together, even though he could barely stand up. But he felt someone take hold of his arm and say, "It's over, Nadir, the story has ended."

He looked up; it was Ahmad Basim. It was the same large, strong body. His beard had lengthened, but the prayer beads were still in his hand.

"Thank God for your safe return," Ahmad added.

Nadir looked at him in surprise and pain. "You know about it too?"

"We all know, Nadir." Then he smiled and said, "My friend, you're talking as if you were with me yesterday. I've missed you." He embraced him, while Nadir showed no emotion. Ahmad went on, "Come with me."

"Where to?"

"To the Sidi Gabir Friday Mosque. We'll hear a great lesson, the last one I'll ever hear in Alexandria. . . ." Then he laughed loudly. "That is, if I pass, and God willing, I will. I had a beautiful dream that foretold that I would pass, even though you weren't sitting next to me in the exam so I could cheat."

Nadir couldn't stand there any longer. He rushed off, hoping against hope that he would catch up to Yara and the man in his forties. In Port Said Street he saw nothing. They must have taken a car that would make its way from Suez Canal Street to Alexander the Great Street, then to Raml Station and on to Anfushi. He ran the few steps to Suez Canal Street and looked to the right, but he saw nothing. He didn't even know what kind of car they might be in. There was nothing before him but silence, the sun filling the space around him, and its heat over his head.

All there was for Nadir in Alexandria now was his house in Maks, where he practiced his silence and where his mother watched him. If a furtive tear escaped her eye he disappeared into his room, opening books that he didn't read and writing poetry that he tore up. Now he had even forgotten all the poetry he had written in prison. He had forgotten his promise to himself that he would write it all down again.

But it was impossible to stay in the house all the time, because it was the year-end vacation and there were no middle-school or high-school students for him to tutor. So he began to go out to the beach and sit on the rocks, looking at the distant ships coming to Alexandria, or the ships leaving it, also far away. All those ships must be leaving behind them stories of separation and pain.

Directly in front of him were the poorer summer vacationers, and the carters with their horses and donkeys. On his right were the old lighthouse and the little wooden cabins. If he passed among them he found their Egyptian owners, now elderly, sitting in front of them. There weren't many seagulls but they were ceaselessly moving and circling in the air, abruptly diving into the water to emerge with some small fish in their mouths. His mind showed him the picture, even if he couldn't see it.

But why wasn't he seeing Bishr? Bishr had not come again, maybe in order to give him a chance to grieve, and think, and clear his spirit alone. He remembered Bishr now, and Kariman and Hasan. He hadn't seen any of them since they'd gotten out of prison. He knew the telephone number of Kariman's house, of Bishr's house, and of Yara's house. Kariman would say what Bishr would say, that he should be tough and forget. Yara wouldn't answer him; he should not appear in her life again, Yara couldn't bear it. Nawal, into whose arms he might have thrown himself, had become a mirage. Everything around him had turned to ruins, Alexandria was ruins, ruins wherever he went. He remembered Cavafy when he left Alexandria after the English entered it in 1882, when his family left for Istanbul. He remembered the poet's yearning for the city he had left behind in ruins from the war, the ruins that Nadir was seeing in everything around him where there were none. Cavafy and his family had returned to Alexandria, unable to bear leaving it, but now Nadir had to leave Alexandria. Alexandria had fallen into ruins, now, even without a war. The world that had been his was now behind him. Cairo was the future for writers and artists and politicians. This was his opportunity and he should not grieve over what was done. But he made a face, blaming himself, blaming his stupidity. Yara would go with him wherever he went. The ruins would go with him!

He went back to the house to eat, pretending to be happy with the food his mother made him. She even smiled again, and she put a piece of chocolate into his mouth. After he finished supper she followed him into his room. She said, "I know you can't forget. But I also know that time will heal everything, so I say nothing and I'm at peace."

He looked at her with great love. She whispered to him, "I'll tell you something you don't know. In my youth I loved a handsome young man in Dekhela. He was from a rich family, the Rubi family, they're well known there. Of course you've heard of them. His family came between us, and he left me for the sake of his family."

He looked at her in amazement, and smiled. She said,

"Thank God you've smiled! Your father came to propose to me at a time when the whole world seemed dark, black on black. I gave in. I married him not knowing what I was doing. But whenever I look at you and your brother I thank God, who gave me more than I expected. I don't think it would have been possible to have two such beautiful boys from anyone but this good man."

He laughed, really laughed. She said, happily, "Once I ran into this first love of mine by chance in Manshiya. I shook his hand and I laughed. I didn't feel anything move in my heart. When I met him I felt that the story had ended. Believe me, Nadir, love stories are like that." He stared at her in amazement, and she went on: "A day will come when you'll meet her and feel that everything that happened was a dream gone by. It's just that first love leaves a deep wound, but it always ends."

He grasped her hands and kissed them. She was thoughtful for a moment; then she said, as if to herself, "But her name is pretty. Yara." Then, correcting herself, "But love isn't about names."

Thinking about this strange confession from his mother, he said, "I know time heals all things, but I'm thinking about her. Will she be able to bear it? Yara is very delicate, and what happened must have been against her will. She's lost a lot of weight and now she faints all the time."

"At a certain point resistance will appear, and her body will reject weakness. Believe me, even though I'm not educated—life will go on."

He looked at her in astonishment. Her words were beautiful, and seemed convincing. She asked him, "Why doesn't Bishr visit you now?" He did not answer. "Then you should go to him. Get busy with him with what you were doing. Politics doesn't kill, love is what kills."

His astonishment increased. He held his mother's head to his breast and kissed her. "I'll read and write tonight."

She said firmly, "First thing in the morning you'll go to Bishr."

To his own surprise he went to sleep early and woke up early. He made his way to Bishr in Bacos. As he went he began to notice what was around him, especially when he went into Market Street and saw before him the vegetable, fruit, and fish vendors. The neighborhood bore the name of one of the Greek businessmen from Alexandria's past, also the name of the Greek god of wine, and none of these weary people who were buying and selling knew that.

Bishr said, as they left his house, "What do you say to a crazy visit?"

"To whom?"

"Rawayih and Ghada. We left the apartment and the owner closed it, but they're still in their apartment. Don't hold back, it will help you forget, and I'll get rid of my fury."

Surprised, Nadir asked, "Why are you furious?"

"Because you're not forgetting."

They laughed, and went on their way to Tanais Street. His thoughts weren't anything like Bishr's, but there was no harm in dropping in on them with him. Nadir felt that this would be the last visit to the street.

Nadir stood in the living room in surprise as he saw Rawayih burst into tears, saying, "I can't believe it. You're not Si Nadir, you've lost so much weight! What did they do to you in prison, the bastards?"

He said, smiling, "I'm fine."

Ghada said, "It's really good of you to visit us and ask after us. We're going to leave the apartment in a few days."

Rawayih smiled as she offered them tea. "How're things between you and Madam Nawal, Si Nadir?"

Bishr couldn't stop looking at their bodies. They were each wearing a light gallabiya that revealed the arms and shoulders and ended at the knee. A transparent gallabiya that showed the small black slip underneath.

Nadir smiled awkwardly without answering.

"I saw her giving a man named Isa a letter and asking him to give it to you after you got out of prison. I saw tears in her eyes."

Taking her in his arms, Bishr said, "Don't open old wounds, Rawayih. We've come to forget."

Ghada asked, "Will you visit us in our new place in Nuzha? I'll give you the address, both for the apartment and for the shop."

Bishr asked, "Are you really going to sell clothing for women who wear the hijab?"

Rawayih answered, laughing, "Even though I don't know what 'clothing for women who wear the hijab' means, people say that's the merchandise of the future. What matters is that we're not forced to sell underwear!"

Bishr and Nadir laughed, and Ghada said, "It's called *lingerie*, Rawayih, I've told you a hundred times. Be a *lady*, will you, we're going into serious work!"

Nadir and Bishr smiled, and Rawayih went on: "Yes. There's another big store that opened with clothes for veiled women, but on Nabi Danyal Street. Will our little store be able to compete? May God protect us, really and truly, so we're not forced to sell *lingerie!*"

Suddenly Rawayih said, "That's right, Si Nadir, who is this Nabi Danyal? Is there truly a prophet whose name is Daniel?"

Bishr laughed hard, and Nadir smiled. Ghada said,

"I only know Danyal who collects for the electricity. He comes every month."

Bishr set off laughing again, and this time Nadir laughed too. Rawayih said, her eyes shining,

"Thank God! You laughed, Si Nadir. It showed on your face that you've been carrying a heavy load."

Nadir kissed her cheek and stood up. "Thank God, really and truly, since now we know you're all right. I hope you have a better life in Nuzha."

Bishr glared at him furiously. Ghada noticed and said,

"No offense, Si Bishr, but I have my period, and so does Rawayih."

Rawayih said, "Why are you saying that? Tell the truth. We're beginning a new life, Si Bishr. Will you begrudge us that?"

Bishr looked at them, truly moved. He stood up and said, "Of course not." He kissed each of them in turn.

They went out. But as soon as they were downstairs Rawayih looked out of the window and called, "You didn't get the new address."

Bishr answered, "We'll come back tomorrow."

He hurried off with Nadir along the empty street. "Poor things. They really believe we'll visit them in their new place."

Nadir didn't answer; he seemed to have gone into a silence that lasted for several moments, until they emerged onto the Corniche from small Saint Gabriel Street. They were met with the sea air, and the strong daytime sun. Nadir stopped and Bishr stopped also, looking at him.

Bishr said, "It really is a strange world. Can you imagine, now I feel as if I really loved them. I even feel like they're sincere and they really do want an honest life." Nadir smiled. Bishr added, "Thank God, you smiled, and a little while ago you laughed. So there's hope!"

Nadir said, "I want to hear the story from Yara. If I hear it from her, everything will be over."

Bishr looked at him in astonishment. "You're crazy! Come with me to the Wali Café, maybe we'll find Kariman. Who knows, maybe Khalil will suddenly come out of his hiding place."

Nadir said, "Do you know where his hideout is and we don't?"

"I was in prison too, remember? Come with me, I'll tell you what happened to Kariman. I'm really afraid for her."

"I'm going to Stanley Beach now. I must find Yara. I have to hear it from her."

"You're crazy."

"Please, Bishr, leave me alone."

"What's happened, all of a sudden? Okay, I'll come with you. I won't leave you, even though I know you won't get anywhere. Even if you meet her, she won't talk to you. You'll just cause her embarrassment in her new life."

But Nadir just signaled for a taxi; it stopped, and they got in.

At Stanley Beach he and Bishr began to walk among the summer vacationers who were sitting under umbrellas and lying on the ground. Ordinary bathing suits and bikinis were all around them, and Bishr contemplated their owners with regret, saying to himself, all these women and Nadir is looking for Yara! There were women, children, and girls around the ice cream seller. The owners of the cabins sat out in front. Bishr didn't lift his eyes from the women and neither did Nadir, but he was looking for Yara.

They went up to the next level of cabins and to the level above that, walking in front of them as their owners watched them, perplexed. Bishr said, "No one is wearing street clothes except for us. Even the old people sitting in chairs on the beach in front of their cabins are wearing shorts. We look suspicious, God protect us!" Nadir didn't answer.

They walked for more than an hour without finding Yara. As they left the beach Bishr said, "You have to know the details of the story, or you won't be able to rest or stop looking for her. We'll have to sit in a café. I'll tell you what I haven't told you yet."

Nadir gave himself to Bishr, who began talking inside the large Wali Café. Around them were the noisy backgammon players, the children of the vacationers, eating ice cream and running between the chairs, and the air coming from the ceiling fans. The walls enclosed them all.

"Yara never left you. Her family all went after her. The man she married is her father's age. In fact he's the one who interrogated her in the district attorney's office the day they arrested her, and he's the one who set her free."

"How do you know that?"

"From Isa Salamawy. Yara told him everything. She was crying and asked for his advice, but he didn't give her any. As usual, he couldn't."

"Have you seen Isa?"

"Yes, two days ago in Ateneos. Actually I ran into him in front of Amm al-Sayyid's, the bookstand, and he's the one who took me to Ateneos. He said he couldn't tell you—he didn't want you to hate him. By the way he wants you to go to him any morning at the Khafagi Café to collect the letter that Nawal left for you."

Nadir said nothing, despairing. Bishr said, "What happened to you isn't as bad as what happened to Kariman." He told him what had happened to her, and then said, "Kariman doesn't have anywhere to sleep now except the living room of her apartment. I went to see Hasan in Mansura; he's decided to live in Cairo and come back at the end of the next school year to take the exams. He'll depend on me to follow the lessons and to tell him what our syllabus is, and what's not on it. The professors don't change what they assign, usually, and next year's syllabus won't differ much from this year's. I told him frankly to marry Kariman and take her with him to Cairo."

Nadir looked at him in surprise, and Bishr said, "In Cairo he'll begin a new life as a writer of stories and plays. He'll make his way in the literary world. With her with him they could both work in the independent press. In Cairo there are Arab press offices where a lot of young people work who can't find any opportunities in the government press. What matters is that they struggle together."

"What did he say to you?"

"Nothing. He had no comment." Bishr was silent for a few moments, and then said, "It seems that he changed in prison without our knowing."

They were both silent for several long moments, until Bishr spoke again. "You too—if you went to Cairo that would be therapy for you. Frankly the best advice in these situations is for you to move on to another girl."

"What do you mean?"

"There are a lot of girls. Move on to another one, forget Yara with her, then leave her."

Nadir looked at him in surprise, then smiled and shook his head. Bishr said, "That's what everyone does who's disappointed in love."

"What if the other girl gets attached to me?"

"It's perfectly natural, life is full of painful stories. Anyway you can leave her before she gets really attached. And I can nominate one for you."

Nadir was astonished by Bishr's talk. Bishr went on,

"What do you think of Wafaa?"

"You know her?"

"Naturally. I sometimes go to Cairo without telling the rest of you. I met her once and she said nice things to me about you. Which means the way has been prepared."

"You're crazy!" Nadir cried, shaking his head in surprise and anger. Bishr said, "Then spend the rest of your life crying over spilled milk."

Silence held them for a few moments. Nadir could not believe what he had heard. Then Bishr spoke again, laughing. "Or go to Nawal in France." He laughed again. "A poet like you has a beautiful girl before him in Cairo, and a beautiful woman in France, and you're crying over a lost love in Alexandria. You'll drive me crazy."

Nadir stood up and said peaceably, "I've had a good time with you, Bishr. But I should go home."

Strange that a man should feel that he wants to put his head through a wall in front of him that he cannot see. That's what Nadir's wandering thoughts came to, as he looked at nothing and shook his head, sadly.

He found that the solution was to go out, to walk in the streets. In Manshiya and Raml Station. He found himself standing in front of women's clothing stores there, or standing in front of well-known coffee shops, going into them and coming out again. For a moment he imagined that he was walking through the Alexandria that Isa had told them so much about. He smiled, mocking himself; he knew that he was looking for Yara. He went into the Elite, Pastroudis, Asteria, Santa Lucia, Délices, and Chez Gaby. It occurred to him that the elegant man in his forties might be among the patrons of the Syrian Club, since it was an aristocratic club, as they said. He went to it and at the door the security guard asked him if he was a member or not; he was embarrassed and then said no, and the man shook his head, sadly.

Once he thought that the man in his forties might take her to an elegant lunch at the Seagull. Another time he asked himself why he wasn't visiting the restaurants in Bahri and Anfushi. Then he wondered why it had not occurred to him that she might have left Anfushi with her husband for another quarter, which could well be in Raml, or in the Smouha area, where apartment buildings had begun to increase in number. In a moment of weariness he thought about the absurdity of what he was doing. She might have traveled to Europe to spend the summer with her husband, since he seemed to be from the upper class. But Nadir kept on going out, and every day his mother said to him, with a laugh, "Don't tell your father what I told you!"

He would laugh and kiss her cheeks, and she would say, "May our Lord protect you and give you patience, son. God willing he'll make it up to you with someone better."

So this kind mother knew about his sterile walks, or at least she sensed them.

In the *al-Ahram* newspaper he read an item about the closing of the *Vanguard* magazine, but there were no details. He was overcome with anger; Sadat must have shuttered it for good because it was a Communist magazine.

He realized that his poem had not been published. So now it would never be published. He thought about going to Cairo, to Café Riche, to meet the important critic, so he could think with him about what could be done. That same evening Bishr visited him, to inform him of the need to go and bring back more publications. For a moment he thought that Bishr was doing this just so that Nadir would see Wafaa again. Maybe he would be inclined toward her, and forget his sadness. He found himself saying to Bishr, "Spare me the trip, this time."

"But you're the only one who does that."

He thought a moment and then said, "Wafaa has never come to Alexandria. Her father likes to go to Ras al-Bar in the summer. Have her bring the publications to Alexandria so she can see the city."

Bishr thought about it, then said, "I'll try, but you'll be the one to meet her." Nadir said nothing. Bishr went on, "I'll tell you when and where."

Nadir gave him a mocking look. "The solutions you've offered me, Bishr, aren't right for me. I won't cure my heartbreak by breaking others' hearts. And it's hard to go to France. Maybe I'll go someday, to study or to work. I promise you that I'll recover. I'll get control of my spirit, that's what's driving my body through the streets."

Bishr looked at him, pleased. "Then I'll go myself. The best thing for you to do now is to meet Isa and get Nawal's letter from him. You'll definitely find something to please you in it. Maybe she's given you her address in Paris. Forgive me for my bad thoughts."

Nadir was waiting for the day when the results of the exams would be posted. He would go to the college several days in a row and maybe Yara would appear on one of them, just the way it had happened last year.

In fact he did go to the college. A few students were coming in, and there were a few in the cafeteria. For the first time he felt conclusively that he was really naive.

"The story's over, Nadir," he said to himself, and started making his way back to Raml Station. "The story's over." He began repeating the words as he walked, then he stopped when he felt that his voice was rising and that his lips and even his hands were moving. He would not let himself go mad. He slowed his pace and no longer said anything. He thought that in spite of what had happened he had read a lot in recent days, and had written a lot of poetry, too. So he was strong. He yearned to announce that to everyone, right now, in the street.

He stopped on the sidewalk in front of the people sitting outside Ateneos, vacationers drinking tea and coffee and juice, vendors of peanuts and pistachios moving among them. All of a sudden he wondered whether Isa might be there now, when he usually spent his days in the Khafagi Café. It would be a wonderful coincidence. If he found him he would stay with him until he went to his house to get Nawal's letter, which he had forgotten all this time.

He went inside and, to his surprise, he found Isa sitting at the end of the room near the window. Perhaps Isa had even seen him on the sidewalk. But if he had seen him, why hadn't he called to him?

Isa stood up, extending his hand to him and saying, "At last you've remembered me!"

There was a small book in English in front of him; Nadir read the title and found that it was the memoirs of Isadora Duncan. He smiled. He had seen the beautiful film about her life, with Vanessa Redgrave in her role. He had seen it in the Alhambra Theater on its first run, years ago. Seeing this as a chance to get out of the state he was in, Nadir sat down and said, "I've read a lot this week about the Futurist School in literature in Russia, before the Bolshevik revolution. I especially liked Mayakovsky, Alexander Blok, and Yesenin." Then he pointed to the book. "By the way, Isadora Duncan is the one Yesenin loved."

Isa said happily, "I went to a lot of trouble to find this book. Isadora is the greatest dancer of the twentieth century." He signaled to the waiter, saying, "Lunch in an hour when Christo comes. Now a beer for my dear friend. . . ." He turned to Nadir. "Since you've returned to reading."

Nadir relaxed a little. Isa said, "Tell me which one you liked, as a poet—Mayakovsky or Yesenin or Alexander Blok?"

"All three. But Mayakovsky's poem, 'A Cloud in Trousers,' really affected me. It's magnificent, and powerful. It saved me from sadness for some time."

Isa looked at him thoughtfully. "Poetry is your therapy, Nadir, reading it and writing it. Believe me. But tell me what you remember from this magnificent poem—I've almost memorized it."

Nadir looked at him in surprise. He began to feel a little real happiness.

"I didn't memorize any of it, but I heard it echo around me as he was shouting the name of the Virgin Mary. His language is surpassing. As he says, there's a man wresting himself free and taking off from inside himself and he can't find any refuge. It's a greater poem than anything the Communists produced after that, no offense, Ustaz."

Isa smiled. "That's true, it really is. It's epic and full of life, beyond the ordinary. Those Futurists were greater than their surroundings."

Nadir said, sadly, "Yesenin committed suicide, and Mayakovsky after him."

Isa smiled. "Many writers have committed suicide. Hemingway, and before him Stefan Zweig and Virginia Woolf. Even in Egypt Ismail Adham committed suicide at the beginning of the forties."

"The author of the article, 'Why I'm an Atheist?'"

"Yes. Even though he published it at the end of the thirties and no one accused him then of blasphemy or of being an infidel. All that happened was that writers and intellectuals answered him with articles which they collected in a book entitled *Why I'm a Believer*. Four or five years later he committed suicide, not because of the article. He was greater than his surroundings. The poet Fakhry Abul Saud also committed suicide during the Second World War."

Nadir said, surprised, "I know that. He was the romantic poet who translated *Tess of the d'Urbervilles* by Thomas Hardy. He must not have been able to bear the war and the destruction in the world around him."

"He was married to an Englishwoman. When the war began she was in England. His young son drowned in the River Thames in London and he was cut off from news of his wife, so he committed suicide. Certainly his romanticism was one of the reasons for his weakness."

Nadir thought to himself: Who could withstand the loss of his wife and child? But he was also happy with the conversation, and with his ability to talk to someone. He said, "It looks to me as if the Soviets in Russia abandoned Mayakovsky."

"No. Writers' suicides don't have anything to do with political regimes. They commit suicide if they feel that the universe is smaller than they are. They might also feel that way if they've lost someone dear, as in the case of Fakhry Abul Saud, or if they've failed in love, for example."

Nadir was embarrassed and Isa noticed, so he continued immediately:

"But the strong don't commit suicide. Life doesn't stop for any-one's sake, and smart people know that if they lose something beautiful they will certainly find something more beautiful somewhere else. Life is given to us only once, and it's worth living. I advise you to read the novel *How the Steel Was Tempered* by Ostrovsky. He's the one who said that."

Silence fell for a while, then Isa went on:

"We've talked a lot about suicide today. What's most important is that you read Mayakovsky's poem again and memorize as much of it as you can. It will change your feeling for poetry and your view of it. By the way, do you know what its original title was?"

"Yes, 'The Thirteenth Apostle.' But imperial censorship rejected the title because there were only twelve apostles."

Isa said, "Really, how could Mayakovsky be an apostle? In the view of the censors he's just an ordinary mortal, that's why they gave it a new title. He really was a cloud but in trousers, in the form of a man. He passed the way clouds pass; but the poem, poetry, they've made him eternal, like the apostles."

Nadir looked thoughtful for a few moments. Then he said, in a low voice as if he were talking to himself,

"The sky over Moscow is always cloudy and overcast, and the sky over Alexandria is clear, most of the time. But now there are clouds over Alexandria."

Then he fell silent again, while Isa wondered in confusion what else Nadir might come up with. He had surprised him. Finally, Nadir smiled. "But what's strange, Ustaz Isa, is that you're reading writers who didn't agree with Communism."

Isa smiled, feeling somewhat reassured about Nadir. He said, "Communism isn't a religion, Nadir. The writers who didn't agree with it had larger ambitions, as I told you. They weren't capitalist politicians, either! What matters is that reading poets like Mayakovsky will make a big difference in your skill in poetry."

Nadir began to feel that now he needed more conversations of this kind. Yes; that's how he would return to the world again, despite the clouds, if only little by little. But all at once Isa said, "Are you unhappy with me, Nadir?"

"Why, Ustaz?"

"Because I didn't tell you about Yara. I wasn't able to. I told Bishr everything."

"Let's consider that what happened was fate. But tell me, do you have any news of Nawal? Has she written to you?"

"Of course not. Nawal was always a past, as long as I've known her, but her present is now in Paris. She will forget us all, this woman who never forgets her own past."

"I'm going to stay with you until you go home and give me her letter. Do you mind?"

"On the contrary, I'm happy to see you today! Even if I'm sad that you all didn't visit the Greek Museum with me."

"Wow, Ustaz, that was before the January uprising! You still remember?"

"That's the one past I want you to know. Don't believe anything else."

"Then I will go with you one day, Ustaz."

A beautiful young girl wearing the hijab came in with a young man her own age. They sat down cheerfully, across the room. Isa was very surprised. He whispered to Nadir, "A girl wearing the hijab coming into Ateneos with her boyfriend!"

Nadir smiled and said nothing. Isa went on: "I'm not surprised. I know the Egyptian people well: they'll fall in line behind the Wahhabis because the political regime is giving them room, but in the end they'll fool them. The hijab will become an ordinary piece of clothing and not a sign of Islam. The beard and the gallabiya will be a way for a lot of people to manage in life and to deceive others."

Nadir couldn't believe what he was hearing. "The Egyptian people aren't swindlers, Ustaz!"

"I know. But they want life to go on, in some fashion. What matters is that it goes on." He laughed, "Don't worry about the Egyptians!"

Nadir said, "Maybe the new parties will be able to resist these strange ideas."

"No. They're parties just for show produced by the regime, and it won't allow them to be anything else. But the Muslim Brothers and the Islamic Group aren't just for show. Egypt will pay a heavy price, but it won't cease to exist. Just when it seems that the fruit has ripened and the time has come to pick it, so that Egypt will be a state subject to the Arabian Peninsula, the Egyptians will throw off the ideas and the clothing they've put on. I might not see that day but you certainly will, and you'll remember me."

Then Isa laughed loudly enough to astonish Nadir, who smiled in turn. He thought about how he could turn the conversation to another intellectual topic, since he had begun to feel pessimistic again. But then Christo appeared in the distance and Isa said, "This Christo is one of God's saints! Mention him and you'll find him in front of you. I was just now thinking about him."

Christo came up to them with his camera slung over his shoulder. He looked exhausted; he hadn't taken off his suit jacket in spite of the heat. Isa said,

"This is Nadir, the poet, Christo. You've seen him before, of course?"

Christo put his camera on the chair beside him and said, "It's over, there's no more As You Like It." Isa looked at him in surprise, and he went on, "It's over. As You Like It was sold to Kentucky, and closed. Now they're getting it ready for chicken. Poor Seif Wanli won't be sitting there any more."

Nadir smiled, and Christo went on: "A European restaurant has become an American chicken place. Never mind. Seif Wanli also sits in the Elite, Christina likes him."

It was clear that Christo wasn't going to stop. He poured himself a glass of beer from the bottle in front of Nadir and said,

"This Alexandria is crazy. Yesterday I saw a guy walking in front of the Alhambra Cinema and the Strand hawking medallions he had for sale. He was saying that the medallion had the picture of the believing president, and it cost five piasters. Today I saw him just now also walking and selling the medallions, but he was saying in a loud voice that they had the picture of the crazy president, and they were free."

Isa laughed loudly, and Nadir couldn't keep himself from laughing too. As the sound of their laughter rose, people sitting around them turned and stared at them. Isa said to Nadir, "Come and sit here with Christo every day and you'll forget everything."

Christo shook his head and in a sad voice he said, "It's over, khabibi, there's no more Christo." Isa looked at him in surprise and Christo continued, "It's over, khabibi. Christo's not staying in Alexandria. It's final, Christo's going to Athens."

Silence engulfed them for a moment, then Isa asked, "Are you really going?"

"I have to, 'cause my wife's here. Yes, she arrived a week ago. I thought she's going to live with me, she never forgot me! She told me she's afraid I'll die here and be buried some place they don't know where."

Isa said, "In the Greek cemetery. And anyway you're still young, Christo."

"No, khabibi, I'm seventy. I'll take the pictures with me and sell them in Athens. There's a lot of Alexandrian Greeks there who'll buy them. Here, it's over, there's no one who buys old pictures."

Silence descended on them again for several moments, until Christo said, "My wife told me I'll meet a lot of Greeks in Athens, so I'll be right in Alexandria. My wife no tell me lies, I know her."

Silence returned, this time for longer. Nadir was looking out of the open window and saw a large number of people rushing in the same direction, some running on the sidewalk on the far side of the Corniche. The cars were also slowing down. Isa looked in the same direction and asked, "What's this?"

Nadir said, "Maybe it's an accident."

Christo looked out of the window, looking left in the direction the people were heading. He said, "No, khabibi, that's really a lot of people. I have to go take pictures. It's not important to eat right now."

He picked up his camera and rushed off. As usual, he looked as if he was rolling on his way out. Isa asked Nadir, "What do you think?"

"Christo cheered me up. I don't want to see anything that might upset me."

Isa stood up and said, "On the contrary, it looks as if what's happening is unusual. Let's go look, we'll find out that there are troubles in the world bigger than love and separation."

Nadir hesitated but stood up and went with Isa, who was saying to the waiter, "Leave everything where it is, we'll be back soon."

They left Ateneos. As soon as they came out onto the sidewalk they found that the crowds were increasing, with people coming from Sa'd Zaghlul Square and from the other side of the Corniche. As they got closer the crowds increased, blocking half the street and the whole of the sidewalk opposite. They heard a woman weeping and saying "You poor dear, you poor mother's darling!" A man said, "May God punish the bastards who caused this!" and a bearded man in a gallabiya was saying "All power and all strength belong to God, suicide is forbidden, my daughter." They heard one teenager saying to another, "That's a really pretty girl, God, what a shame!"

Christo was trying to push through the crowd. When he wasn't able to he drew back and began taking pictures of the crowd itself.

The body belonged to a girl wearing jeans and a top, which the seawater had lifted so that a lot of her belly showed. A woman was shouting, "Oh God, she's pregnant! May God forgive us."

One of the men answered her: "Don't insult her, lady, she's just swallowed a ton of water. Shame on you!"

A girl appeared plunging through the crowd, determinedly opening a way for herself with her hands, until she got to the body. She sat beside it on the ground and put her ear to the heart briefly, and then grasped the wrist, motioning to everyone to be quiet. In a moment she seemed to feel a faint pulse. She cried,

"She's alive, she didn't die!"

She began to massage her chest as the others stood looking on in amazement, applying pressure to the girl's belly so the water came gushing out of her mouth. People began shouting, "God is great! God is great!"

Isa and Nadir were trying to break through the crowd. When they succeeded they stood looking at the body in disbelief. Nadir's voice sounded strangled from the terrifying shock:

"Kariman! It can't be!"

Shock tied Isa's tongue and showed in his eyes also. Nadir said, "Please stay with me! Don't leave me."

Nadir expected that Isa would disappear, as he usually did in any difficult situation. In fact Isa had been thinking about retreating and then disappearing. Nadir sat on the ground and raised Kariman's back, resting it on his chest, as the water kept pouring out of her mouth in spurts. Kariman began to breathe, and then she took a long breath. Isa yelled at the people, "Make some room, give her room! Let the air get to her!"

Kariman rested on Nadir's chest, and he didn't know if she realized he was there or not. She closed her eyes again. A police van had pulled up, and a young officer got out with two municipal policemen, who asked people to let him through. A young man was standing in the crowd holding a leather purse in his hand, all of his garments soaked. As soon as the officer came up he said to him,

"I'm the one who saved her, officer, sir. I saw her putting this purse among the rocks, then she jumped into the water. I pulled her out and put her here, then I went back to get the purse."

They heard an ambulance siren, so the officer said to one of the policemen, "Take the purse and bring this young man with us to the station after the ambulance takes her." Then he looked at the crowd and asked, "Do any of you know her?"

They were all silent, and some of them began to move away. Nadir hesitated for a moment, but then he said, "I know her." Isa also hesitated but then said, "I also know her, officer."

The officer looked at them in surprise. "Then you two will also accompany us to the police station."

Two medical technicians got out of the ambulance carrying a stretcher, on which they placed Kariman. The officer said to one of the policemen, "You go with her to the hospital. Don't let her leave after they treat her until I tell you myself."

In the Manshiya police station Nadir and Isa sat in the superintendent's office waiting for him to come in. The young man with the wet clothes was standing in embarrassment, because he couldn't sit on the chairs with the water still dripping from him. The officer had taken the purse and put it on the superintendent's desk. As soon as the superintendent came in he took one look at the dripping young man and said to the officer,

"Get him a wooden chair so he can sit down."

Then he looked at Isa and Nadir and asked, "You know her, you said that to the officer?"

Isa answered, "She's our classmate in the college. The Humanities College."

The superintendent asked, "You're a doctor, sir? I mean, a professor?"

Isa was embarrassed. He said, "No, I'm a student. We're all candidates for the *license*." The superintendent seemed shocked; he nearly laughed. But Isa went on, "I'm an affiliate student. Before that I was an affiliate in the College of Business and the Law School. My name is Isa Salamawy."

He brought out his identification card and presented it to the superintendent, who said,

"How strange! So you, sir, are an amateur student then!"

Isa did not answer, so he asked Nadir, "Are you also an affiliate?"

"No." He presented his identification card.

The superintendent thought for a moment and then asked them, "What brought you to the scene of the accident?"

Isa spoke up quickly: "We were sitting in Ateneos, Nadir and Christo and I, and we saw people running. We went out to see what had happened and we found her."

The superintendent marveled, "Christo! Who is this Christo?"

"A Greek Egyptian."

The superintendent smiled, then laughed. "Are there still Greeks in Alexandria? I seem to have madmen before me. Tell me something else, Ustaz!"

Nadir was embarrassed but Isa said, "You must believe us, sir. And don't forget that I've studied law, and that means I'm a lawyer, which means I know my rights and my duties."

The superintendent did not seem to care about what Isa said. He opened the purse and overturned it on the desk to empty it. A lipstick; a pack of cigarettes; a Ronson lighter; a few bills of small denominations, ten cents or a quarter of a pound; a small telephone book with a few numbers in it; a small sealed envelope.

Isa said, "Excuse me, sir. The district attorney's office should be the one to examine the victim's possessions."

The superintendent's face betrayed some anger. "You're going to teach me my job, Ustaz? It's not enough that you're still an affiliate student, at your age? I'm asking you to please hold your peace. When I ask you something, answer!"

He opened the envelope, to Isa's increasing distress. Nadir was also beginning to be angry. The man extracted a letter from the envelope and began to read:

"Please don't be angry with me, my beloved Hasan. Don't be angry with me, Mother. Maybe someday you'll thank me. Today I'm going to kill your evil husband who's always harassing me. I've failed to prevent him. I listened to him and put on the hijab so I would have a place to live among you, but there's no use. Don't be angry with me, my friends, Bishr, Nadir, beautiful Yara, I never see her any more but she will surely learn of it from the papers. Don't cry, Yara—I wasn't destined to live. Forget me, all of you. I'm the one who hasn't been able to forget all of you, all this time. He nearly defeated me the last time, that animal who doesn't deserve to live. I'll kill him and I'll kill myself. I've prepared everything."

Nadir was dazed by what he heard, as was Isa, whose eyes kept twitching and widening in surprise. The superintendent pressed a button affixed to his desk and the young officer hurried in. The superintendent shouted,

"Someone has been murdered, my esteemed officer! The girl killed her stepfather. There's no indication of her address, she doesn't have an ID card." Then he looked at Isa and Nadir and asked them, "Do you know her address? Your names were in her letter."

Nadir hesitated, then said, "I don't know it."

"Do you have the telephone number of any of the others whose names were mentioned, so we can call and find out?"

Again Nadir hesitated. Then he said, "Yara." He felt regret at bringing Yara into this. This isn't the right way to see her, Nadir! But a policeman came in, saluted the superintendent, and said,

"Your excellency, I have news from my colleague Abdallah who went to the government hospital with the victim. He called and said that she'd regained consciousness and confessed to killing her stepfather, and she gave him the address. He dictated it to me, sir."

He gave a small piece of paper to the superintendent. Nadir sighed in relief. They would not have to call Yara.

The superintendent shouted at the officer: "Inform the central administration and have them send a team from the Muntaza station to the house in Mandara where the murdered man is. Thank God it's not in our area." Then he looked at the things on the desk and said to the officer, "Take this to the district attorney." Then he looked at the others. "As for you, you may go. Goodbye."

Nadir and Isa stood in the street, in the open air and among the people who were moving as if they had just sprung up from the street. The young man with the wet clothes had moved off and disappeared. Each of them was looking straight ahead, in shock. Isa's face showed confusion, and Nadir was very afraid. Kariman would be tried for murder. He said,

"What will we do now?"

Isa said resolutely, "We'll go to the hospital. We won't abandon her."

Nadir said, "I mean about her killing her stepfather."

With the same resolution, Isa said, "I'll defend her, and I'll pay everything I have for top lawyers to save her. I'm not going to live life just by watching it any more."

They made their way to Raml Station and to the government hospital.

In the hospital, a soldier had been added to the policeman who had come with the ambulance. Isa and Nadir sat in the waiting room in front of the ward where Kariman was being held. They were not allowed to go in to see her, but they remained sitting in the hope that they would be allowed in later. The district attorney would surely come, if only that evening, and then maybe it would be possible for the attorney to allow them to see her. But suddenly the policeman standing with the soldier at the door motioned to them. He said, smiling, "I have good news. The police found her stepfather alive, and he's now in the hospital, in surgery. He has a concussion and a large knife wound to the head."

Isa exclaimed in excitement, "God is great! Then it's a crime of attempted murder, not murder. But given the sexual harassment, it's meaningless. Sexual harassment from a man who professes Islam! I for one won't leave him in peace, I'll spend everything I have to see him in jail. Five years at least." Then he looked at Nadir. "You can leave me and go home. I'm alone at home or alone here, it makes no difference."

Nadir looked at him with great affection. "I'll stay with you, Ustaz."

Isa said with a laugh, "Don't worry. I'll meet you later and give you Nawal's letter."

Sadly, Nadir said, "I'm not thinking of anyone but Kariman any more, Usatz. Kariman is the only one who's left for us, now, for all of us."

Then he left Isa and went to sit alone, trying not to cry.

11

"WHAT YARA HAS NOT READ of Nadir's poetry, and what she must now read."

He said to me:
If it were not for the Mediterranean Sea,
there would have been no *Odyssey*.
I said to him:
Odysseus returned
and our labyrinth began.

He said to me:
The Great Sea,
the Hinder Sea,
the Hellenic Sea,
the Sea That's Near Us,
the Roman Sea,
the Inner Sea,
the Mediterranean—
great names for our sea.
I said to him:
A sea whose waters
flow from the tears of lovers.

He said to me:
Alexandria in its day

opened its arms to strangers.
I said to him:
Alexandria does not realize, now,
that the strangers of today
know nothing of trees.

He said to me:
Why are you always staring at the buildings in the streets?
I said to him:
They have all turned into question marks.

He said to me:
If God loves a man
he puts him to the test.
I said to him:
If God loves a man
he puts in his path a woman to love him.
Anything other than that
is chasing the wind.

He said to me:
The seagulls come with the ships
and leave behind them.
Seagulls love coming
and rejoice in leaving.
I said to him:
Seagulls leave no one behind them.

He said to me:
Why do you not leave the beach?
Darkness has descended.
I said to him:
These ships with shining lights,
when will they stop leaving?

He said to me:
Don't look for Yara after today,
refrain from walking the streets
after her shadow.
I said to him:
At home I grieve.
She is the one who walks the roads before me.
He said to me:
Don't look for Yara after today.
She has come to have a house and a husband.
I said to him:
And I no longer have a country that is home.

He said to me:
You have a city to which men come in droves.
I said to him:
Men who don't know the meaning of a homeland,
they now settle in this city.

He said to me:
There is upon this earth that which makes living worthwhile.
I said to him:
And I am suspended between the earth and heaven.

He said to me:
Music is your passion, so why do you flee it?
I said to him:
It's far away now in the night, and fading.

He said to me:
Love always begins bearing with it its end.
I said to him:
No one ever learns that, except at the end.

He said to me:

Every lost love
can be forgotten in a love that's new.
I said to him:
Except for first love.
Whenever you remember,
it fills the room around you.

He said to me:
People pass, but the cities remain.
I said to him:
And what would remain for people,
were the cities to pass?

He said to me:
Don't call it separation;
the story has been completed.
I said to him:
Stories of love are not completed,
except by the death of the lovers.

He said to me:
Why do you go up to the roof
so early every morning?
I said to him:
I dream of Yara returning,
sweeping away the clouds of black
from the city.

He said to me:
Why also do you go out so early to the beach?
I said to him:
I dream of Yara returning,
spreading the rainbow
above the sea.

He said to me:
All of this is caused by love?
I said to him:
All of this is caused by separation,
and our separation is caused by outlaws blocking our paths.

He said to me:
You're young, my lad,
the world is wide before you,
catch any wave.
I said to him:
There is no wave before me to catch,
there is no wave behind to bring me back.
The sea has cast me out, alone
and retreated from the city.

He said to me:
Nawal's life is a story of lost love.
In Paris she met Rushdi,
and he too is a story of lost love.
Heaven put omens in your way,
why did you not see them?
I said to him:
Glad tidings
are what hang always before lovers,
hopes,
white clouds that they alone can see.
Lovers do not understand omens.

He said to me:
Then cease, today, to weep.
I said to him:
But today has no end.

Let no one blame me.

I know that autumn brings the quail,
but it's sadness also
coming at its appointed time.
I know the earth turns
and does not stop for anyone.
But that's because we
do not sense its turning.
I know the world is wide and its confines broad,
but I have become like Mayakovsky,
a cloud in trousers.
I leave my spot every morning,
yet every evening I return.
Yara alone
now gives me hope,
makes me feel strong.
I know that she
will not leave my spirit
as long as her phantom has a face and a body.
We are liars, my friend.
We always talk with a masculine mind,
we walk after women in the roads
and the story of my lost love becomes mixed
with a people that was happy,
having nothing to do
but cock fighting,
wine drinking,
making fun of the rulers.
Today the desert wind
is raging over them,
and that sheikh who threatens
women with hell
does not know that stories of love
are formed by fire.
That idiot who closes the windows and the doors
does not know

that he has closed them
upon the lovers,
that they have room for lovers' phantoms.
Those men don't know the secret of windows:
they were made for light and air,
then desires took control of them from behind,
open or closed.
And these new washed garments
spread upon the line
to the sun and the wind
are stories that walk in the roads.
The old man mounted the filly
to outrun time;
the filly will reach her destination
without the old man on her back.
Yara will remain with me
in my waking and in my sleep,
a butterfly as I have known her,
joyous under heaven,
because she flits about my face,
looking for open windows
to come and go
with beautiful stories
to spread as smiles before me.
Above the roof tops and the roads
Yara is in my heart
that will not stop beating
with her name.
I hear her now calling to me:
do not turn back,
go on your way.
The gods have given me joy enough,
and what was lost of my joy
remains with you.
Make of it your store,

and be certain that you are with me.
There is still a woman
in the universe who loves you,
even if she is no longer with you,
a woman who sends her tenderness to you
through the ether,
laden with the scent of Paradise.
One woman in the universe
who removes the barriers from your way.
You will not leave my eyes, ever,
my beloved.
So I hear her.
She asks me,
Do you want to see me?
How do you not see me
when you hear my laughter?
Go on your way,
for you alone are the one
who will write the story of our love.
Don't be like my father and my mother,
amateurs of old things,
for I, too,
I will be with you always,
and our story will never be faded or worn.
Don't forget the day I saw the quails with you,
coming with the autumn,
and I asked you where the quails come from.
You told me, From Europe, the cold,
looking for a warm breast.
I said to you, Poor things,
many of them die on the journey.
What if they stayed where they are?
You told me, Then all would die.
So leave this city,
so that if you write our story

you will write its story with us.
You will not write the story of the city
while you are in it.
And if you found me
you would not write our story,
ever.
Not ever.

Translator's Acknowledgments

THIS TRANSLATION IS DEDICATED TO Farouk Abdel Wahab, in loving memory. I am also very grateful for the generosity and kindness of Neil Hewison, Lucy Shafik, and Johanna Baboukis at AUC Press, without whose support this project could not have been completed; to Hala Abdel Mobdy, for patience and expert advice; and to Wendy Munyon, for her wisdom, her sharp eye, and the gift of endless hours of editing.

∗

hoopoe is an imprint for engaged, open-minded readers hungry for outstanding fiction that challenges headlines, re-imagines histories, and celebrates original storytelling. Through elegant paperback and digital editions, **hoopoe** champions bold, contemporary writers from across the Middle East alongside some of the finest, groundbreaking authors of earlier generations.

At hoopoefiction.com, curious and adventurous readers from around the world will find new writing, interviews, and criticism from our authors, translators, and editors.